DATE DUE	
MAR 15 2007	FEB 24 2007
APR 18 2007	MAY 05 2007
MAY 12 2007	JUN 16
JUN 14 2007	JUL 12 2007
DEC 19 2011	AUG 30 2011
JAN 13 2013	

RCH (*see page* 135

The Motive from the Deed

Also by Patricia Wynn

The Motive from the Deed

URBANA FREE LIBRARY

PATRICIA WYNN

PEMBERLEY PRESS
CORONA DEL MAR, CA

The Motive from the Deed
3rd in the Blue Satan Mystery Series
Featuring Blue Satan and Mrs. Kean

First Edition
Cover design: Kat&Dog Communications
Art: Edward Collier (fl. 1662-1707), Still Life. 1699.
By permission of Tate Gallery, London/Art Resource, NY

LCCN 2006938222
ISBN 0-9771913-3-8
ISBN13 978-0-9771913-3-8

Publisher's Cataloging-in-Publication Data

Wynn, Patricia
    The motive from the deed / Patricia Wynn. -- 1st ed.
        p. cm. -- (Blue Satan mystery series ; 3)
    Summary: "Hester Kean's brother is implicated in the murder
of a notorious London bookseller in the shadow of St. Dunstan's
Church." "[summary]"--Provided by publisher.
    ISBN 978-0-9771913-3-8 (alk. paper)

    1. Great Britain--History--George I, 1714-1727--Fiction.
    2. Brigands and robbers--Fiction. 3. Historical fiction.
    4. Adventure fiction. I. Title.

                                        2006938222

ℰ

In Memory of

My Mother

Marguerite Johnston Barnes

Acknowledgements

I am forever indebted to the poet Alexander Pope for the verses used in this book. They are taken from his *Moral Essays, In Four Epistles to Several Persons*. A great deal of my information about Pope, Lady Mary Wortley Montagu, and Edmond Curll has come from Peter Quennell's excellent work, *Alexander Pope, The Education of a Genius 1688-1728*.

I could not write the scenes in London with such detail without Walter Thornbury's *Old and New London*, a nineteenth-century work in six volumes, made available to me by the University of Texas Libraries in Austin. This series could never be written without the resources of these libraries, including the Harry Ransom Center with its priceless treasures.

My knowledge of the Oglethorpes comes almost exclusively from a work by Patricia Kneas Hill, suitably entitled *The Oglethorpe Ladies*, published in 1977 by Cherokee Publishing Company of Atlanta.

For information on the justice system, such as it was in 1715, I am greatly indebted to J.M. Beattie and Oxford University Press for *Policing and Punishment in London 1660–1750*, to Peter Linebaugh and Cambridge University Press for *The London Hanged, Crime and Civil Society in the Eighteenth Century*, and the University of Chicago Press for its four-volume facsimile of the 1765–1769 edition of William Blackstone's *Commentaries on the Laws of England*.

My other references are too numerous to list, but I am thankful for them all.

Historical Background

As the story goes, in 1715, at the end of August, at a royal drawing-room, his Majesty King George I delivered a cut direct to the Earl of Mar. In a fit of pique, supposedly, that very night Lord Mar left his wife and his house and headed immediately for Scotland, where he called together the Scottish clans and launched a rebellion.

The rebellion, known later as the "Fifteen", was one of many waged by the Jacobites (followers of James Stuart) to regain the thrones of England and Scotland for the Stuarts. The best remembered of these took place in 1745 and involved Bonnie Prince Charlie's bid for the crown. In that uprising the Scottish clans were defeated at the Battle of Culloden, and subsequently crushed. But unlike that later, frequently-romanticized rebellion, the "Fifteen" also involved English Jacobites and was the nearest the Stuarts, in the name of Charlie's father James, ever came to regaining their throne. For months leading up to it, the Jacobites in London, Oxford, and other cities fomented riots, Jacobite agents infiltrated King George's army and recruited soldiers to the cause, and in the West, English aristocrats collected secret stores of arms and ammunition. As soon as Lord Mar raised James's standard and proclaimed him King of Scotland, Jacobites in the North and West of England also rose for James. It was due only to a series of well-timed events that the rebels were foiled at putting their darling James on the throne.

George had been King of England and Scotland for only one year, but he was very well served by the Whigs who had seized the royal palace in his name. Among his ministers was Robert Walpole, whose astuteness would one day make him the first prime minister of Great Britain. In the year 1715, he earned his trusted place by operating a Committee of Secrecy charged with investigating the previous Tory ministry. This committee not only unearthed irregularities in the conduct of the former ministers, but also uncovered the Jacobites' plot. The question was not *if* the Roman Catholic James Stuart would try to wrest the throne from his Protestant cousin George, but *when*. With the government firmly in Whig hands, Tory papers were seized, the mail was opened, freedom of speech and dissent were curtailed, and spies were paid to keep the Crown informed of James's and his chief followers' movements.

As an exile, James had to rely for his intelligence on the men who flocked to his side. By and large they consisted of malcontents, among them: Irish who had fought on behalf of his father James II; Roman Catholics, including priests, who'd been stripped of their rights; and, young adventurers to whom James had promised a peerage if and when he triumphed. The trouble with these people was that they had nothing to lose in England, and everything to gain if James became king. Desperation and frustration turned them into loose cannons, quick to assume authority they did not possess, grasping at every vague opportunity to advance the cause, gullible in their attempts to win converts, less than truthful with themselves and others, and extremely indiscreet with James's plans. James did not have the maturity, the resources, or the strength to restrain them.

These were the men James had to rely upon to keep him in touch with his followers in England and Scotland, substantial people with property and estates. Among these were true believers in the divine right of kings, men, and women, too, who were willing to risk everything for the cause that inspired their loyalty for whatever personal reason. One was his cousin and childhood friend, illegitimate son of Charles II, Lord Derwentwater of Northumberland, who had been raised at St. Germain with James.

Without the ability to look into the heart of each of James's adherents, it's impossible to know all their motives. Clearly, there were some very powerful men who had secretly courted James just to ensure their own survival in the event he managed to retake the crown. If George had offered them a post in his government, who knows whether the "Fifteen" would ever have taken place? But the Whigs demonized the Tories so successfully that George made it clear from the instant he took the throne that he would have nothing to do with them.

In fairness, these Tories sealed their own fates by corresponding with James and conspiring against the Act of Succession, the act of Parliament that had named George the next King of England. The Earl of Mar did not launch the rebellion simply because he'd been publicly insulted by King George. He had already promised to rally the clans to James's cause, and George's snub was a sign that he had better make haste to rally them or he would suffer the same fate as two of James's other correspondents, the Duke of Ormonde and the Viscount Bolingbroke.

Under the plan the Jacobites had concocted, as soon as enough arms had been collected and secreted away near Bristol and Bath, the Duke of Ormonde, an experienced general, very popular with the army, was to call for the rising. James's agents had been fomenting discontent among the troops, who would, it was assumed, flock to Ormonde's call. As soon as Ormonde gave the signal and turned the army, James would make his way to the French coast and take ship for the west coast of England with whatever troops he could muster in France. Simultaneously, the Earl of Mar would rally the clans, take Edinburgh, and begin the march south.

It was a good plan and it might have succeeded, if Walpole's spies had not stayed at least three steps ahead of the Jacobites. Earlier in the spring, charges were brought against the Viscount Bolingbroke, who escaped them by fleeing to France. Then in the summer, before Ormonde could call for the rising, the government reacted to the riots thrown in his name by issuing an order for his arrest. Forsaking glory in favor of safety, Ormonde, too, fled the country, leaving the Jacobites without a military leader. Only Lord Mar remained to carry out the plot in Scotland.

When George cut him at the palace, Mar must have realized that the game was up. He could run, as Bolingbroke and Ormonde had done, or he could proclaim James King of Scotland and try to keep

King George's troops at bay until James and Ormonde landed in the West. But loose lips betrayed the existence of ships full of armaments that had been financed and armed by Louis XIV of France. Then Walpole's men uncovered the caches of arms in the West. When Ormonde tried to land in the West, the weather threw him so far off course that it was assumed he had drowned. And King George's spies defeated all James's attempts to reach the coast of France.

Without military leadership or arms, the risings in Oxford and the West were quickly quelled. The only English rebels who marched to Mar's call were the Jacobites in Northumberland and Lancashire. In spite of the thousands of clansmen who had rallied, without a proper military leader, the rebel armies floundered. The cold, and lack of food, when reinforcements failed to arrive, drove many Highlanders to desert. The English rebels were defeated before they could join up with Mar, who retreated for the winter. By the time James managed to land in Scotland, his troops were depleted. He was so pale and listless as to disenchant many of his followers who had never seen their prince. After being chased over Scotland by King George's troops, he was forced to escape again to France.

Bolingbroke, Mar, and Ormonde spent the remainder of their days in exile. If their risk had paid off, as it almost did, it is their names that would be familiar to us now instead of Walpole, Marlborough, and George.

In vain the Sage, with retrospective eye,
Would from th'apparent What conclude the Why,
Infer the Motive from the Deed, and show,
That what we chanced was what we meant to do.

Yet more; the difference is as great between
The optics seeing, as the object seen.
All Manners take a tincture from our own;
Or come discoloured through our Passions shown.
Or Fancy's beam enlarges, multiplies,
Contracts, inverts, and gives ten thousand dyes.

CHAPTER I

August 13, 1715

As the horns began to trumpet, a light hush fell over the fleet of little boats upon the Thames. Watermen's wherries and aristocrats' gilded barges bobbed like corks about the Royal Shallop, on which King George and the Prince and Princess of Wales lounged in regal splendour.

To either side of this dazzling concourse towered the masts of his Majesty's sailing ships: the fifty-gun Worcester, the Shrewsbury with its three large decks, the Blenheim and the Prince George with ninety guns each. Square-sailed merchants of every tonnage and type stood moored along both banks of the river, impervious to the waves that lapped against the pleasure craft, splashing their passengers with drops. Silent and still in the long summer twilight, these sentinels had framed the King's journey from the base of London Bridge to Lime House where the music was to be performed.

Hester Kean, waiting woman to her cousin Isabella, Countess of Hawkhurst, had the privilege of witnessing all this from the forward bench in Lord Hawkhurst's barge. Tonight, she could not help feeling a measure of respect for King George, no matter what a dolt she might otherwise think him. His presence at this event showed a complete lack of fear concerning the security of his throne. Surely, no one observing him now, as he reclined under a splendid gilt pavilion, would think he had a care in the world—certainly not that the kingdom he had so recently inherited might soon fall under attack.

The magnificent display—from the carved and painted barges to the enormous ships boasting the colours of Great Britain—conveyed an impression of might, which, perhaps, was the reason King George had commanded this performance. If the Pretender and his French allies were planning an invasion, as believed, they might have second thoughts after seeing such a demonstration of power.

The danger had not yet come, but no one doubted that it would. Rumours that the Pretender had left his place of retreat to lead his exiled troops were heard daily. The lord bishops of the Church of England were so convinced of his coming that, in reaction to the tumult in the streets, they had formally assured King George of their faithful support. And, though the rioting in London had been halted by the camping of troops in Hyde Park, every week arrests were made of people who had cursed his Majesty or spoken dangerous words against the government. Meanwhile, prodded by his Whig advisers, King George continued to insult the Tories he would do better to charm.

Tonight, however, his Majesty betrayed no sign of concern as he tapped his fingers to the music floating over the water.

Hester relaxed against the cushions lining the barge and prepared to enjoy a respite from the tensions that had hounded the Court all summer. The gentle rocking of the barge, the inspiring music by Mr. Handel, and the splendid summer night created an illusion of peace.

The tranquility was instantly shattered by a shriek from Isabella behind her. "How dare you, sir!" Hester's cousin whispered loudly, ending her show of outrage with a giggle.

Her start had been so violent as to rock the barge. Reluctantly, Hester turned to see what had provoked it and found her cousin mopping water off her bosom with a lace handkerchief. Under the heavy pavilion in the middle of the barge she lay propped on cushions between her husband Harrowby and their guest, Lord Kirkland. Lord Kirkland had been one of Isabella's swains before her marriage, and was her current flirt.

With a look of assumed innocence, Lord Kirkland dried the water from his fingertips. "My lady, I protest! How can you accuse me of sprinkling your breast, when drops are raining down at us from all sides?"

"Fie, you naughty, naughty man!"

"Shall I call him out, my dear?" Harrowby's coyness added to the merriment of the jest. Isabella and Lord Kirkland had maintained a steady stream of this nonsense all evening, regardless of Isabella's delicate condition.

Just recently, Harrowby's physician had confirmed Isabella's suspicions that she was carrying a child, but impending motherhood had only mildly restrained her spirits. As yet, except for a few weeks of nausea, she had not suffered much from the nine-month sickness. Her energy was unimpaired—which meant the only drawback had been the restriction against sexual intercourse during the first four months of her gravidity to keep from dislodging the babe. The four months were nearly up, as she frequently reminded her husband in the hearing of Hester, and the entire household.

Normally, at this time of year, Isabella and Harrowby would have been disporting themselves at a place like Tunbridge Wells, instead of being trapped in London, but the Court had been forced to stay in town all summer to support the King. The peers had sacrificed their summer pleasures to ensure that the first Hanoverian king would remain on his throne, and that *they* would not fall under suspicion of working for the Pretender, James Stuart. At least this evening's outing on the Thames had spared them the suffocation of another royal drawing-room at St. James's

The Prince and Princess of Wales had moved their households to Kensington Palace for the summer, which had afforded some aristocrats the excuse to escape their London houses during the months of dangerous heat, when the small pox was more likely to spread. Harrowby had been one of the fortunate few to secure lodgings for his family in the small village of Kensington close by. But with Parliament not yet granted a recess, he had to spend most of his days in the House of Peers voting on measures the King believed necessary to secure his reign, leaving Isabella to amuse herself.

The Prince's court was much more diverting than his father's. Unable to understand English, King George had no interest in plays or even conversation with most of his subjects, who spoke neither German nor French, and he had no patience for the kind of public entertainments that had always made the English Court the centre of aristocratic life. He preferred spending the evening alone with his German mistress. In contrast, the Prince of Wales, who spoke a heavily-accented English and had enthusiastically embraced his new country, hosted the sort of balls and assemblies where gentlemen and ladies might flirt to their heart's content.

The King's appearance upon the water tonight was a rare public event. For this reason, his courtiers had crowded about, their vessels exhibiting varying degrees of wealth. The Hawkhurst barge was naturally one of the more magnificent. Like the King's, its pavilion was roofed with crimson carpets, laid over ornate posts with gilded carvings. With eight liveried oarsmen to propel it, and banners waving from bow to stern, it cut an impressive swath through the water.

The oarsmen were at pains to keep it near his Majesty's shallop, however. So many of the Thames watermen had crowded the river in their little wherries, they had left the larger vessels little room in which to ply their oars. The constant motion of the concourse had chopped up waves so rough that even the King's shallop rocked occasionally from side to side.

Over a flourish of trumpets, hautboys, and double curtails, Hester heard Harrowby complain to his bargeman, "If this rabble don't take care, they're going to make us tip! Why the devil don't you make 'em back away?"

"We'll try, your lordship." Samuel's tone was skeptical, but he called out an order to his crew.

Harrowby was not the only one becoming nervous, Hester realized, as an occasional gasp or shriek reached them from the other barges. The number of little boats had been increasing, as his Majesty's subjects up and down this stretch of the river came to take advantage of the musical treat. One could hardly blame them when they would rarely have heard such splendid music. Performances like these were only given in the chambers of dukes and kings.

For all his faults, King George sincerely loved music, and wherever he chose to amuse himself, the musicians and composers were certain to be the best. Hester leaned back against the cushions again and strained to hear the notes drifting over the water. But with the increasing cries of alarm from the audience, the constant lapping of the water, and the occasional crack of oar upon oar, the music was all but drowned out.

The barge gave a sudden lurch, a convergence of waves rocking it to within an inch of tipping. Isabella screamed, and Hester turned to see her pretty cousin, her golden locks askew and her blue eyes wide, grabbing fearfully onto her husband's arm.

Lord Kirkland tried to distract her with another jest, but the brow beneath his massive periwig was far from tranquil. Hester held on to the bottom of her seat and subdued her quickened pulse.

Isabella's anxious wail carried over the music. "What if the boat does tip, Harrykins? I cannot swim!"

"If it does, your ladyship," Samuel ominously advised, "you must take a-hold of the bark. Even if she's upside down, she'll float."

"But I do not wish to be soaked! Harrowby, let's leave!"

"Hush, my dear! If you don't take care, his Majesty will hear you."

As yet, King George had not permitted the spreading alarm to disturb him, but clearly his beefeaters were growing worried. Dressed in their usual garb of red tunics and caps, with purple stripes and gold lace, they braced their feet in the shallop, pikes clasped in front of their strained faces. But, in spite of these Yeomen of the Guard, the listeners' boats pressed closer and closer to the royal barge, pushed by the increasing number of other vessels behind them.

The music played on, even when suddenly the Guard turned their pikes upon the encroaching boats, whose oars could not find space to row away. The beefeaters had cause to feel uneasy, since one assault on the King had already been attempted. How could they be sure there was not another Irish madman or a Jacobite spy in one of the vessels? If King George had wished to place himself at risk, he could not have chosen a better way.

From the anxious looks on the faces around her, Hester knew that her thoughts were shared. The music was soon forgotten as fear flew like sparks from barge to barge.

Eventually, whether the King recognized the general concern, or the Royal Bargeman advised him to return, his Majesty finally signaled for the musicians to stop. While his Yeomen used their pikes to clear other vessels out of the way, his oars attempted to cut a path through the water.

The tide was rising rapidly. Hemmed in by smaller boats, the barges of the nobility struggled to turn their forty-foot lengths. Collisions led to altercations as the passengers vented their fright, adding fury to the chaos. Not even the royal oarsmen could find enough room to swing their oars. The best they could do was use them to ward off other boats, as the tide slowly swept the fleet of little vessels back up the Thames.

Harrowby's party fared no better. As the Hawkhurst oarsmen struggled to turn, Hester was buffeted about. A sudden push carried them straight towards the Royal Shallop. Unable to halt, they cringed, expecting a crash. Hester swallowed a cry as a beefeater's pike was thrust in front of her nose. She retreated as far as the boat would permit, with Isabella's shrieks and Harrowby's oaths ringing loudly in her ears.

Turning to peer through the gathering dusk, she spied the boat that had knocked them into the Royal Shallop, a common wherry, bearing a woman and three men. Two of the men were dressed shabbily, like the desperate souls who might try to do away with the King.

With a start, one of them leapt to his feet, rocking their boat perilously from side to side as he clambered over the seats. He aimed straight for Hester, as if intending to leap aboard Harrowby's barge. Grasping onto their benches, his friends cried out in alarm, but he seemed oblivious to their warnings as he lunged Hester's way.

For one terrifying moment, she believed she was caught between the King and his assassin.

Then the ruffian opened his mouth, and her brother Jeremy's voice came joyfully over the water. "Hester! Is that you?"

℘

Earlier that evening, a short way up the river, on the southern bank near Vauxhall Stairs, Thomas Barnes rode a tall, lanky horse through the gate to his master's house and headed for the stables. Both he and the animal were weary, for they had travelled all the way from the coast in Sussex. No less than his mount, Tom hoped to find a good meal waiting, although Katy, who kept house for him and his master, had no reason to expect him back tonight.

Tom's master, the outlawed Viscount St. Mars, had bid him recover the horse, so Tom had ridden to Rye, where the thief who had stolen it had found a smuggler to take him into France. Tom had discovered the animal abandoned in a livery, the liveryman eager to relinquish it in exchange for his unpaid bill. The whole business had been accomplished so quickly that Tom had started home that very same day, spending only last night on the road. As he crossed the yard in back of the house, he wondered if Katy would be as glad to see him as he would be to see her.

During the past few weeks, with his lord in France, Tom had come to a momentous decision. He still feared that Katy might give him the pox, for before St. Mars had hired her, she had been an innkeeper's wench. For months Tom had fought his growing feelings for her, but eventually his contempt had changed to love, and even respect, for he had come to understand that she had only sold her favours to survive.

Katy had never been a thief. Nor had she ever shown a wish to continue her sinful life. Instead, she had begged Tom to help her get a decent post in St. Mars's household, and she had fulfilled it beyond his highest expectations. Her faithfulness, her skills, and her modesty had made him forgive her past and admit the desire he had felt since first seeing her.

When St. Mars returned from France, Tom meant to ask his permission to wed her. He thought she might have him, for marriage would give her back the respectability she had lost. From the glances Katy sometimes threw him when she did not know he was watching, he hoped she might want him for another reason, too. But his longing raised a fear that haunted him whenever he recalled his father's agonizing death from the pox. Then, he wondered if he should—or could—ask for nothing more than her cheerful companionship.

He pulled his mount to a stop in front of the stable door, wishing Katy would come out to greet him, but a glance at the house through the lingering twilight caught no sign of stirring. With a grimace of disappointment, he started to dismount, just as a pig came snuffling from behind the wash house.

Before he could even wonder whose pig it was, the horse beneath him gave a piercing neigh. Flattening its ears, it charged at the swine, whose startled squeals rent the air.

With his foot caught in the stirrup, Tom reached for the pommel and held on for dear life, as Looby—the horse St. Mars had so aptly named—tried to snatch the little animal with his teeth and trample it into the ground. With every muscle in his body straining, Tom maintained his grip, as the outraged horse lunged left and right through the yard after the scampering pig. His nails were torn by the leather with every jerk. His neck threatened to snap. Unable to pull on the reins, he fought to throw his leg back across the horse, but every time he nearly did, Looby cut sharply to the right and almost swung him off.

The pig ran in ever wider circles. Tom cursed loudly at all swine as he swung helplessly on the stirrup.

Eventually the neighs and squeals drew Katy from the house. With a shriek, she ran and flapped her apron to chase the pig away. Her efforts made Tom's situation worse, for Looby's turns grew even wilder. He was shouting for her to stop, when the horse made a broad swerve and slammed him into the stable wall.

His sweat-slicked fingers lost their grip. His back hit the ground with a bone-rattling jolt, just as mercifully his left boot broke free of the stirrup. The breath left his body with a whoosh. He struggled to regain it. Lying with his chest in a spasm, he thanked God that he hadn't been dragged. Then the thought that Katy could be trampled made him sit up with a jerk.

As he raised himself, he saw her running towards him, the pig nowhere in sight. Looby had come to a stop outside the door to the brew house, and was beating upon it with one front hoof. It looked as if the pig—whosoever it was—had managed to squeeze inside it and shut the door.

Tom fell back and closed his eyes. He had forgotten that Looby hated pigs. But even if he hadn't, a pig was the last thing he had expected to see.

"Mr. Barnes, are you hurt?" With a puff from her skirts Katy fell to her knees in the dust beside him.

His breathing was still laboured. He couldn't answer at once, which seemed to alarm her. She tenderly lifted his head and laid it in her lap. If he had been able to talk, he might have spoken angrily to her. He would have demanded to know where the cursed pig had come from. But neither he nor St. Mars had bothered to tell her what a lunatic Looby was around pigs.

With a cool, light touch, she combed his hair back from his forehead. Her lap felt as soft as a clover-filled meadow. All at once, a sigh of happiness eased the tightness in Tom's chest.

Then her hand touched his cheek, and all thoughts of Looby and the pig fled from his mind.

"Tell me, please, Mr. Barnes," she said again. "Are you hurt?"

With joy welling up inside him, Tom gazed up into her pretty face and smiled.

⚷

Almost as suddenly as Hester's brother had appeared, he vanished, his boat knocked away by another. But before he was carried off, he raised his voice above the hubbub to ask for her direction. When she called back that she was living with their cousin Isabella, now Countess of Hawkhurst, a stunned look came over his face. Then he broke into a beaming smile, as if no piece of news could have pleased him more. As his wherry floated away, he promised to visit her in Kensington the next week, before his boat was swept out of sight.

Hester fell back against her seat and struggled with a sense of unreality. She had not seen her brother Jeremy in over five years. She glanced at her companions in the barge, but with their attention focused on the King's boat, no one seemed to have noticed her encounter with Jeremy.

As darkness gradually fell, the crush of little boats continued to block the King's oars. In the end, the royal barge only managed to return to London Bridge by driving with the incoming tide. Fatigue, relief, and discreetly suppressed anger could be seen on every aristocratic face when, finally, his Majesty's courtiers set foot on Tower Wharf and started picking their way to their waiting carriages, leaving their oarsmen to shoot the treacherous waters under the bridge alone.

Hester was unable to absorb the shock of encountering her brother after so many years, until she stood safely ashore, but as she picked up her skirts to follow her cousins and their guest into Thames Street, a range of conflicting emotions stirred her breast. She waited for the footman to hand her into the coach and took her place across from Isabella before giving into her confusion.

Her first sensation of relief, that she was not to be spitted on an assassin's sword, had been followed by a deeper one of thanks to learn that her brother was well. She loved Jeremy, and the joy of seeing him alive had brought tears to her eyes.

Now those feelings were threatened by others that pushed and shoved at her ease. It was impossible not to feel angry, for, if not for an accident of fate, she might never have learned not only that Jeremy lived, but that he dwelt not far from her in London. And with that anger came the old anxiety, the kind a mother must feel about a wayward child.

Hester had not heard from Jeremy since he had run away from their father's house. The night before he had left, he had informed her that he did not want to study for the Church as their father intended. Instead, he planned to seek his fortune. He rather thought he might take ship for the colonies—or become a seaman, he wasn't precisely sure which— but whatever the case, he knew he was not fashioned for the clergy if it meant sitting through endless lessons day after day.

Hester had always known how much her brother hated and resisted their father's tutoring, which was often enforced by a whipping. It was not that Jeremy could not read his lessons, but that his mind would wander in every direction. He read everything that came in his way, but the more fanciful and adventurous the material, the greater its appeal. He found no use for Latin or Greek or even the worthiest of sermons, but the stories that were told by Betty or John, their servants, would send him spinning day dreams for hours. It was his absent-mindedness that had driven their father to frustration.

Hester had not tried to persuade her brother to turn his mind to his studies. She had offered to plead with their father to apprentice him for different work, if that was what he wished.

But Jeremy must not have believed in her ability to sway the Reverend

Mr. Kean, for in the morning he was gone, and after the first burst of fury from their father, nothing more of Jeremy had been said.

Hester could not help loving him, but in leaving her behind, he had shown no concern for her dismal future. He had not even made the empty promise to come and fetch her when his fortune should be made.

Knowing him as she did, Hester had not expected anything to come from his venture. She had thought he would return when he grew tired of being hungry, or at least when their father died. She had tried to talk him out of leaving, certain he would get no farther than the first town before someone either cheated him out of his meagre store of coins or tricked him into some foolish act. For the Jeremy she knew did not have a suspicious bone in his body. He was cheerful and generous to a fault and had the uncomfortable habit of making fast friends with anyone who struck up a conversation with him. He had an innocent faith in his fellow man, and whenever anyone disappointed him, his shock and outrage were so great as to be comical.

He lived according to his principles, which in a less-grasping age would have been considered Christian, but were thought foolish and imprudent by most Englishmen—certainly by their father who, in spite of being a clergyman, had little inclination to share. Even Hester, who admired her brother's generosity, found it irritating at times. He had no ambition, and the fact that he had survived on his own all these years astonished her. She dared to hope that he might have learned a little bit of prudence.

Unfortunately, the brief glimpse she had caught of his clothes, and his dubious state of cleanliness, had not conveyed a sense of prosperity. She had mistaken him and his companions for ruffians. And now that Jeremy planned to call on her at Hawkhurst House, where he would present himself as her brother and Isabella's cousin, she could not help feeling nervous about the reception he would get.

It was not that she would ever be ashamed of her brother, even if he was perfectly capable of embarrassing her deeply at moments, but her position in Isabella's household was that of a superior servant. True, they were cousins. But without a penny to her name, Hester would always be a dependent. And in the Hawkhurst household, her security must depend on the goodwill of Isabella's husband, who had enough to worry him with the importunities of Isabella's mother, brothers, and sisters without the welfare of her cousins, too. Though not mean in the accepted sense, Harrowby did possess a natural degree of selfishness. And he was understandably nervous about his position. Having been granted his cousin's title when the Viscount St. Mars was accused of murder, and conscious of the Crown's suspicion that the former Lord Hawkhurst had been a Jacobite, Harrowby worried about the need to preserve the best appearance.

Hester somehow doubted that he would find the sight of Jeremy particularly reassuring.

Fortunately, during their brief encounter on the Thames, neither of her cousins had noticed her brother's boat. Now, on the way to their rented lodgings in Kensington, both were giving vent to their relief by reliving every hair-raising moment of their outing.

"I don't wonder that it gave you palpitations, my love," Harrowby was saying. "I confess, I was a trifle agitated myself. I don't know why his Majesty had to go all that way just to hear a bit of music, when he might have had them play for him at Kensington or Hampton Palace. After all—" he gave an amused snort— "it's hardly likely they would have refused to come! But to drag us all to a place where every jackanapes among them keeps a boat!—well, I doubt that he will do it again."

"It certainly did seem ill-advised," Hester agreed, judging it best to abandon her silence. "But I suspect King George had no concept of the interest his concert would arouse, or that the watermen at Lime House would think to join us. Remember how shocked he was to discover that his subjects could enjoy his park at St. James's?"

Her speech seemed to remind Harrowby of the risk he took in appearing to criticize the King, for he said hastily, "Well, no harm done." Then, remembering Isabella, he added, "Assuming, of course, that *you* took none, my dear. We mustn't upset the little mother now, must we?" Isabella's interesting condition had given her husband brilliant hopes of an heir.

"Oh, lud, no!" his little woman replied. "Though I was vastly scared when the Guard stuck their pikes in my face! But, now that it's past, I feel completely well. I wonder if anything is going forward at the Palace tonight."

To Isabella, Hester knew, it was intolerable to think of retiring this early in the evening. Her pregnancy had not diminished her desire for pleasure in the least. It had restored her husband's attention, however, and for that Hester was glad, even if the prospect of an heir who would take the Hawkhurst inheritance farther from its rightful owner was a travesty she could hardly bear to contemplate.

The Earldom of Hawkhurst rightfully belonged to Gideon Fitzsimmons, the Viscount St. Mars. Hester knew for certain, as few did, that St. Mars was innocent of the murder that had led Parliament to declare him an outlaw and bestow the title on his cousin Harrowby. She also knew that the only bit of proof that might clear him had either been destroyed by Isabella's mother or been hidden away in the event it should prove useful to her later. There was nothing Hester could do to help St. Mars regain his title, unless she found that letter, so chances were that if Isabella was delivered of a son, her child would be Earl of Hawkhurst one day.

Isabella's child would be Hester's blood kinsman—and Jeremy's—a grandchild of her Aunt Mayfield's, a conniving shrew of a woman for whom Hester felt neither affection nor pride.

Fortunately, Mrs. Mayfield was not living with them just now. She and Isabella's brother Dudley had been sent packing to Dudley's country seat the moment Harrowby had seen the size of the house they were to rent at Kensington. Mrs. Mayfield's presence was scarcely tolerable in a house as vast as Hawkhurst House in Piccadilly. It would be too much for any son-in-law, even one who had always been vulnerable to her flattery, in such a confined space.

Hester was glad she would not have to present Jeremy to their aunt after all these years, when Mrs. Mayfield could never refer to him without calling him a wastrel. Jeremy might be heedless and irresponsible, but his better qualities would always be lost on a woman as grasping as their aunt.

Hester could not be sure of Harrowby's welcome for her brother either. So she made plans to alert the footmen that if Jeremy should appear, they should ask him to wait downstairs and fetch her privately to him.

Not always Actions show the man: we find
Who does a kindness, is not therefore kind . . .

CHAPTER II

Jeremy did not come on Monday. Nor did he appear the following day or even the next.

Hester had waited eagerly, if nervously, to greet him. She was curious to discover how her brother had maintained himself, and whether those five years had matured him. But when he did not come, she was torn between the notion that she had only imagined their meeting, and the lowering reflection that Jeremy had never been good at keeping his appointments.

She had plenty of time to fret. Since the family had moved into the house in Kensington Square, her days had rarely been filled. Occasionally, she accompanied Isabella on her daily walk to Kensington Palace, but since the King rarely came there, Isabella had no need for Hester to interpret his French, and she often left her at home. It was undoubtedly more amusing for Isabella to go into company without her, since Hester could not help being dismayed by Isabella's flirting, which promised more than it should. Hester tried to hide her disapproval, but her cousin's swains resented her restrictive presence. And since one of those swains was now the Prince of Wales, Hester was glad not to have to act as chaperone.

The vast gardens of Kensington Palace, which had been laid out for

Queen Anne, offered any number of spots for a *tête-à-tête*. The first time Hester had strolled them, she had been struck by the notion that the walks and spirals seemed designed as if for nothing else. If not for the gentlemen's duty to spend the daylight hours in Parliament, she suspected that even more assignations would be made. Fortunately for Hester's peace of mind, his Highness the Prince of Wales—as a member of his Majesty's Council—often had to be at St. James's.

Harrowby and the King's other courtiers travelled back and forth to Westminster daily using the King's Road—virtually free of robbers now, since the army had built its encampment in Hyde Park. This route between St. James's and Kensington Palace was so brightly illuminated that everyone felt safe using it, even at midnight. Even the ladies still ventured into town. Plays were still being performed, ambassadors were received at Court, and visiting went on, even if fears were high.

It was a time of finger-pointing and whispering. No one would say if more arrests among the nobility were planned, but the general opinion was that Mr. Walpole and the King had not finished purging either the Court or the army of Jacobites. King George had issued a call for all seamen to enter the navy and all the soldiers in Ireland to report to their forts. He had sent a regiment of Foot into Scotland and inspected his troops in Hyde Park every week. Clearly, his Majesty was preparing for civil war. With more arrests ordered every week, all his courtiers could do was wait to see where the King's Messengers would strike next. And, since nearly every one of them had neighbours or relations who were Stuart supporters, it was hard to find anyone whose nerves were not on edge.

Isabella would always be the exception, of course. Hester reckoned she was fortunate to live in a house whose lady would never be suspected of having a treasonous thought. Isabella could not be suspected of having many thoughts at all.

Without many duties to perform, or access to the library at Hawkhurst House, Hester had to find other ways to occupy herself. For exercise she either walked to the palace grounds or strolled up the High Street to peer in the shops. When she did have the chance to go inside the palace, she wandered through the former queen's apartments to admire Queen Mary's collection of japanned furniture and China dishes.

Other than these pursuits and her ever-present needlework, she had little to do except to daydream about St. Mars—a tendency she greatly deplored—and to read the news-sheets sent out from London.

On Thursday afternoon, she sat in the drawing room to peruse the weekly papers as well as the *Daily Courant*. She had just read a fascinating report of a large cloud, which had descended to earth near the town of Cambridge, drawn up several tons of water into the form of a spout, and then rained it back on the village of Harson, when James Henry, the Hawkhurst receiver-general, appeared in the doorway.

When he saw her, he paused. "Ah . . . Mrs. Kean. I hope I do not disturb you."

"Not at all," she said, setting her news-sheets aside. She would always be happy to see him, were she not painfully aware of the secrets she must keep from him. She was the only member of Harrowby's household who knew that James Henry was the illegitimate son of the former Lord Hawkhurst. She had learned that fact from St. Mars, but James Henry must never know of her friendship with his half-brother St. Mars, or that St. Mars was the mysterious highwayman Blue Satan.

Taking her gesture as an invitation, James Henry entered the room but did not sit. "I have just returned from the Essex estate and had hoped to find my lord at home, but the footman tells me Lord Hawkhurst has not yet come back from the House of Peers."

"I expect he will be here shortly. He usually stops to see if Isabella is at home before riding on to the palace."

"And my lady?"

"She's been to call on their Highnesses these three hours or more."

"She is not too easily tired?" His frown told Hester that he knew of her cousin's delicate condition. She hoped he had not heard of Isabella's flirting as well.

Hester felt the need to come to her cousin's defence. "Isabella is in fine fettle, and her confinement will come soon enough."

A hint of colour crept up James Henry's neck. He gave an abrupt nod and quickly changed the subject. "So . . . what have you learned from your reading? I did not stop for news on the road."

As he moved to stand by the empty fireplace, Hester took up the papers again. She told him the tale of the water spout.

He knitted his brows. "It's hard to believe that such an extraordinary occurrence is not some kind of omen."

Hester restrained a smile. She knew that many people would consider it a sign that the Pretender was coming, though why such a portent should appear in a village no one had ever heard of, she could not imagine.

"If you are seeking an omen, I should think this one more likely." She located the paragraph that had caught her eye just before he had entered the room. "A shepherd has discovered a treasure of a thousand ancient coins in an earthen vessel near Rapton."

"Indeed! I should not be surprised if someone's future soon changed for the better."

Hester laughed. "Yes, the shepherd's at the very least."

James Henry looked taken aback, before giving a sheepish laugh. "You find me superstitious?"

She smiled kindly at him. "I beg you will forgive me. But I do not put much faith in signs or omens. It must come from being a clergyman's daughter."

"You think it blasphemy?"

"No." Gazing at his earnest face, Hester could not help thinking how much like St. Mars he was, and yet how different. The same hawk-like features were there, but she would not have had to explain her thinking to St. Mars. "It is simply that I often heard my father's parishioners ponder the meaning of this sign or that. And, inevitably, none of their fears came to pass, so they would seize on a later occurrence and say that *it* must have been the reason for the omen."

"But what if it was?"

"Then, the error was mine. But it always seemed that people—in our village, at least—were too eager to use signs to cast aspersions on the neighbours they did not like."

While James Henry digested this, Hester went back to the news-sheet and read of the sentencings recently handed down at the Surrey assizes. Six people had been condemned to death, including a woman who had killed her baby, and another by the name of Trolly Lolly, who had apparently caused the authorities repeated grief. Seventeen others were to be burnt in the hand, another seventeen to be whipped, and twenty-one transported to the Colonies in America.

The next item stated that a person carrying letters from the Rainbow Coffee-House at Fleet Bridge had been assaulted at ten at night in Cheapside and his bag of letters taken.

"Is there anything else of interest?" James Henry asked. "What does it say about King Lewis of France?"

Hester read to him of the attempts to save the life of Lewis XIV, and wondered if that king would live. She knew very little about him, except that he was extremely old, having outlived all his legitimate sons and grandsons, and extremely rich, if the stories of all his palaces were true. His physicians' prescription, that he take the waters of Bourbon, seemed of questionable benefit, unless the waters of that place were much more restorative than those at either Tunbridge or the Bath.

She did not read aloud the following paragraph, reporting on the movements of the former Lord Bolingbroke and the Duke of Ormonde, for St. Mars had been in communication with Ormonde before he had left for France. Just thinking of St. Mars could quicken her pulse, and she would not wish his brother to wonder why she was discomposed.

James Henry asked if any more arrests of Jacobites had been made.

Grateful for a reason to keep her gaze averted, Hester skimmed the *British Weekly Mercury* until the word "Newgate" stopped her. "Yes, here," she began. "It says—"

Then she froze, as a name leapt off the page and made her gasp. Her heart constricted within her breast, and her vision wavered, causing her to lose her place. Searching frantically for it again, she prayed, *No, dear Lord, please let it be a mistake!*

With her pulse drumming in her ears, she did not hear James Henry speak, until his voice came from above her head. "What is wrong, Mrs. Kean? Why do you stop?"

She found her place again and read.

"Mrs. Kean?"

Her hands trembling so violently she could no longer hold up the page, she raised unseeing eyes.

"It says—" she faltered, then in a faraway voice, said— "that Mr. Jeremy Kean has been taken to Newgate for writing a pamphlet in support of the Duke of Ormonde."

Jeremy was not the only person committed to Newgate on the charge. The news-sheet also named a bookseller by the name of Edmund Curry, said to own a bookstall up against St. Dunstan's Church.

Before Hester could speak again, James Henry called for a servant to bring her a glass of wine and insisted she drink. Sitting beside her on the velvet settee, he held the glass to her lips.

Its fire revived her, but, shocked and unable to think, Hester could barely form intelligent replies to his questions.

"This Mr. Kean is a relation?"

She nodded dumbly. "My brother."

"Did you know of his being in London? I have never heard either you or anyone in your family mention him."

Hester gathered her wits to tell him how she had encountered Jeremy on the Thames. She told him that no one else in the family was aware of her brother's presence in London and that, until this moment, she had known nothing about how he had supported himself in the five years since she had last seen him.

"He was to visit here this week, but he did not come. This is the reason, of course. What shall I do? I must see him—help him!" She turned to beg for his advice. "You do not know my brother, but I can assure you, he does not deserve *this*. I suppose he could have done something foolish—but he would never knowingly do anything to get himself sent to gaol. He has convictions, but he doesn't possess the character of a rebel. Not *this* sort of rebel."

James Henry's expression was far from encouraging. The skepticism on his face frightened her, even more than its grimness. "I do not know what can be done," he said at last. "I shall have to ask my lord's permission, but I should be able to get you into Newgate to see your brother, at least."

"Oh, yes! That is what I must do, of course! But once that is done . . . then what?"

He urged her to be patient. "We can determine that after we have seen him."

At his use of the word *we,* Hester felt a surge of relief. "You mean, you'll go with me?"

His lips curved into a faint smile. "You certainly must not go by yourself." Then he frowned again. "I have never set foot in Newgate, but I fear you will find it very distressing."

She could feel herself blanch. "That cannot be helped. I must see what I can do for my brother."

He was staring at her, and his expression changed, betraying an emotion that looked surprisingly like guilt. "Of course," he said gently. "I suppose that is what a dutiful sister or brother should do."

He stood abruptly, and his attitude seemed to have altered as well. "On second thought, instead of waiting for my lord, I suggest we leave him a note with word of our errand. I will explain the circumstances later."

Hester eagerly agreed. If Harrowby took it into his head to forbid them, she would have to disobey him and walk all the way to the gaol. So it was infinitely better not to wait for his decision.

She ran upstairs to fetch her shawl and bonnet. Then, on her way back down, she recalled how thin and almost . . . *mangy* Jeremy had looked on Saturday, and she ran to the kitchen to pack a basket of meat and fruit, before meeting James Henry at the front door.

He had used the time to call for a hackney coach, which stood waiting for her in the square. With barely a glance at her basket, he handed her into the vehicle and told its driver to take them into London.

Hester was grateful that he had not shouted out directions to Newgate Prison. The fewer who knew of her brother's arrest the better it would be. Harrowby was more likely to help Jeremy if she could convince him that no one at Court would ever hear of the scandal.

Less than half an hour later, as their coach pulled up in Newgate Street, Hester gave a prayer of thanks for James Henry's escort. If not for him, her courage might have flagged. He had directed the coachman by way of Little Queen Street and Holborn, sparing them the delays from traffic in the Strand. As he handed her down outside the keeper's house in front of a massive gate, Hester was momentarily reassured by the sight of four carved figures representing Liberty, Peace, Security, and Plenty. But before James Henry could even pull the bell, a stench, greater than she had never smelled, assaulted her nose.

Waves of nausea weakened her, and she clutched at James Henry's sleeve. He put a muscular arm about her waist, and she leaned against him for support. The urge to retch nearly overpowered her, but with every ounce of will she could muster, she forced it down.

"Are you sure you wish to do this?" he asked, his head leaning towards hers.

Hester managed to nod. Then she forced out, "I'm sure I'll grow accustomed to it . . . . There, it's more tolerable already." Feeling a little better, she gently freed herself and urged him towards the gate.

At James Henry's summons, the keeper, a slovenly brute, stumbled out of the lodge, and gave his name as William Pitt. When Hester asked to see the prisoner Mr. Jeremy Kean, he looked them shrewdly up and down, taking note of the quality of their clothes. His own were dirty and unkempt, and as they waited for his reply, he repeatedly scratched at his groin and arm pits, leaving Hester in no doubt that he was covered in lice.

He demanded to know their business with the prisoner, and whether they had come to pay Jeremy's rent. Unless they had, he informed them in a bullying tone, he would not trouble himself to bring Jeremy up from the Stone Hold.

The word *hold* sent a shiver through Hester, but she conquered her impulse to turn to James Henry and beg for Jeremy's keep. She was not so naïve that she did not recognize Pitt's attempt to frighten money from her, and she refused to fall prey to his tactics. But Jeremy would certainly need money for food and drink, and her own funds were so meagre that she knew they would not buy him much.

In the next instant, however, she learned that James Henry was not a man to be easily intimidated. For the past few years, he had managed Lord Hawkhurst's property, consisting of six large estates in five different counties. With the earl's name behind him, he oversaw the stewards, collected the rents, and disbursed the money—even to the earl himself— routinely dealing with all manner of men. He said, "We shall arrange for Mr. Kean's keep once we have seen him and ascertained his needs, but it would be useless to discuss them beforehand. You will take us to see him immediately, or I shall lodge a complaint with the Sheriff."

He did not bother to mention his connection to Lord Hawkhurst. And Hester doubted that even his threat to complain to the Sheriff was necessary. The natural authority in his voice was enough to convince Pitt that he was not to be bullied.

The keeper held his ground, however, when it came to admitting them to the hold. He insisted they would have to speak to Jeremy through the press yard grill.

He grinned wickedly at Hester. "If ye wants ter visit 'im inside, or move in wif 'im, ye'll 'ave ter pay fer a room in the Guv'nor's House. But that'll be five 'unnerd pound up front, and twenty-two shillin's a week—*if* 'e's even 'ere that long."

Hester's heart sank at the thought of such an exorbitant sum, but she obeyed when he gestured for them to follow. After a few paces down the street, he pointed to the end of the building, where several people stood clustered in front of an iron grill. He told them they should wait there. Then he ducked back into the lodge, releasing, as he went through the door, a blast of raucous voices, slurred with drink.

Even with the thick stone wall between them and the prisoners, Hester was nearly overcome again by the horrific odours. As James Henry conducted her down Newgate Street, she held her handkerchief pressed to her nose, wishing she had thought to sprinkle it with some of Isabella's perfume. But she had scarcely remembered to bring food for Jeremy, which was far more important than her queasy stomach. She wondered how her brother could bear to be in such a filthy place, when he had always been more squeamish than she.

As they reached the end of the street, the crowd, consisting mostly of women, reluctantly made room for them closer to the grill. A few of the women had the listless air of people who had waited for a very long time, but most appeared to be vagrants who had come to taunt the prisoners through the bars. Some seemed inclined to beg, but a dark look from James Henry scared them away.

The stench had grown worse the nearer they had got to the grill, as a door from the gaol opened directly onto the yard. Several prisoners were standing or taking exercise in the narrow space, which could not have been over fifty feet in length and less than ten in width. The only sun that managed to reach it was a faint patch of light along the eastern wall, and it was there that many of the men, a few with their wives, leaned with their faces up to receive it.

The prisoners' condition was not as miserable as Hester had feared. Some appeared to be reasonably well-dressed. She turned her gaze away, however, when one of the women stared resentfully back at her, making her realize how horrible it would be never to have any privacy.

She and James Henry had not waited many minutes before a door opened onto the yard. Two of the women gasped and covered their eyes. One of the men sprang forward and hastily removed his coat to offer it to the person poised to come outside.

Instinctively, Hester felt a stab of fear. She craned her neck for a better view into the yard, just in time to see Jeremy stumble through the door with a turnkey clutching his arm.

His chest and shoulders were bare, as well as his legs. If not for the other man's coat, which he had wrapped about his waist, she had no doubt he would be standing in front of the assembly without a stitch of clothing.

He was pale, frightened, and dirty. And as Hester noted the raw, red marks at his wrists, neck, and ankles, a rage such as she had never known mounted inside her until she shook.

In spite of his filth, Jeremy was trying to bear himself with dignity. Squaring his shoulders, broad and strong on his tall, lean body, he bowed to the man who had provided him with covering, before turning to see who his visitors were. The sight of Hester, peering at him through the grill, clutching the iron bars in helpless anguish, seemed to astonish him. But in the next moment, he came striding towards her with eager relief.

"Hester! I thought Mrs. Curry had come to see me! How did you hear—?"

"I read it in the news-sheets. Jeremy, how did this happen? Are you hurt? Where are your clothes?"

This last question raised an expression that was half-shame, half-outrage. "The turnkeys took them when they discovered that I did not have enough money to pay for my fetters to be removed. I was taken so suddenly, you see, that I came away without a penny in my pockets, and there is nothing in this place that one does *not* have to pay for.

Since my clothes were all I had, and I could not bear to be weighted down by the irons, I had to surrender them in payment. But I couldn't even stand up in those irons!

"I regret having to appear this way," he said, with offended dignity, "but they've put me into a crowded hold with no bedding or even a chamber pot. Not even a bucket!"

"Oh, Jeremy!" Hester could barely speak over the painful lump in her throat, "But what about this charge? What can we do to help?"

He shook his head, his baffled eyes staring back at her with their usual frankness. "They say that someone laid information that I had written a treasonous pamphlet, which I swear I never have! And that Mr. Curry printed it, which he never did. For the life of me, I cannot imagine who would have said such a thing or why."

He noticed the basket hanging from her arm, and his attention was suddenly diverted. "Have you anything to eat in that basket, Hester? They don't give us anything in here but bread and dirty water."

"Oh, yes!" She hurried to rifle through it. "I'm so sorry, I forgot. All this is for you." The basket would not fit through the bars, so Hester handed him a pullet's leg, a wedge of cheese, and an apple, which Jeremy began to devour on the spot. She wondered if she could trust Pitt to see that Jeremy got the rest, but she had so many worries, she did not even know where to begin.

A stirring at her elbow reminded her that she had not made her brother known to James Henry. As she made the introduction, Jeremy saluted him cheerfully with the chicken bone, and apologized for not greeting him in a more gentleman-like fashion.

Noting that the turnkey was growing restless, Hester broke anxiously into this speech. "How much will you need for bail?"

Recalled to the seriousness of his situation, Jeremy sobered. He said quietly, "Thank you, Hester. But there is no bail in a case of treason."

Hester's stomach plunged to the ground. For a moment she remained speechless, but she soon composed herself to ask, "Then how much will you need to get your clothes back and to be moved into a decent cell? You can have everything I own, but I shall have to bring it tomorrow."

James Henry interrupted before Jeremy could reply. "No need to wait, Mrs. Kean. I brought money with me."

Jeremy gaped at him. Then, as if a welcome notion occurred to him, he gazed back and forth between James Henry and his sister, and beamed. "That is very good of you, Mr. Henry. I shall hope to pay you back, of course."

Suspecting the error her brother must have made, Hester felt an uncomfortable warmth creeping up her body.

She was relieved when James Henry corrected Jeremy's misunderstanding by saying politely, "You have my lord to thank, not me. He would not wish his lady's cousin to be lodged so poorly."

Hester doubted whether Harrowby would care very much how her brother was lodged, but Jeremy accepted this statement with his usual ingenuousness, not realizing that James Henry would have to explain the expenses he had made to his employer.

James Henry went on, "But your sister and I shall attend to that. Before we do, what can be done to defend you against this charge?"

"I truly do not know." Jeremy's moment of cheer vanished. "I do not even know what Mr. Curry is doing to defend himself. He was not put in the Stone Hold with me. He had money with him, you see, so they put him upstairs in the King's Bench Ward."

"And there truly is nothing to the charge? You did not write the pamphlet in question?"

"I don't even know what pamphlet they're talking about! The King's Messengers simply appeared at Mr. Curry's shop and said that information had been laid against us. Then they seized all the pamphlets in the shop, but I never saw anything like the one they described. Mr. Curry doesn't usually deal in political matters," Jeremy said. "He says there is no profit to be made in politics. What I write for him has more to do with interesting occurrences—hangings and drownings, and so-forth."

"This is how you've been earning your living?" Hester asked.

"Yes." Jeremy flushed—whether from pride or shame, or a mixture of both, she could not tell—but when the turnkey stepped forward to take him back to the hold, his colour fled, leaving him pale and frightened.

He turned his guileless gaze on Hester, and said anxiously, "You will come to see me again, will you not?"

Devastated by the fear in his eyes, she promised to visit him again at the first opportunity, and reached through the bars to grasp his hand, before the guard could take him away.

"I will see what can be discovered about the evidence against you," James Henry said hurriedly. "If you are innocent, you should have nothing to fear."

Jeremy visibly latched onto these words, as he was dragged backwards towards the door. He managed to raise one hand in farewell before the turnkey shoved him inside.

The moment he disappeared, Hester went weak in the knees. Her anger over her brother's mistreatment had shaken her so fiercely as to rob her of strength. She would have been glad for the support of James Henry's arm, but his frown told her that he was preoccupied.

After a few seconds' thought, he said, "I believe it would be best if I put you into a carriage. I cannot predict how long my negotiations with Pitt will take, and you should not wait here alone."

As he took her elbow to usher her outside the gate, Hester declared, "How can I ever thank you enough?"

He looked surprised, but pleased, when he responded, "You must not give it the least consideration. As I said to your brother, I am certain my lord would wish me to see to his comfort."

If James Henry truly believed that, Hester thought, she would not be the one to disabuse him of the notion. His conviction that it was Harrowby's responsibility to care for her brother would carry much more weight with the earl than hers.

"Is there nothing we can do to get these charges removed?"

James Henry regarded her soberly. "Let me see what I can discover, first. We'll discuss the next step when we know more."

Fortunately, Harrowby had gone straight to Kensington Palace from Westminster that evening, so Hester was able to wait for James Henry's return before suffering Harrowby's reaction to the news.

James Henry found her in the withdrawing room, where she had tried to keep herself from fretting by occupying her hands with needlework. He started in immediately, telling her that he had ordered

Jeremy's clothes to be returned, and that he had stayed to see him moved into a more comfortable ward. He had scarcely been with her a few minutes, when they heard the earl's horse pulling up in the square.

The footman in the hall must have acquainted Harrowby with the news that his receiver-general was upstairs, for he joined them at once, and not perceiving Hester's anxious expression, asked James Henry how he had found things on the Essex estate.

"Fairly dull, I should say?" Harrowby ended, on a laugh.

"Not at all, my lord. The draining of the fens is quite an interesting process. If your lordship would like, I should be happy to describe the work to you."

Harrowby gave him a startled glance. "No, no!" he said hastily. "I'll take your word for it. Not much in the farming way myself, you know. Besides, mustn't keep you. You'll want to be off to the Abbey tomorrow, I expect."

James Henry darted a look at Hester, before sucking in a purposeful breath. "Perhaps not *quite* so soon as that, my lord."

"Oh?"

As Harrowby raised an inquisitive brow, James Henry said, "I gather that your lordship did not stop here on the way to the palace. I left a message for your lordship explaining why Mrs. Kean and I were obliged to take a carriage to Newgate prison."

"Newgate!" Harrowby exclaimed, transferring his gaze from James Henry to Hester and back. "What the deuce took you there?"

Hester opened her mouth to speak, but James Henry forestalled her. "I am afraid Mrs. Kean received some very distressing news. She read in a news-sheet that her brother, whom she had not seen for many years, was taken up by a Messenger."

Harrowby turned an alarming shade of pale. He put a shaking palm to his forehead, and said faintly, "Treason? He was taken up for treason?"

"He has been accused of writing a pamphlet offensive to his Majesty's government. But Mr. Kean assured us both that the charge is completely unfounded. With your lordship's permission, I will see what evidence there is against him and get the matter sorted out."

Harrowby's face changed from a ghostly white to an angry red. "Of course he said it was unfounded! What else would the blackguard say?"

James Henry pulled his brows together in a formidable line. He cast Hester an apologetic glance, before saying, "I am certain that he spoke the truth, my lord."

"Indeed, my lord!" Hester found her voice to say emphatically, "Jeremy would never even think of lying! If he had written anything treasonous about the government, he would be much more inclined to announce it proudly. He was never one to conceal his opinions."

She saw at once that hers had not been a fortuitous speech.

Harrowby gasped. "I hope neither of you mentioned the connection between us—not that I acknowledge any relation to this brother of yours, Mrs. Kean! I never even knew of his existence."

"We said nothing, my lord," James Henry said. "We both endeavoured to keep your lordship's name out of the business. But surely you will wish me to see what can be done to clear up the confusion? The sooner we can establish that Mr. Kean knew nothing about the reported pamphlet, the better it will be for all concerned."

When Harrowby seemed on the point of forbidding him to involve himself, James Henry continued smoothly, "Naturally, if Mrs. Kean's brother were to be convicted and sentenced, people would soon discover the connection to this family. So we must avoid a trial at any cost."

The protest Harrowby had been about to utter died on his lips. His brain seemed full of imagined horrors, as he gaped at them both.

"I have taken the liberty of having Mr. Kean moved into a more comfortable ward. I was certain you would wish me to see to his comfort."

Hester doubted that Harrowby had registered a word of this last speech. His mind still appeared to be fixed on the terrifying prospect of being linked in any way to a convicted traitor.

Finally regaining a portion of his senses, he adjured James Henry to clear the matter up at once. "And without once mentioning my name, do you hear? I tell you, this is all that was needed. First, the old gentleman, and now this Jeremy fellow! What sort of maggots have people got inside their heads? Don't they see how dangerous it is to involve themselves in intrigues of this sort? Have they no thought for their relations? Or do they want us all to end with our heads on London Bridge? Look at Lord Oxford! And now, poor Thomas Harley has been committed to the Gate-House."

"I am certain that Jeremy is innocent, my lord. You have nothing to fear from his kinship to Isabella," Hester said. "Why, no one could have been more astonished by the charge than he!"

"That had better be true, Mrs. Kean," he said indignantly. "After all that I have done for you, I should think you would know better than to introduce a scandal into my house."

He gave her an anxious look. "I don't suppose you will feel it necessary to visit him again? Not if Mr. Henry is taking care of the situation?"

"I should like to be able to visit him. Until this week, I had not glimpsed my brother in more than five years, and at times, I even feared that he was dead. If there is any possibility that he . . . that something . . . ." Hester found it hard to go on. "I should like to spend more time with him if I may."

For all his foolishness, Harrowby was not without a heart. He could not summon the cruelty to refuse her.

"Well, if you must see him," he said, "then you had better return to Hawkhurst House. You, too," he said to James Henry. "I can't have the two of you traipsing back and forth from Newgate to this house. Someone would surely begin to wonder what all the coming and going was about."

Bowing her head in relief, Hester made him a curtsy. She would have to invent a tale for Isabella, for it was not to be supposed that her cousin could keep such a secret.

"I shall escort Mrs. Kean to Hawkhurst House tomorrow," James Henry said. "Would you wish me to report to you daily on the matter, my lord?"

Harrowby shook his head most emphatically. "No! I should rather know nothing about it at all. Though I suppose you should advise me if the fellow's going to be hanged, so I can try to smooth things over with the King. I can honestly say that I've never set eyes on the villain."

Hester bridled at this description of her brother, who for all his faults, was certainly *not* a *villain,* but she could not afford to make an enemy of Harrowby. It was Hawkhurst money that would keep Jeremy housed and fed during his imprisonment, and Harrowby's receiver-general who would work to get her brother set free. If St. Mars were in

England, he would help her, but he was gone. And being an outlaw himself, he could hardly inquire about the evidence in Jeremy's case. So she bit her tongue.

James Henry, however, cleared his throat. "I do not think you should regard Mr. Kean in that light, my lord. There is certain to be an innocent explanation."

Hester gave him a look of genuine gratitude. It was easy for her to defend her brother, because she knew him and his character. James Henry could have no basis for making such claims on a stranger's behalf. That he had done it amazed her. She could only admire him for his courage in standing up to his employer and his fairness in giving Jeremy the benefit of the doubt.

Now, she only prayed they would be able to prove Jeremy's innocence.

Yes, you despise the man to Books confined,
Who from his study rails at human kind;
Though what he learns he speaks, and may advance
Some general maxims, or be right by chance.
The coxcomb bird, so talkative and grave,
That from his cage cries Cuckold, Whore, and Knave,
Though many a passenger he rightly call,
You hold him no Philosopher at all.

CHAPTER III

It was not until the next day, when she was seated in a carriage next to James Henry, armed with a larger basket of food and three bottles of sack for Jeremy, that she confided her greatest fear to him.

"I know that Jeremy would never plot against the government," she said. "Even if he did have sentiments about the Stuart cause, which to my knowledge he never had, I cannot believe he would risk his safety like that. If he had been accused of drinking a toast to the Duke of Ormonde, I suppose it could have been possible. Not because he's a Jacobite, or even a Tory, but because in a certain situation, he might consider it the polite thing to do. But when we both lived at home, he never demonstrated the slightest interest in politics."

Her companion's smile told her that he was not perfectly convinced. "You do not think he might have changed in the years since you last saw him?"

"No. If we had not seen him yesterday, and he had not denied it so forcibly, I might have wondered. But the man we saw in Newgate is the same Jeremy I've always known, and he would never lie to me."

She clenched the hands in her lap. "That is not what concerns me. What I fear is that Jeremy could have been imposed upon by someone else."

"You mean, he might have been tricked somehow?"

She nodded, biting her lip. "Either that, or much more likely that someone found a way to cast the blame on him. I cannot believe he would have written such a pamphlet. Jeremy has his foolish moments, but he's not that kind of a fool. He would have recognized the danger of writing anything in support of Ormonde. Unless there was some overwhelming reason to write it, he would have refused. In fact, the Jeremy I know would have been outraged if someone had asked him to do such a dangerous thing.

"No," she said again, musing aloud. "The only circumstance I can imagine is that someone who knew Jeremy decided to employ his name."

Next to her, James Henry frowned again. "But I don't see any need for that. It's the custom for writers to assume false names. Why should anyone use your brother's?"

"That is not precisely what I meant. It's only that . . . knowing Jeremy, and how quick he is to trust complete strangers . . . I have to wonder if he might somehow have laid himself open to being used." Hester heard the confusion in her voice. "I cannot pretend to know how, but that is the possibility that worries me most. And it could be impossible to prove if he is taken to trial."

James Henry said nothing, but his expression told her that she had given him something more troubling to think about.

They arrived at Newgate and, after paying the driver, rang the keeper's bell. Pitt sauntered out of the lodge, taking his time, and scowled when he saw who had rung him.

"We are here to speak to Mr. Kean again," James Henry said, "and this time, his sister would like to be admitted to see him."

"Well, yer a bit too late fer that," Pitt said. "They took 'im away just after you were 'ere."

The blood drained from Hester's face. "Took him away? But why?"

She could not believe that her brother had been tried with no warning. Warring with the fear that he had already been hanged was a stubborn conviction that it was simply impossible for the sessions to have been held.

"How should I know?" Pitt growled. "I suppose ye've come ter git yer money back. Well, ye'll 'ave ter come again. Can't say as I could put me 'ands on ev'ry penny of it just now."

"You cannot mean that Mr. Kean was taken for trial," James Henry said sternly. "So speak clearly, man! Who came for Mr. Kean, and where was he taken?"

"T'was their lordships sent ter 'ave 'im discharged." Pitt shrugged. "Said as 'ow they didn't 'ave no evidence ter 'old 'im."

"He's been discharged?" Hester's heart gave a leap of joy. "You are certain it was my brother, Mr. Kean, who was released?"

Pitt cleared his phlegmy throat and spat near her feet. "It were 'im all right. I thought ye must've 'eard and come fer yer—"

He caught himself before completing his sentence, but he had obviously believed they had come for the money James Henry had paid for Jeremy's keep. Now that Hester's shock had passed, she saw this, but she wondered why Jeremy had not come to tell her of his release.

The same question must have occurred to James Henry, for his harsh, aquiline features bore signs of annoyance. He looked down at Hester, and noting her embarrassment, eased his expression into a smile.

"I daresay he was so relieved, he could think of nothing but going home and to bed. A message will likely be waiting for you in Kensington Square."

"Possibly," Hester agreed, but she feared it was all too unlikely. It would be just like Jeremy to neglect to send her word. "I should feel much better if I could speak to him, though, before I return to Isabella. I do not wish to burden you any further with my brother's affairs, so I will not ask you to accompany me. But I think I should find him and discover what the trouble was all about."

"It's no burden. And I confess that I should like to hear the story myself. My lord is not at ease with regard to this affair."

James Henry had every right to accompany her if he wished, but Hester could not help feeling nervous at the prospect of his seeing Jeremy again, particularly if no message was waiting for her in Kensington Square.

They summoned another hackney coach and instructed the driver to carry them to St. Dunstan's in the West. There, Hester hoped to find the bookseller's stall belonging to Edmund Curry, Jeremy's patron, who should be able to direct them to her brother's lodgings.

The medieval church of St. Dunstan's had been constructed long before the need for city streets or the invention of carriages. The church was so large that it protruded some thirty feet into Fleet Street, blocking the carriageway, and hampering the flow of horses, vehicles, street vendors, and pedestrians that used the busy thoroughfare. Shops with projecting wooden signs had been constructed along its eastern and western walls. The Great Fire of London had halted just three doors east of the church, so the west end of Fleet Street between St. Dunstan's and Temple Bar was still overhung by the upper stories of ancient houses.

The driver whose hackney carried them from Newgate cursed and fought his way through the snarl of traffic, putting Hester's nerves on edge. The joy that had filled her on hearing that Jeremy had been saved was fading at the prospect of locating him in this chaos. But James Henry and Hester had no sooner stepped down from the vehicle in front of St. Dunstan's than Hester spied the sign of the Bell and Bible to their right.

On any other errand, Hester would have taken the opportunity to gaze up at St Dunstan's clock, with its two massive giants who struck the hours with their hammers—one of the most wondrous sights in London. Now, however, she had but one purpose, which was to discover how Jeremy had won his release and why he had not immediately sent her the news.

Mr. Curry's bookshop—if, indeed, this was it—stood at the beginning of a long row of stalls erected against the eastern wall of the church. Most of the stalls were devoted to the booksellers' trade.

James Henry opened the door to the tiny shop, and the first thing that met Hester's gaze was her brother, leaning against the wooden counter. He appeared to be lounging, and was speaking to the pretty creature behind it, a woman with a pleasing youthful figure and light brown tresses under a modest cap. Behind her was a wall hung with long wooden rails, draped with unbound folios of every size and shape.

When James Henry and Hester entered, the woman glanced up with a guilty start. Then, perceiving two strangers, she gave them a welcoming smile.

Jeremy turned and saw them, and pleasure lit his handsome face. "Hester! And Mr. Henry! Good day to you, sir. I was just telling Mrs. Curry how you came to my rescue." He turned and extended one arm towards the pretty woman. "But I must make you known to one another. Hester, this is Mr. Curry's wife, Mrs. Sally."

He pronounced her name with such reverence that Hester was left in no doubt as to his sentiments. Suppressing her dismay, she politely acknowledged the introduction, hoping she had not betrayed her concern.

Jeremy presented James Henry as the gentleman who had been so generous as to pay his lodging in Newgate. He beamed on Mr. Henry as if he had just discovered the perfect Christian soul.

"Jeremy," Hester said impatiently. "We just came from Newgate, where Mr. Pitt informed us that you had been discharged."

"Yes, isn't it marvelous, Hester? It was all a terrible mistake. Someone accused Mr. Curry and me of producing a treasonous pamphlet, but when the justices looked into the charge, there was no such tract to be found. They said it must have been either a misunderstanding or a prank."

"Did they say who laid the information against you?"

"No." He shook his head, his face befuddled. "They received it in an anonymous letter. If there were not so many illegal pamphlets being printed just now, they said, they would have ignored it—or at least examined us first. But with the Pretender's agents stirring up trouble, they're acting quickly on every report.

"They were most apologetic—said they would send a notice to the news-sheets to clear our names. I think that was very decent of them, don't you?"

"Wonderfully decent." Hester tried to keep the irony from her voice. "But did you not think of advising me of your release? When that horrible man Pitt told me that you had been taken away . . . Jeremy, I feared you had been hanged and quartered!"

"Oh, my poor Hester!" His face drooped in heartfelt sympathy, but it did not occur to him to apologize. "What a fright you must have had! But I am perfectly well, as you see."

He added ingenuously, "To tell you the truth, I could not help feeling concerned for Mrs. Curry here. I feared she must be completely overturned by all that had passed. So, as soon as I washed the filth of that place off me, I came here straight away to let her know that all was well." He relayed all this with a confiding air, as if looking out for Mrs. Curry's welfare was a duty that he had selflessly taken upon himself.

Mrs. Curry had the grace to blush. Peering up at Hester from beneath her lowered lids, she stammered, "Of course, it was very kind of Mr. Kean to concern himself. But since my husband was discharged at nearly the same minute, there was really no need for him to worry on my account."

Throughout this recitation, James Henry had observed the pair and said nothing. Now he asked, "Does your husband know who might have slandered him, ma'am?"

She gratefully turned to him and shook her head. "No, sir. But my husband is forever making enemies, so it was likely only someone who wished to do him harm."

"Making enemies?" Hester said. "Whatever for?"

"Well . . . this is not the first time that he has been carried off to gaol, you see. He sometimes publishes things that other people do not wish to be printed."

"What sort of things?" Hester grew anxious again at the thought that her brother could be involved in any unsavoury business.

"Oh, any manner of things."

This was said in an airy tone that Hester did not quite know how to interpret. It seemed to indicate either a wish to avoid explanation, or else a remarkable lack of concern.

Mrs. Curry went on, "Sometimes there are letters that come into his hands—written by the poets, you know, like Mr. Pope. And he publishes stories by authors like Mr. Kean, only not under their names, so it makes people guess who wrote them."

Hester turned to her brother. "What about you, Jeremy? Have you made any enemies with your writing?"

"I don't think so." He seemed genuinely astonished by the notion, which gave Hester some comfort at least. "But I don't write about anyone important, and I never claim to be anyone real. I just invent my own stories."

Hester could not understand why her brother had been accused of treason if what he said was true. But, perhaps, the person who had laid charges against them had been too furious with Mr. Curry to care if he endangered Jeremy, as well.

She was on the point of questioning him further, when the shop door opened and a cheerful voice said behind her, "There he is, looking as sweet as if he hadn't just spent the last pair o' nights in a privy! Bless you, my boy! But it's a pleasure to see you!"

Hester turned and beheld a tall, slender man of middle-age, rather carelessly attired in the garb of a solicitor's clerk. His face was long, with a wide forehead and a pointed chin. He wore a short brown wig, and his skin was lightly freckled. There was a slight lilt to his voice that she could not immediately place.

Jeremy greeted him with a laugh and presented him to Hester and James Henry as Mr. Sullivan of the Temple.

Mr. Sullivan gallantly raised Hester's hand to his lips. "*Joseph* Sullivan, at your service, mistress."

Hester had the curious feeling that she had seen him before. The mystery was soon resolved when he said, "I nearly had the pleasure of making your acquaintance last Saturday night, when the four of us took the air upon the river."

Then, she recalled that he had been one of the men in Jeremy's boat—the only one who had *not* been dressed like a ruffian.

"It was due entirely to Mr. Sullivan's kindness that we found each other," Jeremy explained, "for he treated me and Mrs. Curry to the outing."

"Your other companion was Mr. Curry, then?"

"No, that was Tubbs. He writes things for Mr. Curry, too. A good fellow, Tubbs. We share lodgings, so you will be sure to meet him. Mr. Curry did not join us that evening. He doesn't care much for boats."

A movement at her elbow reminded Hester that James Henry had been patiently waiting. She squirmed when she realized that Jeremy had said nothing about repaying him. They could not discuss his debt with an audience, however, so Hester gave James Henry a rueful look before turning back with the intention of drawing Jeremy outside.

A lively banter had started up between Mr. Sullivan, Jeremy, and

Mrs. Curry, who evidently were on the friendliest of terms. Before Hester could catch her brother's eye, however, the talk took an uncomfortable turn when Mr. Sullivan joked, "It's a shame you were taken with Mr. Curry, my boy. It would have been a great chance to have a go at his wife."

Mrs. Curry turned a ghastly pale, and Jeremy's cheeks went red. They exchanged mortified glances, as if wondering whether the other had heard.

Plainly, neither one had any notion of the other's regard. As Mrs. Curry bent to fumble beneath the counter for a book, Jeremy uttered an uncomfortable laugh.

With surprising tact then—though it came with a broad wink for Hester—Mr. Sullivan added, "If I'd known ya *both* were in gaol, I might've had a try at the widow myself. But there's just my luck! I didn't know ya'd been arrested until ya'd already been cleared.

"What's it like in there, my boy?"

Jeremy seemed relieved to have the subject changed, but, out of respect for Mrs. Curry's feelings, he refrained from describing the worst horrors of Newgate.

"I had visited Newgate once," he said, "to take down the last words of a condemned man, but I had never seen the vilest part of it. It's a scandal! Not even the most heinous villain should be kept the way those prisoners are kept! Someone really ought to do something about it. I hope to persuade Mr. Curry to publish a pamphlet about the conditions in the gaols. I shall have to convince him, though, for he did not see the worst of it himself. He was lodged more comfortably upstairs."

As Jeremy spoke, Mrs. Curry abandoned her fumblings beneath the counter to peer up at him with worshipful eyes. But the moment he mentioned her husband, she abruptly dropped her gaze. The shift in her position attracted Hester's notice, and she turned in time to catch the woman's anguished look.

Feeling Hester's eyes upon her, Mrs. Curry did her best to cover her unhappiness with a smile. But as Hester returned it, she felt far from tranquil.

Jeremy was speaking to James Henry now, and his words immediately drove any other thought from Hester's head. "I was thinking that perhaps Lord Hawkhurst would wish to contribute to the publishing of such a tract," he said. "As generous as he was to me in my distress, I am sure he would wish to know about the unfortunate men imprisoned with me. In fact," he confided, "I was hoping you might be able to advance me a sum to improve those men's situations now, before—"

"Jeremy!" Hester strove to keep her tone polite. "We must not become so indebted to Lord Hawkhurst that we can never repay him."

She was relieved to see a trace of amusement on James Henry's face, even if it was nothing other than the pressing of his lips to hide a smile. Her brother's speech had taken him slightly aback, but apparently he could appreciate the selflessness of Jeremy's request.

Jeremy was so guileless, it was clear he believed that the kindness he'd received was due to the generous benevolence of Isabella's husband, as James Henry had said.

What had amused James Henry, Hester thought, was probably the sheer ingenuousness of Jeremy's proposal, for her brother understood nothing of money, neither the ways of earning it, the burden of sharing it, the responsibility of maintaining a family fortune, nor the restraints upon spending it that an employee like James Henry must respect.

Jeremy accepted her interference unquestioningly, however, merely demonstrating his surprise with raised eyebrows and a rounding of his lips. He was as ready to take her lead as he had ever been, so he smiled at James Henry and said that he had instructed Pitt to direct the rest of the money James Henry had given him to the comfort of his fellow ward-mates, not for once believing that Lord Hawkhurst would wish to have it back once he heard about the misery of their condition.

Concealing her exasperation—for Jeremy would be incapable of understanding the delicacy of her position—Hester turned to James Henry with a pledge to repay Harrowby poised on the tip of her tongue.

She was forestalled by Mr. Sullivan, who, peering out the window, murmured in a secretive voice, "Better mind your P's and Q's, friends. Here comes the law."

Following the inclination of his head, Hester looked outside and spied the beadle, making his stately way to the door of the shop. He parted the pedestrians before him like Moses with his staff. Opening the door, he stepped into the Bell and Bible, and eyed their little group with intense disfavour.

Wondering what they had done to annoy an officer of the ward, Hester glanced at her brother. But he had turned to exchange a conspiratorial grin with Mrs. Curry, whose answering smile seemed a little bit forced.

"What's this? What's this? Not up to any more trouble now, I 'ope!" the beadle boomed as he pushed past them into the shop.

"No trouble at all, Mr. Simpkins, and a very good day to you, too," Jeremy said.

Dividing his scowls evenly between Jeremy and Mr. Sullivan, Mr. Simpkins ignored James Henry and Hester and swept off his wide-brimmed hat to make a deep bow to Mrs. Curry.

The removal of his hat exposed his features to light: a small pair of eyes and a bulbous nose in a pock-marked face. The skirt of his coat was much too short and rode up to reveal a portly physique. The warmth of the afternoon had made him perspire, leaving stains under his arms and down the middle of his back.

Over the top of his head, Mr. Sullivan gave Jeremy a mischievous wink.

"I 'ope these men 'aven't been disturbin' you, my dear?" Mr. Simpkins addressed this remark to Mrs. Curry in a distinctly tender tone. He would have possessed himself of one of her hands if she had not clasped them both behind her back.

Foiled, he straightened, giving Jeremy a forbidding look. "Sir, I wonder that you're still loiterin' about this shop after the disgrace you 'ave brought upon this poor woman's 'usband!"

"Hold just a second there, Mr. Simpkins!" Mr. Sullivan said. "Have ya not heard that our Jeremy's been cleared? It seems the authorities took him up in error."

"Indeed," Mrs. Curry said earnestly. "Neither Mr. Kean nor my husband was guilty. It was all a vicious lie!"

At her defence of Jeremy, an angry flush spread over Mr. Simpkins's face. "You're far too trusting, my dear, as I've told you many times afore. It is my duty as beadle of this precinct to keep a lookout for vagrants, and you shouldn't encourage them to laze about." He tried to catch hold of the hand she'd let fall, but Mrs. Curry snatched up a pamphlet and used it to fan her face.

"I protest this slander, sir!" Jeremy's laugh rang with incredulity. "How can you accuse me of vagrancy when Mr. Curry is my employer? Where else should I be every day, if not here?"

"And my business is equally clear," Mr. Sullivan said, picking up a book that lay upon the counter. "I doubt that Curry would thank you for chasing off his customers."

Mr. Simpkins struggled with a response, but, reluctant to offend Mrs. Curry, he mastered his temper. Searching for a new target, he looked about and spied James Henry and Hester.

"And 'oo might these strangers be?" he asked, raking them up and down with a suspicious glint.

Jeremy presented them, making a point of mentioning their connection to Lord Hawkhurst, as well as his own.

Hester could hardly blame her brother for boasting of the relation when Mr. Simpkins appeared to suspect him of every kind of evil. Wondering if James Henry would take offence, she glanced at him and was relieved to see that no flicker of annoyance disturbed his features. On the contrary, the look he gave Mr. Simpkins seemed to challenge him to object to their presence as well.

"While we *are* here," he said, turning to Mrs. Curry, "I should like to see what books you have, and perhaps I can interest Mrs. Kean in making a purchase."

Mr. Simpkins swallowed the rebuke he had been planning, and bowing deeply to Mrs. Curry again, begged her to excuse him, as he had important business to attend to. As he puffed out his chest and stalked out, planting his staff loudly with every step, Mr. Sullivan had to restrain himself to keep from chuckling.

Even James Henry looked as if he might have enjoyed a laugh, but, instead, he asked Hester, "What do you say, Mrs. Kean? Isn't there something here you would like?"

Caught unprepared, Hester gazed longingly at the books hanging from their rails. "There must surely be something," she said regretfully. "But I know that Mrs. Curry will forgive me if I do not make any purchase today." She gave a smile, as if she might buy something later, when the truth was that she never expected to have an income that would stretch to cover books.

She was astonished when James Henry turned and whispered in her ear, "Please, I insist! I have been meaning to speak to my lord about making you an allowance. As my lady's cousin, that would be more fitting than paying you wages."

"Oh, no!" Hester said. "You mustn't—"

"And, pray, why not, when you perform so many duties for them both?"

"But I already receive—"

"Your lodgings and food, yes. But so do we all, and still we receive our wages. Why should you not have any money for yourself?"

Hester couldn't tell him that she did not wish to be a further charge on the estate, which rightfully belonged to St. Mars. Nor that she hoped it would one day be his again. One of her greatest fears was that Harrowby and Isabella would run through all of St. Mars's money before he could be restored to his title. And how could she face him if she took even a penny, when he received none of it himself?

Mistaking her pause for acquiescence, James Henry smiled with a look of genuine pleasure before taking her elbow to draw her closer to the counter.

Mrs. Curry pulled down books to show them. Seeing that they were occupied, Mr. Sullivan made a cheerful bow and took his leave. Jeremy waved him off before joining Hester at the counter.

She had noted with some surprise that among Mr. Curry's books were a few written by names she knew. One slender volume was by that new poet who was so popular, Mr. Alexander Pope and another was attributed to "A Lady of the Court". When she asked Mrs. Curry about the latter, she told her the verses had been penned by Lady Mary Wortley Montagu.

Hester found herself unable to resist James Henry's encouragement. "What have you written, Jeremy?" she asked.

Mrs. Curry set down the thick set of folios James Henry had asked to see entitled, *The Adventures of Telemachus, the Son of Ulysses,* and left him looking over them, to place several chapbooks in front of Hester. With her face lit, she gazed proudly from Jeremy to Hester, who read,

"News from the Dead: Or, The Monthly Packet of True Intelligence from the other World." The small volume purported to contain an *account of the Helliopolitan Junto, and some Transactions that pass'd therein; a consolatory letter to a Person of Quality, from her Daughter now in Heaven, with a Description of that happy Place, and of her Arrival there* (advice touching the education of children); a piece on *the character of a Devil of a woman*; and a *Daily Exercise for Libertins, with some occasional Devotions. Enigmas to be solv'd.*

It had supposedly been written *by Mercury. For the Month of August* and *printed for E. Curry at the Bell and Bible, against St. Dunstan's Church in Fleet-Street, where may be had the other Parts pr. 6d. each.*

Hester flipped through the stack below it and found more installments of *News from the Dead*, including *An Account of the Abbot Soyer, who began to preach in the 6th Year of his Age, with his first Sermon here faithfully inserted* and other pieces, such as, *Reflection upon Death bed Charity.*

Swallowing an inclination to smile, Hester said, "These are splendid, Jeremy! Where do you get your ideas?"

He squirmed, uncomfortable with the praise, but gratified as well. "I truly couldn't tell you, Hester. They just occur to me when I'm least expecting it—the ones that are *mine,* at least. Mr. Curry does suggest a subject to me every now and then, like the one to the lady of quality from her daughter in Heaven—he thought it might please Lady Whitwood, you know, because her daughter recently died, and I thought it might give her comfort, so I wrote it. The stories from Greece are the ones I learned in my studies. And you would recognize the devotions, Hester, for they are Papa's, or as near as I can remember them."

"Well, I must have some of these," Hester said, in as hearty a tone as she could muster, "as long as you can promise me that I won't be frightened by them."

Jeremy flushed and gave an embarrassed laugh. "Oh, I doubt there's anything to scare you—as if I could! You never were the sort to take fright. But don't be fooled by the title—that was just Mr. Curry's idea. He said that a title like this would draw readers, and I believe it has, for Mrs. Curry tells me that my books sell very well."

"Indeed!" Mrs. Curry happily agreed. "We sell twenty of these for every other book."

"Mr. Curry says that if I keep writing this well, he wouldn't be surprised if he could increase what he pays me for them before long."

His innocent comment suddenly seemed to rob Mrs. Curry of the pleasure she had expressed. The dimples that had burrowed into her cheeks disappeared, and a hint of shame dulled her eyes, before she turned to James Henry to ask if he would like to look at anything else.

He had decided upon the history of Telemachus, and insisted on buying all of Jeremy's tales for Hester, in spite of her protests.

As Mrs. Curry added up their purchases, he pulled a handsome watch out of his vest pocket and told Hester that they had better return to Hawkhurst House.

Outside in Fleet Street again, Jeremy chased them down a hackney and stood beside it to hand his sister in. "Don't look for me to visit you in the coming week," he said, kissing her on the cheek, "for I'll have to write even more than usual to make up for the days I was in gaol."

As he closed the door behind her, Hester was struck with a sudden impulse to beg him to take care. But, putting this down to his recent peril and the general unrest in the kingdom, she restrained herself and merely waved him goodbye.

Court virtues bear, like Gems, the highest rate,
Born where Heaven's influence scarce can penetrate:
In life's low vale, the soil the Virtues like,
They please as beauties, here as wonders strike.
Though the same Sun with all-diffusive rays
Blush in the Rose, and in the Diamond blaze,
We prize the stronger effort of his power,
And justly set the Gem above the Flower.

CHAPTER IV

Far away from London on the edge of Paris, Gideon Fitzsimmons, the outlawed Viscount St. Mars, brought his horse to a halt before the Porte St. Denis. The guard who stepped forward to demand his papers took one look at the embroidery on his silk waistcoat, the Spanish lace at his wrists and throat, and the luxuriousness of his shoulder-length *peruque* and hastily waved him through the busy gate. Apparently he had learned that it did not pay to insist on doing his duty when an aristocrat was involved, even if this one seemed willing to stop.

Outside the Porte St. Denis, along both sides of the bustling road, narrow houses of three, five, even six stories stood jammed together, sharing walls. It was not until Gideon's horse clopped across a wooden bridge over a canal and passed through the Grille St. Denis that he got his first, welcome whiff of country air. From this point onward, with the city of Paris behind him, and the Church and Monastery of St. Lazare on his right, the dusty road that stretched before him was lined with high, stone walls, protecting the gardens and orchards that fed Paris.

The house Gideon sought was only a league away. When he reckoned he had ridden that distance, he beckoned to a boy, who was herding a sow with a switch, and asked to be pointed to the house belonging to

Monsieur Vaugirard.

Within a few minutes, he had located the house, handed his reins to a groom in the yard, and made his way through a flock of pecking chickens to the door, where he was admitted to a cool, flagged hall. At the door to Monsieur Vaugirard's *salon,* a lackey announced, *"Le vicomte de St. Mars,"* and Gideon walked in to make his bow to the two gentlemen who stood to greet him: James Butler, the former Duke of Ormonde; and Henry St. John, the former Viscount Bolingbroke.

Both men were of exceeding height, and they dressed with the same degree of elegance, from their expensive French *peruques* to the diamond buckles sparkling on their shoes. Both had been impeached by Parliament, and their estates had been attainted by the English Crown. But all resemblance between them ended there.

Although both were considered to be handsome, Bolingbroke's features were much smaller and his complexion much fairer than the Duke's. His pale-lashed eyes conveyed a shrewdness that Gideon had never found in Ormonde.

And—for the moment, at least—Bolingbroke seemed free of the guilt that had swept the Duke's expressive face the moment Gideon's name had been announced.

His Grace soon recovered his poise to welcome the visitor with an imitation of his former warmth. "So, it's you, St. Mars!" He invited Gideon to take a chair and assumed an avuncular tone to cover the uneasiness between them. "You received our message, I see. No trouble in finding us, I hope?"

"None, your Grace. Your letter neglected to appoint a time for my visit, however, so I may have come at an awkward time." He had noted with annoyance that both men were dressed to go out.

Just yesterday he had received a letter from Bolingbroke, requesting him to call at this address, as he was preparing to set out for Bar-le-Duc in Lorraine. Bar was the only refuge James Stuart had found when the English had forced the French to expel him from their territories. Anyone wishing to speak with him directly had no choice but to journey to Bar, and Gideon felt that he owed James a report on the impressions he had formed about the Jacobite enterprise in England before returning there himself.

But he was impatient to go home. Though still an outlaw in England, he had found that the only time he could forget his misfortunes was when he was with Hester Kean. Recent occurrences had made him worry how near she had come to entrusting her heart to a certain gentleman, as ruthless a person as Gideon had ever met. While she had said nothing of her feelings, her expressions had revealed enough to cause Gideon doubts. And the villain himself, now rotting in a French prison, had had the effrontery to suggest that there might have been something between them. Gideon knew he would not be easy until he could speak to Mrs. Kean and satisfy himself that it wasn't so.

But Bolingbroke had recently accepted the seals as James's secretary of state, and Ormonde had been named his general. It would have been foolish, and perhaps a waste of Gideon's time, to press on to Bar without first seeing what they wanted. Unwilling to delay his journey one day more than necessary, and sensing an urgency in their summons, he had ridden here at once. Now, it appeared that he had erred.

Ormonde hesitated over a reply, but Bolingbroke smoothly filled the breach. "We *were* engaged for the evening. But if his Grace will make my apologies to Mrs. Trant, I shall be grateful if you will stay and sup with me."

The Duke was plainly delighted by this solution, which would spare him from explaining why he had suddenly quitted England without advising Gideon—or, indeed, any of his fellow conspirators. To Gideon's polite protest that he had no wish to overturn their plans, Bolingbroke replied that it would suit him much better to remain at home.

He did look tired, as Gideon noted the moment the words were out of his mouth. Bolingbroke's natural pallor had masked his fatigue, but now that Gideon examined his face more closely, he saw the black shadows under his eyes.

Ormonde took a hasty leave, first assuring Gideon that Bolingbroke would tell him how his Majesty's business stood. This they all understood to mean the Pretender's plans for an invasion. Then Gideon found himself alone with the man who had, last year at the age of thirty-six, governed England as Queen Anne's most powerful secretary of state.

It was Bolingbroke whom Gideon's father had blamed for the Tories' failure to restore James Stuart to his throne. In the chaos surrounding

Queen Anne's death, the Tory leaders had failed to seize the government in James's name. Instead, the Whigs, with the authority George had given them in Hanover, had swept into the Palace to claim and hold it for George.

But the Queen's death had come hard on the heels of a bitter fight between Bolingbroke and Robert Harley, Lord Oxford, for control of the government, a lengthy quarrel which had left their party with no aim. Their rivalry had cost the Tories their power, leaving them to the mercy of vengeful Whigs. For the last six months, they had been forced to defend themselves against charges of abusing their authority while in office. And, with those charges bearing the name of treason, with death as the penalty, both Bolingbroke and Ormonde had fled to France.

Ormonde had always been at the centre of the Jacobite plot to restore James Stuart to the throne. What had not been clear before was the extent of Bolingbroke's involvement in the cause. But, however little he might have taken part in James's plans before, he was critical to them now.

Perhaps, like Gideon, accused of a crime and unable to prove his innocence, Bolingbroke had grasped the only opportunity available to regain his position in England—working for James in the hope that, once he was King of Great Britain, he would reward them with restitution of their titles and estates. As Bolingbroke called for his servant to bring them wine, Gideon reflected that, bereft of his own home, he would be the last to blame his host for this motive.

He waited for the servant to quit the room before asking why he'd been summoned.

Leaning forward to fill his guest's glass, Bolingbroke directed him a questioning look. "We heard you were at St. Germain, and leaving soon for Bar."

Gideon took a sip of the claret before nodding. The look on his host's face had alerted him that the news he was about to hear would not be welcome.

"You have heard of King Louis's illness?" Bolingbroke asked.

"Yes, we received the news at St. Germain."

Bolingbroke took a deep, bracing breath. "I have just been advised that there is no hope for his recovery. Louis will die. Which means that

James will lose the best friend he has in this world."

He did not wait for Gideon's response, but carried on in a weary voice, "Louis's physicians have insisted on prescribing him the waters of Bourbon. Fifteen covered waggons and upwards of sixty horses are to be sent to fetch the water for his bath, with horses laid upon the road for frequent changes to speed the journey. Six Couriers of the Cabinet are gone to bring, one after the other, the water that his doctors have ordered him to drink along with the baths.

"No effort or expense is to be spared—when it's as certain as night follows day that his Majesty will not live out the month." Bolingbroke's eyes met Gideon's over his glass. "He is suffering from a great mortification in his legs, and from that there is no cure."

Bolingbroke threw back his head to empty his glass, and poured himself another. Although he had spoken without a hint of bitterness, it was clear how devastating Louis's death would be to James and his followers. His Most Catholic Majesty Louis XIV was the king who had welcomed James as a baby to his exile and who had given his father, James II, the Palace of St. Germain to use as his own. It was Louis who had educated James and paid him an allowance at the expense of France, and who supported James's mother, the former Queen of England, Mary of Modena. And it was Louis upon whose generosity hundreds of James's supporters lived.

Twice Louis had outfitted ships with arms and armies to help the Catholic Stuarts regain their throne. It was only after France's utter defeat in the long war with England and her allies that Louis had conceded to England's demands and banished James from his lands. In that treaty, he had solemnly promised not to assist James to launch an attack upon England or Scotland, but no one believed he had abandoned his support for a Stuart restoration in England. And now Louis was dying.

No wonder Bolingbroke was downing his wine with no apparent appreciation for its bouquet.

"You wish me to carry this news to James?" Gideon guessed, finally.

"Yes . . . but there is more." Bolingbroke, who was noted for his eloquence, seemed to struggle for words. "I fear you must convey to his Majesty the dismal state of his affairs vis-à-vis the Court of France."

With a mounting sense of dismay, Gideon waited for him to elaborate, which he did, after taking another gulp and refilling both their glasses.

Leaning back against the velvet cushions of his divan, he began, "You must know that from the moment of my accepting the seals from James, I have begged and pleaded with the government of France to lend us the men and arms we need to bring about the rebellion. I was advised by a leader of our movement at home that our people were ready to rise, but that our enterprise would not be successful unless James arrived with twenty thousand arms, a train of artillery, five hundred officers with their servants, and a considerable sum of money—all of this, when France was reduced to the ebb of her riches and power.

"Even with the greatest will in the world, Louis could not afford to send an army into England. Still, at his own expense, he permitted the fitting of a ship to carry James and his guards. I had hoped to persuade him to help us more when he saw the results—the rallying of thousands of Englishmen and Scots to the Stuart standard.

"But that—" Bolingbroke paused. "That was before his Grace of Ormonde appeared on my doorstep." He gave a laugh, which did not disguise his frustration.

"Imagine, if you will, the effect on the French, when the man who had been touted as the leader of James's army—the man about whom all the English Jacobites were supposed to rally—turned up here, unexpectedly and without explanation. Since Ormonde arrived, I have not been able to get even *one* of Louis's ministers to take us seriously. Those who are not openly hostile simply regard me with pity. All my remaining hopes were with the King, and now Louis is dying, and not one of his ministers will commit to an action that his successor might oppose.

"I see no remedy for it, but to wait to discover who amongst them will survive into the next government, and hope that a regent can be made sympathetic to our cause. Without the help of France, I fear we shall never recapture the momentum that's been lost."

In the silence that followed this speech, Gideon asked, "Why *did* Ormonde choose to flee? With all the turmoil in the streets, why did he not just call for the rising?"

Rubbing a hand over his eyes, Bolingbroke sighed. "Forgive me if I can barely speak of it and keep my temper in check. There is no doubt that our greatest chance has been lost. If he had called for the rising then, I believe that the army would have rallied round him. But no matter how great a campaigner he may be, I'm afraid he lacks decision. Whatever reasoning he *did* use was exactly as I told you. He was convinced that no rebellion would succeed without troops from France. Too many of our English nobles have insisted on that commitment from James before they will agree to support him."

Gideon could not doubt this. His father had made the same condition.

"Then, of course, he was impeached and thought he dared not wait any longer for Louis's response. That should have been his signal to act." Bolingbroke gave the ghost of a smile. "But, as much as I bemoan Ormonde's arrival, I can hardly blame him for evading a trial."

Nor should Gideon, even if no army would have come at either his or Bolingbroke's call. He simply wished the Duke had been honest with him about the conspirators' need of aid from France. But it was possible that Ormonde was incapable of handling such a difficult situation. His talent on the battlefield was said to be prodigious, but that did not qualify him to lead a conspiracy.

"But if you knew that the cause was hopeless without those arms, why did you permit the Jacobites in England to betray themselves? You must read the news-sheets! Hardly a day goes by that some Jacobite is not arrested for openly defying King George. How much longer will it be before every one of them has been thrown into Newgate? And then, where will James's rebellion be?"

His teeth clenched, Bolingbroke said, "Do not, for one instant, expect me to accept the blame for those incidents! *Or* for the total lack of discretion that has warned the government of every one of our movements. If I had known that every Irishman on both sides of the Channel had taken upon himself the office of ambassador—that every lady who is titillated by the notion of aiding a prince had assumed the role of spy—I should never have accepted this post.

"But that has been the state of James's affairs both here and in England and Scotland since long before I became involved. The Jacobites in France believe that the whole of England is ready to rise in James's favour, and they take every burning of a meeting house, and every toast made to James over a mug of ale, as proof of his strength. Add to that the cursed Catholic priests, who have adopted his restoration as the next Crusade, and you have scores of letters crossing the Channel back and forth carrying our secrets. Without the first suggestion of caution, James's plans are discussed in every coffee house and over every lady's tea table. And what we have in the way of organization is no better than the chaos to be found in a theatrical pit!

"No, St. Mars, I will not take the blame for the lamentable condition of this undertaking! If you would like to blame his Grace of Ormonde, pray be my guest. But it is not only *his* loose tongue that has worked the mob into a fever pitch. You would have to blame each and every one of James's adherents for that."

Gideon saw that his impression of James's enterprise, though far from favourable, had been far too generous. The conspiracy was every bit as poorly managed as he had seen and worse.

He looked his host squarely in the eye. "Have you considered telling James to give up hope?"

Bolingbroke started, as if Gideon had uttered the unspeakable. But a hint of humour, and respect, entered his gaze.

"Yes," he admitted, after a pause, "but I doubt I ever shall. Not until the last hope from France is exhausted. And even then—" He shook his head. "No. There are others who could help us." He did not explain this last remark, but looked straight at Gideon and appeared to speak truthfully. "I have committed myself to James's service and have nowhere else to go. But I shall not lie to you, St. Mars. From nearly the moment of accepting the seals, I have wondered at my rashness in getting involved in the Chevalier's misfortunes."

"You do not rate his chances high, then?" The very fact that Bolingbroke called James by his French title "*chevalier*" rather than "his Majesty," as Jacobites always did, was proof enough of his reservations.

"Honestly . . . ? No, I cannot put much faith in them. But if I am ever to return to England, what choice do I have but to throw my fortunes in with his?"

Gideon had come to the same conclusion, yet he had not been quick to embrace the cause. Bolingbroke believed they shared the same motives. But with Louis's death imminent, Gideon was forced to question his decision again. To bring civil war into his country with no greater goal than recovering his own estate . . .

But this was neither the time nor the place for reflections of that sort.

He brought Bolingbroke's confidences to a close. "So what precisely do you wish me to say to James?"

"Tell him—" Bolingbroke weighed his words. "Tell him that his Majesty King Louis is dying. Even before you arrive in Bar, the King may be dead. Then say that Ormonde and I will be working to gain the confidence of the regent for the young prince. But make him understand that all of this will take time. His adherents in England say that in no way should he come before the end of September, at the earliest. But it will take much longer than that to get the regent to commit the arms we need."

Gideon agreed to convey the message, though he knew how disappointed James would be to receive it.

Depressed by all he had learned, he did not tarry over supper, but took an early leave.

He would set out for Bar in the morning. But, even with several days of travel before him, he doubted it would be enough time to find the right words to deliver such dismal news to James.

℘

The news-sheets duly reported that Jeremy and Edmund Curry had been released from Newgate and all charges against them dropped. Hester would have liked to remain at Hawkhurst House. But since her brother had no immediate need of her, she was obliged to resume her waiting duties in Kensington.

The next week brought a flurry of news concerning his Majesty of France, who was said to have received the last sacraments. The news-sheets reported that he had named the Duke of Orleans sole Regent for the Dauphin. Then on the 24th of August, one of the King's Messengers arrived from Paris with an express from the Earl of Stair, which said "the Most Christian King, Lewis XIV" had died on Sunday morning last, the first of September, New Style, in the 73rd year of his reign.

Lord Stair, the British Ambassador, pressed King George to recall him from France. And, in a move that might have been connected, a reward for the capture of the Pretender—alive or dead— was funded at £100,000. Parliament also formally passed the acts of attainder against the Viscount Bolingbroke and the Duke of Ormonde.

None of these events prevented the King from attending the opera in the Haymarket on Saturday night. The Prince and Princess of Wales chose to take the air on the Thames instead. Since, on this occasion, they planned to remain above London Bridge, Harrowby and Isabella ventured out in their barge again, though Isabella had vowed she would never set foot on it again. Hester would have loved to see another one of Mr. Handel's operas, but her cousins always chose the Prince's court over the King's. Hester did not think they were wise to show their preference for the Prince, but, as with most things she could not change, she kept this opinion to herself.

They did accompany King George to the Thames on Monday at five in the afternoon, when he went down to see a most amazing experiment. A colonel in the army by the name of Becker had invented a new engine for diving and had arranged a demonstration for the Court.

A large party of courtiers and military men met above Westminster Stairs, and, leaving their carriages and sedan chairs, descended to the river's edge, where three chairs had been set out for the King and the Prince and Princess of Wales. Hester and Harrowby ushered Isabella down the bank, a task made tedious by her physician's prescription to walk slowly, and her need to be fanned every few steps. The summer heat, more oppressive today with a threat of rain, afflicted her more than others, though in every other respect, she seemed as healthy as before.

Reminded of the impending blessed event, Harrowby recalled a thought, "By the bye, my love, have you heard the news concerning the Marquess of Linsey? That his lady has borne him a son?"

"No," Isabella said, between pants. For a lady who spent her days at

Court, she was woefully short on gossip. But, since most of her time was spent flirting with gentlemen, she often missed it.

"Well, she has. And what's more, they have christened the boy George. The King and his Grace of Rutland stood as godfathers and the Princess as godmother." Harrowby raised a meaningful brow. "I've been thinking that it might be a very good notion to name our boy George, too."

"Oh, pooh! And *I* thought Richard was the name I should like."

Richard was Lord Kirkland's name, but fortunately Harrowby failed to draw a connexion.

"I'm sure Richard's a very good name in its way, but I can't help believing that it might be wise to honour the King. Then we could ask him to act godfather to our brat, too."

"Not the Prince?" Isabella seemed ready to pout. "When his Highness has been so good to me?"

Harrowby chuckled uneasily. "I'm afraid not, my dear. Not the first child, at least. We mustn't offend his Majesty, you know. And there is certain to be another we can use for the Prince. And you can name that one Richard."

"Oh . . . very well. If that is what you should like."

Giving in to an evil temptation, Hester interjected brightly, "And what if the child is a girl?"

Harrowby gave a violent start and nearly lost his footing on the sloping ground. "Egad! You're right, Mrs. Kean! That *is* a possibility. We shall have to think of something else in the event such a calamity occurs."

"You might consider calling her 'Georgiana.' It has a rather pretty ring."

"Indeed it does! And, you may not have noticed, but it has the advantage of sounding very much like George." Harrowby beamed across his wife at Hester. "By gad! I believe you have solved the problem. If it's a girl, then all shall not be lost. Well done, Mrs. Kean!"

Hester thanked him, adding that it would always be her pleasure to serve him in these small ways.

By this time, they had reached the riverbank, where they drew to a halt with the other courtiers. The royal family took their chairs, and the Court gathered tightly about.

After throwing a wary glance at the ominous sky, Hester craned her neck to see Colonel Becker's strange contraption. Her view was partially obscured by the gentlemen-in-waiting to his Majesty. But from what she could manage to see, the colonel appeared to be uneasy, for he repeatedly cast nervous glances at the water lapping against the bank.

The royal nod gave permission to start. Colonel Becker explained that the engine he had devised—unlike Mr. Halley's famous diving bell—would allow him to walk and work underwater. The apparatus he held up consisted of a leather-covered chamber, only slightly larger than a man. It had a metal sphere for a helmet with a small glass porthole in front for viewing, while the body sported two leather appendages for arms. Three leather tubes protruded from the top of the helmet. These would extend above the surface, two to supply Colonel Becker with fresh air pumped down by several large bellows, and the last to carry out his exhaled breath.

A rumble of thunder made everyone glance anxiously up at the gathering clouds. The King made a gesture, urging Colonel Becker to make haste.

With the help of his assistant, Colonel Becker began to enter the chamber as if he were diving head first into a suit of clothes.

His face had just reappeared in the porthole, when Hester heard someone behind her calling her name. She turned, and saw Jeremy, looking only slightly more presentable than the last time she had seen him. His plain black coat and breeches she recognized as being the clothes their father had last bought him. Over the past five years, they had lost all their crispness. It also appeared that Jeremy had grown, for the sleeves to his coat ended a good two inches short of his wrists, exposing the frayed cuffs of his shirt.

These were details that Harrowby was certain to notice. Ashamed of these reflections, however, Hester smiled as she made Jeremy known to Harrowby and recalled him to Isabella. As she had feared, their cousins stared at him in open-mouthed amazement.

Jeremy seemed oblivious to their dismay, as he favoured them with his broadest smile. His teeth were unusually white and straight, like Hester's, and his smile was disarming. He made Harrowby a perfect bow, reminding Hester of the grace he had always shown. Then he kissed Isabella on both cheeks and drew a giggle from her when he told her how beautiful she was.

"I had hoped to find Hester here," he said, addressing them all. "But I am particularly glad for the opportunity to thank you for your immense generosity to me during my recent misfortunes, my lord."

Harrowby received his thanks with a nervous look, which Hester read as half-gratification, half-fright at the thought that Jeremy might be overheard. He stammered, "N-not at all! Mustn't think of it! Would be terribly grateful, indeed, if you'd refrain from mentioning it again!"

"You are far too modest, my lord." Jeremy glowed with the affection and esteem he felt for his new cousin. But sensing Harrowby's discomfort—even if he mistook it for modesty—he changed the subject.

"My lord, Isabella, Hester—if you will permit—my patron Mr. Curry has requested the honour of being presented to you."

As she'd witnessed the inevitable effects of Jeremy's charm, Hester had begun to relax. Now, a feeling of dread stole up her spine as a man stepped forward to be introduced, with another close behind. The moment Harrowby's eyes lit upon the first he uttered an outraged, "Zounds!"

The man who approached them was the most unattractive person Hester had ever met. No two of his constituent parts seemed to match. His pronounced irregular features included goggle eyes, a broken nose, and—most repellant of all—a right ear, which looked as if its upper half had been ripped off and left to heal itself. In addition to these, his lanky body had knock knees, splayed feet, and over-large hands.

Hester had never shrunk from deformities. It was not the sight of this man's imperfections—or even of his ear—that made her take an involuntary step backwards, but the strong, foul odour that wafted towards them as he drew near. He seemed not to have washed either himself or his clothes in years. His jacket was so torn and disreputable, it made Jeremy's look as if the King's own tailor had sewn it. And his wig, made of the cheapest horse-hair, failed to cover his long, dirty hair.

This, it appeared, was Mr. Curry.

'Tis from high Life high characters are drawn;
A Saint in Crape is twice a Saint in Lawn;
A Judge is just, a Chancellor juster still;
A Gownman, learned; a Bishop, what you will;
Wise, if a Minister; but if a King,
More wise, more learned, more just, more everything.

CHAPTER V

A t the sight of him, Hester's thoughts flew to the bookseller's pretty wife, and she repressed a shudder at the notion of her being married to such a man.

Harrowby was so appalled by the introduction he was struck speechless. Isabella gave a whimper of distress and sought relief from Mr. Curry's odour by shielding her nose with a scented handkerchief.

"A pleasure, Lord Hawkhurst." Curry made an ungainly bow. "A very great honour indeed. When I learned that my *protégé* had such illustrious relations, I had to beg the favour of this meeting. You may not be aware, my lord, but I have published a number of what one might call 'casual scribblings' by some of your lordship's friends."

Taking advantage of Harrowby's strangled state, he went on, "You seem astonished, my lord, but upon my oath, it is true. Yes, quite a number of his Majesty's nobler subjects have tried their hand at verse from time to time. You must know the Lady Mary Wortley Montagu— his Majesty's current favourite. It has been my good fortune that some of her most charming efforts have fallen into my hands. Yes, even the ladies are not too bashful occasionally to put their pens to paper."

He peered at Isabella with a prurient interest. "What about you, my lady? Do *you* ever dabble in verse?"

Isabella had steadily retreated behind her husband, and she answered with a distressed shake of her head. "I do not feel at all well, my lord! Let us go!"

Hester did not wonder that her cousin found Mr. Curry's odour intolerable, especially in her condition.

"Indeed, sir!" Harrowby protested. "You press too close!"

"My cousin is in a delicate way," Hester said, stepping between them. "You will have to excuse us, but she must not be distressed."

She glanced imploringly at Jeremy, whose guilty expression revealed that he quite understood the problem. His eyes begged her to forgive him for a situation he'd been powerless to prevent.

"What a pity!" As Harrowby and Isabella turned and walked away, Mr. Curry's tone held an edge of anger. "But I am more acquainted than you might think with the delicacy of ladies." He turned his goggle eyes upon Hester. "What about you, Mrs. Kean? Do you share your brother's talent for writing, for I assure you, his is considerable. Have you ever thought of composing a satire on your friends at Court?"

Hester was too astonished by this change in direction to form a rapid reply, so he continued, "I can promise that if you have even a fraction of Mr. Kean's skill, I will be happy to publish anything you might wish to say about your noble companions."

At last, she found her tongue. "No, Mr. Curry, I have not. Nor would I ever consider writing anything satirical about my family or my friends."

Misunderstanding the nature of her affront, he protested, "Oh, I should never betray your identity, I assure you, my dear Mrs. Kean! You must not think that I would expose you to your friends. I am the last one to be indiscreet, as I'm certain your brother will attest." He threw a fond smile Jeremy's way, before adding, "You have, perhaps, noticed my ear. The damage occurred when I was placed in the stocks for a misperceived insult. I had no intention of offending anyone. But the public can be very cruel to the unfortunate, my dear Mrs. Kean."

In spite of the revulsion he raised in her, Hester winced to hear that his ear had been torn as the result of such a barbarous act. The mob would insist on throwing garbage at the people locked helplessly in the stocks, and they did not seem to care how hard the things they threw might be. She tried to express sympathy without encouraging him, but only a mumble came to her lips.

When she did not take up his offer of publication, he looked disappointed. "I quite understand that you would not wish to write about your cousins," he said, unconvincingly. "One sees that your principles are every bit as lofty as your brother's—very admirable, of course. Nevertheless, I feel compelled to point out, as I have to your brother many times, that the readers in London will pay ten times for bits of gossip what they would pay for the keys to St. Peter's gate.

"But I can see that I have failed to persuade you. Perhaps you could coax a few verses from her ladyship, instead. Even if *you* penned them, I doubt she would mind if you attributed them to her. She might even enjoy the notoriety. And readers are known for preferring the work of aristocrats over anyone else."

Hester demurred, not troubling to tell him that no one who knew Isabella would ever believe she had written a poem. She cast a glance over her shoulder, and saw that Colonel Becker had entered the water. The river did not seem to be very deep, for his face was still showing through the porthole, and the water had barely covered the tubes for his arms.

The Court was still looking on expectantly. Isabella and Harrowby had moved only a short way off. As long as they gave no sign of leaving, Hester was trapped with Jeremy's friends. She turned back and, hoping to end her speech with Mr. Curry, looked beyond him to the second man, whom Jeremy had never had the chance to introduce.

He did now, giving the man's name as Tubbs. Hester remembered he had said that Mr. Tubbs shared his lodgings.

Still shaken by Mr. Curry's unpleasant nature, Hester was relieved to see that Mr. Tubbs—whom she now recalled seeing in Mr. Sullivan's boat—was a more self-effacing individual. Short in stature, he had a cringing posture that lessened his height even more, and his clothes seemed to be in an even more pitiable state than Jeremy's. But at least he was clean, and he had made an almost desperate attempt to groom himself. His threadbare coat was buttoned tightly about his neck, presumably to conceal the absence of a shirt. He was wigless, too, but he had combed his mousy hair and tied it ruthlessly back with a ribbon.

"Tubbs is a very good fellow, Hester," Jeremy said, as if she might doubt it. "And he has prodigious talent. Why, you could put one of his translations next to a piece by Mr. Pope or Mr. Swift and be hard put to know the difference!"

Tubbs squirmed sullenly under this praise. Before Hester could think of anything kind to say, Mr. Curry interjected, "But Tubbs is no match for your brother, Mrs. Hester, neither in learning nor in rank. He does well enough for who he is, but Tubbs knows his place. He does not expect to have the same success as a gentleman like your brother here, with his superior connections."

His ingratiating manner was so offensive that Hester wondered how Jeremy bore it. Tubbs, too, seemed less than enamoured with his patron. At the moment he was glaring at Curry from beneath a heavily furrowed brow. And his look darkened more when Curry added, with a peculiar emphasis, "I will grant him one *special* talent, however, and that is a very light touch."

Hester would have done something to break away at this point, but Mr. Tubbs gave a sudden jerk of recognition.

"Mrs. Kean . . ." he pondered her name aloud, as if he'd just recalled something. Then he blurted, "Are you the Mrs. Kean who was kidnapped by the highwayman, Blue Satan?"

His choice of words, as well as the unexpected topic, startled Hester and made her flush.

Mr. Curry's ears picked up, and Jeremy's eyes grew wide with shock. "That's right!" He frowned in recollection. "I remember we heard about a Mrs. Kean who had been abducted. You asked me, then, if I knew her, Tubbs. But I had no reason to believe it was you, Hester. Was it? And did the villain harm you?" His face wrinkled in concern.

Hester hid her agitation with a shaky laugh. "No, I wasn't harmed. And there was no abduction . . ." she faked a grimace . . . "unless you count being taken up for a shield 'an abduction'." She tried to sound as nonchalant as possible. The last thing she wanted was to be questioned about Blue Satan in front of Mr. Curry. "He set me down as soon as we were out of range of the guns. The most trying part was making my way to the inn where my cousins had stopped."

Mr. Curry had listened eagerly to this exchange, and now he said,

"But, this is excellent! You must tell your brother all about your horrific ordeal, Mrs. Kean. It will make a wonderful book. The story of your abduction and how you managed to escape ravishment by a gentleman of the road—with moral exhortations and cautions for the fairer sex, of course. I can imagination no more gripping a tale—and with your talented brother to write it—"

Flustered, Hester could not stem the flow of his enthusiasm. Even Jeremy's eyes had lit at the prospect of relating her adventure, though he did have the grace to direct her a questioning look. When he saw the protest forming on her lips, his excitement faded. He would never press her to do anything that would make her uncomfortable, but it was clear that a story about Blue Satan would be a great boon to his work.

Mr. Tubbs was sulking, for it was he who had brought Hester's adventure to Mr. Curry's attention.

A loud clap of thunder made them jump. A sudden gust of wind alerted them to rain and sent all the spectators scurrying for cover. This mercifully spared Hester from further intercourse with Mr. Curry, who turned and fled.

Glancing about, she spied Harrowby and Isabella hastening before her up the bank with the Court, as the first large drops began to fall.

"Come, Hester." Jeremy took her elbow and started to lead her behind them. "I'll see you to your coach."

The sky opened up. Within seconds the weather changed from sticky and warm to wet and chill. As they ran through the heavy fall, the water turning the bank into deep, slick mud, Hester had to shout to be heard above the shrieks and curses coming from the others caught in the downpour. "What happened to Colonel Becker? Did the new engine work?"

Jeremy shouted back, "Didn't you see? He had to cancel the experiment. The tide was too low."

That explained why Colonel Becker had appeared nervous. This outing had resulted in nothing but a series of vexations.

Irked beyond speech, Hester was relieved at least to find Harrowby's carriage still waiting for her. As offended as he must have been by the presentation of Mr. Curry, she had half-expected him to leave her to walk home. When Jeremy opened the door to the coach to hand her in, the pout on Harrowby's face told her that the goodwill she had gained with him earlier that day had been completely effaced. As she gathered her sodden skirts about her to avoid dripping on him or Isabella, he barely gave a nod in response to Jeremy's cheerful farewell.

On the way home, Hester was forced to submit to a lecture, which started the instant the carriage began to roll. As much as it grieved her to hear Jeremy criticized, she could hardly blame her cousins for their reactions to Mr. Curry.

"Never in my life have I encountered such a vulgar mountebank!" Harrowby exclaimed, the injury to his self-conceit still raw. "His patron, did your brother say? Wasn't he the fellow who was taken up by the Messengers?"

When Hester admitted as much, he huffed, "Well, I don't wonder at it! As villainous a fellow as I've ever met! Why, his face alone is an affront!"

Isabella ignored the reference to the Messengers. "And he smells!"

"Indeed." Hester apologized for submitting them to such a distasteful figure. "But as repulsive as he is, Jeremy assures me that he's never published anything treasonous—in fact, nothing of a political nature at all."

"Humph!" Harrowby snorted. "Your brother is a fool if he believes that. Why, the fellow has 'traitor' written all over him! Mark my words, he'll find himself at the end of a noose someday. And I will not have him visiting you, Mrs. Kean! Let us be clear on that!"

"I would not think of allowing such a thing, my lord. I shall advise Jeremy that he is not to bring his associates to your house."

She hoped that Harrowby would not notice the distinction she had made between Jeremy and his friends, but for once he had kept pace with her. He eyed her disapprovingly.

"I am not at all certain that your brother will be welcome either. Not if he consorts with villains like that."

"I understand your reservations, my lord, but I can promise that he will never inflict them upon you again."

"But his taste is abominable! Isabella, did you see his coat?"

"Yes, it was dreadful! But he could buy another. And if he were well-dressed, I think he should look very handsome, don't you? You could give him the name of your tailor."

"I shall do nothing of the kind! I would never insult my tailor by sending that ragamuffin to him!"

Biting her lip, Hester tried to conceal her offence, but Harrowby must have noticed, for he said reluctantly, "I beg your pardon, Mrs. Kean, but I am only speaking the truth. You think my name is illustrious enough to make up for your brother's deficiencies. But if people were to see him dressed like that, they would be certain to believe those charges against him. And it's not just his coat. He needs a great deal more polish than that."

As they had now reached the house in Kensington Square, Hester did not argue further, judging it best to leave the matter unsettled until Harrowby's temper had been given time to cool. But her heart sank at the possibility that Jeremy would never be welcomed at Hawkhurst House. With his current employment, he could never purchase better garments, no matter how many of his *Notes from the Dead* were sold.

A few days later, Colonel Becker conducted his experiment in the Thames. The journals reported that he walked underwater all the way from Westminster Stairs to Queen Hithe, without once bringing his head to the surface for air.

But this time, no one was there to witness his feat. Reports that the Earls of Hume and Wigtonn had been committed to Edinburgh Castle, as well as more rumblings from abroad, kept everyone, including Hester, close to Court for the next several days. The news-sheets recounted an extraordinary flurry of meetings between Ormonde and Bolingbroke and the Pretender's agents—from his mother the Queen Dowager, to his private confessor—leading everyone to believe that an invasion was imminent. Hester marveled at the speed with which the intelligence reached England. She could only conclude that King George had spies trailing the former Tories night and day to be so certain of their movements.

Amid these reports, there was one that particularly caught her eye. Her heart sank when she read that "the outlawed Viscount St. Mars" was rumoured to have left St. Germain for Bar-le-Duc in Lorraine.

℘ ·

A week after his meeting with Bolingbroke, Gideon found himself standing at stiff attention in the centre of a close formal chamber, nearly smothered by the stale air of its ancient tapestries and the oppressive heat from an unseasonable fire burning within its great hearth. As he waited to receive the Pretender's response to his news, his mind wandered to his Thames-side house and the pleasant breeze that freshened it.

Although Mrs. Kean had never visited him there, he could picture her standing on the lawn, peering across at the view he found so soothing. But the image was spoiled by a feeling that something was not right at home. He wondered how long it would take him to find a ship to smuggle him back into England and prayed that this trip to Bar-le-Duc would not lead to more delays.

He had arrived in Bar that morning. After relinquishing his weapons at the gate and passing a thorough examination by the guards, he had been forced to undergo a third inspection before being ushered into James's withdrawing chamber. Concerned about the risk of assassination, his Majesty's gentlemen were reluctant to allow anyone into his presence, unless at least one of them could vouch for the person's identity. Even after the Pretender's secretary, James Murray, recognized Gideon, they had still asked him to send his message through a courtier. But Gideon had insisted on speaking directly to James, not willing to trust any of the Pretender's gentlemen to relay his message faithfully.

James had greeted him eagerly. But once Gideon had begun to deliver his news, the Pretender's smile had disappeared.

Gazing respectfully at the man seated in front of him, Gideon tried his best to conceal the shock that had rocked him on first seeing James. But as he steeled himself for the questions that were sure to come, he wondered what had caused the dramatic alteration in the prince's appearance.

The last time Gideon had seen him was nearly three years ago at St. Germain. That was before James had suffered the indignity and disappointment of his expulsion from France. As little as Gideon had cared for James's courtiers then, he had still been drawn to the shy prince who was nearly his own age. James had been blessed with the straight nose and firm chin of the Stuarts, but he lacked their infectious warmth. Even the large, lustrous eyes he had inherited from his Spanish mother failed to offer any window into the privacy of his thoughts.

Gideon had been prepared to meet the distance in James's stare. What he had not expected to encounter was his extraordinary pallor, made even more conspicuous by an enormous black periwig and the dark circles beneath his eyes. Perspiration shone on James's forehead, and, despite his obvious attempts to hide them, he fought an occasional shiver.

None of the Pretender's servants seemed perturbed by the ague that gripped him. When Gideon had first suspected a fever, he had glanced at the attendants ranged about the room to see if MacDonald, James's Gentleman of the Bedchamber, would signal him to keep his audience short. MacDonald had returned his glance with an enigmatic look, so Gideon had pressed on with his unwelcome report, speaking in French so there would be no risk of a misunderstanding.

James had listened to him in heavy silence, his eyes rimmed red with fever and his face white with strain. After a lengthy pause, he asked, "You had this directly from Lord Bolingbroke?"

"Yes, your Majesty. Everything I have said concerning his Majesty King Louis of France and the advice from your men in England is a message from Lord Bolingbroke. The observations on your Majesty's organization in England, however, are my own."

A gentleman behind him started forward. "You lie! We've all seen—"

James cut him off with a movement of his hand. With his rheumy eyes on Gideon, he said, with no inflexion, "We thank you for your report, *Monsieur de St. Mars,* and wish you a safe journey, which you will start immediately. My faithful MacDonald will accompany you to the door."

With a curt nod, he consigned Gideon to the custody of his gentlemen, without the customary offer of his hand to kiss.

Shaken by the abrupt dismissal, Gideon could only make a profound bow before retreating from the chamber in the wake of the glowering MacDonald. Once they had exited the audience chamber, he was scarcely surprised then to be passed off to a lackey, with instructions to escort him from the palace.

So. After all his troubles, he was not to be offered so much as a meal or a bed for the night. As he was ignominiously led to the gate, indignation and anger built inside him. His feelings were only partly assuaged by the knowledge that he would have spent an uncomfortable evening in the company of gentlemen who considered him a traitor or a coward—possibly both. Wryly, he recalled Bolingbroke's reaction to his suggestion that James should be told the true state of his affairs in England. But, in spite of the reception he had just received, Gideon knew that what he had done was right.

He had ridden just a few miles out of Bar, wondering where he could safely pass the night, when the sound of pounding hooves closing on his rear caused him to spin his horse about.

Fearing treachery, he drew his sword, and kept it out, even when the rider hailed him by name. In a few seconds James Murray had brought his heaving mount to a halt, and set it to prancing a few paces away.

He had a sealed paper in his hand, which he cautiously held out to Gideon. "This message is for you from his Majesty."

Gideon took it, keeping a wary eye on James's messenger. "Do you wait for a reply?"

Murray bent his head to examine his horse's reins. "His Majesty expects no reply." His embarrassment alerted Gideon to the probable contents of the letter.

When he did not open it immediately, the Scot turned to leave. Gideon spurred his horse forward and blocked his retreat.

Alarmed, Murray would have drawn his weapon, too, if Gideon had not moved instantly to forestall him. He poised the tip of his sword within an inch of Murray's throat.

"Do not attempt it." He spoke through clenched teeth, furious at how poorly he had been treated. "I shall only detain you for a moment. But before I am so *shamefully* dismissed from his Majesty's service, there is a question I should like you to answer."

Murray stared defiantly back. "And if I refuse?"

Faced with the young Scot's pride, Gideon's anger quickly vanished. He gave a twist of his lips. "Then I shall be forced to ask someone else.

But, considering the months I have wasted in James's service, I should like to know the truth . . . . How ill is his Majesty?" he demanded.

Murray was leaning as far from Gideon's sword as his spine would allow. Now his face betrayed a ruddy flush. His defiance wavered, though his tone was still firm. "He is not so ill that he means to give up!"

Gideon ground his words between his teeth, "Tell me what is wrong with James. What is the fever that afflicts him?" Then, recalling that none of his gentlemen had seemed to be worried, he added, "Has he been ill before?"

With a hasty glance at the blade Gideon had jabbed towards his nose, Murray spoke reluctantly, "His Majesty suffers from a quartan fever." He added earnestly, "But his physicians are all agreed that he is unlikely to die from it. They say it is only a mild form of the malaria."

Incredulous, and feeling suddenly very tired, Gideon released a disillusioned sigh. "How long has he suffered from it?"

"He first became afflicted when he was fighting for King Louis against the Dutch, but as you saw, it does revisit him, particularly when he is anxious."

And yet, his men expected him to lead them in a war. "What you are admitting," Gideon said bitingly, "is that James becomes ill whenever he exerts himself?"

Murray bristled at his sarcastic tone. "His Majesty will not be denied his rights just because of an illness! He will not allow it to divert him from regaining his throne!"

"I am not questioning his courage," Gideon said wearily. "Merely the honesty of his friends."

Not bothering to wait for Murray's response, he dug his heels into his horse's ribs and galloped towards home. The abruptness of his motion startled Murray's mount, which reared and backed, giving Gideon the lead he would need if the Scot decided to give chase. Before he had turned completely, he had caught the look of astonishment on the other man's features, followed by a flash of chagrin.

Gideon rode away from Bar, with his sword grasped in his right hand, and James's letter crushed in his left with the reins.

Late that night, as he drank in the taproom of an inn, he read the

Pretender's message by the sputtering light of a tallow candle. Its wording was terse. With no thanks for the risks Gideon had taken on his behalf—no mention of the life Gideon's father had sacrificed to his cause or the promises he had made to restore Gideon to his title—the Pretender informed him that he had no further use for his services.

The fury Gideon felt was due mostly to one thing—James's complete disregard for his father's death. Nothing else really mattered. If not for his father's loyalty to the Stuart cause, Gideon would never have acted for James. It was guilt that had driven him to accept a commission. Now that his commission was over, in spite of his resentment, he felt a lifting of the burden that had weighted his chest, as if he had finally begun to atone for his part in his father's death. He had served James as honourably as he knew how, and if his services had been spurned, it was not for any fault of his own. It was because James, as sick and weak as he was, was as determined to redress the injuries to his father as Gideon had been for his. The difference, he believed, was that James would listen only to the advice he wanted to hear.

And, suddenly, the sheer absurdity of his anger hit him.

He had been dragged into the Pretender's conspiracy against his will and in defiance of his better judgement. But, once having pledged to serve James, Gideon had carried out his task, regardless of considerable peril to himself. He had postponed the fulfillment of his own wishes in order to inform James of the barriers to his quest, hoping to spare him more disappointment in the cause of such a futile endeavour.

And for what? To learn that truth and honour would never be prized above flattery and greed?

Gideon knew he had a right to feel outraged, but strangely what he felt now was a strong desire to laugh. Now, he could go home with his guilt assuaged. Or he could, as soon as he paid his last respects to King Louis of France. He would attend Louis's rites as a duty that came with his French estate. Then, he would find another ship to smuggle him into England.

"Odious! in woollen! 'twould a Saint provoke,"
(Were the last words that poor Narcissa spoke)
"No, let a charming Chintz, and Brussels lace
Wrap my cold limbs, and shade my lifeless face:
One would not, sure, be frightful when one's dead—
And—Betty—give this Cheek a little Red."

CHAPTER VI

When the French, Spanish, and Sicilian ministers prepared to put their households in mourning for the French king, Isabella fretted that King George would do the same. Determined to divert herself as much as possible until then, she vowed to spend even more time at Kensington Palace with their Highnesses. Hester, too, worried that she might find her own freedom restricted in future. So, with the intention of warning Jeremy of the rules Harrowby had set for his visits, she made a journey into town.

She left early in the morning to arrive just after the shops had opened, in order to return with the carriage in plenty of time for Harrowby to set out for the House of the Lords. Her errand ostensibly was to obtain a copy of the *13ᵗʰ Edition of the Practical Scheme* at Mrs. Garways's at the Royal Exchange, a reference work, which their excellent housekeeper, Mrs. Dixon, had long been wanting. On her way to Cornhill, Hester hoped to find Jeremy at the Bell and Bible, but in case she did not, she had written a note to leave with Mrs. Curry. She would have posted the letter to him, but her pride had revolted at the thought of asking Harrowby to frank any message to her brother, and she doubted that Jeremy would have a penny to spare for the charges.

By the time the coach reached Fleet Street, the early shoppers had already taken to the thoroughfare, where they clustered on the pavement, waiting impatiently for the shops to open their doors. To avoid the worst of the tangled traffic, Hester instructed the coachman to set her down west of St. Dunstan's so he could turn the carriage while waiting.

Weaving a path among the shoppers, ballad singers, and fruit vendors, she made her way to the east side of the church and was surprised to spy Jeremy at once, standing in the midst of a small crowd in front of the bookseller's stall. At first she was relieved that her errand would be so easy. As she drew nearer, however, she could see that something was amiss.

The door and shutters to the bookstall were still firmly closed. Mrs. Curry was standing outside the door with Jeremy, and both appeared to be worried. When Hester joined them, Jeremy distractedly explained that Mrs. Curry had come to the bookstall that morning and had found it locked.

"She came to me, not knowing what else to do. When she left her house this morning, she assumed that Mr. Curry had risen early to open the stall, for the key was gone from its hook."

"Couldn't he simply have stepped away?"

Mrs. Curry and Jeremy exchanged anxious looks, before he replied, "We would like to believe that, Hester, but Mrs. Curry doesn't think that her husband ever came home last night. She's afraid he might have met with an accident."

The bookseller's wife was finding it hard to meet Hester's gaze. "You may think it strange that I did not note his absence before, but I often fall asleep before Mr. Curry comes in. He always closes the stall at night, and I work so many hours during the day . . . ."

Hester could easily believe that Mr. Curry's wife would seize upon any excuse to be asleep when such a husband came home, but she tried to display no more curiosity than the situation demanded.

"And you have no other key?"

Mrs. Curry shook her head.

Hester did not ask Jeremy what they planned to do, for they were clearly undecided. If they broke the door and Mr. Curry did arrive, they would have to get it repaired before nightfall.

"If you'll forgive me . . ." She stepped forward to satisfy herself that the door was not merely stuck.

When she rattled it, she found it was securely locked. Shaking the door had only parted it from its jamb a fraction of an inch.

But the tiny crack let out a whiff of air—and with it, an odour that Hester instantly recognized. She took a hasty step backwards, involuntarily raising a hand to cover her nose.

Behind her, Mrs. Curry uttered a gasp.

Jeremy swore. Quickly pulling Hester out of the way, he said, "I shall have to break it in. Hester, would you please take Mrs. Curry home?"

"No!" Mrs. Curry violently shook her head. "No, I must see!"

Jeremy gave his sister an agonized glance. She said soothingly, "You *will* see, of course. But we should step back to give Jeremy the space he needs."

She led the other woman a short distance away, while Jeremy hurried up Fleet Street in search of a tool with which to force the door. A shop was being altered just a few houses over, and he quickly returned with a carpenter, armed with a crow bar. When the carpenter balked at the order to break into the stall, Jeremy removed his coat, took the bar himself, and wedged one end between the door and the jamb. Then, with a loud squeak of straining hinges and splintering wood, he ripped the two apart.

A few people had gathered to see what Jeremy was about. Before Hester could stop her, Mrs. Curry dashed forward. Hester caught up with her just as the small crowd parted to let her through.

A woman screamed. With her stomach in knots, Hester tried to step in front of Mrs. Curry to block her view, but as the path to the doorway cleared, they both saw what had happened to her husband.

Mr. Curry lay motionless on his back, splayed against the counter of the stall. From his bulging eyes and swollen tongue, it was plain that he'd been throttled to death.

In the chaos that ensued, several things occurred at once. Mrs. Curry let loose with a whimper and turned to bury her face on Hester's breast. The woman's scream had attracted more people, and before anyone could stop them, scores of onlookers elbowed their way forward to gape at the body, while those who had already seen it clapped their hands over their noses and tried to flee. Within seconds, it looked as if a riot had started outside St. Dunstan's Church.

After his first moment of shock, Jeremy was startled out of his paralysis by Mrs. Curry's cry. When he saw that Hester, though shaken, had her well in hand, he snatched his coat from the carpenter and hurried in to lay it over Mr. Curry's face.

One of the men attracted by the noise was their friend from the Temple, Mr. Sullivan. He came running out of a nearby house and pushed his way through the crowd. When he peered into the shop and saw the body stretched out on the floor, he raised a hand to his forehead as if in prayer before noting the ladies' presence. Then, despite an unnatural pallor in his cheeks, he had the presence of mind to herd the crowd away from the door.

He had barely begun to do this, when the booming voice of the beadle carried to them from up the street. "'Ere, 'ere, I say! What's all this 'ubbub about? Step along! Step along, before I call for the constable and 'ave the lot o' you thrown into the Poultry!"

By the time he had pushed his way through with the aid of his staff, most of the spectators had flown, leaving Mr. Sullivan, Jeremy, Mrs. Curry, and Hester to meet him in the open doorway.

"'Zounds!" At the sight of Mr. Curry's legs, sticking out from beneath Jeremy's coat, he halted, and a succession of emotions passed across his face. Astonishment, horror, and a dawning comprehension were quickly succeeded by a malicious flicker of satisfaction and an unconvincing look of outrage.

He wheeled on Jeremy. "So! It's just as I said it would be! Yer wickedness and yer idleness 'ave finally led to this!" He shook his staff in Jeremy's face and shouted, "Just 'old there, you knave, till the constable can be fetched!"

Eyes wide in disbelief, Jeremy protested, "No, you mistake! I had nothing to do with Mr. Curry's accident. I merely found him when I forced the door." When these words seemed to have no effect on the beadle, who threatened him with gaol, he looked to his friends, and said, "Tell him, please!"

Mr. Sullivan and Mrs. Curry both tried to explain at once. Hester remained silent, fearing that a sister's testimony would not be believed, although the urge to leap to her brother's defence was almost impossible to resist.

Mr. Simpkins silenced Mr. Sullivan, and in a tender voice begged Mrs. Curry to tell him what horrible thing had occurred.

She related the events that had led to Jeremy's breaking into the stall, ending with, "Mr. Kean would not even have been here if I had not gone to his lodgings to ask for his assistance."

Nothing about this tale pleased Mr. Simpkins, particularly the last part, which made him screw up his lips as if he had bitten into a green persimmon. His tone was no longer coaxing when he narrowed his eyes, and said, "Now, why would you want to fetch this young scoundrel, when you could 'ave called on an officer of the ward?"

Taken aback by his insinuating tone, and still suffering from shock, Mrs. Curry could only stare at him in stunned silence.

Jeremy hurried to fill the breach. "Mrs. Curry had every reason to believe that her husband was well. And when she found the stall locked, she came to see whether he had called on me or Tubbs and simply forgotten that he had removed the key."

As honest as Hester's brother was, he could not manage to make this account sound very convincing, though the fact that Mrs. Curry had turned to him had been innocent enough. Hester doubted that the bookseller's wife would have called on Mr. Simpkins for assistance unless she had no friends at all.

During the argument, Mr. Sullivan had entered the shop and moved behind the counter, where he examined the floor with quick searching glances. Finding nothing there to interest him, he returned his attention to the conversation, a modicum of his colouring restored.

Mr. Simpkins was shaking his head at Jeremy's explanation. "Don't try to cut a wheedle with me! I've been onto your tricks ever since you first set foot in my ward. You could've done Curry in last night, so I'm calling for a constable and taking you before a magistrate right now."

Hester joined the others in protesting this loudly. She had to raise her voice considerably to be heard. "You have no reason to suspect my brother! What possible proof can you present to a magistrate?"

Mr. Simpkins had started to take a clearly shaken Jeremy by the arm, but her question made him pause. He scowled furiously at her. "I misdoubt but what some proof will be found."

"Until you have any, if I were you, I should think twice about making charges against my brother. A magistrate will expect you to present proof." As he appeared to hesitate, she added, "And, of course, you will be expected to bear the costs of the prosecution, including paying the witnesses to come forward."

This reminder of how costly a prosecution could be finally had an effect. Jeremy threw his sister a grateful look.

Mr. Simpkins turned to Mrs. Curry and said coaxingly, "Come, my dear! Surely you don't want this scoundrel gettin' away with killin' yer 'usband now, do you? Don't you want to lay the charges against 'im yourself?"

She shook her head and held both her hands to her cheeks. "No, of course, I don't! I don't believe for a minute that Mr. Kean did it!"

The beadle felt so thwarted that he pounded his staff on the floor. He rounded on Jeremy. "Well, you can *kimbaw* 'er, but you can't fool me, you rogue! I'll find proof, you can bet on that! You won't get away with this murder. I'll see you 'anged—just see if I don't!"

With that, he turned and stamped outside, leaving them with the stench of Mr. Curry's unwashed body permeating the tiny shop, for indeed, *this* was the odour that Hester had recognized.

Mrs. Curry shuddered and began to cry.

Jeremy would have put his arm about her, but Hester took charge of the widow, saying, "I believe the coroner should be called. And the constable should be alerted, as well. I can take Mrs. Curry home and, if they have questions for her, she can answer them there."

Jeremy agreed with this plan. Following the two women to the door, he called out to a couple of boys in the street and dispatched them— one for the constable and one for the coroner—before Hester and Mrs. Curry left.

He would have preferred to join them, but Hester advised him in a whisper, "Stay, until you tell the constable what happened. If you don't, Mr. Simpkins is likely to make up his own version of the events, and I fear he meant those threats."

Jeremy raised both eyebrows and formed his lips into an "O," letting her know that he understood. Still Hester feared that he was incapable of realizing just how much ill-will Mr. Simpkins bore him and how capable the beadle was of doing him harm. For, as she'd noted on first meeting Mr. Simpkins, he was plainly jealous of Jeremy for the respect—and possibly the stronger feelings—that pretty Mrs. Curry bore him.

The Currys' house stood in Bell Yard, a dark, narrow alley just east of Temple Bar. Its location was fortunate, since on her way there Hester noticed the Hawkhurst coach, drawn up to the raised footpath in Fleet Street. She had forgotten she had told the coachman to wait.

She paused just long enough to instruct him to return to Kensington with a message for Isabella that she had been detained. Then she asked him to call for her later, whenever his lord had no further need of the coach, giving him the Currys' direction in Bell Yard as where to find her.

Under the circumstances, Hester did not let the notoriety of the Currys' street discourage her from entering their house, although on a different occasion she might have hesitated to brave it alone. Still a relative stranger to London, even she had heard that the area round Shire Lane had an unsavoury reputation, which appeared to be confirmed by the sinister condition of its ancient houses.

Fortunately, the stairwell up which Mrs. Curry led her had been swept clean, and the tiny parlour, though spare of furnishings, was reasonably tidy, in spite of the lingering odour of Mr. Curry. Instead of stopping at the first landing, however, Mrs. Curry led her up another flight of stairs to a cosy bedchamber where Hester found, in addition to the bed, a small, elegant table with a pair of wooden chairs, a washstand next to a rather handsome wardrobe, and in a far corner a shelf with an astonishing number of bound books. From the feminine appearance of the bed hangings and the toilet articles on the washstand, Hester got the impression that this was where Mrs. Curry—and Mrs. Curry only—lived. If this had been the bedchamber she had shared with her husband, there was certainly no trace of a masculine influence, least of all Edmund Curry's.

She begged Mrs. Curry to lie down and offered to bring her something restorative to drink, but the widow declined, saying, "I could not bear to rest. Not with the image of him still in my mind. I shall have to stay busy if I do not wish to lose my sanity."

In the end it was she who fetched them each a dish of tea. Hester followed her back down two flights into the kitchen and watched as she unlocked the caddy. Hester had been unprepared to find such a luxury in the bookseller's house, but she hid her surprise and, once back upstairs, sipped at the tea gratefully, while waiting for Mrs. Curry's nerves to settle.

The emotion the woman revealed did not appear to be grief as much as a mixture of horror and shock. She drank her tea with a great deal of sugar, and gradually a rosier colour returned to her cheeks.

"Mrs. Curry . . ." Hester began.

"Please don't call me that!" The widow shivered as if with revulsion. Then shameful tears filled her eyes. "I beg your pardon, Mrs. Kean. I should not have spoken so sharply. But when I hear his name, I see that face with the tongue hanging out, and it is all I can do not to burst into hysterics."

"Of course," Hester said, although she thought there was more behind the widow's reaction than she let on. "What shall I call you, then?"

She wiped her eyes on the cotton apron she had forgotten to remove and, gave a sniff. "Call me Sally, please. That is what my family used to call me. Sally Cadagin was my name."

"And where is your family now?" Hester thought that perhaps one of her relatives should be fetched.

Sally gave her an uneasy glance, then peered down at the hands fidgeting in her lap. "They live in the North. My parents do, at least. My—Mr. Curry—" She said his name hurriedly. "He paid for them to move back home last year. It's cheaper to live there than in London, and my father . . . . Well, since you are Mr. Kean's sister, I'll tell you . . . .

"He had lost everything here. I do not want you to think ill of him, though. He is a furniture maker and very good at his trade. He makes very fine pieces. But he moved us here hoping to make tables and beds for the nobility, and he did not realize how long it would take to win their custom, or how much it would cost us to live. He wanted the best for his children, he said, and the best was here in London. He sent us all to school—even us girls. But when the guild refused to let him join, his trade suffered, and he ended up in the Fleet."

A debtors' prison. Hester winced in sympathy for Sally's family. Now she understood something that had puzzled her before, Sally's careful way of speaking. If she had come from the North, she had likely had to work hard to lose her accent, which would not have helped her in her trade in London.

"That is where Mr. Curry found me." Sally said, forcing her chin up, as if daring Hester to find fault. "He offered to settle my father's debts and help my family get home, if I would marry him, keep his house, and sell books in his stall. He saw me reading to my father, you see, when he was there writing a story on one of the other inmates, so he knew what I could do."

Hester saw that Sally had really had no choice but to accept Mr. Curry's offer, if it was the only way to get her father out of the Fleet— or, indeed, *all* of her family, for without any money, they had all lived in the gaol with him.

"He even bought some of my father's pieces when they were sold at auction. My bed, this table and chairs—everything in this room, except the shelves—my father made." The pride in her voice was heavily tinged with regret.

Hester sincerely complimented her on her father's work, before asking if she wouldn't like to have an apothecary called. "He could give you something to help you sleep."

"No." Sally was adamant. "I want to wait till Mr. Kean comes."

At Hester's startled look, she flushed and added, "I must hear what the coroner said. I won't be able to sleep until I am certain that Mr. Simpkins hasn't done your brother a mischief."

"Then you think he meant those threats?"

"I wouldn't doubt it for a moment." With indignation, a trace of her northern accents crept into Sally's voice. "He's been making sly remarks about your brother for ages now. Just because I won't have nowt to do with him, he blames Mr. Kean. He's got to have someone to blame for his own conceit, but as polite a gentleman as your brother is and always has been—" She was too angry to go on.

Hester was proud, and greatly relieved, to see that in this respect her brother had not changed. No matter how attracted to Sally he was, the

Jeremy she knew would never ask a woman to betray her wedding vows. His code of honour was chivalrous, which occasionally led to his detriment, but in this instance it had guided him correctly.

She decided it would be wise to change the subject. "I fear your husband must have been robbed," she said. "In my rush to get you away, I did not think to ask you if anything was missing."

Her remarks brought a puzzled frown to Sally's face. "I did not think about it then, but now that I do, I am certain that the books were there. If it was a robber who did it, he would not have got very much. Mr. Curry always brought the day's earnings home before taking my place. He said he did not want me walking through the streets with money in my pockets, even if it meant he had to make the trip twice. If the robber found any money, it would only have been what Mr. Curry made last night before closing up. That could be why the robber throttled him," Sally added, in a small voice. "Perhaps he was angry to discover so little."

They heard a knock downstairs, and Sally jumped to her feet. Hester advised her to stay in the room in case the caller was someone she did not wish to see, and Sally allowed her to answer the door.

It was Jeremy, looking tired and strained. He gave Hester a grateful smile, before asking anxiously how Mrs. Curry was doing.

"She's well enough, but she refuses to rest until you tell her what occurred after we left. Who did it, Jeremy? A robber?"

He shrugged and grimly shook his head. He did not speak again until they had joined Mrs. Curry in her bedchamber, where he paid her his condolences. She accepted them with trembling lips and downcast eyes.

Throughout this painful scene, Hester waited impatiently. The moment she decently could, she pressed Jeremy for more answers.

"Nothing appears to have been stolen," he said, "except the key to the stall. The constable arrived just after you left and when he searched Mr. Curry's pockets, he found money still in his purse. He said I should bring it to you," Jeremy told Sally, reaching into the pocket of the shabby coat he had used to cover Mr. Curry's face and extracting a small leather purse. "The constable said he would make a note of the amount, so it is quite all right for you to have it. There are fifteen shillings and a few pence."

Sally took her husband's purse with a confused look. "But why would a thief leave this?"

"Perhaps he heard someone coming. That's a very public place. It's a wonder he had the time to—to do what he did," Jeremy finished his speech hastily, not wishing to upset her.

"And then locked the shutters behind him?" Hester asked. "In that case, then someone might have seen him."

"That's what the constable hopes," Jeremy said, "though no one must have witnessed the murder or surely he would have set up a cry for the watch. The constable said he will tell the beadles to post a notice asking for any witness who saw a man in front of the Bell and Bible late last night to come forward."

It was possible that someone *had* seen the murderer lock the shop, but Hester could not believe the killer was a thief. If his purpose in attacking Mr. Curry had been to rob him, then surely he would have returned for the purse later, when no one was about.

A second knock at the door announced the arrival of the Hawkhurst coach. Hester was reluctant to leave, but Sally assured her that she would be all right, and Jeremy said he would stay to make certain she was.

Hester asked him to walk her down the stairs, so she could have the opportunity to say, "Jeremy, I do not think you should remain here alone with Sally. Mr. Simpkins intends to make trouble, and he might be believed if the neighbours see you here alone. The gossips will talk. And we can't be certain that a magistrate won't believe Mr. Simpkins's word over yours and Sally's."

Jeremy's nostrils flared. "I know. I didn't want to say anything in front of her, but he came back while the constable was there, and you would not believe the accusations that puff-pigeon made. As if I would ever . . . You know I would never—"

Hester patted him on the arm. "I know you perfectly well. There's no need to convince me. But, if you are charged, my opinion will not count. I have seen innocent men accused of crimes they did not commit. People are quick to jump to conclusions, and in a case of murder, they are particularly hasty. How did the constable react?"

"Well, at first he was inclined to listen to the beadle, as you might imagine, but when he realized there was no evidence, he took a more prudent position. He said the Lord Mayor would not be happy if he brought such a weak case into his court, and that he would not take the risk of a suit against him for abusing his authority."

"That is a great relief, but anything might occur to make him change his mind. Please swear to me, you will be careful!"

He promised to arrange for a woman to stay with Sally. "Though I hate to shock her by telling her why she needs one," he said, dreading the embarrassment.

Concealing a smile, Hester refrained from telling him that Sally knew more about Mr. Simpkins's motives than he realized.

As she prepared to step into the coach, he stopped her. "I don't know how anyone could think that I would kill Mr. Curry, when he was my only patron. I don't know how I'm going to manage to live!"

The anguish in his voice caused her a genuine pang of worry, until a possible solution to his problem came to her. "Does Mr. Curry have any children?" she asked.

"No."

"Then can't Mrs. Curry publish your work? The Bell and Bible should be hers now. Even if he has other heirs, most of his estate should come to her."

Cautious relief came into his face. "Yes . . . of course! At least . . . I believe she will. I shall have to ask her. Thank you, Hester! I should have thought of that myself."

"If you run into any trouble, you must come to me. Can you pay the fare to Kensington?"

"If not, I can walk. No, don't look like that." He laughed. "It's not very far. But I would hate to leave Mrs. Curry to manage the bookshop alone. She may need my help."

Hester saw that he was determined to stay close to the widow, regardless of Mr. Simpkins's threats. So, resolving to come again as soon as she could, she took her leave.

As the carriage pulled into Fleet Street, the tolling of the passing bell at St. Dunstan's began to ring, and the morning's events finally caught up with her. Alone in the carriage, being bounced over cobblestones, she started to shudder. She clasped her arms tightly about her and retreated into a corner of the coach. Trying to rid her memory of the sight of Mr. Curry's hideous corpse and the stench of his body, she reached into her mind for fortitude and began to consider all she knew.

It was only then that she recalled the jest Mr. Sullivan had made hardly more than a week ago in front of the Bell and Bible—that if he had known Mr. Curry was in Newgate, he would have tried his luck with "the widow."

But grant, in Public Men sometimes are shown,
A Woman's seen in Private life alone:
Our bolder Talents in full light displayed;
Your Virtues open fairest in the shade.
Bred to disguise, in Public 'tis you hide;
There, none distinguish twixt your Shame or Pride,
Weakness or Delicacy; all so nice,
That each may seem a Virtue, or a Vice.

CHAPTER VII

Hester realized she might have to give testimony at the inquest, which, given the season, would have to be held soon, even if the worst of the heat was behind them. She also knew she would have to inform Harrowby of the murder if she wanted to ask for leave to visit Sally again. But afraid of his reaction, she waited for a propitious moment. Unfortunately, recent news had put him in a very testy mood.

Reports that a great meeting of the clans had taken place at Aboyn had prompted the King to send more troops into Scotland. His Majesty's Council was said to be preparing for the worst. Fears of war had cast a pall over Court, leading many of his Majesty's courtiers to plan for the safety of their families. And, since the absence of the Prince of Wales, in meetings with the Council, had left the entertainments at Kensington Palace flat, even Isabella had a reason to stay at home.

That afternoon in Kensington, they dined *en famille,* a rare enough event. With Harrowby fretting over the rumours, Hester would have been glad for James Henry's assistance. True to his word, however, before his departure for Rotherham Abbey he had managed to leave her ten shillings, with a note saying merely, "Allowance for Michaelmas last." That would give her some resources at least in case Jeremy needed help. She could think of a dozen things she would like to do with the money, but until Mr. Curry's murderer was discovered and her brother safe, she would put them out of her mind.

The board was laid out in the withdrawing room. Harrowby stayed frowning down at his plate until the footmen left.

Then, looking up, he said, with an ominous sigh, "They say the Earl of Mar called the meeting of those Highlanders. It looks bad. Very bad. Someone ought to tell him that he's put himself in a dangerous position. His Majesty takes a very dim view of these goings-on."

"If his property is in Scotland, why shouldn't he meet with them?" Isabella asked, taking a large spoonful of syllabub onto her plate. As a result of her condition, her appetite had doubled overnight.

Her lord was not the least taken aback by this display of ignorance. He gave his wife a confiding look. "His Majesty don't like it because the Stuarts are Scots, my dear. He thinks they are up to something. And I don't give a fig for their chances if they are."

"Then why would Lord Mar wish to displease him?"

"Ah . . ." Harrowby nodded sagely. "There you have it, little woman! I posed that very same question myself.

"Do you recall the levee the King held on the old Queen's birthday? Well, I did not see it, but some would have it that his Majesty turned his back on Lord Mar. Gave him the cut direct! And even if one cannot blame his Majesty—for Mar's always been a havey-cavey sort of fellow, if you ask me—why it's easy to see why Mar might take a pet and take off for Scotland in a huff.

"Very proud, Lord Mar. Very high in the instep—expects to be rewarded for negotiating our union with Scotland. I'm sure the old Queen made over him tremendously. But King George, you know, he doesn't truck with Tories." Harrowby sighed heavily again. "But this current business—it looks very bad. Very bad."

As shaken as she had been all day, Hester felt an instant concern for St. Mars, which had nothing to do with the similarity of his name to the Earl of Mar's. When she'd last seen St. Mars, he had been on his way to France, and the news-sheets had later reported his attendance at the Stuart Court at St. Germain. The English considered him a Jacobite and a traitor. Although he had not discussed his involvement in the conspiracy with her, she knew he was tied to James in some way. She hoped he would never risk joining a rebellion, but with no other means of being restored to his place—the earldom that Harrowby now held—she would not be astonished if he did. She only wished she could speak to him first and try to dissuade him, for she believed that King George had taken such a firm hold on his Crown that it would prove impossible to wrest from him.

There was nothing she could do for St. Mars now, however. So sick at heart, she told herself to deal with one set of troubles at a time.

A footman entered the room and came to bow at Harrowby's elbow. "The news-sheets have just arrived, my lord."

Harrowby snatched them up before the servant could complete his bow. "Ah, here they are! Good man! You may run along." Turning to his wife, he explained, "I told the servants to send them up directly. It won't do to be behind with the news, y'know."

"Is anything good at the theatre?"

Harrowby ignored her question and, forgetting to beg her pardon for reading at the table, scanned the papers for news.

For a few minutes, the only sound they heard from him was an occasional grunt, but something suddenly made him exclaim, "Well, I never! What arrogance!"

"What arrogance is that, Harrykins?"

"Oh, it's nothing to be frightened about, my dear. Not as long as there's a sea between us, which I believe there is. But it says here that a group of savages, calling themselves the Sable Indians, has taken a few of our fishing boats in Boston and is holding our colonists prisoner. They're asking the Crown for forty pounds for each one!"

Isabella puzzled idly over this while she gnawed on a pullet bone. Then she asked, "Why should the King pay ransom for them when we sent them there to get rid of them in the first place?"

Peering up from his paper, her husband blinked, before breaking out in a laugh. "Oh, that's excellent, Isabella! Yes, very droll, indeed! I wish his Majesty could have heard it. I daresay it would have given him a laugh. You won't mind if I repeat it for him next time the opportunity presents itself? I imagine his interpreter can make it clear." He chuckled heartily again and downed his glass of claret.

Clearly in the dark as to the cause of her husband's delight, Isabella gave him a distracted smile and contented herself with draining her glass as well.

Judging this to be the best moment she was likely to have, Hester begged both their attentions and, as briefly as she could, informed them of what had transpired that morning.

"I fear there is no doubt that he was murdered," she concluded, bracing herself for Harrowby's angry disapproval.

To her surprise—although he had frowned on learning of her visit to the bookseller's stall—his expression cleared with relief.

"I don't wonder that he was. If you recall, Mrs. Kean, I told you the fellow would meet with a violent end. And so he did. Why, any fool could see it coming, as offensive as the blackguard was! Well, we shan't have to worry about his calling here, then, shall we?"

With a satisfied nod Harrowby resumed reading his papers, as if there could not possibly be another word to say upon the subject.

Isabella, however, who had gasped at Hester's pronouncement, questioned her avidly about the discovery of the body. She proclaimed her horror with theatrical shivers and little cries, but it was clear her interest in the Currys was merely prurient. Hester did her best to satisfy her cousin's ghoulish curiosity, though she would rather have blocked the images from her head and dwelt on who could have committed the murder, and why.

"I should like to make a visit of condolence to Mrs. Curry," Hester finally said, "and to sit with her during her husband's funeral."

Isabella gave a little pout. "I do not see why you should be obliged to. With a husband like that, she is certain to be coarse."

"One might expect so—however, it is far from the case. Mrs. Curry is a very pretty creature. I doubt she cared for her husband overmuch."

"Huh!" Harrowby snorted, laying his papers down to take up his fork. "She would be a strange sort of female if she had. Shouldn't wonder if she didn't make off with the fellow herself."

Alarmed by this careless statement, and anxious to stem any gossip that might result from it, Hester said, "That is out of the question, my lord. Mr. Curry was throttled, and his wife is too small a woman to have done it."

"Well . . . I'm afraid I cannot let you go," Isabella said fretfully, "for you might be murdered, too, and then I should have no one at all to keep me company."

Hester knew it would be useless to press the point. Her duty was to her cousin, and according to the books she had read, Isabella should not be distressed for fear the baby could be injured. She agreed to postpone her visit until her absence would not be felt.

Then Harrowby surprised her saying, "We can carry you into London later this week, if you like. There's a notice in the news-sheet that a pair of sea creatures may be seen at the Duke of Marlborough's Head in Fleet Street. You'd like to see the monsters, wouldn't you, my dear?"

Although Hester would have preferred to waste no time, she could hardly refuse Harrowby's generous offer. Fortunately, her testimony was not required at the inquest. And two days later, a letter came from Jeremy saying that given the condition of Mr. Curry's body, he had been buried in haste. Jeremy, along with several stationers and booksellers, had acted as Mr. Curry's pallbearers.

Concealing her impatience then, the next afternoon Hester accompanied Isabella and Harrowby to Lord Kirkland's lodgings, where they took him up for the outing. On the way into town Harrowby and Lord Kirkland chatted about the various monsters they'd seen, and Harrowby read yesterday's notice about the two sea creatures.

Purportedly from New Zealand, they were five and seven feet in length. They were described as having heads like bull-dogs, beards like tigers, spots like leopards, talons on their forefeet like lions, and tales like hares, with "two wonderful feet behind, which no other creature was known to possess." Hester would have liked to get a glimpse of the curiosities, but knew she must take advantage of the opportunity to check on Jeremy. Certain that Isabella would be perfectly content in Lord Kirkland's company, she reluctantly left them at the Duke of Marlborough's Head, informing them that she would take a hackney home. Then she quickly made her way to the Bell and Bible.

At the bookstall, she found Sally working alone behind the counter, looking pale in black bombazine from head to toe, but exhibiting no other sign of grief. Hester watched as a customer completed his purchase, then lingered with the apparent intention of flirting. As Sally greeted her, the man gave Hester a sheepish look before tipping his hat and taking his leave.

Sally seemed to want to explain the man's behaviour, but, believing it was no business of hers, Hester forestalled her. "I shouldn't have interrupted your business, but I hoped to find Jeremy here, and I only have a little time."

"Mr. Kean left for his lodgings a few minutes ago. He has a story to finish, so you ought to find him there." Sally tried to hide her pleasure when she added, "I am going to publish another of his books. They have sold very well, and he was kind enough to say that he would rather I publish them than any other bookseller of his acquaintance."

"I am certain he would. Then you will continue your husband's business?"

As Sally's smile faded, her trepidation became clear. "Mr. Kean believes I can, and I hope he is correct. I had never thought of running the business myself, but it is true that I have learned nearly all I have to know by observing Mr. Curry. And, if I don't keep on, I shall have to sell the bookstall and move away like my parents."

"You have no wish to go home?"

Sally gave a firm shake of her head. "Not if I can manage to stay. I like the bustle of London, and I love dealing in books. Mr. Curry could see that about me. That was one of the reasons he married me."

"I perfectly understand. There is no greater pleasure than a book." Hester did not ask her what Mr. Curry's other reasons were, though Sally's comment had intrigued her. Instead, she said goodbye and promised to call on the widow again soon.

She was turning to go, when through the shop window she spied the now-familiar form of Mr. Simpkins, making his way towards the door.

Sally spotted him at the same time, for she hastily said, "Pray do not leave me yet, Mrs. Kean. Not until Mr. Simpkins is gone, if you can spare the minutes."

Nothing could have persuaded Hester to leave. She wanted to discover whether Mr. Simpkins was still of a mind to accuse Jeremy of Mr. Curry's murder.

The beadle entered the shop. When he saw Hester, his hopeful look changed to a scowl, but he made a deferential bow, sweeping off his soft-brimmed hat as he did. The top of his wig revealed thin spots where the hair had fallen out, making her think that he had either owned it for many years, or else had bought it from a used-wig merchant. Wearing a wig was an affectation for a man in his position, but Hester believed she knew his motive for doing it.

"Good day to you, mistresses. I've just come 'round to see if there's any service I can do for you, my dear."

This last comment was directed solely at Sally, who gave a frosty nod, and said, "No, there is not, Mr. Simpkins. I am getting along quite well and will not be needing your assistance."

His gaze narrowed, and his looming body stiffened. "I'll wager you're not turning away all such offers, mistress. I warn you, you'll be sorry if you trust a stranger with yer 'usband's affairs."

"I shall trust whomever I please, and I'll thank you to keep your accusations to yourself, Mr. Simpkins!"

The beadle's face reddened. The knuckles around his staff went white.

Hester wished Sally had shown more tact, but there had been a touch of hysteria in her voice, probably a result of the week's shocking events.

Mr. Simpkins looked so furious, Hester wondered if he might have throttled Sally if she had not been there to bear witness. But he could not murder the widow in front of her, as he apparently wished to do. Instead, his tone was menacing when he said, "I think there's a spot o' knavery going on 'ere. There's something mighty suspicious about a wench who don't care if 'er 'usband's killer gets caught."

"But I do care!" she protested. "I simply will not permit you to accuse a gentleman who's innocent!"

"And 'oo's to say that 'e is? You wouldn't be thinkin' of sharin' yer in'eritance with 'im now, would you? That could look pretty bad to a magistrate, I'd say, 'specially when nobbut a few days ago, it seemed like you was favourin' a different man altogether?"

Sally's flush revealed both anger and humiliation, but she drew herself up. "A few days ago, I was a married woman with no thought of anyone but my husband, Mr. Simpkins! But, if you must know, I do not plan on sharing my husband's business with anyone yet."

This seemed to assuage some of his rancour, for a spark of hope lit his eyes. He gazed at her warily, however, as if uncertain whether to believe her. "A 'andsome woman like yerself will be wantin' to marry again. And soon, I shouldn't wonder, or you'll be lonely in your bed, which would be a cryin' shame. But if I was you, Mrs. Sally dear, I'd give some thought to 'oo I picked, if I didn't want to give the magistrates somethin' to chaw on. They might think you were a mite 'asty to replace yer 'usband."

Sally's voice shook. "And I shall know who started the evil rumours if they do!"

Mr. Simpkins raised his eyebrows, but his smile was malicious. "Now, why would anyone want to cause you trouble, my dear? Didn't I come 'round to see if there was aught you needed? I'm only sayin', you should take a bit o' care in choosin' yer friends, or else you might be suspicioned of something wicked, that's all. Most women can't be trusted, as their lordships know. If they're not cheatin' their employers, they're temptin' men to do their stealin' for 'em. There's even some wot tempts a man to kill their 'usbands."

When Sally did not dare reply, he laughed. Then he held out a hand, waiting to be given hers, until she was forced to let him kiss it in order to get rid of him. Then he finally took his leave with a promise to visit her again.

"Vile clown!" she exclaimed, shuddering as soon as he had closed the door. "I beg your pardon, Mrs. Kean, but I cannot bear to be alone with that man. And you heard what he implied about Mr. Kean! If it were not for your brother's kindness . . ." She pulled a handkerchief from her apron pocket and buried her nose in it.

"How long has Mr. Simpkins been harassing you?"

Sally sighed. "Not a day goes by that he doesn't stop and try to touch me. Mr. Curry said I should be flattered by the attention, but I cannot like it, particularly not from Mr. Simpkins. And he never buys any books, so I see no reason to pretend that I do."

She looked down at her hands, folding and unfolding the handkerchief nervously. "Do you think he could cause trouble for Mr. Kean and me? Serious trouble, I mean?"

"I can't be certain, but I fear it. Sally, he clearly fancies himself in love with you. Do you think he might have murdered your husband in the hope of winning you for himself?"

Her eyes filled with tears. "How should I know? If he did, it was not because I encouraged him. You must believe me! I tried to be pleasant without letting him get too near, but he would have to be mad to believe I would accept him as a suitor."

No, Hester reflected, not mad. Not after seeing the first man Sally had wed. But she did not point this out, saying merely, "Unfortunately, some men are capable of that kind of self-delusion. Some women, too, I shouldn't wonder."

She had added this last comment with nothing particular in mind, so she was taken aback when Sally bristled, patently hurt. "That may be, but I assure you I am not one of them. Whatever Mr. Simpkins suspects . . . well . . . you must not imagine that I have deluded myself!"

She busied herself then, taking up some books left on the counter and replacing them on the rails behind her. Chagrined, Hester realized that Sally had taken her remark as a warning that she should not expect an offer from Jeremy. Their admiration for each other was so obvious, it had never occurred to Hester that either one could doubt it. She would have laughed at Sally's blindness and assured her of Jeremy's regard, had she not been acutely aware that it could be dangerous for Jeremy for her to do so.

All she could do now was ask permission to visit Sally again at home, which she did with all the warmth she could muster. Then, feeling that she had done what she could to smooth over the misunderstanding, she left in search of her brother.

Her walk took her north up Fetter Lane. When she emerged at Holborn, she peered in both directions, searching among the many wooden signs up and down both sides of the street, until she spied the one with the Pewter Platter not far to her right. As she approached the house, she noted that, unlike the imposing Staples Inn or the even larger Furnivals behind her, the Pewter Platter was small and sadly in need of repair. Then her impression grew worse when she entered the taproom and asked the landlord and his wife to direct her to Mr. Kean's chamber.

"So now it's anovver one, is it?" The landlord looked her up and down. "Well, ye can tell 'im I don't see 'ow 'e manages the lot o' ye wiv vem ovver culls about."

A moment passed before his meaning became clear to Hester, and by the time it had, the landlord's wife had come from behind the counter and was advancing upon her with rolled-up sleeves and a broom raised threateningly in her hands.

It took all of Hester's character to stand her ground, but she gave her name and demanded to see her brother.

The firmness in her voice made the woman halt long enough to take in her appearance. Squinting in the poor light from the street, she finally said, "She do 'ave a look of 'im, Dick. And she's got 'is fancy way o' talkin'."

"Humph!" was all her husband said, but he made no complaint when his wife set her broom aside and jerked her head to indicate that Hester should follow her up the stairs.

The steps were sadly worn and uneven, and little light shone to guide their way. At the second landing, the woman broke off and, passing one door, halted at the next and knocked.

It opened immediately, but to Hester's consternation, it was not Jeremy's lean face, but Mr. Tubbs's square one that met her eyes. He gaped at the women with a mixture of astonishment and dismay.

"I beg your pardon," Hester said, speaking quickly. "I do not wish to disturb you. I only came in search of my brother."

"Hester?" Before Mr. Tubbs could open his mouth, Jeremy appeared in the opening behind him. "Is anything the matter?"

Hester released a grateful breath and assured him that she was merely there on a visit. Mr. Tubbs mumbled something inarticulate and moved aside to let her pass. Thanking the innkeeper's wife for showing her upstairs, Hester stepped inside.

A look about the cramped room revealed more than she could be happy knowing about her brother's situation. She saw one bed, a scarred oak table, three upright chairs, and nothing else in the way of furnishings. Except for the rumpled bed, the room resembled a workshop more than a place to live. Two of the chairs had been drawn up to the table, where stacks of parchment and bunches of crow and turkey feathers competed for space with two penknives, two inkwells, and a shaker of sand. A small coal fire burned in the grate—more for curing the men's quills, Hester suspected, than for heat—and the sheen of undried ink on two pieces of parchment revealed that she had interrupted their work.

She apologized for disturbing them. Pulling on his hair, Mr. Tubbs attempted to deny any bother, while Jeremy, admonishing her not to be silly, drew up the third chair and invited her to sit.

As she lowered herself into it, Hester spied two piles of men's belongings in opposite corners of the room. With a feeling of dismay, she realized that Mr. Tubbs and her brother shared the dreary space. And the third chair was explained when Jeremy referred to a third lodger who had recently left.

"Was Mr. Woods also a writer?" she asked.

"Yes, he wrote for Mr. Curry, too." Seated again, Jeremy looked about with a hint of embarrassment. "It was Mr. Curry who put us up here. I suppose we ought to write Woods and tell him what occurred."

Grasping at this piece of information, Hester inquired when Mr. Woods had left, wondering if his departure could have had anything to do with Mr. Curry's murder. But it appeared that he had set off for Bristol several weeks ago.

"Poor Woods got discouraged. He was frustrated by his lack of success." As he spoke, Jeremy reached for his penknife and started trimming his quill. "He thought he should go home and try his hand at something more profitable."

Mr. Tubbs squirmed miserably in his chair. Hester looked questioningly at him, but whatever he was thinking, he said nothing.

"I suppose it is an unprofitable business," Hester agreed, "although Mrs. Curry lives comfortably enough."

Jeremy's face lit. "Yes, that is one piece of good news. It seems that, for a while at least, she will not have to worry about money. Her husband has left her a tidy sum—enough to give her time to learn the business."

Mr. Tubbs made a strangled sound and sprang from his chair, his face a picture of distress. "What's this?"

Startled, Jeremy gave his friend an apologetic look. "I didn't think it was my place to tell you, Tubbs, but after the will was read, Mrs. Curry went into her husband's chest and found a considerable sum of money. I don't know what he planned to do with it, and neither does she. He always said he didn't have much."

Tubbs was so livid, he shook. "The filthy dog!" He balled his hands into fists. "Should've known he was lying!"

"Here, here!" Jeremy spoke with a mixture of concern and offence. "Mustn't speak ill of the dead, you know!"

Tubbs gave a ragged laugh. "That's just it!" His features were contorted, and words came spewing from his mouth. "You still don't understand, do you? *That's* the reason Woods left. It wasn't his writing. He saw what Curry was, and the tricks he was playing with his wife!"

Stunned, Jeremy looked up at him. Unconscious of the knife he gripped, he started out of his chair. Hester restrained him with a hand on his arm.

"What do you mean, Mr. Tubbs?" With a shake of her head, she silenced Jeremy, who wanted to halt his speech.

Pulling at his hair, Tubbs apparently regretted his outburst. He peered anxiously at Jeremy and wriggled some more. The voice he used to answer was even more of a growl than his usual mumble. "Don't mean to insult her—Mrs. Curry, I mean. Doubt if Curry gave her any choice. Used people abominably, Curry did. Knew how to play them along."

"If you're suggesting that Mrs. Curry had anything to do—" Jeremy started.

"Not saying a word against *her*. But he knew he could get his way with people, as long as she was there to smile at 'em."

"Smile at whom?" Hester asked. When he darted an uneasy glance her way, then down at his chewed fingernails, she added, "At Mr. Woods, you mean?"

Tubbs gave a meaningful glance at Jeremy and nodded. "He could tell Woods those lies about his books not selling and Woods'd believe 'im because he wanted to! He didn't want to offend Curry as long as that pretty wife of his was making up to 'im!"

He cringed when Jeremy shot out of his chair again as if meaning to shake him by the collar.

Hester spoke quickly. "Mr. Tubbs has expressed himself badly, Jeremy, but indeed, it is no more than Mrs. Curry told me this morning herself!"

He turned and stared at her as if she'd dealt him a mortal blow. Mr. Tubbs had not needed to point out that Jeremy had fallen into the same trap as the unfortunate Woods. The difference, Hester believed, was that Sally returned Jeremy's affections.

Before her brother could speak, Hester pressed on with Tubbs. "So you think he paid Jeremy and Mr. Woods poorly because he could get away with it?"

He nodded and screwed his face into a grimace. "They weren't the only ones Curry used."

"Would Mr. Simpkins be one of the people you mean?"

Stung, Jeremy raised his voice. "But Mrs. Curry can't abide Simpkins!"

"I know she cannot, but it is clear that he is dangerously mad for her. I just came from the Bell and Bible, and he was there, making veiled threats."

Jeremy leapt up again. "I must go there then! If he—"

"Sit down, Jeremy, and listen to me. You will not help Sally by behaving this way." Seeing that he was turning red, she hastened to explain. "I do not mean that Sally was ever a willing party to Mr. Curry's machinations. I doubt she knew how her husband was using her, as Mr. Tubbs said. But she told me that he insisted she be kind to Mr. Simpkins. He even told her she should be flattered by Mr. Simpkins's odious attentions. I think Mr. Tubbs could be right when he says that Mr. Curry may have used his wife's appealing face and cheerful nature to distract some men from noticing how they were being abused."

As Jeremy slowly subsided into his chair, she turned to Mr. Tubbs again. "What did Mr. Curry want from Mr. Simpkins?"

He grunted. "That's easy! Any man who'd been in the stocks as many times as Curry, would want the beadle for a friend."

Hester recalled that Mr. Curry had lost part of his ear in the stocks. "Why was he arrested so often?"

But here, Tubbs glowered and refused to say anything more. He mumbled disjointed phrases. "None of your concern . . . years ago . . . too indelicate for a lady's ears . . ."

Hester refrained from pressing him. Jeremy was growing restless, apparently yearning to rush to Sally's aid. Laying a hand on his sleeve,

Hester cautioned him not to be rash.

"Mr. Simpkins is a serious threat, my dear. He clearly perceives you as a rival for Sally's affections. And, if you provoke him, I shouldn't be surprised if he did charge you with the murder."

"I can't let him bully her on my account!"

"No, but neither will it do her any good to have you carted off to Newgate again."

He blanched, but his stubborn look made her add, "You said yourself that she will need your help with her husband's business."

"And there is one other thing." Hester selected her words carefully. "The more that Sally is forced to defend you from Mr. Simpkins's accusations, the angrier he gets, and I know you would not wish to make Sally the object of his rage. She has enough to contend with as it is."

Hester did not wish to tell him of the insinuations Mr. Simpkins had made—that Sally might have conspired with Jeremy to kill her husband—though he was bound to hear them eventually. For the moment he did not need another reason to run to her defence. There was nothing he could do for Sally right now but stay at arm's length or he could precipitate an act of vengeance from Mr. Simpkins.

She wondered if the way Mr. Curry had exploited his wife's attractions could have led to his murder. She did not know how to get more information, for she doubted Mr. Tubbs would ever talk to her this freely again. If he had not been so enraged by Mr. Curry's lies, she doubted he would have revealed as much as he had. He was an odd creature, uneasy in society and strangely inarticulate for a writer, though anger had briefly made him loquacious enough.

Hester wished St. Mars were here. He had a way of prying information from other men. Or failing St. Mars, James Henry, who might be able to give her advice. As she prepared to go, she asked Jeremy to escort her to a hackney stand, and together they walked downstairs and into the street.

Hester waited until they had left the Pewter Platter before confessing, "Jeremy, I'm afraid I may have offended Sally unintentionally." She recounted some of the details of Mr. Simpkins's visit and the comment she had made. "I believe she thought I was warning her not to count on your regard."

Jeremy's expression—a mixture of eagerness and fear—betrayed his feelings so clearly, it would have been comical if Hester had not loved him so much. "Hester, I have to tell you something. It's a secret I have had to keep, even from myself. And—Sally—Mrs. Curry—has absolutely no idea.

"I love her," he said, and the words seemed to come from so deeply inside him that Hester could have no doubt of his feelings, even if she had not witnessed them first. "I believe I have loved her since the first day I saw her. But of course, I never let myself contemplate, even for one moment, that I might be free to court her one day."

Concern for his safety struck Hester with fear. "I know you wouldn't have, Jeremy. But you must keep those feelings to yourself. You must not give in to them until Mr. Curry's murderer is discovered." Reluctantly, she told him about the threats she had withheld just a few minutes before. "I am convinced that if Mr. Simpkins believes that you and Sally have formed an attachment to each other, he will find a way to charge you with murder."

His look was desperate. "But what if . . . Hester, she is a widow with a business and a fortune! The jackals will be circling to get their hands on her money. But it's not the money I want. It's Sally herself! What if someone tries to trap her into marriage before the murderer is caught?"

His fears were not that unreasonable. Some scoundrels would go to great lengths to trick heiresses into marriage, even for relatively small fortunes like Sally's. She did not point out a more likely truth—that the killer might never be captured. But even Jeremy knew that was a strong possibility. The panic in his eyes frightened her. It seemed as if he had waited as long as was humanly possible and could not bring himself to wait a second more.

"I don't believe that Sally will rush into another marriage. From what I have gathered, her first was not a very happy one, and with the money to support herself and the bookstall, she has no need for a husband. And she seems intelligent enough to avoid the kind of rogue who would try to trap her for her business. Besides," Hester said, cutting him off before he could express more anguish, "you will be nearby to protect her from that sort. And, even if I did not already suspect her of being very fond of you, I know she will never find anyone as attractive as my brother."

Jeremy smiled wanly, unable to believe her.

Hester said firmly, "Jeremy, you must hold back. I know you, but others do not. If you are seen to court her, someone is certain to suspect you of killing Mr. Curry to win his wife *and* his money. They might even accuse Sally of helping you. You have to wait, or it could ruin you both."

This last argument finally persuaded him. He nodded, sighing in defeat.

She had one last piece of advice. "Since Mr. Curry did leave some money, I think Sally should hire a constable at least to make some inquiries. Someone should do it, and she cannot count on an unpaid constable to take any interest. It is not his job."

Jeremy agreed and said he would mention this to Sally as soon as he saw her next.

As he hailed a hackney for Hester, she asked, "Do you have enough to live on right now? Mr. Henry has persuaded Lord Hawkhurst to make me an allowance. It is small, but it is yours if you need it."

He smiled and gave her an affectionate embrace. "That won't be necessary. Sal—Mrs. Curry intends to pay me more for the copies of my books that sold. She found Mr. Curry's ledgers, too, and it seems more of them sold than he realized. He had never added up the sales of the first before offering me payment for the rest. I doubt he was very good at figuring. If the others continue to sell, I should do well enough."

The hackney pulled up in front of them, so Hester did not respond as acerbically as she might have. "Does that mean you can move out of that dreadful inn?" she asked, as he lowered the step for her.

"Oh, I mustn't do that!" His tone was shocked. "I couldn't leave poor old Tubbs to fend for himself."

He handed her in and shut the door. Too tired to argue, Hester merely waved goodbye and collapsed against the seat, wondering when, if ever, her brother would learn the first thing about self-preservation.

In spite of her parting advice, she doubted that a constable would turn up any evidence or even any clues. If there had been a witness to the killing, surely he would have volunteered information by now. Hester had made the suggestion primarily in the interest of silencing any rumours that Mr. Simpkins might start about Sally's indifference to her husband's murder.

She feared it would be up to her to discover who had killed Mr. Curry, or else she would constantly be confronted with Jeremy's misery. With her shop to run, Sally clearly had no time to make inquiries, and Hester doubted that Jeremy had a sufficiently skeptical nature to suspect anyone. If he did try to find the killer, he might find himself outmatched. Worse, if he could not refrain from declaring his love for Sally, Hester knew she would never sleep at night for fear of finding him in Newgate again.

But she did not know if she would have the freedom to pursue an investigation. It was almost certain that King George would put the Court in mourning for King Lewis of France, and she feared that Isabella's resulting boredom would keep her tied to her cousin's apron strings.

But, as true as this soon proved to be, its effect on her plans paled in comparison to the news that greeted her when she stepped into the house in Kensington Square.

The rebellion had started.

But grant that Actions best discover man;
Take the most strong, and sort them as you can.
The few that glare each character must mark,
You balance not the many in the dark.
What will you do with such as disagree?
Suppress them, or miscall them Policy?
Must then at once (the character to save)
The plain rough Hero turn a crafty Knave?

CHAPTER VIII

The Earl of Mar had set up the Pretender's standard in Scotland and had named himself Lieutenant General of James's forces. On learning this, King George sent the Duke of Argyle into Scotland with troops to confront them.

The next few days brought more disturbing news. The Jacobites had nearly taken Edinburgh Castle with the assistance of some of the soldiers inside it.

When Ormonde and Bolingbroke failed to surrender themselves to the Tower, the House of Lords razed their names from the List of Peers and ordered an inventory to be made of their possessions. The Court soon learned, however, that the Duchess of Ormonde had sold their house in St. James's Square and Richmond House to the Duke's brother, the Earl of Arran, to avoid forfeiting them to the Crown under the Act of Attainder.

This was all Hester could glean from Harrowby over the succeeding week, as he relayed news to his family in anxious, disjointed speeches between hurried trips to St. James's Palace and the House of Lords. The reports in the news-sheets were clearer, but brief. The King was in Council at St. James's with the Prince and Privy Seal, Mr. Secretary Walpole, and the other powerful gentlemen of that body. Lord Powis had been committed to the Tower for undisclosed crimes. And, somewhere in the North, a ship had been sighted unloading men with horses, who then had made their way to the Highlands.

Harrowby sent immediately for James Henry, ostensibly to ask what his receiver-general would do to protect his property in the North, but, as Hester suspected, more likely to beg his advice. Harrowby was torn between the inclination to cling to the protection of his Majesty's troops in Hyde Park and the fear that he would do better to bury his face at Rotherham Abbey until the outcome of the rebellion became clear. But King George had still not granted Parliament a recess, so Harrowby had no choice but to remain where he was.

His fears were partially calmed by a report from abroad that the Regent of France had refused an audience to Bolingbroke and Ormonde.

"Serves them right!" he said angrily to his wife, as they sat in the withdrawing room, waiting for James Henry to arrive. "They should be hanged for causing this fuss! At least, they'll be getting no aid from the Frenchies this time."

The news-sheets had come with the afternoon post. The same mail had brought Hester another letter from Jeremy, who wrote that Sally had engaged a constable to investigate Mr. Curry's murder, and had even offered a reward for information about the crime. Hester hoped this would deter the gossips from suspecting that Sally had had any hand in her husband's death. Unfortunately, no witnesses to the murder had come forward, which made it stranger still that nothing had been stolen from the bookstall. It appeared that the constable had uncovered nothing, but Jeremy assured his sister that he had kept his promise. His wording was circumspect, but Hester could read his meaning between the lines. He had not declared his feelings for Sally.

Mr. Simpkins continued to mutter threats and accusations, and Jeremy now feared that others in the street had started to believe him. He sounded unhappy, but he warned Hester not to risk a trip into town. "The public is understandably on edge, for no one knows where the Pretender's men will strike. So take care of yourself, Hester, and do not worry about me."

Isabella, who had been struggling to decipher a letter from her mother, looked up from her page and said, "Mama says everyone is terrified the Pretender will come and murder them all their beds. She begs me to send the coach for her."

Harrowby gave a twitch of alarm. "Nonsense! James may be a Papist, but he *is* a gentleman. He won't go murdering ladies, just because their husbands were Whigs. I hope she's not planning to bring all your brothers and sisters with her?"

"I don't think so. She just mentions herself."

"Humph!" he muttered. "If she truly believes the Pretender is coming, I wonder that she could think of leaving them. Better write and tell her to stay where she is."

For once Hester was in perfect accord with Harrowby and even offered to write the note. The last thing she wanted was Mrs. Mayfield there to order her about.

"Poor Mama! I know she worries about me and the child."

"Your mother can come in January when the child is due," Harrowby said.

"She had better come within the month or the roads will be too deep to travel."

Hester did not dare to hope that Mrs. Mayfield would get trapped in the country until the roads dried next spring. She could only be grateful for every moment of relief she was given from her aunt.

Harrowby was eyeing Hester with a speculative look. He turned to his wife then, as if to propose an alternative. But another hurried glance at Hester made him colour, and he seemed to think better of his notion, for he turned back to Isabella and sighed. "Very well. I suppose you must have her. You may tell her to come when we move back into Hawkhurst House. But not a day sooner, mind! Tell her you'll inform her when we are there."

The door opened to admit James Henry, fresh from his horse. His face looked hot and dusty and his boots were muddied from the road. He took a few steps into the room and bowed.

Harrowby pounced upon him before he had a chance to raise his head. "There you are, Henry! I wondered what was keeping you. What do you make of all this business, eh?"

Correctly interpreting this to refer to the rebellion, James Henry spoke in a soothing voice. "I am certain there is nothing to worry about, my lord. The news is very disturbing, of course, but I believe King George has matters well in hand."

"You do? Well, of course he does! What else should one believe? But what if the Pretender's men make it down here, eh? Then, what?"

Oblivious to his own contradictions, Harrowby plied his receiver-general with anxious questions until his most pressing worries had been laid to rest. After nearly an hour of this, when he finally appeared to be satisfied, James Henry begged leave to go to Hawkhurst House to change his clothes.

Harrowby waved him off. With a feeling of frustration, Hester saw that she would have to wait to ask James Henry about his plans, for she could hardly demand his attention as Harrowby had. Her impatience had been building all week, for with Isabella insisting on her company, she had no liberty to help Jeremy. Someone with the freedom to come and go would have to investigate Mr. Curry's murder, and with St. Mars still in France, she had no one she could ask for help.

It was the next day before she managed to intercept James Henry, just inside the front door. She begged a private word with him before Harrowby learned of his arrival.

Detecting the urgency in her voice, he frowned and gestured towards the stairs, prepared to follow her. They retreated to a small withdrawing room at the rear of the house, which neither Isabella nor her husband tended to use.

By the time they reached it, Hester found she hardly knew where to start. She realized how presumptuous it would be of her to ask for more of James Henry's help. Turning to face him just inside the room, she fumbled for words, and ended by asking him instead whether he thought the uprising could spread to Rotherham Abbey.

He peered at her strangely, as if suspecting that this was not the subject she had originally intended to broach. But he did not press her. "It's not the Abbey that worries me," he began, before he caught himself up. Then, noting her expression, he realized that he had given himself away, for he reluctantly admitted, "I did not wish to alarm my lord, but I am concerned about the Northumberland estate. The neighbours are Papists, as are many of the tenants. Stuart sympathies are strong in that region, and it is possible that some of the men will join the rebellion. If they do, they might try to seize the estate, or at least take the stock and fodder."

"What will you do?"

He smiled ruefully at her. "All I *can* do, which is to see the situation for myself. I can speak to the tenants and try to assess their leanings. But my instinct tells me that they will be more likely to remain loyal if they sense my lord's presence, even if only in the person of his agent."

Hester saw that she must not distract him from so important a journey. The Northumberland estate was part of St. Mars's patrimony. She would never forgive herself if it was lost because she had kept James Henry from his duty.

"When do you leave?" she asked, careful to hide her disappointment.

"Tomorrow, if my lord will agree. Obviously, I shall have to make him aware of some of my concerns." James Henry looked questioningly at her from beneath his heavy brows. "Is there anything particular that worries you, Mrs. Kean?"

She gave him a grateful smile and lied. "No, nothing at all. You have told me all I need to know."

She would have made a light farewell, but he surprised her by taking her hand and saying earnestly, "Pray do not let yourself be frightened by this conflict. As long as his Majesty's troops are near, I am certain you will be safe."

He had misunderstood the reason for her questions, which was just as well. His kindness, when added to all her deceptions, however, made her flush uncomfortably. Not knowing where to look, she mumbled something stupid—later, she was certain that it *was*—and made a quick curtsy, which forced him to release her hand.

With a hint of shyness, he bowed and quitted the room, leaving her to wonder how much of what she was feeling was pleasure, and how much chagrin.

When, that afternoon, Isabella went for a drive in the park with Lord Kirkland, Hester sat at the writing desk in the withdrawing room and composed a letter. She addressed it to Mr. Mavors, the name St. Mars had assumed in London, in care of the King's Head in Lambeth, where Tom collected his master's post. Then, she sealed it with a wafer and walked into the High Street to post it herself.

✍

Tom had made it almost his daily practice to drink a mug or two of ale at the King's Head whenever he was installed at his master's house on the Thames. There was seldom any post to collect, but if St. Mars ever did wish to reach him, this would be the only way. Tom had reckoned it safer to make friends with the innkeeper than just to stop in to ask for letters, when the arrival of so few could arouse his suspicions.

Tom was considerably surprised, therefore, when as soon as he walked in, Mr. Bailey hailed him with the news that his master had two letters waiting.

He paid the postage, then sat down to drink his beer before taking the letters outside to read. Too much haste on a master's errand could look suspicious, too. Before putting the letters in his pocket, he noted that one was from St. Mars, and his heart gave a skip to know that his master was still in France and at least well enough to write. Since the news from Scotland had arrived, Tom had feared to read in the newssheets that St. Mars had joined the rebellion. Now, he prayed that his master hadn't written to tell him just that.

The other letter, he saw, had been posted in Kensington, which aroused his curiosity. Only a few people knew how to reach St. Mars, and most of those worked for the Pretender. Eager to read both letters— for he had St. Mars's leave to open any message that came for him— Tom downed his mug in a few huge gulps, wiped his mouth on his sleeve, and left to take horse.

His mount today was far more placid than Looby. Tom knotted the reins loosely about Beau's neck and left it to the horse to find their way home. As the big animal plodded along, Tom dug the letters out of his pocket and broke the seal on St. Mars's first. Beau's stride was fairly smooth. Swaying gently in the saddle, Tom found it easy to make out his master's hand.

St. Mars had written in his usual fashion, as from Mr. Brown to Mr. Mavors. He wrote that his business in France was now concluded, and that he looked forward to seeing his friends soon in London. He would be taking the packet from Calais to Dover at the first opportunity, and hoped to find Mavors and his family well at home.

Tom released a deep sigh and relaxed his features in a smile. Nothing in his master's letter hinted at any trouble, which surely it would if he meant to join the rebellion. The channel crossing would pose far greater dangers than his letter allowed, of course, for St. Mars could not take the packet. With a price on his head, he would have to find an illegal way to enter England. But with nothing left to worry about except his master's crossing, Tom could turn to the second piece of mail with a lighter heart.

He hesitated before breaking the seal. Even with St. Mars's orders clear, he could not feel right to open it. But if, as he thought, it *was* from Mrs. Kean, St. Mars would never forgive him if he failed to respond.

Shaking off his qualms, he unfolded the sheet of paper and searched for the signature. A breeze curled the two top corners, but he could see "Hester Kean" written at the bottom. Spreading the letter back open, he stretched it over Beau's neck and started to read.

As near as he could make out, Mrs. Kean was asking St. Mars to meet her as soon as he came home from France. She wrote of finding her brother in London and of some trouble he was having. Mrs. Kean knew as well as St. Mars that the government was reading the mail, so she had not stated the nature of her problem. Knowing her a bit by now, though, Tom had the feeling that her brother's trouble would turn out to be much more serious than just a toothache or a pile of debts.

After reading St. Mars's letter, he had been ready to ride for Dover with the happy thought of meeting him. Riding back to London together would give Tom the chance to ask St. Mars for his permission to wed. But he reluctantly discarded that plan. If Mrs. Kean needed his master's help, then St. Mars would want Tom to offer his in his stead.

Back at the house, he stabled Beau and brushed him down, wondering how he should go about getting in touch with her. Mrs. Kean had given an address in Kensington Square. As St. Mars's groom, before his arrest, Tom had come to know that area well enough, but now he could not afford to be recognized by any of Lord Hawkhurst's servants.

In the past St. Mars had used Katy to take messages to Mrs. Kean. But Katy had posed as a fruit peddler, hawking her strawberries in Piccadilly. If anyone from Hawkhurst House recognized her, he would surely ask himself what she was doing in Kensington. Tom believed that any man with two eyes in his head would recall Katy's face instantly. Rufus, the porter at Hawkhurst House, had certainly ogled her enough!

No, he was the one who would have to go. He would just have to employ some of his master's wiles. Maybe Mrs. Kean's problem would keep him busy, so he wouldn't have time to worry about St. Mars.

ॐ

Bundled in a cloak and muffler, Gideon huddled against a warehouse on the quay in Calais, fighting his impatience. He had been seeking a passage to England for the past three days.

The previous week, the embalmed corpse of King Louis XIV had been carried with magnificent pomp all the way from Versailles to the royal tombs at St. Denis north of Paris, his entrails preceding the rest, and his heart conveyed to the Church of the Jesuits of St. Louis. The procession had started at nine o'clock in the evening and had arrived at eight the following morning, its train so long that it took an hour and a half to pass. Hundreds of thousands of people had lined the route to see it—not out of grief, Gideon believed, so much as shock. Gazing at the throng, he had wondered how many of the French, whom Louis had impoverished, had believed that their king—who had claimed the sun for his own, had outlived most men, and had usurped the Parliament's right to oppose him—had been immortal.

The Duke of Orleans's Regency had been ratified by the Parliament, which had voted to nullify the old king's will. The royal dukes, Louis's bastards, had fought for guardianship of the boy-king and lost. The Regent had taken immediate steps to reduce the expenses of the royal household, savings which should ultimately amount to more than thirty million *livres.*

More important to the English, he had dismissed Bolingbroke's friend, Louis's foreign minister, the Marquis de Torcy.

Gideon was still at St. Denis when news of the rebellion in Scotland arrived. His surprise was reflected in the stunned faces of James's gentlemen who had come to represent him at Louis's funeral, seeming to demonstrate that the Earl of Mar had acted alone. Bolingbroke and Ormonde immediately pressed their request for an audience with the Regent, who steadfastly refused to see them. Now there was talk that the Jacobites might even be expelled from France.

How long it would take James to reach the coast and make passage to Scotland, Gideon could not guess, but it was certain that English ships would be lying in wait for him. The British Navy would be patrolling the Channel, which would make Gideon's own crossing more hazardous.

He had hastened to Calais, but his fears had already come to pass. No smuggler was willing to chance being caught with a Jacobite aboard his sloop. Rumours that spies were reporting their movements to the authorities had all but shut down their trade. The risks of free trading were great enough without rebellion added to the charges. So, for the past three days, all Gideon's inquiries had been met with curt refusals, making him chafe.

He could not shake off the disturbing feeling that he was needed at home. He was oppressed by the notion that something had happened to Mrs. Kean, though he could not imagine what it could be. Just knowing that war was about to start made him imagine all sorts of ills. He comforted himself with the reminder that as long as Harrowby possessed the earldom, the Hawkhurst household would enjoy King George's protection, for Harrowby would never think of endangering his life for a cause.

A change in the weather, expected at this time of year, promised to make his crossing even more of a challenge. In the past few days, autumn had blasted in on gusts of cold wind. Blowing into his cupped hands to stay warm, Gideon pondered the remaining choices he had. Earlier, he had even considered buying a boat and hiring his own crew, but he had rejected the plan as foolish for he would have to abandon the boat offshore and lose the considerable money he'd spent. Now after three days with no success, this idea recurred to tempt him seriously. So, he left his shelter and headed up the wharf to look for a boat.

With his face muffled up over his nose to avoid detection, he was just passing the packet office, when he spied a familiar face through the window. Stopping to peer inside, he saw a young lady, accompanied by her maid and groom—and apparently no one else. Even if he had not met Fanny Oglethorpe again recently at St. Germain, Gideon would have known her anywhere by her likeness to her sisters.

The moment he saw her, his mind gave a leap. Quickly he turned and strode to the door.

He paused just inside the office at the sight of so many passengers—most, if not all of them English—but ignoring the knot in his stomach that warned him to hide, he carved a path through them to accost the young lady with a bow.

"Your servant, ma'am." His gaze seeking hers, Gideon kept his voice to a low murmur.

He was relieved to see a spark of recognition come to her face, even if the glances she threw at her fellow passengers revealed how little she relished meeting him here. She took a quick step forward and offered her hand to be kissed, bending near to whisper, "You must address me as Mrs. Barker, my lord."

He straightened to find that she had recovered her poise. A mischievous gleam lit her eye, giving him hope that what he intended to propose would not meet with an instant refusal.

He offered "Mrs. Barker" his arm and invited her to take a promenade along the wharf. As they made their way back through the crowd, a coquettish arch of her brow told him that she was more than a little intrigued.

Gideon led her a safe distance away from the office, past the fishing boats that were docked there. Her maid followed discreetly. He threw the woman a significant look over his shoulder, but his companion said, "Do not mind Marie, *monsieur*. She is French and a Catholic. You cannot believe that Mama would engage another English maid? Not after what happened to Anne!"

No, Fanny's mother, Lady Oglethorpe, would be far too clever to make the same mistake twice. Years ago, the English servant her daughters Anne and Eleanor had taken with them to France had converted to the Roman Church and entered a nunnery. Later, perhaps regretting her decision, she had written to her mother and insisted that she had been carried off against her will and forced to take the veil. Worse still, she had made up the story that the Pretender was not truly James Stuart, but the Oglethorpes' child, who had been substituted for the real prince when he died of convulsive fits at the age of five or six weeks. The story had been published by the Whigs and was still widely believed. There had never been a shred of truth in anything the girl had claimed, but as a result of it, Anne Oglethorpe had been taken on a warrant of high treason for taking the girl to France in order to subvert her to the Roman Catholic religion.

If not for the protection of her lover, Robert Harley, Earl of Oxford, she might have been executed. The fright she had suffered, however, had stopped neither her, her sister Eleanor, nor their mother from conspiring to put James Stuart back on the throne.

Now, it appeared that the youngest daughter, Fanny, had joined the family cause.

"I don't suppose I need ask why you are travelling incognito," Gideon said, guiding her away from a man who was pushing a loaded wheel-barrow along the wharf.

She gave a little skip, and said, "No, isn't it marvelous! I'm sure you've heard the news!"

"Yes. I confess it took me aback."

She nodded, squeezing his arm with barely suppressed glee. *"Nous, aussi!* We had no warning at all! I doubt that my Lord 'B' and his Grace of 'O' were ever so confounded! But I think the Earl of 'M' is vastly courageous, don't you? And I know that Cousin Jonathan will be so pleased." Cousin Jonathan was the name Jacobite spies used for James Stuart in their correspondence.

Since he needed her help, Gideon bit back the words that sprang to his tongue—*Did she think it was a game to be played with men's lives?*—and asked instead, "Did your mother send you the news?"

"No, we read it in the news-sheets. But what of you? How did you learn of it?"

Gideon told her the truth, that the news had reached him at St. Denis. But he kept his story short. Obviously, she had not heard that James had dismissed him, and she might not wish to help him if she knew, especially if she feared her mother's wrath. Lady Oglethorpe was called "Lady Fury" for good reason.

By this time, they had reached the end of the wharf. Turning back, Gideon gave a look about, but although the docks were crowded with porters and scavengers, no one was close enough to hear.

He asked Fanny if she would help him get back into England. He explained his plan.

From her bright looks, he could see that his scheme had appealed to her adventurous nature. When he finished, however, she treated him to a mock pout and said, "So that is why you approached me! I should have known it was not for the pleasure of gazing into my fine eyes! But, if you must have it that way, of course I shall help you. I know how fond his Majesty is of you."

Gideon gave an inward wince. He did not like having to deceive her, but James and his followers owed him this much at least.

They dined together, not at Madame Grandsires's house, where most English passengers took their meals, but at a small cross-timbered inn around the corner on a side street, which Fanny said would be more secure. Taking a surreptitious look at the men in the taproom, Gideon was relieved to note that most of them appeared to be French. Under English rule until the last few years—and in reality Flemish—Calais could claim many inhabitants besides the French. The number of English and Dutch on her streets was enough to give any Jacobite pause.

They took a private parlour for their meal. Then Fanny sent her maid to fetch her groom. And, before the next packet sailed, her manservant—dressed in St. Mars's clothes—returned to the house of Fanny's sister, Eleanor de Mézières, and Gideon took his place next to Fanny, disguised as her groom.

They were fortunate in that the captain judged the weather fair enough to sail. Gideon paid the oarsmen who rowed them out to the packet boat and held the ladder while Fanny climbed aboard.

He thought he should take a position aft so as not to raise suspicions, but Fanny insisted on keeping him close to her. "I shall say that I cannot be left alone with none but my maid to protect me from gentlemen's attentions," she whispered, with a wink.

He followed behind her at a respectful distance until she found a place along the rail from which to gaze out. Then, glancing over her shoulder at her fellow passengers, she beckoned him to her side.

Gideon threw her an exasperated look. "If you cannot be made to take this more seriously, I doubt this masquerade will work."

"If anyone comes too close, you can fall to your knees and pretend to be searching for my fan."

"A fan? With this chill in the air?"

"Oh, very well—my glove, then. But I hope you do not intend for me to spend the next seven hours or more with no one to speak to?"

Relenting with a sigh, he moved to rest his forearms on the rail. In truth, he had not looked forward to sailing under such dismal conditions. Though usually a good sailor, he doubted that anyone was entirely immune to the rocking of a boat.

"So you have decided to follow in your sisters' footsteps?" he asked, unable to curb his curiosity. He knew that Anne and Eleanor Oglethorpe had crossed the Channel on the Pretender's business many times as the "Barker" sisters.

Fanny turned her face into the wind and scoffed. "Hardly! I'm very venturesome on my own, you know. Besides, his Majesty's cause is as much mine as anyone's. I took instruction from the Abbé Fénelon. And, for converting, his Majesty King Louis gave me a pension of two thousand francs." She screwed her face into grimace. "I'm afraid *Monsieur d'Orleans* has plans to take that away from me, and all the other converts, too."

"Is that why you are returning to England?"

Some of her dark hair had escaped its ribbons, and she brushed it away from her face. "Oh, no. I'm carrying a message of encouragement to the loyal."

"Fanny—" Gideon began on a rush of concern.

She laughed. "It's not a letter, silly! I daren't do that, not wishing to be carried up in *ceremony* to London like Anne—you *must* put it once and for all in your head that I am a very reasonable creature—I'm by far the least violent of the family. Sometimes I think Eleanor's brain will turn if James is not made happy soon. I'm a very moderate person in comparison to her and her husband."

"The marquis? Is he truly that ardent?"

"Oh, yes! There is nothing he will not do in James's behalf. He truly is a dear! But they will need me back in France soon. Eleanor cannot write in English, and neither can Eugène-Marie. So, if they wish to write to Lord Mar, they will have to rely on me."

She said this so smugly that Gideon had to laugh. It seemed that Fanny had the sense of humour the other members of her family lacked.

"How will Anne take the news?" he asked. The last he had seen Anne Oglethorpe, she had been suffering from the worst fit of fury he had ever beheld. She had just learned that the Duke of Ormonde had fled England, leaving her lover Harley, Earl of Oxford, alone to brave the accusations of the Whigs.

"I am certain she will be very happy. She has been sending Lord Oxford's messages to James. Oxford is ready to join us now, so I know she is working to gain his freedom." Fanny giggled. "She refers to him in her letters as 'Mr. Primrose' or, sometimes, 'Mr. Carnation.' Do you not wonder why she chose such ridiculous names?"

"Anne is carrying Harley's messages? But how does she do it? Do you tell me that she has been visiting him in the Tower?"

Fanny nodded, giving him a triumphant look. "Oh, you must never doubt Anne! I cannot tell how she's accomplished it, but where there is a will, there is always a way. I heard that two of the Tower guards left their posts. They tried to climb the wall at midnight to return, but both fell to their deaths. I do not say that Anne bribed them, but who knows?"

Gideon had read that report in a news-sheet that Tom had mailed to him. The paper had said that the men had dashed their brains out on the paving stones.

"What other devilry are your sisters and mother up to?" he said, not in jest.

Fanny laughed and tossed her head. "I misdoubt I should confide in you. But it is fortunate for his Majesty that he has us acting in his interest. Sometimes I think no progress would be made at all, if not for the ladies who are loyal to him."

Gideon did not press her to name any of the others. He had a notion that Ormonde's friend Mrs. Trant had a hand in the enterprise. Recalling what Bolingbroke had said about James's self-appointed diplomats, however, he cautioned her not to do anything without Bolingbroke's approval.

She stoutly refused to agree, saying, "I am sure Lord Bolingbroke is doing the best he knows how, but as he doesn't seem to be accomplishing anything at the moment, I do not see why the rest of us should be shackled by his failures."

There was a strong sense of indignation behind her speech. When Gideon stared persistently at her, she shot him a sideways glance and finally blurted, "He called me a teaser! Just because I would not entertain his gallantry, if you please! I hope my purpose is nobler than that! You must know he believes himself the greatest statesman the world has ever known and the most successful rake, as well.

"Besides," she said, with a pout, "I do not intend to make the same error Anne made. She will never marry now. And poor Molly . . . She would be a very different sort of woman entirely, if only our mother were not such a tyrant."

Gideon did not try to extract any more information from her. The Oglethorpe ladies were so different from ordinary women that he could hardly decide how he felt about them. Their devotion to the Stuarts was unmatched, as was their courage. That Fanny would enter into the conspiracy when one of her sisters had nearly lost her life in the cause seemed more foolish than he could imagine—until it dawned on him that he had done the very same. His father had been murdered working in the cause of the White Rose, and Gideon had not allowed that fact to discourage his own decisions. He could thank God that he was out of the business now, but he knew he would always feel guilty that he had not measured up to his father's ideals. Perhaps that was how it was for Fanny, too, for in what other endeavour could she ever win her mother's approbation.

They spent more time at the rail, then strolled about the windy deck until Fanny was driven below by the cold. Gideon could not accompany her to her berth, so he joined the servants and poorer passengers standing aft, where they struggled to stay dry and warm through the long voyage ahead.

Some nine hours after they had left Calais, they were not far off the Dover shore when their boat was hailed by a sloop in his Majesty's Navy. The captain cursed the delay, but he gave orders to cut sail and prepare to receive boarders.

As the sloop hove to, Gideon huddled deeper into the group of common passengers, lowering his head to mask his height. Finding an opening amid the shifting view of shoulders and hats, he peered out in time to see two officers climb over the side and onto the packet's deck.

They conferred briefly with the captain. Then, one marched aft and started herding the common passengers against the rail. The captain called down to the wealthy passengers below, ordering them up from their berths, while the second officer demanded to see everyone's passport.

With a pulse drumming loudly in his ears, Gideon pulled his woolen muffler higher on his face and hunched his shoulders as if from the cold. He kept an eye out for Fanny, while turning over in his head what he should say. Wondering what Fanny would do if they questioned her, he barely noticed the gentleman in a bagwig who emerged from below deck, until he called an officer to his side and pointed a finger straight at Gideon's group. Whatever he said made the officer raise his head with a jerk. He turned a piercing gaze on the group, eventually bringing it to rest on Gideon.

Gideon felt an instant urge to run. But, even with his legs thrumming and his innards twisting into a knot, he knew that jumping overboard would do him no good. The boat was too far out for him to swim to shore. Even if he could make it, and still had any strength left to run, the sloop would fire its warning guns and he would be greeted on the beach by a regiment from the castle.

The officer strode briskly towards him, his sword unsheathed. Gideon's heart raced and, despite the cold wind, beads of sweat broke out on his forehead. His hands were clammy with the desire to flee, but he willed himself to stay where he was and to conceal his fear. The passengers between him and the officer fell back and gasped, but the officer impatiently shoved them aside.

He pointed his sword at Gideon, then swept it in an arc towards the bow. "You, sir! Please step forward! There is a gentleman here who would ask you some questions."

The courtesy he used made Gideon's heart thump. It meant that the gentleman who had reported him was under no illusion that he was a groom. Wondering how he had been recognized, Gideon allowed a bit of fear to show, for in this situation even an innocent man would be alarmed.

Swaying with the rocking of the boat, the officer took him by the elbow and marched him to the bow, where the mysterious gentleman, the other officer, and the captain stood waiting. The captain's face was strangely pale.

Before Gideon had a moment to wonder why he looked so frightened, the senior officer, who'd been speaking to the gentleman, said to him, "This is Mr. Northcote, a Messenger in his Majesty King George's service. He will take you into custody as soon as we make shore."

Gideon's stomach gave a lurch, as if he'd been dropped from a great height. If he had been on land, he would have fought for his life, but this was definitely not the place. He tried to tell himself he would have a better chance on solid ground. But on this occasion he would not have Tom to help him escape, and his guards would be experienced soldiers from the castle. They would carry him into London and throw him into the Tower, and he would lose even the limited freedom he'd enjoyed as an outlaw.

"Have you nothing to say?" the officer asked him. Then, turning to Mr. Northcote, he said, "But perhaps he does not speak English?"

Gideon's brain gave a start. Why should they suppose he might not speak English? Perhaps, they had made a mistake, and did not really know who he was.

"I can, too, speak the King's English!" he said, feigning indignation in a countryman's accent. "An' I don't see what you gen'lemen are all on about!"

The men's eyebrows shot up as if one. They exchanged doubtful glances. The captain even looked relieved, but the Messenger, Mr. Northcote, merely smiled. "I heard this gentleman speaking fluently in French and English to his lady companion. Do not be fooled by his attempts to disguise his speech."

"But I heard—"

"You will simply have to trust me, Captain," Mr. Northcote insisted. "I saw this man, dressed as a gentleman, in speech with the young lady. Then I followed them to an eating establishment, where they dined together. When they emerged, he was wearing her servant's clothes, and her servant left in his. So you see that I have good cause for my suspicions."

He turned his attention back to Gideon. "Where is your passport, sir?"

Gideon remained silent. A moment of relief had eased the knot in his belly. So, the Messenger had suspicions, but had no clear notion of Gideon's identity. It would be better to hold off on speaking until Fanny was questioned, which she certainly would be. Gideon hoped she could not be prosecuted for helping him, but he could always swear that she had no idea who he was.

He expected Mr. Northcote to confront her then with his accusations, but he had underestimated the Messenger.

"Hold him apart from the lady." Mr. Northcote gave this order to the captain. "I do not wish to give them the opportunity to confer on their story. There is a gentleman scheduled to arrive in Dover late tomorrow who should be able to give us this person's name."

Ask why from Britain Caesar would retreat?
Caesar himself might whisper he was beat.
Why risk the world's great empire for a Punk?
Caesar himself might whisper he was drunk.
But, sage historians! 'tis your task to prove
One action Conduct; one, heroic Love.

CHAPTER IX

B ored and listless, in spite of her doctor's instructions to avoid all carriage rides, Isabella decided to pay a visit to the Duchess of Grafton, who was recently delivered of a child. The King had stood grandfather to the boy—another named George—with the Duke of Richmond and Dowager Duchess of Grafton as the baby's other godparents. Isabella had a notion that the baby might provide some form of diversion.

By chance, their arrival at her Grace's house coincided with a visit from the Princess of Wales, so Hester had to remain downstairs to ensure enough places in the bedchamber for her Highness's ladies-in-waiting.

Hester would have liked to see the child. In the past year, not many babies had come in her way. As long as she had lived in her father's house, there had always been some woman in the parish with a newborn in need of her attention.

On the way home, she mentioned this to Isabella, who merely said, "Lud! Then next time *you* can pay the visit for me! I have never found anything so tedious. Do you know, there was not a gentleman to be seen in the house! I hope when my child comes that Harrowby will not leave me all alone like that."

"Her Grace was alone? Did she not have her lady with her?"

"No, silly! Of course, she had a lady with her. A chamber full of ladies! But all they did was coo over the child. I daresay he was as pretty a child as I've ever seen, but a party without gentlemen is bound to be dull, isn't it?"

Hester restrained the sigh that often came to her when she considered the future of Isabella's child. Sometimes hints of anger and resentment rose up in her, too, for she had begun to have yearnings of her own that were unlikely ever to be fulfilled. It was hard enough to resign oneself to a life without a husband, harder still to give up any hope of children.

Hester stepped down from the carriage in front of the house in Kensington Square and turned to offer Isabella her hand. Isabella took the assistance she offered but quickly relinquished it in favour of her footman's. Will was a strapping, red-haired lad with a great deal of impish charm, which he had quickly learned to use on his pretty mistress.

"Here, let me help you, milady. I doubt but what you've tired yourself."

Isabella heaved a sigh. In truth, she did look a trifle worn. The black of her mourning was not flattering to a lady with her golden complexion. "I am rather listless, Will. But you will see that I get into bed for a proper rest."

Hester would have followed them into the house if Isabella had not said, with a wave of her hand, "Do not bother to accompany us, Hester. Will can see to everything I need."

The languishing smile she gave him raised a flame in the footman's freckled cheeks.

Comforted by his terrified look, Hester refrained from following them inside and turned to search the carriage for anything Isabella might have left. Experience had taught her that this could spare her the trouble of looking later for things her cousin missed.

As she turned again to enter the house, a boy surprised her by running up and presenting her with a note.

It bore no seal. If it had, Hester would have assumed he had mistaken her for someone else, but recently she had learned to examine first and to ask questions later.

With a quickening heart, Hester opened the paper and read, "Follow the boy." It was signed, "Mr. Mavors's servant." The hand that had penned it was rough.

She gave a cautious look about. The coach was clattering away, the second footman hanging on behind. The door to the house was already shut.

The boy was waiting for her to respond.

She told him to lead her to the sender of the note, and the boy took off, making for the entrance to the square.

Hester did not cast any looks behind her as she followed him into the High Street. The boy walked fast, so she was obliged to hurry to keep up. He moved uphill, weaving in and out among the shoppers, until she was afraid he might lose her, but she did not dare run for fear of attracting unwanted attention.

Then, suddenly, he disappeared. Arriving breathlessly at the spot where she had last seen him, Hester peered cautiously round the corner of a building and spotted him several yards beyond inside a court. He had stopped to speak to a thick-set man, dressed in the clothes of a merchant.

Uncertain, she started to draw back, but the man raised his face and revealed himself to be Tom.

He tossed the boy a coin and, sending him on his way, walked quickly over to meet her. When he reached her, he removed his broad-brimmed hat and bowed.

"Thank goodness, it is you, Tom. For a moment, I did not know you."

He was wearing a short, brown wig and a black, knee-length coat over a well-made shirt and waistcoat. Her comment made him lower his head, the look on his face something between a grin and a scowl.

"I don't wonder you didn't know me, Mrs. Kean. Not in these fancy togs. But I thought it best to be safe in case we're seen. I've been about this place, y'see."

She assured him she did, then asked, "Have you come at your master's bidding, Tom?"

"No, mistress. That is, he don't know about your letter yet, but I knew he'd want me to answer it for 'im if I could. So here I am."

Hester did her best to hide her disappointment. Even though she had cautioned herself not to expect St. Mars, she had still hoped to see him.

She smiled and thanked his proxy, wondering whether she should proceed. It did not seem proper to involve St. Mars's servants in her troubles, but Tom looked ready to receive her orders. And with a feeling of relief, she realized she must have someone in whom to confide.

She told him of her discovery that her brother lived in London, about his work for Mr. Curry, and concluded with Mr. Curry's murder. Without exposing her brother's feelings for the bookseller's wife, she gave Tom to understand that Jeremy was in danger of being charged with the crime.

Tom listened throughout with a sober mien. When she had finished, he asked her how he could serve her before his lordship returned.

"I would not wish you to take any risks," Hester said, "but with the rebellion started, I am finding it hard to get into London. My cousin is frightened about the Pretender and requires me to stay at her side. We should be moving back into Hawkhurst House within the week, but even there, I fear my movements may be confined to the house. I was hoping that someone could watch the Currys' shop and tell me if anything of a suspicious nature occurs."

As she'd talked, Tom had worked two fingers beneath his wig to scratch at his scalp. Pursuing the itch while he pondered the problem, he said doubtfully, "I can do it, I guess. But I can't say as I know what sort of suspicions you mean."

"Neither do I," Hester admitted, with a feeble smile. "But the murderer must be someone Mr. Curry knew, for he was not robbed. Someone had a reason for wishing him dead that had nothing to do with money. And I suspect that whoever it was had something to do with the bookstall. Either a customer, or someone else who had a reason for visiting the shop. And, if I am correct, he may visit it again."

She did not tell Tom of her theory—that the killer might have wished Mr. Curry dead in order to win his pretty wife, a woman even more attractive as a widow with a business. It would be better for Tom to reach his own conclusions in case she limited his deductions with the little bit of information she had managed to collect.

"So you want me to keep a watch on the place? And maybe follow somebody, if any of 'em raises my hackles, like?"

"Would you, Tom? If you would, I should be immensely grateful."

The wig now askew, he bobbed his head and mumbled, "It wouldn't be no trouble." Then, he asked her how he should report his findings to her.

"We shall have to meet again then, but only if you discover something I should know. I will send you word the day we've returned to Hawkhurst House. Then, if you wish to see me, send Katy with a note. Tell her I shall take a walk to the Palace every morning at six o'clock, so she can find me on St. James's Street at that hour. Then I will tell her where you and I can meet."

Tom agreed to reach her if he discovered anything of use.

Hester thanked him. Then, anxious to get back, she turned to go. But, before leaving, she permitted herself one tiny indulgence. "By the way, Tom, has your master sent any word of when he means to return?" She hoped she asked this with the right note of nonchalance.

Tom's face lit up. "Oh, didn't I tell you, mistress? He's on his way home right now."

✆

It was nearly dusk, when Gideon was bound and borne ashore, trussed like a boar for the spit and hoisted upon the shoulders of three burly marines. In a cold misting rain, they lowered him into a small boat and ferried him closer to shore, where the townsmen, who were scarcely better than pirates, exacted money from the passengers to carry them onto the beach.

From the shore, he was bruised and bounced as his porters made the long, steep climb to Dover Castle. They carried him through the Constable's Gateway, across the inner bailey, over the moat that guarded the keep via a drawbridge, and into the keep itself. Then, instead of tossing him into a cell, as Gideon had expected, they hauled him up a wide, vast staircase to the second story, where the King's apartments were, and set him down in a furnished chamber, where his wrists and ankles were finally cut free.

He would have asked why they had deposited him in such fine rooms, if he had not feared betraying clues about himself. Grateful to be standing on his own two feet, he looked about the well-appointed chamber and decided he would be wiser to remain dumb. If, by some stroke of good luck, the person who was expected to know him did not, then he could still pretend to be Fanny's servant.

He had glimpsed her once that morning as he'd been lowered into the boat. Then again on the beach with her maid, where their porters had set them down before placing them in sedan chairs for the climb. The officer had suggested that she, too, would be kept in the castle, until a decision about Gideon was made.

As soon as his guard shut the door, Gideon wasted no time, but looked about for a means of escape. The door was heavily built of ancient oak and was locked. His only window revealed a drop of well over a hundred feet with nothing to cling to on the way down. Through it, under grey skies he could see past the massive fortifications of turrets and walls, to houses and pastures many miles away. Dover Castle had been constructed on a formidable site to make it impregnable without— and inescapable from within. It would take an army like Cromwell's to break him out.

He paced, but before he could come up with a plan, he received a surprising visit from the bailiff of the castle, who hurried in, accompanied by two guards. He bowed very low and, in a curiously gracious manner, asked if everything was to Gideon's liking.

Confounded by the man's politeness, Gideon said nothing, but frowned, imagining how taken aback a servant would be to receive such attentions.

The bailiff accepted his silence, almost as if he'd expected it. He made no attempt to engage Gideon in conversation, but assured him that a meal would be prepared and brought up to him shortly. Then, abjuring him to tell his guards if there was anything he lacked, he bowed himself out.

Gideon would have been amused by the episode, had he not recalled tomorrow's threat. Clearly he had been mistaken for someone else. A person of importance, but a fugitive, too. The danger would come, not from clearing the confusion, but from the strong probability that whoever was coming would also know him.

He did not know who the current Governor of Dover Castle was. The Duke of Ormonde had just been stripped of that post, along with the other positions he had held. Busy with his own affairs, Gideon could not remember seeing an announcement of the Duke's replacement. But whoever the governor was, he was certain to be a courtier and a peer. If it was the governor who was expected to arrive tomorrow afternoon, there was virtually no chance that he would not recognize the Viscount St. Mars.

In the morning, the hours passed with excruciating slowness. Never at ease when inactivity was forced upon him, Gideon paced the length of the vast chamber again and again, pausing occasionally at the window to peer out at the bailey far below. The weather had slightly cleared, but an angry fog hovered in his mind. His whole body seethed with nervous frustration. Certain that he would prefer taking his chances in flight, he formed a plan for jumping his guards. His best chance would come when they brought in his visitor. If he could make it past them to the door, he might be able to close it behind him and give himself a few moments' head start.

The awareness that a large company of soldiers would be waiting in the bailey irked him so that he struck the wall with his fist. If there was one thing he should have learned, it was to think before he acted, to try to find a cleverer solution. He tried to think of one now, and recalled that Tom would be expecting him. If he was dragged to London in chains, Tom would hear of it and do everything he could to free him.

Gideon realized, too, that Mrs. Kean would never abandon him to his fate. She would speak in his behalf. She knew who had killed his father and why. If not for the disgrace it would bring on his father's name and the attainder of his estates, Gideon would have tried to clear himself before now. He wondered if a sentence of death would persuade him to change his mind about keeping those secrets, but even now, the notion seemed an unforgivable betrayal of his father. He shoved these considerations aside, however, knowing it was useless to worry about them in advance. If he was recognized and imprisoned, he would have ample time to ponder them then.

Before he was disturbed again, his chamber had taken on a chill. The sky had turned grey again, the sun having lost its eternal battle with the north wind.

At the sound of a key in the lock, Gideon resigned himself to luck and turned to face the massive door through which his accuser would come.

The guard threw open the door and stepped aside to let a procession enter. Gideon saw Mr. Northcote, the King's Messenger, and the bailiff, with several officers in their train. But his gaze went instantly to the gentleman who preceded them into the room.

With tension gnawing at his stomach, Gideon did not know whether to feel relief or horror, for the gentleman who had been brought to identify him was his father's eccentric friend, the Earl of Peterborough, a man whose only predictable trait was capriciousness. From his habit of shopping for his own vegetables, to his occasional preference for wearing women's clothing, he defied all attempts to comprehend him.

Since his escape from the law, Gideon had been hoping to find his father's friend and convince Lord Peterborough of his innocence. Independent in judgement and honourable, Lord Peterborough, he had believed, would listen to his story and decide whether to help him with no regard for the political consequences of his decision. But, whenever Gideon had imagined a conversation with the earl, he had envisioned it taking place in private, somewhere safe where he could speak openly about his father's affairs.

Not here. Not with all these witnesses, when he could not reveal a thing.

Dressed with his usual predilection for paint and patches, lace, and satin, Lord Peterborough gazed at Gideon with astounded eyes. After a moment, he gave a grunt that betrayed a hint of relief. Then, turning to Northcote, he said, "This is the young cub you wished me to name?"

The Messenger's face fell, as if he'd expected a distinctly different reaction. "Yes, my lord. I hoped you could name him for us."

Peterborough looked Gideon over with a weighing gaze. Gideon felt the blood drain from his cheeks. He had to clamp his jaw shut to keep from speaking out in his defence. He endured his lordship's stare, meeting his gaze with no shame.

The earl finally spoke. "Well, I hate to disappoint you, but this is not the man you seek. The Pretender's hair is black and his eyes are dark. This man's hair is as yellow as a Canary bird, and any fool can see that his eyes are blue. So, you may take my word for it and let him go."

Relief coursed through Gideon like a warm shower, but his danger was not yet past.

"But—my lord!" Mr. Northcote was not willing to relinquish his other suspicions. "I accept that he is not the Pretender, of course. But this gentleman is travelling incognito, for I saw him exchange places with the lady's groom. He dined in Calais with her as an equal. I even believe I heard her address him as 'my lord.' With the Pretender's men coming over from France, I cannot permit him to go until I'm convinced that he has no evil intent towards his Majesty."

Peterborough pulled a gold and ruby snuffbox from his pocket and laid a pinch of tobacco on his sleeve. Pausing with his arm in front of his nose, he cocked one eyebrow Gideon's way. "Well, sir! Have you any evil intent towards his Majesty?"

As Peterborough sniffed, Gideon addressed him sincerely. "No, my lord. On my honour, I swear I do not."

"There." Giving a violent sneeze, Peterborough turned to face the others. "On his honour, he said. Fellow's given you his oath that he means no harm whatsoever to his Majesty."

"But the disguise, my lord! His silence—and the lady's deception! What am I to make of all that?"

Glancing at Gideon, Peterborough closed a painted eyelid in a wink which he made no attempt to hide from the gaolers. In fact, his wink was so broad as to encompass the whole room.

Surprised, and still uncertain of his lordship's plan, Gideon could do nothing but wait to hear what the whimsical earl would say next. The muscles in his belly were still taut, but at least, Lord Peterborough had given no sign of wanting to throw him to the wolves.

"I do know this young gentleman," Peterborough said. "And I hope he will not live to rue this day. But it's none of my business who the young fool marries. His parents will have the burden of dealing with him, for if—as you say—the couple has just returned from France, then I have to suppose the deed is done, and no friend can say them nay.

"You should be ashamed of yourself, my boy," he said, frowning sternly at Gideon. "If a son of mine disobeyed me like that, I should thrash him within an inch of his life. I understood the match was expressly forbidden, but I suppose the worst you will suffer is a few hysterics and tears. I've always said that you were shamefully spoiled."

Gideon bowed his head, in part to hide his relief. But a piece of his mind wondered if the earl had meant the end of his speech. He said, contritely, "Yes, my lord."

"Then, this was simply an elopement?" Mr. Northcote was so mortified that Gideon pitied him. The Messenger had done his job well, but he could not question the testimony of an earl.

Gideon hoped that Northcote would not expect Lord Peterborough to swear to his story, for he doubted the earl would take a false oath. But the Messenger seemed defeated at last. And, just in case he should pursue it, the crafty earl forestalled him by saying, in a confidential tone, "Now you see why I mustn't give their names. Lady's reputation at stake. And even if the minx deserves it, her papa is a mean swordsman, and I'm too old for that sort of nonsense. If you want my advice, you'll let them go on their way." He gave Northcote a meaningful nod.

And, with that, he turned, ready to saunter from the room, having washed his hands of the whole lot.

"My lord!" Gideon called to his retreating back.

Peterborough turned. His frown said, *What the devil does the boy want with me now?*

"I should like to request a private word with you, my lord."

Shaking his head, the earl pivoted again. As he walked to the door, he waved a lace handkerchief over his shoulder. "Not today, I'm afraid. I must get to town. Quite a deal going on, as you must know. And I mustn't miss the opera tonight. Mrs. Robinson singing, don't ya know. Wonderful voice that woman has!"

At the door, he glanced back. "Come and see me at home if you like. But not too soon, if you don't mind. I've got worries enough to occupy me now without adding yours to them."

With a feeling of disappointment, swept away on a wave of melancholy, Gideon watched his father's friend disappear from view.

When, later, he told Fanny about Lord Peterborough's performance, she laughed until her eyes filled with tears.

Released near dusk, Gideon had arranged for the hire of three horses, and with Fanny and her maid had ridden as far as Ashford before stopping for the night. On the way, he had asked her how she'd been treated and whether she had feared arrest.

Though she confessed to feeling a bit of alarm, she insisted it had only been on his account, since she hadn't been able to think of a charge they could bring against her. The bailiff had seen to her comfort, so beyond asking the reason she had been detained—which Mr. Northcote had refused to give—she had waited to hear the outcome before deciding how much of a scene to make.

"You should consider yourself fortunate," she said, with a teasing smile, "that it was me and not Anne or Mama who was taken with you. Either one of them would have thrown such a tantrum that all the constables in the Cinque Ports would have come running to see what the fury was about."

Having seen Anne in a temper, Gideon could only agree.

After that, they spared their breath in order to put as many miles as they could between themselves and the castle that night.

Gideon had never broken a journey in Ashford, so he felt reasonably safe from detection at the inn where they stopped for the night. Still, this time he refused to join Fanny for supper and insisted on sleeping in the stable, for he would not take a chance of being seen with her in public again. He could not leave her until he'd escorted her safely to her mother's, but he was anxious for them to part. He was grateful to Fanny, and her cheerfulness made for pleasant company. But he still had not confessed that James had dismissed him from his service, and that he would refuse to be drawn into it again.

He had not needed the reminder about her mother's famous temper to dread Lady Oglethorpe's reaction on seeing him, if the news of his dismissal had reached her. Chances were that James's followers were too busy trying to get him into England to give Gideon any thought. But he could always count on Lady Oglethorpe to press him with an urgent task, and he did not look forward to the moment when he would have to refuse her.

The next day, they travelled west, leaving the inn before dawn.

Fortunately, Fanny's maid proved to be a competent horsewoman, for their route carried them over rough country roads. Gideon did not need to encourage Fanny to haste, for her devotion to James's cause inspired her. They stopped only briefly and changed horses often to increase their speed, Fanny driving them on with more energy than many gentlemen would have shown.

Leaving Kent in the afternoon, they rode into the hills of Surrey and arrived in Godalming in time to see its church steeple bathed in the gentle glow of dusk.

Westbrook Place, the Oglethorpes' manor, stood atop a low, broad hill on the edge of a woods not far from the village. At the end of the long day, the large, red brick house, framed by a thick stand of trees, was as welcome a sight as Gideon had ever seen. With night waiting to close in about them, the air had turned very chill, and, after many hours in the saddle, his body was too tired to fight the cold.

Pulling up his mount at the end of the drive, Gideon considered parting from Fanny here, but the droop of her shoulders told him how craven it would be to leave her to face her mother's wrath alone. He kicked his horse into a trot and arrived before the house in time to help her dismount.

He raised his arms to lift her down, but, as he did, she spoke beneath her breath. "We shall have to maintain the masquerade a little longer. The house may be watched. If you will take the horses round to the stables and hand them to one of the boys, I shall go in and admit you by the back door."

Gideon set her down, holding her elbow as she took her first steadying steps. Then, touching his forelock to her, he watched her climb the stairs, before unlooping the horses' reins and leading them round the side of the house. The boy in the stables asked no questions, merely nodding when Gideon told him where the horses should be returned. Then giving the brim of his felt hat a tug, he went to meet Fanny at the back door.

The moment he saw her expression, he knew that something was amiss. Agitated and pale, she signaled for him to follow and rapidly preceded him up a staircase to the first floor. Afraid he knew what news had greeted her, he prepared to defend himself as they wove through a series of paneled rooms in search of her mother.

Inside the door to Lady Oglethorpe's bedchamber, they found her pacing the floor, from the far wall, which was hung with a portrait of King James II, to the near one, which bore an image of his queen. She scarcely glanced up when they entered, and it was clear from the distracted look she gave Gideon that it was not knowledge of his dismissal that had distressed her.

Fanny quietly closed the door behind them, before turning to say gravely, "Some dreadful news reached Mama today. The government has learned of his Majesty's ships that were outfitted at Havre-le-Grace. The Earl of Stair advised the Regent, and the Regent ordered them to be stopped. They've unloaded all the arms and ammunition that were destined for our troops in Scotland."

Gideon had not been aware of the ships, but he knew at once how important they were to James's invasion. This was exactly the kind of aid the English Jacobites had demanded from France. Without those arms, the English might not rise. He could only imagine the effort it had taken to raise the money for their purchase.

Hardly knowing how to respond, he said the first thing that crossed his mind. "Then Bolingbroke and Ormonde have failed to convince the Regent."

Lady Oglethorpe paused to utter a harsh laugh. Her handsome features were screwed into a furious grimace. "They've not only failed to convince him, the idiots have managed to get themselves banned the French Court! Oh, if only Louis had lived just a little while longer!"

Her eyes filled with angry tears. Fanny tried to get her to sit, and gently pushed her towards a cushioned chair. Fanny herself was so white with fatigue that Gideon wondered how she could stand. She had ridden hard all day, elated by the news of the rebellion that she and her sisters had given their whole lives to achieve, only to be met with this devastating news. Gideon pitied her, even as he felt the truth of what Bolingbroke had said—that James's supporters were also his worst enemies, unable, in their zeal, to keep his secrets. If not, how had King George's spies uncovered the existence of those ships?

A knock at the door caused them all to jump. A liveried footman entered and, bowing before Lady Oglethorpe, said, "Another messenger has come for you, my lady."

She snatched at the note he proffered and without waiting for him to pass from the room broke its seal.

Her dark, outlined eyes devoured the words on the page. As she read, Gideon thought he could see despair and anger waging war across her face. She slumped in the chair, and when she spoke again, she seemed for once too stunned to rage.

"Warrants have been issued for Sir William Wyndham, Sir John Packington, Thomas Forster, and three more of our men. Two have already been taken into custody."

Fanny started, but her mother continued in the same dull voice, "That is not the worst. They've arrested my Lords Landsdowne and Duplin. And if they know about Landsdowne, they must know about the arms he's been gathering. That means that Ormonde cannot land in the West as planned."

Next to Gideon, Fanny let loose with a cry and covered her mouth. He threw his arm about her waist, but she did not faint. Her back was as stiff as a suit of armour as she whispered, "This cannot be!"

Gideon, too, had suffered a shock, for of the names Lady Oglethorpe had read, three had been known to him since childhood. They had all been his father's friends. Charged with treason, they would have little chance of escaping the gallows.

As he stood there, holding onto Fanny, a worrisome notion struck him. He turned to Lady Oglethorpe and urgently asked, "My lady— forgive me—but are you and Fanny in any danger? Is there any chance the Messengers will come here?"

Against his shoulder, Fanny's head gave a jerk. She peered anxiously at her mother, but Lady Oglethorpe gave a listless shrug.

"What would it matter?" All the fire had gone from her voice. "The White Rose is lost. I have nothing to live for now."

Appalled by her indifference to her daughter's safety, Gideon saw that, for the first time in their acquaintance, Lady Oglethorpe was showing her age. With her tall, slim figure and handsome features, it had always been easy to forget that nearly thirty years had passed since James II had entrusted her with the Great Seal of England and bid her to carry it to him in France. She, as well as her daughters, had worked indefatigably for the White Rose, suffering imprisonment, yet returning again and again to conspire for the cause, but this most recent disappointment seemed to have conquered her at last.

Gideon felt Fanny stir within his arm. She freed herself to march angrily to her mother's side.

"We will not give up," she rasped. "We will not forsake his Majesty now—not when he needs us most. There is still the rebellion in the North. We'll find a way to transport him to Scotland, and once he leads his men to victory there, France will give him the arms to fight in England."

Her words reminded Gideon of the wan prince he had seen so recently at Bar. James would be far too ill to lead his troops in battle. Even if he recovered from this last bout of malaria, how would the stress of a Channel crossing affect his health?

At the moment, though, Gideon's purpose was not to crush Fanny's hopes, but to make certain they were safe.

"Fanny—my lady—we should prepare for a visit from the Crown. You are both too well known to be sympathetic to James to doubt that they will come searching here. If the government is making sweeping arrests, they could have information that could put you both in danger. And if they discover me here, they will take my presence as proof that you are involved in illegal activities."

Lady Oglethorpe had regained a modicum of spirit. She still moved slowly, as if wading through a bog, but his words must have made some sense to her, for she waved a hand in the direction of the door. "Show him out, Fanny. He is right. T'were better he were not found here."

"If there is anything I can—"

Fanny cut him off with a shake of her head. "There's no reason to worry about us, but since we do not know where the Messengers will strike next, you had better go." Picking up her skirts, she turned to lead him out.

Gideon moved forward to take Lady Oglethorpe's hand and carry it to his lips. Then, seeing that she hardly appeared to note his touch, he released her gently and followed Fanny from the room.

That each from other differs, first confess;
Next, that he varies from himself no less:
Add Nature's, Custom's, Reason's, Passion's strife,
And all Opinion's colours cast on life.
Our depths who fathoms, or our shallows finds,
Quick whirls, and shifting eddies, of our minds?
On human actions reason though you can,
It may be Reason, but it is not Man . . .

CHAPTER X

Fanny led him down the main set of stairs and into a hallway, which was lit by a pair of sconces. A footman seated on the floor leapt to his feet.

"Open the door for this gentleman, Patrick. And hurry! We must send him on his way."

The servant stooped to roll up a small Turkey carpet that covered a section of the floor, while Fanny crossed to one of the sconces. Taking a candle from it, she waited beside Gideon, as Patrick bent over the exposed oaken floor and, prying at a notch Gideon couldn't see, pulled open a trap hidden in the boards. He stepped back to allow Gideon to pass, holding onto the door, which had no hinge.

As an earthen smell rose up to greet them, Fanny handed Gideon the lighted candle. "This passage will take you to the King's Arms in the village. The keeper is one of us. He will lend you a horse."

Gideon took hold of her hand and bent to kiss her on the cheek. "You have my gratitude, Fanny. If you ever have a need—for yourself, and no one else—I hope you will call on me." He wanted to tell her not to think too badly of him when she heard the reports about him, but this was not the moment to deliver another blow.

She returned his kiss and, with a smile that was almost normal, bid him take care how he stepped.

The passage was not very deep at this end. Handing the candle to Patrick to hold, Gideon laid a palm on the edge of the opening and jumped down. Then, as he straightened to retrieve his candle, a motion in the hall above caught his eye.

A man he had not noticed moved out of the shadows to join Fanny, who turned to greet him just as Gideon reached up for the light. The stranger's voice came in urgent undertones, and, though Gideon could not make out the words, he caught a part of Fanny's response. He heard her address the man as "Father."

Then, Patrick handed down his candle and prepared to lower the trap. Before the darkness closed about Gideon, Fanny altered her position slightly and he caught a fleeting glimpse of the stranger's face.

It was grave—even angry. In the scant degree of light, Gideon could not see whether the visitor was fair or dark, but his eyes shone brightly in a face that was lean and harsh.

That was all Gideon saw before the door closed over his head and darkness shrouded his sight. Cupping a hand to shelter the flame from a waft of air raised by the replacement of the trap, he gave his eyes a moment to adjust to the gloom. His wait revealed a dirt path which disappeared beyond the glow of his candle. Accustomed now to facing the invisible, and too exhausted to care what creatures he might meet on the way, he laid one hand on the earthen wall and, stooping, walked as quickly forward as the flickering of his candle would allow.

✿

In the evening after her meeting with Tom, Hester accompanied her cousins to the Mathematical Water Theatre at the bottom of Piccadilly near Hyde Park. With the Court in mourning, this was one way Isabella could find entertainment.

The performance had been offered as a benefit for the widow of the ingenious Mr. Winstanley, who had devised the theatre with all its delightful tricks, including the glorious Barrel, which served up fruit, sweet flowers, cakes, coffee, and tea, as well as several sorts of hot and cold liquors, while somehow managing to keep them all separate.

Harrowby had taken a box at the three-shilling rate, so they had the best view of all the scenes that were played. Sipping on her tea, Hester nearly choked with amazement as she watched Venus's return from Mount Ida with the Golden Apple. Doves and swans, reportedly sent by Cupid, attended her descent, while the Graces looped her with garlands. A handsome Adonis, bathing with his Daphne, was turned miraculously into a tree before their very eyes, and Narcissus was transformed into a flower. The number of sea gods and goddesses was truly magnificent, and Hester applauded them, gladly putting aside for this one evening all the turmoil in her world.

The incense that drifted through the theatre lightly clouded her vision, making it impossible to see how the various cascades could fall side by side with bursts of fire. She rubbed her eyes, looking downward in the hope that tears would clear them. Then as she took a look about to test them, she caught a glimpse of two familiar figures leaning over from the sixpenny seats in the upper gallery.

The couple straining to see the stage were none other than Tom and Katy. Tom was dressed in his merchant's garb, and Katy, who had no fear of being recognized, was wearing a becoming yellow gown. Tom looked happier than Hester had ever seen him as he gazed at Katy's enraptured face.

Hester smiled, happy to see them enjoying a bit of pleasure. Then she had to chastise herself for the pang of envy that followed. Jeremy's troubles had made her miss St. Mars even more than usual. She had grown accustomed to sharing her concerns with him, and, no matter how much she tried to tell herself that it was a foolish habit to make, she had not been able to stop yearning for his return.

Tom's news, that St. Mars was on his way home, had caused her heart to take such a leap that she'd feared it would fly right out of her breast. Her giddiness had been hard to hide, so she had been doubly glad to come to this place where she could let her pleasure show.

Neither Isabella nor her husband had noticed the change in her, of course. Harrowby was dreading tomorrow, when the gentlemen of the Court were expected to accompany the King to Woolwich to see the launch of two new men-of-war. It would be a long day of speeches and parades, with loud salvos of guns, and nothing but a dinner with the Earl of Orford to entertain him.

The only thing that had cheered him at all was the rumour that his Majesty was finally going to grant Parliament a recess. Harrowby, and Isabella, too, were looking forward to moving back into Hawkhurst House. The cool weather would make it comfortable again, even for a lady in Isabella's delicate condition. They would not make a journey into Kent, for reports of the smallpox there made the peril too great for Isabella and the child.

Hester would have been disappointed not to be visiting Rotherham Abbey, which she had begun to love, but for her desire to work on Jeremy's troubles. She was relieved that her duties would not take her so far away from him now.

She had just received another letter from him in the afternoon post.

In addition to the danger posed by Mr. Simpkins's threats, he now had other cause for worry. As he had predicted, various suitors for Sally's hand and her bookstall had begun to linger about the Bell and Bible, and it appeared that Mr. Sullivan of the Temple might be one of them. The constable Sally had hired to investigate had asked questions at every house within sight of the bookstall and had turned up nothing, so Sally had been obliged to let him go.

Hester had tried to think of something she could do to free herself of her current constraints. She thought of ways to persuade Isabella and Harrowby to make trips into the City, but with the rebellion underway, she doubted they would risk it. They had experienced one of the London riots earlier that year and would not want to be caught in another. With Parliament in recess, it was possible that Harrowby would provide some companionship for his wife, but he was far more likely to spend his time in a coffee house, leaving Hester to entertain Isabella.

With a sigh, Hester told herself that she would simply have to wait for an opportunity to present itself. Her eyes were cleared of the smoke now and, as she swept them over the audience one last time before attending to the performance, the sight of someone among them dislodged a memory.

Harrowby and Isabella were not the only members of Court to come to the Water Theatre that evening. In a box at the other end of the stage, Hester spied Lady Mary Wortley Montagu with James Cragg and a few other young Whigs, who usually spent their evenings entertaining his Majesty.

The comment Hester had recalled was from Mr. Curry. He had boasted that he had published some of Lady Mary's work, and Sally had said something about how it "had fallen" into his hands. Having met Mr. Curry, Hester could not imagine that Lady Mary had ever willingly had anything to do with him, which made her wonder how he had gained possession of the lady's writings. If she could speak to Lady Mary, she might find out something about Mr. Curry's other dealings.

Hester tried to recall all she knew of the lady, a woman of tremendous wit and beauty. Her father, the Marquess of Dorchester, had recently been elevated to Duke of Kingston, though he had nearly disowned her after she had married Mr. Edward Wortley against his wishes. According to rumours, Lady Mary had her own reasons to regret her marriage, for Mr. Wortley had proved to be a passionless bore.

Both the King and the Prince of Wales had been strongly taken with her: the King because she conversed charmingly in French; the Prince for her beauty, though the gossips reported that Lady Mary had scorned the Prince's advances. Fortunately, his Highness had halted his pursuit when he learned that she attended his father's supper parties. Since Hester's cousins greatly preferred the Prince of Wales's court to the King's, she would not be able to approach the Lady Mary there.

Lady Mary's sister Frances was married to the Earl of Mar, the leader of the rebellion in Scotland. The gossips said that he had left her behind without a penny to spend. Her father, the Duke, was so selfish and irascible that it was doubtful he would come to her aid. A Whig himself, he had married Lady Frances to a Tory as a form of "insurance," it was said, which had turned out to be an even bigger mistake than Lady Mary's marriage.

Lady Mary was certain to be distressed by her sister's situation, for political if not for sympathetic reasons, though reportedly they were fond of each other. Hester wished she might be able to persuade Isabella to make a visit of compassion, but she knew that Isabella would find Lady Mary and her friends extremely tedious. Their brand of humour was far too subtle for her to comprehend, and Hester doubted they would welcome anyone as foolish as Isabella into their circle. After all, Lady Mary had made friends with the poet, Mr. Pope, who was surely a great wit.

Now Hester recalled that Sally had mentioned Mr. Pope when speaking of the enemies her husband had made. She had intimated that Mr. Curry had published some of Mr. Pope's work against his will. Hester had never had a chance to meet the poet. She had heard that, when in town, he lodged with the portraitist, Mr. Charles Jervas, another of Lady Mary's friends. They all were said to meet occasionally in the artist's studio.

It was this recollection that inspired Hester with an idea. Isabella had never been painted. With her fun curtailed, and her confinement looming, what better time to have a portrait made than now?

She would need Hester to entertain her while she sat. Even if Lady Mary never came to the studio when they were there, chances were that her friends would have something to say about her dealings with Mr. Curry.

As an option, it did not promise much, but at least it was something Hester could do to try to find a motive for Mr. Curry's murder.

When Gideon reached the end of the underground passageway and knocked at the wooden barrier, he was admitted to the cellar of the King's Arms by a drawer. The boy bade him pass, then closed the entrance to the tunnel, careful to hide it again behind a door banded with shelves.

Eager as Gideon was to go home, he bespoke a bedchamber from the innkeeper, and remained in Godalming until the following afternoon. Then, borrowing another horse, he used the back roads and arrived at his house on the Thames an hour after dark. He could have covered the ground more rapidly by day, but with troops moving in and out of London, he judged it prudent to wait until the shadows could protect him.

Tom came running out of the house to take charge of his mount, and greeted him with a mixture of pleasure, relief, and a curious nervousness. Accustomed as he was to his groom's moods, Gideon knew there was something different about this. He searched Tom's face, but the changes in his trusted features defied Gideon's ability to read them.

"It would appear that you have much to tell me," he said, handing his reins to Tom. "As soon as you've stabled the nag, come inside—unless there is something I should know right now."

Tom shook his head and flushed. "It's nothing that can't wait, my lord."

Gideon was secretly relieved. For a moment, he'd feared that Tom had something unpleasant to tell him about Mrs. Kean.

Inside, Katy greeted him with a bobbing curtsy. Gideon allowed her to help him off with his coat and bore with her exclamations of distress over the poor quality of his disguise. He told her that he'd been obliged to leave one of his better jackets behind in France, but that it couldn't be helped. She wanted to burn the groom's clothes, but he told her to save them, for they might come in handy again.

She urged him upstairs then, saying that Tom would be up directly with the water for his bath. Interpreting this to mean that he needed to wash, Gideon meekly obeyed.

Over an hour later, after several buckets of water had been poured over his head and he'd made a liberal use of soap, he was in better condition to listen to Tom's news.

His concern for Mrs. Kean had proven warranted, but that did nothing to mitigate the feeling that he should have been there the moment her brother's trouble occurred. Gideon pushed this useless thought from his mind, however, to focus on what could be done.

Wrapped in an Indian robe and seated in an armchair in front of the fire, he said to Tom, "So you did what she asked?"

"I did, my lord. Not but what two days weren't long enough to see much. I kept watch both days outside the bookstall. I even went in and bought one of Mr. Kean's books — and a queer set of tales they are, my lord, I don't mind saying! — just to get a good look at the place. But 'cept for that beadle she told me about, and another strange-looking fellow, I can't say as I noticed much at all."

"What did the beadle do?"

Tom snorted. "It was just like Mrs. Kean said. He strutted in all puffed up like a cock of the walk, but it was plain that the widow wanted nothin' to do with him. I've seen his kind afore. They go daft for a woman, then they ends up bein' so jealous that they hurts 'em."

"Or murders their husband?"

Tom raised a speculative brow. "Could be, I guess."

"What about this other fellow you saw? Who was he?"

He shrugged. "Don't know. But the widow knows 'im, sure enough. He weren't there to buy no books, but they talked and talked. Seemed like he was tryin' to sell her on some notion he had or another, but I couldn't tell if she took him up on it or not."

"What was so strange about him?"

Tom thought for a moment. Then, with a puzzled look, he shrugged again. "Can't say exactly. Just somethin' odd. One minute, he'd look like he was a-beggin'. The next, I'd swear he was angrier than a poked bee, but he never raised his voice nor a hand. They was friendly enough at first, but then she didn't look so happy. I got the feeling, maybe he was askin' her for money."

"Hmm . . ." Gideon pondered, frowning. "Well, I shall have to see the widow for myself. When she was talking to the last man, did she seem furtive at all? As if she were afraid of being overheard."

Tom screwed up his eyes and shook his head. "A little irked, maybe, but not afraid."

"Then I doubt the queer cove was demanding payment for having killed her husband. That doesn't mean he didn't do it, of course, just that she was not involved if he did."

"She don't look much like a murderess to me."

Gideon grinned. "I won't ask you what a murderess looks like." Then, sobering, he added, "Although it may be that your judgement is good enough. What does Mrs. Kean think of Mrs. Curry?"

"She didn't tell me, my lord. But even a fool could see what her brother—Mr. Kean, that is—thinks of 'er. He's that smitten, he is."

"Ah . . . ." Gideon leaned back and began to stroke his chin. "That complicates his problem now, doesn't it? And ours, too, if we're to help him. I shall have to have a look at Mrs. Curry to see what kind of siren has him in thrall." Gideon sighed. "I suppose I should get a glimpse of her before I speak to Mrs. Kean."

He asked Tom what arrangements he had made to contact her. As Tom related Mrs. Kean's instructions, a pleasant notion popped into Gideon's mind and made him smile.

He was so elated by it that he failed to notice the heavy sigh Tom emitted when he lumbered from the room.

⌀

A few days later, at sunrise, Hester slipped outside the gilded iron gate of Hawkhurst House, telling Rufus the porter that she was stepping out for a walk. In the chill morning mist, she strolled briskly along Piccadilly and turned left into St. James's Street to head towards the Palace.

Her cousins had moved back into Hawkhurst House just yesterday, and she had posted Tom a note to that effect. This was the first morning stroll she had made, and she did not expect to see Katy. She doubted that Tom would have found out anything of use yet, but she had promised to watch for Katy every morning, and today was the day she would start.

She decided to go down one side of the street and up the other to insure that she did not miss the maid. There were few people strolling St. James's at this early hour, although some gentlemen, out to exercise their horses, were making their way to the park. Servants were bustling in and out of the houses, carrying market baskets and emptying the pots of night soil. The few vendors in the street were hawking milk and the services of a sweep.

Not meeting Katy on her way down, Hester turned and hurried across the street several yards short of the Guard house, not wishing to seem a loiterer. Soldiers had been posted there, in addition to the Guard, and they were bored enough to make a nuisance of themselves to any lady walking alone. She did not consider herself much of an attraction, but Katy was pretty enough that if she had been near, they would have tried to get her attention, causing a spectacle that Hester should have remarked by now.

She was a quarter of the way back up St. James's Street when she thought she spied Katy ahead of her, moving in the same direction. Hester quickened her steps, afraid of missing her, though she tried not to appear in pursuit. The distance between them was closing when Katy glanced back over her shoulder and hurried her pace.

Hester was so astonished, she faltered before resuming her stride. She believed Katy had seen her, but she could have been mistaken. Then, wondering if Katy had a reason for not wishing to be overtaken yet, she continued more sedately.

She was passing the narrow entrance to a court, with Katy only five yards ahead, when her elbow was suddenly hooked from behind and she was twirled into the passageway. The next thing she knew, a man's chest was pressed along her back, his arm was firmly about her waist, and a hand was clamped over her mouth.

She would have screamed—and indeed, a squeak had escaped her, before she'd caught a glimpse of her assailant's blue eyes. St. Mars held her snugly against him for a few moments, the warmth of his body seeping into hers. When he eventually spoke, a tremor, as if from laughter, made his voice come huskily in her ear.

"Should I attribute your failure to struggle to the fact that you know who I am?"

Hester's heart was beating as fast as dragonfly wings, not from fear or even surprise, but from the tingling his embrace had aroused. His breath tickled her neck, spreading gooseflesh up and down her spine. She could not think of an excuse for prolonging this delicious position much longer, however, so she nodded.

To her wonder, St. Mars did not immediately release her. He whispered, "Before I let you go, am I forgiven for accosting you this way? I should hate to free you and discover that you were angry. After all, you might have a weapon hidden beneath those skirts."

The laugh that burst from her broke his hold. She could not regret it, though, when she turned and saw his handsome face smiling down at her.

"You would deserve it if I had, my lord," she said. Then, as she recalled the difference in their ranks, she curtsied, which made him grin even more widely.

"My dear Mrs. Kean . . ." He shook his head. "Always so polite."

Hester rose from her curtsy. "I hardly think so, my lord, when I nearly threatened you. Fortunately for me, you know that I do not possess any weapons."

"Ah, but that's where you are mistaken. You have weapons aplenty, of which I doubt you are aware."

The look that accompanied his remark made her legs quiver like two plucked bows. Her confusion must have shown, for he instantly seemed contrite.

"Pray forgive my teasing, Mrs. Kean. I've been away too long. I'm simply glad to be home. I regret I wasn't here when you needed my help."

Now, they were on more familiar ground. For a moment, Hester had believed he was flirting with her. Even now, she could not entirely dismiss the feeling that he was as pleased to see her as she was to see him, which made it hard to restrain her smiles.

She thanked him for coming and assured him that Tom had been ready to assist her in his stead.

The sound of footsteps on the pavement behind them reminded her of the danger he was always in. With a price on his head, St. Mars must not be recognized. He had scarcely disguised himself this morning, except for his clothes, which were suitable for a coachman. His breeches and coat were cut loose and made of homespun, and he wore a large felt hat, which he pulled lower on his brow as the pedestrian approached.

As soon as the man had passed them in the narrow alley, Hester said, "You have taken too great a risk in coming here, my lord."

"Not at all. I chose this spot expressly for the security it offered. To my recollection, I do not know anyone who resides in Fox Court. And you must have noticed that I avoided any spot within view of the Palace or the coffee houses."

"But to get here, you must have passed by either the Palace or Hawkhurst House! I cannot be sanguine about this, my lord."

"Neither can Tom," he said, with a wondering lilt. "It is strange, but you have that in common."

"Can you not be serious?" Anguish infused her voice. He seemed incapable of feeling any fear for himself.

"I can be as serious as you like, as long as we talk about your brother's problems. So, perhaps we should start."

Hester felt some relief, though she knew that every second must count, for she could not keep him standing in this vulnerable place. What if someone who remembered him had moved into Fox Court during this past year? And when he left it, how could he move through the streets without being seen?

"Very well," she said, nervously brisk. "We shall be as brief as possible. Has Tom seen anything suspicious?"

St. Mars took her arm and drew it through his. "Let us stroll," he said, drawing her deeper into the alley. "We will be less remarked this way."

They walked slowly, keeping to the shadow of the long brick wall that lined one side of the alley.

"Tom related to me the particulars you gave him. And he's made a few deductions himself." He told her that her brother appeared to be enamoured of the bookseller's widow.

She heard a question in his tone and sighed. "It is not the marriage my father would have wished for Jeremy, but it is probably much better than he deserves." Then, knowing how unfair she'd been, she shook her head. "No, I should not have said that. They are both deserving, and I would hate for you to believe otherwise."

She went on to describe Jeremy for him, being honest about his good traits as well as his weaker ones. "I should have said that without an income other than from his writing, Jeremy will never be able to aspire to a greater rank. To be truthful, Mrs. Curry—Sally—is now a woman of means. She is certain to be courted, and she can afford to be fastidious in her choice, or choose not to marry again at all. But I believe that she's in love with my brother, too, so the best thing for them both, I believe, would be marriage to each other."

Hester gave a little laugh. "They might even make each other's fortunes, for she has a bookstall, and Jeremy has the imagination and the ability to write. His *Tales from the Dead* are selling well, I believe."

Gideon smiled. "Yes, they shocked Tom considerably. But then Tom has a Puritan streak."

"He must not have read the one that has my father's sermon in it— or Jeremy's recollection thereof, which could be faulty, I admit."

They had made a tour of the tiny court, which few houses faced. Still, the servants who had walked in and out of the doors had eyed them warily, for they were strangers with no business there. Hester knew they would draw even more attention if they circled the court again.

"There is so much I have to tell you, my lord, that I do not know where to start," she said, frustrated by their restraints. "And I must get back."

"When can I meet you again?"

Hester's pulse rose eagerly. She worried her lip. "I am not that free to wander about. Not with the Pretender on his way here, and Isabella—" She had been about to say, "Isabella's delicate condition," but then she remembered that he did not know about the child. That was one of the things she would have to tell him. She dreaded having to do it, but it would not be fair for him to read it in the news-sheets first.

He had not noticed her awkward breach. "While you are thinking of a time to meet, let me tell you the little I know.

"Mr. Simpkins, the beadle, is still coming round the Bell and Bible. He's apparently angry that he's been rebuffed, but Tom says that his anger is directed more at Mrs. Curry than at your brother. He appears to be smarting from the impression that she encouraged his advances before her husband's death, and although he is jealous of your brother, he blames her for what he calls her deceit."

Hester knew that to most men the woman would always be at fault. Women were merely temptresses in their eyes, the personification of sin since the first bite of the apple. When she thought of poor Sally having to bear with this kind of resentment, she grew alarmed. "Do you think he might do Sally a mischief?"

He grimaced. "Tom could not be sure, of course, but he believes that is the kind of man Simpkins is. The question is, did he want Mrs. Curry enough to commit murder to get her?"

"What does Tom think?"

He smiled. "I shall have to ask him. It's my opinion, though, that Simpkins would have taken a huge risk to kill her husband before he was sure of her. And if he *did* believe she was encouraging him, he could have expected to have her just as easily whether she was married or not."

Hester was disappointed, but she couldn't dispute his reasoning. It made too much sense.

"Then, if not Mr. Simpkins, who?"

St. Mars described a visitor to the bookstall, whom Hester recognized as Mr. Tubbs. He related a scene Tom had witnessed, when he formed the impression that Mr. Tubbs had asked Sally for money.

Hester told him of Sally's discovery that her husband had more money than anyone had realized, and how Jeremy had revealed this to Mr. Tubbs.

"She has already promised to pay Jeremy more for the books he has written. I shouldn't be surprised if Mr. Tubbs asked her for more, too. He was very upset to learn about the money. He said he knew that Mr. Curry had been cheating his authors. And if it is true that he was, it is very reprehensible. You should see the miserable conditions in which they live!"

"If he was angry enough, wouldn't that have been sufficient motive for murder?"

She shook her head. "It could have been, perhaps, but Mr. Tubbs only learned about the money after Mr. Curry was killed."

"Your brother learned of it then, but what if this man Tubbs had already discovered it somehow?"

Hester mused. "It is possible," she said, "but I truly believe he did not know of it until that moment. He was so enraged that he said something about Sally that upset Jeremy, which I believe he regretted, for he refused to say more when I questioned him further." She repeated the words her brother and Mr. Tubbs had exchanged concerning Sally and the way Mr. Curry had used her.

"So Curry encouraged his wife to be friendly to the point of flirtation with the men with whom he did business, so they would not press him for money?"

"Yes, and to people like the beadle, too, so he would overlook Mr. Curry's transgressions—his minor ones, I suppose."

"And you are certain that Mrs. Sally was innocent of this trickery?" St. Mars looked skeptical.

"Mr. Tubbs thinks so, and I agree with him." Changing the subject, Hester asked, "Has Tom seen anyone else lingering about the bookstall?"

St. Mars looked questioningly at her, as if he knew she had someone particular in mind. She was surprised that he had not mentioned Mr. Sullivan, if what Jeremy had written about him was true.

"No," St. Mars said. "Is there someone he should have noticed?"

Hester smiled. "If he hasn't, then I should hate to plant an unwarranted suspicion in your mind. Jeremy was simply worried that he had a rival for Sally's affection, but perhaps he does not."

"That leaves us with only two suspects, and not even one convincing motive."

Hester told him about her plan to question Lady Mary's friends about how Mr. Curry had gained possession of her writings.

He frowned, but agreed that Mr. Curry's trade could be worth investigating.

While they had been speaking in quiet voices, the noise about them had increased. More people had entered the streets. Hester knew she must not keep St. Mars any longer.

"Have you thought of a place where I could meet you safely?" she asked. "With soldiers encamped in the park, we dare not meet there again."

"I have thought of something," he said, with a daring look that almost frightened her. "If my cousin is at Hawkhurst House, then I suppose Philippe is there, too?"

It was Philippe, St. Mars's valet, who had ordered the blue satin cape St. Mars was wearing when he was mistaken for a highwayman. Harrowby was so taken with the garment, and so frightened by the apparition, that he had dubbed his attacker "Blue Satan."

Harrowby had always coveted his cousin's valet, for Philippe was a superb practitioner of the art of gentlemen's dress. Harrowby had retained the Frenchman as his own attendant, but Philippe was still loyal to his original master.

"Yes, Philippe is there," Hester said. "Why do you ask?"

"Because I will need his help to gain entry to Hawkhurst House."

Who shall decide, when Doctors disagree,
And soundest Casuists doubt, like you and me?
You hold the word, from Jove to Momus given,
That man was made the standing jest of Heaven;
And Gold but sent to keep the fools in the play,
For some to heap, and some to throw away.

CHAPTER XI

In spite of her most vigorous protests, two days later, just minutes before midnight, Hester found herself making her way down a narrow flight of stairs in a corner of Hawkhurst House. She had left her cousins and their guests upstairs in the withdrawing room, engaged in playing at bassett. With the high stakes involved, she was never expected to take part at cards, and after watching a few hours of play, she had easily been able to slip from the room without being remarked.

The staircase she was descending made a turn mid-way down. The shadows from her flickering candle struck the wall in front of her, and for an instant made it appear that someone was ascending from the floor below, and would discover her where she had no business to be. Hester paused with her heart in her throat, but when no one came to confirm her fears, she chid herself and went on.

She was entering a part of the house where she had never ventured before. The danger of being found here was not really hers, of course, though she had not been able to think of a credible excuse for descending to the Hawkhurst offices at this hour of the night. St. Mars had chosen these rooms for their rendezvous as soon as he had heard that James Henry was out of town. But they were part of a male dominion, where it would look distinctly odd if she were caught.

Downstairs, she crossed the first large chamber, passing through it diagonally as St. Mars had instructed. At the base of this room there was a door, leading into a smaller one, and it was in this smaller chamber that she was supposed to wait.

The advantage to this chamber, she saw, was that its windows looked out upon the neighbouring house, rather than onto the courtyard of Hawkhurst House, so their lights would not be noticed by the servants. It had two doors that closed, which would give them privacy, in addition to a second way out in case they heard someone coming. And any noise they made would be softened by the room abutting this one on the courtyard side.

Hester took a tinder-box from a shelf and sat down with it in her lap. Then she blew out her candle so that no one entering the adjoining chamber would be tempted to investigate her light. Now that she was hidden by the dark, she felt safer, if not more relaxed.

St. Mars had apologized for asking her to wait, but she understood that his arrival would be difficult to time. He would have to lurk outside until Philippe could open a door for him. Hester did not even want to know how they would manage to accomplish this. She had argued strenuously against St. Mars's reckless plan, but he had insisted that he wished to enter his own house, and he saw no better time than now.

For what seemed like half an hour, but was probably much less, Hester listened to the muffled ticking of a clock in the adjoining room. Wrapping her shawl tightly about her, she shivered in her chair, for there was no fire lit in this room. There was not even a hearth, though nothing could have made her light a flame if there had been one.

Faint footsteps outside the other door made her sit up and tense. In a moment, the door was cracked, and Philippe, holding a candle in a dish, entered, followed by a man in footman's livery.

It was St. Mars, of course. With his hair concealed beneath a brown wig, which tied at the nape of his neck, from a distance he looked very much like John, one of the Hawkhurst footmen. As soon as Hester saw him dressed in this garb, she smiled and gave a nod of comprehension.

She waited until Philippe had closed the door behind them before rising, and, as she dipped into a brief curtsy, said, "Now I begin to see how you managed it, my lord. Good evening, Philippe," she added, giving him a grateful glance.

As St. Mars came up to her, his servant said, *"Bon soir, mademoiselle. I am sorry that you were obliged to wait.* That *crétin* Rufus was flirting with a *putain* outside in the street, and I could not get *Monsieur de St. Mars* past him until he fell asleep."

Hester shook her head in distress, but St. Mars's smile turned wistful.

"Do not begrudge me the pleasure of coming in here." He looked about the small room, as if even *it* held pleasant memories for him. "I have not set foot in this house since I left it to go to my father's funeral."

"I do not begrudge you anything, my lord." Hester made a silent vow that she would not utter another word on the subject.

St. Mars turned to Philippe. "You may leave us now, but come back in an hour to lead me out."

Philippe made a perfect bow, but he did not immediately obey. With his nose in the air, he said, "It shall be as *monsieur le vicomte* wishes, of course . . . provided *mademoiselle* agrees."

"Oho!" St. Mars gave a delighted laugh. "So you think she is in need of a chaperon, do you?"

Philippe gave a dignified shrug. "It is not that Philippe doubts the honour of *monsieur's* intentions. It is simply that a *tête-à-tête* at this hour—one that *monsieur* himself has proposed, when Mademoiselle Kean did not think it at all advisable—could be a grave temptation to *monsieur.*"

"You infernal imp! I ought to thrash you for your impertinence." But St. Mars was chuckling all the while.

Their conversation was excruciating for Hester. Squirming, she said, "There is nothing in the least tempting about our meeting, Philippe! My lord has graciously offered to assist me with a family matter, and we could not find enough time to discuss it any other way."

"If *mademoiselle* insists." Philippe bowed to her, then again and more deeply to St. Mars. "I shall return within the hour."

"Be certain to knock when you do," St. Mars called after him. "You would not wish to embarrass us by walking in on a ravishment."

"My lord, please!" Hester whispered, putting fingers over her mouth to hide her painful mirth. "Now I see where Philippe gets his outlandish ideas!"

"Indeed! Though he did seem thrilled to be assisting me in a tryst, so I hope you will not be too adamant about disappointing him. His English has greatly improved, hasn't it? I believe he was glad for a chance to show it off."

"Yes, poor man! He constantly bemoans the fact that your cousin cannot speak a decent word of French."

"Not a word? I'm afraid you must be maligning Harrowby, Mrs. Kean."

"I did not say 'a word,' my lord, but a '*decent* word.' To Philippe there is a world of difference."

They were standing in the centre of the little room, facing each other by the light of St. Mars's candle on the table beside them. As St. Mars stood smiling down at her, Hester's heart swelled with joy, but knowing how quickly the hour would pass, she asked if he would prefer to be seated.

"To business," he agreed, handing her into a straight-backed chair before taking one himself.

Now that he was being serious, Hester tried to present her thoughts in an organized fashion. The small portion of her brain that had *not* been occupied all day with anticipation of this meeting, had been devoted to her brother's dilemma, and she had decided on a slight change of course. It was one thing to be careful about accusing anyone of murder, but quite another not to call attention to a suspect, if his guilt could lead to proof of Jeremy's innocence.

Consequently, as soon has she had finished recounting everything she had seen at the Bell and Bible, she told St. Mars about Mr. Sullivan and Jeremy's worries concerning his interest in Sally. "I believe he may be Irish, for there is a slight lilt in his voice."

"From the Temple, you say?" St. Mars mused. "I wonder why Tom has not mentioned him, when he is usually quick to suspect foreigners. I'll have a look out for him myself, and if he *does* show an interest in the widow, I'll see if I can determine what it's about. Any others?"

"None that I'm aware of. But it must be someone connected with the bookstall. In the first place, the murder was committed there, but more importantly, no money and no books were taken. The killer took the key, so he might have returned at any moment during the night if he had wanted to rob it."

"Then we know that robbery was not the motive."

Hester nodded. "That's why I fear it has something to do with Sally." She told him about Mr. Sullivan's flirtatious comment after Jeremy and Mr. Curry had been released from gaol.

St. Mars raised his brows. "Your brother was arrested? Why?"

"Oh!" Hester clapped a hand to one cheek. "I can't believe I forgot to tell you. But Mr. Curry's killing nearly drove it out of my mind. And I did not like to say anything about it to Tom." Feeling foolish over the omission, Hester told St. Mars about the curious prank that had landed Jeremy in Newgate.

"Is that what you think it was? A prank? Couldn't the two incidents be related?"

"At first I thought they might be, but with the rebellion starting, and my aunt due back, I have not been able to concentrate on Jeremy's troubles the way I should."

She must have betrayed her distress, for he leaned closer and took both her hands in his.

"We *will* get to the bottom of this. But try not to worry about the rebellion. I doubt it will succeed." He said this on a note of regret.

Hester wanted to ask him what his involvement with the Pretender was, but felt she didn't dare. When he did not volunteer any more, she agreed. "Whether the Pretender belongs on the throne or not, I believe King George will hold onto his Crown. The Whigs who serve him are very astute, and he always appears to be at least one step ahead of the rebels—usually more. I do not believe that James Stuart can win, no matter how favoured he is."

St. Mars gave a nod. "King George's organization seems vastly superior, and the French are now entirely on his side. I do not see how James will even manage to cross the Channel."

"The rumours are that he will travel incognito to the coast."

St. Mars gave a rueful grin. "That will be only the first of his trials."

As Hester listened in horrified silence, he told her about being taken into custody at Dover Castle. When he related the story of his release, Hester exclaimed, "No wonder, you did not let a little thing like sneaking into Hawkhurst House deter you, my lord. This was child's play in comparison."

"I won't deny that I worried for my head on that occasion, but it helped me to know that you and Tom would work to free me."

The warmth in his eyes made her glow. He had released her hands, but he took them up again, and the touch of his thumbs on her palms made her tremble.

His candle flame sputtered in a pool of melted wax. Shadows danced all about them.

"We should certainly have tried, my lord, but I trust you will not risk that peril again?"

"Not in that precise way, I won't. I'm of a mind to stay on this side of the Channel for a while, at least until the fighting is over."

Hester was thrilled to hear this news, but not wishing him to see how pleased she was, she straightened in her chair, which had the effect of breaking his grip upon her hands.

He frowned and smiled at her at the same time. "But that is not what we came here to talk about, is it?" Returning to the subject of Jeremy, St. Mars said, "I cannot help believing that we would be helped by knowing who played that prank on Mr. Curry and your brother. And if your brother was a victim of it, why not Mr. Tubbs?"

Hester felt stupid for not having wondered the same. "Why not, indeed! Unless . . ." She mused as a thought came to her . . . "unless the person who did it had a vendetta against Jeremy, and it was Mr. Curry who was the innocent victim on that occasion."

When St. Mars looked doubtful, she said, "Or, if you do not like that theory, which admittedly is weak, what if the person only wished to get rid of Mr. Curry and Jeremy for a while? Whoever did it must have known that the charges would eventually be dropped when no treasonous pamphlet was found."

St. Mars was nodding. "And the reason why Mr. Tubbs was not included . . . ?"

"Is because Mr. Tubbs does not hang about the stall as much as Jeremy does."

"You are saying that person's interest was in the stall itself?"

Hester tilted her head to one side to consider. "That is one possibility, yes. What I meant, however, was that whoever it was might have wanted a chance at Sally, as Mr. Sullivan said."

"Did Sullivan take that chance?"

She frowned, trying to remember Sally's reaction to his comments. "I don't know. She was quite discomfited by the suggestion that Jeremy might have taken advantage of her while her husband was away, but I assumed that was because she felt guilty about her attraction to him. And I was so interested in that reaction, I did not observe her when Mr. Sullivan said the same thing about himself."

"I think you should ask her. Getting a person thrown into Newgate seems more than just a prank to me. What if Curry did have something treasonous in his shop? It's not at all implausible that he would, even if it wasn't the pamphlet the letter described. Then he might have hanged, which is hardly my idea of a jest."

The thought that Jeremy could have been implicated in treason, even if innocent, made Hester blanch. When St. Mars noted this, he quickly said. "But you see my point. The two incidents could easily be connected."

He suggested she try to discover whether someone visited Sally during her husband's arrest, and he promised to uncover Mr. Sullivan's interest in the bookstall.

"We should also try to find out what Mr. Tubbs was doing while his publisher was in gaol, as well as what he spoke to Sally about the other day."

Hester said she would try to get some of these answers from Jeremy. Then, as much as she hated to mention Isabella to him, she explained again how hard it had become for her to get away from the house.

"Isabella is frightened by the idea that the Pretender is on his way. My Aunt Mayfield has written several times, begging to be allowed to come to town before his troops swoop down and capture her. She has persuaded your cousin Harrowby to send the coach for her, and ought to be here within the week."

"If I were Isabella" —St. Mars's eyes danced— "I should be more frightened at the thought of Mrs. Mayfield's coming than the Pretender's."

Hester had to suppress a giggle. Knowing that they mustn't be overheard, she covered her lips. It relieved and surprised her that St.

Mars could refer to Isabella with no sign of hurt or bitterness. Not so very long ago, he had been in love with her, but she had gravely disappointed him. Hester had worried that he might never recover from his infatuation, but with a sudden feeling of elation she realized that he had not betrayed the slightest degree of suffering when he had spoken of Isabella now.

She ended her laughter on a sigh. "I know it is wicked of me, my lord, but I must agree with you. I confess, I dread her coming."

"Might your cousin not feel safer with her mother here? And if she does, could that help to free you?"

"It's possible, but my aunt always has a way of putting me to use." Hester changed the subject, not wishing to waste their time together with talk about her aunt or herself. "Nevertheless, I have thought of a way that I might discover more about Mr. Curry's dealings." She told him that she hoped to persuade Isabella to have her portrait painted by Mr. Charles Jervas, explaining his connections to Lady Mary Wortley Montagu and Mr. Pope, and theirs to Edmund Curry.

He raised his eyebrows in approval. "Well, then, it appears that we each have a few paths to pursue."

This was it, then. Their meeting was nearly at an end. Hester knew that she must convey all the unpleasant news to St. Mars without further ado.

Saddened by the prospect of causing him distress, she delayed the most painful news a moment longer by starting with a more trivial piece. "I have something to confess to you, my lord. Mr. Henry has started paying me an allowance. I tried to prevent him, but he insisted that I should be given something besides my food and lodging. I am very sorry, my lord."

She said this last, because he had frowned with an intensity she had never seen on his face before. He looked displeased—quite angry, in fact—when she had hardly expected him to care. She felt guilty about taking his money when he was not the one to give it, and, in telling him, had merely sought to ease her conscience.

"My lord?" She was about to say that she would return the money, when St. Mars spoke.

"Do you mean to tell me you have not been receiving any allowance from my cousin?"

She blinked. "No, of course not, my lord. Did you think that I was?"

St. Mars stood up so abruptly that his candle nearly blew out. "Of course I've been assuming you were! Didn't your aunt ask Harrowby to provide for you?"

Hester was smiling now, for she saw that his anger was not directed at her, but at his cousin. "No, my lord. But why should she, when she had never made me an allowance herself?"

"Ye gods!" Gideon stared at her speechlessly. He was appalled that he had never thought to inquire into her circumstances. "So, for all the time you have been living in London, you have had no money of your own?"

"No, but I have not been ill-treated."

"You have not?" He scoffed.

"No, how can you ask? I've been well fed and very well housed. And I never lack for clothes, for I receive as many of Isabella's cast-offs as anyone could want—in addition to the other gifts and treats she gives me," she added with a wince after glancing at his stormy face. "Isabella is truly very good to me, my lord!"

He snorted. He wanted to say something cutting about Isabella, but he knew it would not please Mrs. Kean. Besides, it was his fault for not making sure that she was taken care of.

"So, James Henry has taken it upon himself to rectify this abominable situation?" He knew he should feel grateful to his half-brother, but he could not help feeling a pang of jealousy. *He* was the one who should have been Hester's champion.

"He did— My lord, I wish you would not tease yourself over this. I would not have told you about it, if I had thought it was my due."

"I am well aware of that, Mrs. Kean." He scolded her with a shaking head. "And I had not believed you could be so foolish. How much does he give you?" He tried to tone down his ire, but in truth, he was boiling.

She looked almost afraid to tell him now, but she hesitantly did, "He gave me ten shillings for Lady Day, so I presume he means to do that quarterly."

He clamped his jaw shut. *A reasonable sum for a superior servant.* He would have been furious over the smallness of the amount, had he not reminded himself that James Henry was not at liberty to be extravagant with his lord's money. He swallowed the remark he was about to make, and said instead, "That will do for a start, but it is not nearly enough. I shall speak to my banker."

Her eyes grew wide in dismay. "My lord . . . no!" She stood. "I should never have said a word! Now you will be thinking that I was asking for more."

He gripped her shoulders. He wanted nothing more than to give her a big shake . . . except, perhaps, to kiss her. Recalling what Philippe had said, and how she had so vehemently denied that she could be at any risk, he did not give in to either temptation.

Softening his grasp, he brought his eyes just inches from hers, and said very gently, "That is more foolish even than your previous remarks on the subject. I know you too well, my dear. You would never ask anything for yourself. You must allow me to do this, however, or I should never be able to hold my head up again."

She had opened her mouth to complain, but this last phrase silenced her. She gazed deeply into his eyes and must have seen that he meant what he had said, for she looked away and a shy smile touched her lips. "You are very kind, my lord. But please, consider . . . . Will it not look odd if I am suddenly found to be in possession of money? I should find it very hard to conceal its source from my aunt. So difficult, in fact, that I must beg you not to do it."

He straightened, but kept a hold on her shoulders. Not for the first time, he had noticed how very good she smelled, like the freshness of a rose, at the same time, with something that was uniquely Mrs. Kean. Her scent, as much as her nearness, aroused him, which made him loath to let her go.

He smiled down at her and saw the clearness of her eyes, even in this fragile light. "You will not talk me out of this so easily, my dear. The money will be yours, but you will be free not to spend it. I shall have my banker hold it for you, if you wish. Then, whenever you have need of it, all you'll have to do is call upon him."

"Now," he said, releasing her shoulders to put himself a safer distance away. "Philippe should be here shortly. Is there anything else we should discuss?"

"There is one thing more, my lord." The regret in her voice was almost palpable. Her expression told him how much she dreaded being the bearer of bad news. "I'm afraid there is something else I must tell you . . . ."

Dread crept though his limbs, though he knew not of what.

Mrs. Kean faced him with courage and sympathy in her eyes. "Isabella is expecting a child, my lord."

For a fraction of a moment, Gideon wondered why the devil she imagined he would care that her cousin was breeding. He started to frown, to tell her once and for all that Isabella meant nothing to him any more. Then his brain made the connection, and he felt as if a heavy cask had rolled onto this chest and squashed it flat.

Isabella Fitzsimmons, *née Mayfield,* was going to produce an heir for her husband Harrowby. A child who, though innocent of any wrongdoing or conniving, would be yet another obstacle to Gideon's regaining his title and his estates. As challenging as his ambition had been, this pregnancy would make it even more difficult.

The very second the blow had hit him, Mrs. Kean had flinched and her face had been overcome with compassion. It would not do either of them any good if he reacted too strongly. Nor would reacting change the facts.

It would be Harrowby who produced the heir to Rotherham Abbey. All the rest, Gideon thought he could relinquish without too much pain. It was Rotherham Abbey, he realized, that was more than a home to him.

He was glad that Mrs. Kean had been the one to inform him, but he could not bear to stand here any longer with her woman's eyes perceiving every bit of his pain, and revealing her willingness to share it. Not when he couldn't ask her to help him forget it, as he suddenly, so desperately wanted to do.

He mustered a smile. A weak one, he knew. "I cannot pretend that you haven't dealt me a blow, but I thank you for having the courage to tell me."

"I did not want you to read it in the news-sheets, my lord."

"Good Lord, no! I should not have enjoyed that." He knew that his laugh sounded forced. But there was nothing else to be said.

He was searching for a different topic to spare them both this unease, when Philippe opened the door and slipped into the room.

"*Voilà Philippe,*" Gideon said, turning towards him. He didn't know whether to be relieved or saddened by the interruption. But at least it afforded them a change of subject. "You did not knock, Philippe. Does that mean you believed that *mademoiselle* was safe from my lecherous schemes?"

"Ah, no, *monseigneur!* It means that Philippe forgot monsieur's instructions. Would you prefer that I go out and come back in again?"

"No, damn your impudence! I wonder if my dear cousin Harrowby tolerates your impertinence as kindly as I do."

"Alas, *monsieur!* I doubt if *milord 'Arroby* is capable of appreciating Philippe's so excellent wit, even if 'e does 'ave more respect for Philippe's advice than *monsieur le vicomte* ever 'ad."

"*Touché!* I see that is time for me to go, before you subject Mrs. Kean to any more of your Gallic spleen." He turned back to Hester and, taking hold of one of her hands, drew it to his lips.

"Your servant, madam. I shall pursue those questions we discussed and inform you of any answers I find. I presume you will do likewise?"

She was still peering at him as if looking to see if all was right, although on Philippe's entrance, she had masked her compassion. For that he was particularly grateful. He would not have enjoyed having Philippe ask him what the matter was. Nor was it beyond his imagination that Philippe would commit such an impertinence.

Mrs. Kean agreed to their plan. She promised to write him the moment she found anything out. Then, she followed him to the door and, giving him a last, gently sympathetic smile, she begged him to be careful on his way out.

Philippe went out first, then signaled that it was safe for Gideon to come.

Before he closed the door behind them, Gideon leaned back inside the room. "Oh, there is one thing more, Mrs. Kean."

She looked up expectantly. "Yes, my lord?"

"As regards temptation at this hour . . . pray, do not be deceived. I may have been tempted, even if you were not. So in these matters, I should advise you henceforth to speak only for yourself."

He wished he could have made a portrait of her face at that moment, for she looked speechless and confused and—yes, pleased all at the same time. The combination was adorable.

She recovered enough to bob him a curtsy and say with a shy smile, "As you wish, my lord."

He turned and moved quietly through the dark room that looked out onto the courtyard, feeling better than he had a few moments ago, when the last thin shreds of hope had seemed to slip through his fingers.

Harrowby be damned! But he would haunt Rotherham Abbey, if that was the only option left open to him. Mrs. Kean would be there to admit him whenever he liked, and as the secret entrance opened into her bedchamber . . . .

He was obliged to put an end to these alluring thoughts when Philippe made a sign for him to tread quietly. He would have to stay alert if he wanted to leave his house without getting caught.

Minutes later, outside in Piccadilly he ran till he was out of sight of Hawkhurst House. If anyone had seen him leave, they would assume that John Footman had been sent with an urgent message from his lord.

The notion of wearing the Hawkhurst livery had been a stroke of genius. With Philippe as his ally, the clothes had been relatively easy to obtain. He did not doubt they would prove useful again someday.

Still running, he turned and headed for the Thames, where he would find a waterman to ferry him across. As he slowed to a walk, he reflected that he felt remarkably cheerful for a man who could only enter his own house under cover of night. But Mrs. Kean seemed to have that happy effect on him. Of course, he wished he could have seen more, could have walked up into the principal rooms and slept in his own chamber—but curiously, he had been happy enough with his visit confined to James Henry's offices.

His greatest frustration, in fact, had not come from the inability to roam freely in his own house, but from the restraints imposed upon him as a man of honour. And Philippe—that graceless spawn of Satan—

had understood him only too well! Gideon thought that, tonight, even Mrs. Kean had shown a glimmer of understanding when he had teased her on the subject. At times, her innocence astounded him, but he could take comfort from it, too. If she had no more experience at flirting than she had demonstrated, he could probably dismiss his fears that that villain, rotting in a French prison, had met with the slightest degree of success.

As these thoughts passed through his head, he made his way past the Haymarket and Charing Cross. Keeping a wary eye out for footpads and soldiers, he soon descended Whitehall Stairs. Three wherries floated there, waiting for fares. The watermen set up a cacophony for his custom, but Gideon refused to enter into their haggling. Hopping into the first boat he reached, he gave its owner directions to take him to Vauxhall Stairs.

As the boat's oars dipped rhythmically into the river and safety settled over him, his smile faded at the thought of Mrs. Kean's dependent condition. He should have realized that she had no money of her own. With a shrew like Mrs. Mayfield for an aunt, it was hardly surprising that she had been employed on no better terms than a slave.

He wondered how difficult it had been for her to bear. He recalled that, before knowing her well, he had found her clothes ill-chosen and had believed it due to a fault in her taste. Now, he felt not only foolish, but ignorant and self-centred for not guessing what her situation must be. Having been used by the Jacobites himself and discarded by James, he could only begin to imagine the hurt and humiliation to which Mrs. Kean must often have been subjected.

Well, he would see that she would not have to be dependent on Harrowby forever. He would make certain she had funds enough to leave Hawkhurst House whenever she wished. For the moment, however, she was better off in her cousin's house than she would be on her own. And he could not deny that it pleased him to think of her enjoying the luxuries of his estate when he could not enjoy them himself. Perhaps it was selfish, but he needed her to remain in his household, too. She was not only his greatest friend, but the only bridge between his former life and this one, his window into the Court, and his eyes for everything inside the Hawkhurst household.

This last thought reminded him of Harrowby's expected heir. But Gideon was too inured to losses now to let anything depress him for long. He refused to dwell on his disappointment, reminding himself that he was lucky to be back in England. He had just spent a delightful hour in the company of Mrs. Kean. And now he had a purpose, too.

As of tomorrow, he would be on the search for Mr. Curry's killer, in deadly earnest.

His Principle of action once explore,
That instant 'tis his Principle no more.
Like following life through creatures you dissect,
You lose it in the moment you detect.

CHAPTER XII

On the following morning, Gideon set out for the Bell and Bible, disguised as a fop. No one who had known his careless ways with dress before would have recognized him in layers of paint, a scattering of patches, a full-bottomed wig with two elaborate wings in front, and an eyeglass dangling from the end of a ribbon. The coat he wore over a flowered waistcoat was a bright scarlet, the kind of showy colour he had never worn. When set against the blackest of periwigs, it made his skin appear whiter than was usually seen on a gentleman of his outdoor habits.

He took a boat to Temple Stairs and found a chair to carry him the short distance to St. Dunstan's. In Fleet Street he paused at several bookstalls before finally ending his stroll at the Bell and Bible, where he meant to try an experiment of his own.

He needed to assess the honesty of the bookseller's wife for himself. He trusted Mrs. Kean's judgement, but he feared she might have allowed her partiality for her brother and the object of his affections to blind her to a case of deceit. He knew her loyalty well. He had witnessed it in her attitude towards Isabella to the point that he could not tell if she even perceived Isabella's faults. He had also been the beneficiary of her loyalty, when he had done nothing to earn it.

It was an admirable trait, but it might have led her to mistake Sally's character. Gideon wondered if her affection for Jeremy might have interfered with her judgement.

Therefore, the moment Gideon entered Sally's shop, he raised his glass and ogled her through it. "Egads!" he drawled. "What a fair piece to find in such a dreary spot! And all bedecked in black, too!"

Sauntering the few steps to the counter, he lowered his glass and reached for her hand. "I vow, I must protest, my dear! Ye're much too pretty a creature to be slaving behind a counter."

Sally avoided his grasp and made him a bobbing curtsy. His approach had flustered her, and she rose with a hand to her breast and a quiver in her voice. "You flatter me, sir. But, indeed, this is precisely where I should be. This shop was my husband's, and now it belongs to me. These garments you see are widow's weeds."

Gideon admired the adroitness with which she had fended him off. Her practiced response let him know where she stood without offending a potential customer.

She quickly diverted his attention from her person to her wares. "Could I interest you in a book, sir? Perhaps, you would care to buy a tome of witty verse, penned by a lady of the Court?"

She had formed an opinion of his tastes, too, and had used her expert assessment to distract him. Gideon silently complimented her tact and her mercantile sense. If Jeremy Kean did manage to win this woman, he should enjoy a reasonably prosperous life.

It was not Gideon's intention to distress her, but to determine if her motives were mercenary. Since she had done nothing to encourage the advances of a wealthy man, he believed he could absolve her of complicity in her husband's murder—at least with the motive of inheriting his bookstall. There could be other motives, of course, one that he had been especially loath to discuss with Mrs. Kean.

If this Curry fellow was truly as repugnant as Mrs. Kean had said, wouldn't a wife be tempted to do away with him so she could marry her lover? Gideon could not dismiss the possibility until he was certain that no lover existed. The elusive Mr. Sullivan, perhaps?

He made the widow a stiff, slight bow. In keeping with his character's conceit, he gave a partial leer and said, "Recently widowed, are ye?

Well, m'dear, I believe I understand ye. Mustn't give the gossips too much to gnaw on, now, must we? But, I trust y'will think of me kindly when ye've had done with your mourning?"

The smile Sally gave him was distant and cool. No gentleman in his right mind would take it for a promise. It was sufficient merely to keep the door open to sell him some of her wares.

Gideon slowly perused the book she handed him, as if his motive in remaining were to engage her favour. He had determined that a purpose for his lingering would be needed if he was going to keep the bookstall under surveillance. Without one, he would find it impossible to get near enough to see and hear what went on in the shop without arousing the murderer's suspicions.

He lazed elegantly with one elbow on the counter and read the book through his raised glass. As Mrs. Kean had said, it was purported to be by "A Lady of the Court" —according to the Currys, Lady Mary Wortley Montagu. Gideon knew virtually nothing of the lady, since she had arrived at Court only a few months ago. Even if she had been there before his exile, he would seldom have met her since her father, a committed Whig, and his, a fanatical Tory, had been the worst of enemies.

Her verses were written with a great deal of wit, if with a certain smugness. The objects of her satire were not all clear to him, but, then, he had never partaken in the petty personal squabbles that other members of Court found so absorbing.

Assuming that her verses would appeal mightily to a fop, however, he read them with manufactured glee, uttering an occasional, "Oho!" or "Tee hee!" Interspersing these outbursts with intervals in which he ogled Sally shamelessly, he watched while other customers came and went, bought books in folio or tracts, and came to flirt with the widow. Sally always seemed to know which of these were serious customers and which were only there to waste her time. The latter few received none of her smiles and were often turned away with a raised shoulder.

She must have begun to believe that Gideon fell into this category, for she eventually came over and said, "May I wrap that book for you, sir, so you can enjoy it in a more cheerful place?"

So she had not forgiven him for calling her bookstall "dreary." Gideon smothered a smile.

"No, thank you, m'dear. I am enjoying it perfectly well here, but I shall be happy to pay for the privilege of enjoying the view." He gave her a leering wink and produced his coin.

The purchase earned him the right to stay a while longer. He could not stand at her counter all day, and so far, none of the customers he'd seen seemed to have an unusual reason for visiting the stall. Then someone of interest came in—Mrs. Kean's brother, Jeremy.

Gideon examined him with blatant interest, which he could easily do by staring rudely through his eyeglass. Jeremy bounded up with a puppy-like joy to be in his sweetheart's presence, but Sally was plainly distressed by his visit.

The whole time he was there, she fussed about the shop, keeping unnaturally busy, and seeming to avoid his eyes. She appeared to be labouring under a terrible burden, with the result that she did not know how to behave. It seemed to Gideon that whatever disturbed her was greater than either hurt dignity or pride, for she jumped nervously whenever the door opened or a figure shadowed the glass. But it was clear from the way her gaze followed Jeremy when he was not looking at her, that she was seriously attracted to him.

Clear to everyone, that was, except Jeremy, who seemed exactly as his sister had described him.

Warm and ingenuous, as his sister had said, Jeremy had greeted him with a broad smile and had ignored the sneer that Gideon's disguise obliged him to give in response. From then on, his attention had been only for the widow, and if there was the slightest bit of insincerity in his admiration, Gideon could certainly not detect it. Jeremy seemed truly smitten, though he expressed his affection without the commonplace gallantry so fashionable now. Courtesy and consideration were the only attentions he permitted himself to give, but beneath them Gideon sensed a longing to give more.

While Jeremy was still at the Bell and Bible, a customer approached the door. He attracted Gideon's attention because he lingered outside the shop for several minutes, glancing furtively up and down the street before finally stepping inside.

He gave a nervous glance at the two men inside before asking to see a set of sermons. He pretended to peruse it, while Jeremy made his farewell, promising to stop in tomorrow in case Sally should have an errand for him. Then, when it became obvious that Gideon had no intention of leaving, the customer beckoned Sally to his end of the counter and in a whisper asked to see something else.

Whatever his request was, it seemed to throw Sally for a loss. She had leaned forward to hear him, and now she drew back. "I do not understand you, sir. What can you mean by my husband's 'private stock?'"

The look he gave her was both suspicious and cruel. "Come now, girl, don't play the innocent with me! I've been buying off your husband for many a year. And if he's gone and got himself killed and left you this shop, then you must know where he keeps them."

"Keeps what?" she asked, plainly taken aback. "I am aware of nothing, sir, except the books you see here on these rails."

By this time, the man had recollected Gideon's presence and threw him another wary glance. When he tried to hush Sally, Gideon made a point of raising his eyeglass and staring obnoxiously through it at the man.

"What's this? Is this ruffian disturbing you, m'dear? Shall I step out and tell someone to fetch the constable?"

The frustrated man gave a start and backed hastily towards the door. "No need, no need!" he said, giving Sally a parting glare. "Must've mistaken the shop. But I'll have you know, you won't be getting my custom again, wench!"

As he slammed the door, setting the glass to rattling in its frame, Sally gaped as if she had never witnessed such madness. As strong as she appeared to be, the episode had clearly shaken her, coming so close upon the violent death of Mr. Curry, Gideon suspected. He hated to annoy her further, and in his present disguise, any offer of sympathy from him might tip her into tears. So, after expressing his outrage at the man's extraordinary incivility, he took himself off with a promise to return on the morrow.

That evening, at his house, he conferred with Tom who had been set to trail Mr. Simpkins on his daily rounds. Tom reported that the bookseller's widow was not the only female Mr. Simpkins harassed.

"It's a right old lecher he is, my lord!" Tom exclaimed in disapproval.

Gideon was lounging in his small parlour after a particularly filling meal. He had dined late on a tender loin of pork.

Tom had butchered the pig himself. When complimented on its flavour, Katy had looked flustered and Tom, who had also been in the room, had hidden a smile. This was so unlike his faithful groom's usual behaviour that Gideon had prolonged his commentary on the pork in an attempt to provoke a further reaction. But Tom had only ended by scowling and saying, "We can't keep pigs with Looby about. You know that, my lord."

Tom steadfastly refused to share his master's repasts, but he would stand and bear Gideon company while he ate. Dining alone was oppressive to Gideon, so he made use of his meals to discuss his affairs with Tom, and sometimes with Katy. She had left them now, so Tom seemed more at ease.

"Tell me what you observed." Gideon tipped his chair back on two legs, and propped a booted ankle atop the other knee. He had removed his paint and heavy wig, and had gathered his hair in a ribbon on his neck.

"Well, I followed him just like you said, my lord, and he made his rounds just like he ought. There wasn't nothin' wrong in that. But he stopped—oh, three or four times—wherever a pretty wench was workin', and he always tried to lay his hands on 'em. None of 'em liked it, far as I could see, but that didn't stop the old beggar from tryin'."

"Were these married women?"

Tom screwed up his face in thought. "I think maybe two were, but I couldn't get close enough t'see, or he might've spotted me. I can only guess at it, my lord."

"What made you think they were?"

"Them two? They was both workin' alongside a man, and Mr. Simpkins, he was careful not to bother 'em when the men were payin' 'em any mind."

Gideon gave an appreciative nod. "A reasonable deduction. Was he any more forward with the others?"

Tom's eyes lit. "Aye, that he was, my lord! But I can't say as he got any further with the widows or spinsters. They were just that much louder when they refused him." He added hesitantly, "I can say this, my lord. He wasn't near as forward with any of those women as he was with Mrs. Curry."

"Hmm. . . ." Gideon pondered this information, while Tom shifted from one foot to the other. It was possible that Mr. Simpkins had been more vigorous in his pursuit of Sally because she had encouraged him. Not voluntarily, according to Mrs. Kean, but at her husband's insistence. That could account for the depth of his anger when she had finally repulsed him.

"Do you want me to follow him again, my lord?"

Gideon looked up at Tom and was surprised to detect signs of discontent on his stalwart face. He was well accustomed to Tom's grumblings, but they usually stemmed from worry, not unhappiness. "No," he said, keeping his eyes on Tom and crossing the other knee. "I don't know that anything would be served by it. Instead, I propose that we both keep a watch on the bookstall tonight, to see what goes on."

Tom bobbed his head. "Yes, my lord." But his mind was plainly somewhere else.

Slapping his thighs, Gideon brought the legs of his chair back onto the floor with a crash. "All right, that's it," he said. "Let's out with it!"

Tom's head jerked up in alarm. "My lord?"

"I want to know what's bothering you. And don't bother to deny it," Gideon said, as Tom looked ready to protest. "It's been plain since I came home that something is eating away at you."

Tom's back went stiff, but he failed to meet his master's eyes. Tilting his head awkwardly, he said, "It's not that I'm worried, my lord. It's just that—"

When he stopped, Gideon asked, in a voice that he tried to keep calm, "Are you having second thoughts about staying with me?" He had never meant for Tom to forfeit his life in the service of an outlaw.

Tom looked horror-struck. "No, I swear that's not it, my lord! How can you ask me? Me, as has cared for you since you were a little lad!"

Relief filled Gideon's breast. "I cannot pretend to be sorry to hear you say that, Tom." He coughed to clear a sudden roughness in his throat. "Very well. Then, if it's not this life we're leading, what the devil is it?"

Tom squirmed. "I don't know that I'm that ready, my lord."

"Ready? To do what?" Gideon frowned, his anxiety giving way to concern.

"Well . . . to say it, I guess. I can't be sure . . ."

He looked so miserable, that Gideon could not allow him to conceal the matter a minute longer. "You had best tell me," he threatened, "or I doubt either of us will ever have a moment's peace. I can tell it's on your mind, so how can I be expected to forget it myself? Come on, Tom. Let's have the worst of it."

Tom took a bracing breath, but stood staring down at his boots. "I don't know what the worst may be, my lord! And that's what's got me all tied up in knots!" He glanced up and the anguish in his gaze pierced Gideon's heart.

Gideon found himself reacting with anger against he knew not what. He had never seen his loyal groom so distressed, and he felt Tom's pain as if it were his own. In spite of the barriers of rank between them, the affection that bound them together had always been stronger. Without thinking, he stood and placed a hand on Tom's shoulder and gave it a little shake.

His gesture, unprecedented since the days when he had learned the difference between master and servant, brought an astonished look to Tom's face. He swallowed and bowed his head.

He stammered, "I—I had been thinking of asking your leave to marry Katy, my lord."

Gideon felt a jolt of something—Envy? Jealousy?—before relief released the tension in his back. "And this is what has you in such a wretched state? Why, of course, you may marry her, if you wish! And I shall be the first to congratulate you. When is this marriage to take place? You have asked her, haven't you? Is that what has you all flummoxed?"

To his surprise, Tom did not look the slightest bit relieved. He did not seem to know how to answer Gideon's questions, or indeed, which to answer first.

Finally, he blurted, "No, my lord, I haven't. But what's got me worked up is that I don't even know if I should."

"Why? What do you mean, Tom?" He laughed. "Do you want the wench or not?"

Tom flinched as if struck, and a glimmer of comprehension finally pierced Gideon's dullness. He squeezed his eyes shut, cursing himself for the thoughtless fool he was.

He had not meant to insult Katy. In truth, he had forgotten how she had been employed before they had met her and had used the word *wench* to mean nothing more than a serving maid.

Before he could retract it, however, Tom said, so desperately that Gideon could not doubt him. "Yes, my lord, I do. I want her so bad it hurts, but what if . . . What if she's got the pox, my lord?"

Gideon held his breath a moment before heaving a great sigh. He removed his hand from Tom's shoulder and fell back onto his chair. As the full magnitude of Tom's fears struck him, he looked up at his beloved servant and wiped a hand across his mouth. "I . . . see," he eventually said. He felt pity for Tom . . . and for Katy, too. "You fear that because of her past, she might make you sick. Is that it?"

Tom peered into his master's face and nodded. At least, he seemed a little relieved, now that he had confessed his worry.

Gideon pondered the problem, which was not one he had ever considered before, because even when he had worried about the health of the women he had bedded, he had never expected to marry any of them. And it would not be only Tom's health that was at stake, but his children's, too.

At the thought of Tom having children, Gideon could hardly restrain a smile. He could almost see them playing in his yard. With Tom for a father, they would be the most watched and scolded children in Christendom, if he raised them the way he had raised Gideon.

But Tom had noticed his mirth and his expression underwent a series of alterations, from astonishment to a scowl.

"Sorry, Tom." Gideon hastily sat up. "I promise I wasn't smiling over this." He furrowed his brow in thought, then said, "What if we got a physician in to see Katy? If he says she's well, then would you feel safe enough?"

He could tell the instant his idea soaked in, for the lines on Tom's forehead eased. Then his misgivings returned. "But what if that makes her angry? I wouldn't want to shame her. She doesn't even know I want to marry her,"

Gideon started. "She must have some idea, surely!"

Tom's neck turned crimson. He gave a reluctant smile. "I think she knows I fancy her, my lord."

"Well, thank God for that!" Gideon sat back again. "But you needn't worry that she'll get angry, for we won't tell her what the doctor's really here for. I'll tell him to physick you both. I'm sure it's past time that I should have done it, but Robert Shaw always saw to those sorts of things at the Abbey. This housekeeping business is all new to me. I'll get you both physicked, and I can discreetly ask the doctor what he thinks about Katy."

As he expounded this plan, Tom's misery began to lift. He seemed scarcely able to believe that his problem might be so easily solved. "I thank you kindly, Master Gideon," he said huskily, as if a lump had lodged in his throat.

Hearing this address, which Tom had used throughout his childhood, Gideon felt a stinging in his eyes. "Not at all," he said briskly. "It will please me to see you settled so comfortably . . . if Katy will have you, that is."

As Tom grinned self-consciously, Gideon added, "But you'll have to wait until this business with Mrs. Kean's brother is ended, for I'll need your full attention. And, now, if that's all settled, I suggest we give some thought to what we'll be doing in Fleet Street tonight."

When they returned to the City, it was nine o'clock and dark. All the church bells were ringing the hour, and the shops in the shadow of St. Dunstan's were closing for the night. They watched from an alley while Sally shuttered the door of the Bell and Bible and walked with Jeremy in the direction of Bell Yard. As the two strolled past, Gideon noticed how careful she was not even to brush against him.

He had changed his disguise and was dressed as a law student. After instructing Tom to establish himself as a customer at the Mitre Tavern across from St. Dunstan's, Gideon waited in the shadows at the entrance to Ram Alley, bundled up in a black gown, and leaned against the wall with the ostensible purpose of smoking a pipe. Only a generation before, as a precinct of Whitefriars, Ram Alley would have been packed with debtors claiming sanctuary from their creditors. An act of Parliament had stripped them of that privilege, so now the alley served merely to give access to passages leading into the Temple and Serjeants' Inn. The residents of Serjeants' Inn included some of the justices from the highest courts in the kingdom—men definitely to be avoided—so Gideon had darkened his brows and worn a dark tied wig.

In this area of London, there were no travellers' rooms to be had. All the inns here were inhabited by members of the Temple, so Gideon could not install himself nearby as a visitor, newly up to town. Fortunately, Serjeants' did not overlook Fleet Street, so he did not have to fear being spotted through one of its windows. The Mitre was frequented by persons who appeared at Court, so he could not afford to loiter in its taproom.

All was quiet now at the bookstall, though Fleet Street was still strewn with pedestrians making their way home. If not for the occasional armed soldier who sauntered past, it would have seemed that no war was in progress. Stray dogs, vagrant children, and the men and women who staggered out of gin shops still drifted through the streets. The presence of the soldiers had an unsettling effect. Some Londoners seemed reasonably glad to see them, while others strode past them with tightened lips and lowered eyes.

Gideon stood, puffing away on his clay pipe, and watched a pig root in the street, until Tom came out of the Mitre and joined him.

"Wait a few minutes," Gideon mumbled around the stem of his pipe. "Then follow me." He led the way to a more sheltered spot down Fleet Street at the entrance to Falcon Court, directly across from St. Dunstan's, where they could speak without being seen.

As soon as Tom joined him, he asked, "How was the view from the Mitre?"

"Not too bad, my lord."

"Good," he said. "That will give you a more comfortable location from which to observe the shop. Did you see anything of interest?"

"No, nothing, my lord." Tom made a sound of disgust. "Unless you want to know how many of his Majesty's men passed by with whores."

"Nothing else?"

Tom's "no" was accompanied by a sigh.

"I know it may seem unlikely, Tom, but I can't help feeling we will see something here if we keep our eyes open. Mrs. Kean obviously believes so, too, or she would never have asked us to watch the stall. We know that the killer did not steal anything, but he did make off with the key. The lock has been changed, so the key will do him no good. But he must have had a reason for taking it, and if so, he should come back.

"Besides," he continued, "today I witnessed something rather interesting at the shop."

He told Tom about the customer who had asked to see Mr. Curry's "private stock."

"What did he mean by it, my lord—" Tom gave a sudden jump— "unless it's that pamphlet what Mr. Kean got tooken up for!"

"Possibly . . . in which case Mrs. Kean's brother is in worse trouble than we know. The customer's behaviour was certainly furtive enough."

"But if the Messengers turned the place inside out, wouldn't they've found any books like that?"

"Not if Curry had hidden them cleverly enough. I wish we could search that shop. But if there is something hidden there, the killer may know where. That could be the reason he took the key."

Tom nodded and stifled a yawn.

"Just stay with me another hour or so," Gideon said. "Then you can go home to bed."

Tom tried to sound livelier. "I can stay as late as you do, my lord."

"No, that would be a waste of our time. I'll need you to take watch tomorrow when the shop is closed. Then on Monday, I'll pay Mrs. Curry another visit."

Tom wanted to argue, but Gideon hushed him, before taking a position in the black shadow of the building. From here, he could see the front of St. Dunstan's Church, and the corner where the Bell and Bible stood to its right. The shops that abutted the east side of the old building were firmly shuttered for the night. The pedestrian traffic was lighter at this hour, with only the comings and goings from the Mitre Tavern, the calling of the watchman, and an occasional drunkard stumbling past to break the silence. Most people would be readying themselves for bed to save on candles.

A rat emerged from a house and scurried past. Suddenly, a fat tabby appeared from behind a pile of refuse and pounced, bringing the rat's frantic squeaks to a halt in a matter of seconds. Then, as if suspicious that Gideon meant to steal its prize, the cat dragged its heavy meal away by the scruff of its neck.

Grimacing, Gideon hunched his shoulders and wrapped himself more tightly in the gown. The summer had been brief. A cold north wind was sending gusts through the streets.

In spite of his miserable surroundings, Gideon had chosen this late hour for a reason. He doubted it would be of benefit to watch the shop in the early morning hours, when there should surely be too many people up and about for anything nefarious to occur. He would stand watch until just three o'clock, but the last few hours without Tom would seem long.

He was thankful then, when soon the sound of quiet footsteps approached from his left. He scarcely had enough time to pull Tom deeper into the shadows before a man hurried past their hiding place in Falcon Court. Then, pausing, he glanced quickly in both directions, before crossing the street at a silent trot. He moved past St. Dunstan's and disappeared inside the shop on the corner across from the Bell and Bible.

Tom released a pent up breath, and whispered, "Nothing there, my lord."

Gideon was not convinced. The man had behaved as if he hadn't wished to be seen. He'd used no link. And he'd appeared to be carrying a bundle under his arm.

"You may be right, but let's wait and see. That house looks down on the Bell and Bible. I wonder if anyone has asked its inhabitants if they noticed anything the night that Mr. Curry was killed. I must tell Mrs. Kean to ask her brother."

He was about to give Tom permission to retire, when the same man emerged from the shop, locked the door behind him, and, again making sure that no one was about, started back the way he had come.

Gideon put a finger to his lips, and the two men moved silently to press themselves against the nearer wall. They watched as the stranger went past them. Then, as soon as he had, Gideon stepped out from his hiding place.

The stranger kept his head down as he hurried past Temple Bar. He stuck close to the houses, glancing about him as he went.

It always made sense to stay wary when travelling the streets of London at night, particularly when walking alone. Nevertheless, there was something furtive in the man's movements that seemed worth investigating. Gideon motioned to Tom, and together they set off in pursuit.

The man led them past St. Clement's and into the Strand. Following him in the dark, Gideon was frustrated by his inability to see the man's face, but he made note of other details in his appearance. He was tall and angular in build, and his coat was dark. He walked with a slight hunch, as if accustomed to bending over his work, but that could have been nothing more than a defensive posture for walking the streets. At Charing Cross, he veered right, then left into Pall Mall. In a circular beam cast by a lantern he passed, his costume was revealed to be sober. He wore neither jewels nor silk nor expensive embroidery.

Here, in the City of Westminster, there were more pedestrians on the street at midnight, with revelers coming and going from the theatres and coffee houses. It was riskier here for Gideon, who, if he were to be stopped, was more likely to be recognized. But like the stranger they pursued, Gideon kept mostly to the shadows.

As their quarry headed for St. James's Street, however, Gideon's pulse began to race. Any one of the figures he made out in the dark, either calling for a chair or descending from a carriage, might know him.

Tom was growing worried, too. He took hold of Gideon's sleeve, and whispered urgently, "No, my lord! Let me go."

Gideon shook off Tom's hand. He had the feeling they were about to learn something important. "Let's just see where he goes. No one will know me in this rig."

For his master's sake Tom could not risk making a scene, so he grudgingly subsided. They were nearing the corner into St. James's, where the lights were brighter. At the end of the street facing the Palace, the St. James Coffee House, a noted Whig gathering place, was famous for Mr. Cole's Globe Light, which illumined the pavement and everything within several yards. Just before they reached it, however, the stranger turned left and entered a house in the very shadow of the Palace.

Ozinda's Coffee House.

When Gideon saw the man's destination, he gave a sigh of satisfaction. So they *had* learned something to make his risk worthwhile.

He led Tom a short way back the way they had come and stopped when they reached a spot with darker shadows.

"Did you see where he went?"

Both stood with their faces turned away from Pall Mall. As a coach clattered past, Tom threw a glance over his shoulder and nodded.

"Well, we know that he's a Tory, at least, and most likely a Jacobite, for I doubt that many Tories who are not for James will be frequenting Ozinda's just now. Were you able to get a look at his face when he turned?"

"No, my lord."

"Me neither." He paused. "I wonder, Tom, if you could try to spot him in Ozinda's? I dare not go in myself, for I often drank coffee there. But we need to know what he looks like, and I cannot afford to waste this chance. Did you take note of his clothing?"

"I did, my lord. I'll find him, but you should get away from here."

"I will, I promise. The devil of it is that there is nowhere in Pall Mall for me to wait. I'll have to start back. As soon as you get a good look at him, come directly to me. I'll wait for you past Charing Cross, across from Northumberland House, just inside Woodstock Court. It looked quiet enough when we passed. Now, be off with you, and do not stay any longer than you need."

Tom headed back to St. James's. Gideon waited a few moments longer before moving on. The lamps outside the many coffee houses made him want to shield his face with his gown, but any gesture of that sort would draw the very attention he was eager to avoid. So he kept his face bare, merely inclining his head if anyone walked near. The memory of his confinement in Dover Castle was too recent to ignore, but he cursed this intolerable need to hide.

Along both sides of Pall Mall stood fine residences of the nobility interspersed with popular coffee houses, like the Smyrna, where his father had often been entertained by Dean Swift. On the south side farther down, stood the Cocoa-Tree, Gideon's favourite, where he had used to take his morning chocolate and chat with the owner Isaac Norsa, a Jew, about his native Italy—another house in which no Whig ever dared show his face. The Smyrna, a known gathering place for Jacobites, seemed unnaturally quiet tonight.

Dodging a pair of sedan chairs and a group of common street women in their nightdresses, Gideon did not breathe easily until he had successfully reached the middle of Pall Mall, at which point he could slow his pace. Here were the backs of the mansions that faced St. James's Square. This portion of the street was much darker, with fewer people walking about. He hoped that Tom would catch up with him soon, for, unlikely as it was, Tom could also be recognized by someone who happened to remember Gideon's groom.

He thought about the man they had followed. It was unlucky that they had not seen where he had come from before he'd entered Fleet Street, but they had not been aware of him at all until he was almost upon them. His errand near St. Dunstan's was suspiciously brief. He could have been delivering an innocent package, but he was not dressed like a messenger.

There was something vaguely familiar about him, Gideon realized, something about his general shape or size.

He wondered what a Jacobite would find to interest him in that house in Fleet Street, one of only three east of St. Dunstan's to have survived the Great Fire. That made it more ancient than anyone could possibly know. Gideon decided to take a look at it tomorrow and see who its occupants were. For now, he could not recall what sort of shop occupied the ground floor. It might be nothing but a coincidence, but the fact that the house faced the Bell and Bible led him to believe that tonight's discovery could be significant.

Behind him, suddenly he heard a shout, followed by the sound of running feet. As the din increased, he turned to see a group of men, sprinting towards him through the dark. Two ducked into the Smyrna Coffee House, while a third disappeared into one of the older houses in Pall Mall. As the fourth dashed past him on the far side of the street, Gideon saw that it was the man he and Tom had shadowed.

He was about to give chase, when the last of the runners pulled abreast. Tom slowed just long enough to grasp him by the arm and gasp out, "Messengers, my lord!"

Gideon sprang into a run, his longer, younger legs easily keeping pace with Tom. "Are they chasing us?"

Tom panted. "Can't say. They just raided the place! Every man that wasn't nabbed scattered faster than a herd of sheep. I ran for the door and didn't look back."

As he rasped this story out, Gideon tried to peer back, but he could make out nothing through the dark. He could still hear shouts and scuffling noises behind them in Pall Mall, but the sounds were growing fainter. It was likely that the Messengers had caught enough suspects to keep their hands full.

He turned forwards again in time to notice St. Alban's Street just ahead. Grabbing Tom's arm, he urged, "In here! Quick!"

Dashing across the corner of St. Alban's, they hurried into the Carved Balcony Tavern and hid themselves at a table. The high backs of its benches concealed them from other patrons, and gave Tom a chance to catch his breath. When the host came up to serve them, Gideon kept his hat brim low and ordered each of them a mug of beer.

As soon as the man left, Gideon raised his brim and discovered that Tom still looked shaken.

"We've lost them for now," he murmured. "So, tell me what happened."

Tom steadied himself with a deep breath, before leaning his forearms on the table. "I had just gone in to take a good look 'round—I couldn't've been in there any more than a minute, my lord—when three, or maybe four gen'lemen rushed in with a handful of soldiers. They nabbed Mr. Ozinda and a few others, before every man jack of 'em who wasn't in reach made a dash for the door."

"Poor old Ozinda," Gideon said. "I can't believe he was any party to a plot. What about our man? Did you get a look at him first?"

"Yes, I did, my lord."

Tom paused, while the drawer set down their beers. Tom gazed longingly at his mug, until Gideon encouraged him to drink. Even with Messengers on his tail, Tom refused to take a sip without his master's permission.

As he took a few thirsty gulps, Gideon asked, "Will you know him again if you see him?"

"I should, my lord."

"Good. Then, point him out to me if you see him near the bookstall. Tomorrow's Sunday, so the shop will be closed, but I'll see what I can discover about that house he visited. He could be up to something illegal—perhaps the treasonous pamphlets Mr. Kean was arrested for. I wonder if Curry had business with him. It may be nothing, but at least we have something to look into now."

A wench swayed by, followed by a drunkard who staggered close to their table.

Tom eyed them both askance. "Didn't we ought to get out o' this place, sir?"

"There's no hurry." Gideon shrugged. "And we're safer in here. The Carved Balcony has never been considered a respectable place, so we shouldn't meet with anyone we know." He sipped his beer to allow time for all the hubbub to die down.

He felt reasonably satisfied with this evening's work. Surprisingly, he *would* have something to report to Mrs. Kean. Gideon just hoped that the stranger's nocturnal activities would prove to have a bearing on Edmund Curry's death.

How many pictures of one Nymph we view,
All how unlike each other, all how true!
Arcadia's Countess, here, in ermined pride,
Is, there, Pastora by a fountain side.
Here Fannia, leering on her own good man,
And there, a naked Leda with a Swan.
Let then the Fair one beautifully cry,
In Magdalen's loose hair and lifted eye,
Or dressed in smiles of sweet Cecilia shine,
With simpering Angels, Palms, and Harps divine;
Whether the Charmer sinner it, or saint it,
If Folly grow romantic, I must paint it.

CHAPTER XIII

The morning after her midnight meeting with St. Mars, Hester had awakened to find that she had overslept. Even the maid who'd come in to light the fire had not disturbed her slumber.

Her conscience told her that she should get out of bed, but the certainty that Isabella would still be lounging in hers persuaded her to ignore it. A wonderful feeling of languor overcame her as she burrowed more deeply under the covers.

Just once, she wanted to snatch a moment for herself, a break from worrying about Jeremy's troubles, and the rebellion about which she could do nothing. With her Aunt Mayfield on the way, Hester knew how precious her seconds of freedom were, and with St. Mars exerting himself on Jeremy's behalf, she could afford to indulge in a few minutes of drowsy bliss.

The way St. Mars had flirted with her had made her heart skip with joy. She had floated up the stairs to her room without her feet once touching the ground. His words had caught her completely by surprise, but on this occasion she had refused to be confused by his meaning. She had not persuaded herself, as she had always done before, that he must have meant something quite different from what she would have understood if he had addressed his remarks to any other woman.

He *had* been flirting with her. And intentionally, too, which meant that he found her at least moderately attractive and did not mind if she knew it. But why he should want her to be aware of this, when he could not wish for any result to come from his flirting, still had her a bit confused.

She had pondered this question before dropping off to sleep, but the memory of how he had looked at her had been too intriguing to permit any conclusion to be reached that night. The best she had managed was that gentlemen enjoyed flirting as much as ladies did, and since St. Mars had been deprived of the company of ladies of his rank for several months, he must miss the play that came with their companionship.

Hester could not be persuaded that his aim had been anything but amusement, and for that ounce of good sense she thanked the Lord. It would be difficult enough to relinquish St. Mars to the lady he would wed someday without having to end a serious flirtation. But for this morning, at least, she would hug last night's pleasure to her as the most delicious experience of her life.

She wondered whether St. Mars would continue his behaviour, and how she should react if he did. But since this question threatened to overshadow her current happiness, she pushed it aside. She would comport herself the same way she always had towards St. Mars—as his friend— for, in spite of the change in his manner, that was what she was and always would be. She was lucky to be that much.

With this decision made, she spent the next half-hour indulging in daydreams about herself and St. Mars that bore no earthly resemblance to resolution. She did not rise from her bed until footsteps outside her door informed her that Isabella had awakened and was calling for her morning chocolate.

With a sigh, Hester forced herself to get up, washed her hands and face in the basin, dressed, and brushed her hair into a tidy coiffure, before seeking her cousin's room.

She found Isabella sitting up in bed, sipping the sage ale the doctor had prescribed to strengthen her womb, and discussing with her maid which gown she would wear. Now that her belly had begun to swell, she no longer admitted gentlemen to her chamber to watch her toilette, though her breasts would probably have distracted them from noticing the bulge at her waist. Isabella's breasts had always been large, but recently they had swollen to an amazing size.

By way of greeting, she complained of them to Hester and asked if they would always remain that tender and swollen. Hester made soothing noises, preparing to turn the conversation to the idea of her cousin's portrait being painted, when a brief knock was followed by Harrowby's bursting through the door.

His haste startled Isabella, who produced a little shriek. Her husband had not yet dressed, but had covered himself in a glorious banyan of ruby silk embellished with gold thread. His close-shaved scalp was still covered by a cap. Hester would have immediately left the chamber with Isabella's maid, had he not gestured for her to remain.

"Have you heard?" he asked in a breathless voice. "Philippe just brought me the ghastly news. He heard it from Rufus, who got it from one of Burlington's footmen. The Earl of Scarsdale was arrested this morning! Taken by a Messenger from his own bed in Duke Street— before he'd even had his morning chocolate. Taken from his own bed!" he repeated, horror filling his eyes. "If I had not received the news from Philippe, I should never have believed it! And before he had even broken his fast!"

Hester couldn't tell whether it was the invasion of Lord Scarsdale's bedchamber or the early hour of his arrest that Harrowby had found more shocking.

"Did they carry him to the Tower, too?" Isabella inched up higher in bed, clutching her ale to her breast, as if someone might attempt to snatch it from her. "It must be getting very crowded."

Pacing at the foot of her bed, Harrowby shook his capped head. Today was a shaving day, and a thin stubble coated his chin.

"Not to the Tower." He added gloomily, "*Yet*. They say he's been taken to a house in Charles Street. But make no mistake, he'll be guarded well! Since Sir William Wyndham escaped, the Messengers will be taking no chances. A pretty penny they have placed on Wyndham's head, too. A thousand pounds!"

"Maybe Lord Scarsdale will try to kill himself," Isabella said with an anticipatory shiver.

"What?" her husband said. "Oh, you must be thinking of Edward Harley. I very much doubt it, my love. Just because Mr. Harley stuck himself with a knife is no reason to believe that all the others will. They cannot all be lost to the fate of their souls. They may be Jacobites, but most of them are still Christians. Besides, Lord Scarsdale is an earl, so think of all he stands to lose."

Harrowby came to a tottering stop and peered fearfully round a bedpost at his wife. "What worries me, my dear, is that I doubt that all of them have even given aid to the rebels."

Hester gave a start. "The government must surely have reason to believe they have, if it's taking them into custody!" Then she recalled the error they had made in Jeremy's case, and she was not so certain. But nothing could be gained by increasing Harrowby's consternation, so she did not share this thought.

He shrugged, refusing her comfort. "Oh, you know— 'acting on information' —that sort of thing. I believe they are merely taking no chances. Ever since that plot at Bath was discovered, they've been jumping at every squeak. Troops are being shifted from York to Bristol in case the Pretender tries to land there, but he could be anywhere! James has his supporters throughout the length and breadth of the kingdom. That Scottish fellow—what's his name? The one that Montrose says is nothing better than a thief—Robert Roy, that's it— even *he* has joined the Pretender's side."

Hester did her best to calm him. "I am certain his Majesty has matters well in hand."

He gave a mirthless laugh. "But who will he suspect next, eh? Point is—what I want you to do—in case they come for me—is go immediately and ask the King for an audience. I mean you, Isabella! But take Mrs. Kean with you, and let her do all the talking. All you have to do is look pretty, my love, but take care not to cry too much. From what I hear, his Majesty is not easily moved by tears."

"I am certain you have no reason to fear arrest, my lord," Hester protested. "But if the worst should happen, what would you wish me to say?"

He scowled. "I think that should be fairly obvious, Mrs. Kean! Tell him what a faithful subject I've always been. Swear that I've never taken the slightest notice of James Stuart or his rights. I should like to think his Royal Highness would put in a kind word for me, but as wild as he is, who knows? He might do it for you, my dear," he said glumly to Isabella, "but as much as the King hates his son, I doubt if it would help."

Harrowby sighed and turned to say testily to Hester, "If he asks you any questions, I shall expect you to know what to say."

Hester wished she could assure him of his safety. It seemed extremely unlikely that Harrowby would ever be arrested, for to the best of her knowledge he had never flirted with the Jacobite cause. It did not seem reasonable either to suppose that King George would offend someone as powerful as the Earl of Hawkhurst without solid proof. But Jeremy had been gaoled, and for no better reason than that someone had sent the authorities an anonymous accusation.

She promised to help Isabella petition the King, if the unhappy event should ever occur.

She waited until Harrowby had dragged himself to his chamber to receive his barber before broaching the subject of Isabella's portrait. Her cousin did not immediately seize upon the idea, for she doubted it would amuse her to sit still for so long. With her confinement looming, she was reluctant to try anything that seemed the least bit like retirement.

The arrival of Lord Kirkland and his friends later that morning proved a tremendous boon to Hester's plan. No sooner had they heard of the proposed portrait, than they urged it eagerly upon their Diana. They begged to be allowed to attend her sittings and even went so far as to offer suggestions on the way she should be portrayed, arguing volubly between a shepherdess and Venus arising from the sea. The only drawback to their enthusiasm was that they almost persuaded her to have her portrait painted by Sir Godfrey Kneller instead of Mr. Jervas, which would have defeated Hester's purpose. Fortunately, Mr. Jervas was much younger than Sir Godfrey, which appealed to Isabella. So by dinner that day, Hester had been given leave to ask Harrowby for his permission to engage the younger painter.

He gave it absently, when seated with the ladies at the board, adding only to Isabella, "Whatever you do, my love, if you must speak to his Majesty on my behalf, do *not* take your mother with you. I am certain it would be fatal if you did!"

As soon as the meal was concluded, Hester sat at her desk and penned Mr. Jervas a letter, asking when Lady Hawkhurst could come for an appointment. She received an immediate reply, inviting the countess to visit his studio at Cleveland Court on Tuesday morning, at her earliest convenience.

On Sunday, Harrowby proposed that they attend the service at the Chapel Royal at St. James's, to demonstrate their loyalty to the King. When the prayer was said for his Majesty's welfare, Harrowby prayed in a firm, carrying voice, and he maintained this volume throughout the prayers for the success of his Majesty's troops.

At the Palace, they learned that Lady Katherine, Sir William Wyndham's lady, had come from Somersetshire to support her husband. General Wade was gone to the Bath to suppress the rebellion in the West. And in Scotland, Lord Burleigh, who had been taken prisoner with two Jacobite chiefs, had escaped his captors by dressing in his sister's clothes.

Monday brought cold wind and rain. By Tuesday, after two days' boredom, Isabella was almost as eager to visit Mr. Jervas as Hester was. The artist's studio was only a short distance away. Hester would have suggested walking, but Piccadilly was deep in mud, and in her interesting condition Isabella could risk neither a chill nor a fall. She was bundled into a chair, and with the aid of Hester, two footmen, and two liveried chairmen, she was soon set down before the door to Cleveland Court.

Just northwest of the Palace gate, Cleveland Court had been built on the site of the townhouse of the Earls of Berkshire. At the Restoration, Charles II had bestowed it upon his mistress, Lady Castlemaine, when making her Duchess of Cleveland, from which title the house had derived its name. The current building, which was old and cavernous, could be entered by a central courtyard.

As the chairmen gently set Isabella down, one of the footmen pulled upon the bell. She had barely emerged from the chair when the creaking of hinges announced the opening of the door. A servant ushered the ladies within and with a deep bow offered to announce them to his master, who was already at work in his studio.

He showed them into a vast, draughty room with very little in the way of furnishings. Tall mullioned windows gazed out upon a grey day, but with no curtains to obscure them, they permitted a significant amount of light to spread through the room. Leaning against two walls were stacks of large canvases, turned on their edges. A half dozen or so sat propped on easels at which young students worked with their oils.

Giving them instruction and standing with a paintbrush in his hand, was a man of about forty years of age, with a sloping forehead, clear deep-set eyes, and a jutting nose. Thinning hair, cut short, covered his scalp with tight curls.

The moment he perceived his visitors, Mr. Jervas put down his brush and hurried over to greet them, stopping before Isabella to perform a deep bow with a hand held over his heart.

"Lady Hawkhurst, you honour me with your patronage. Surely all of England has heard of your astounding beauty."

This flattery made Isabella laugh. Tossing her curls, she offered him her hand to clasp, but he regretfully demurred, apologizing for the paint on his fingers which he feared would sully hers. With a sweeping gesture, he indicated his students who were filling in the backgrounds of his pieces in progress, and apologized again for the strong pervading smell of mixing paint.

He offered to take her round his studio, so she could see the range of portraits he was in the midst of executing. Isabella took his elbow, and together they strolled from one easel to the next, while Hester followed in their wake.

After gazing at the third and fourth portraits, Hester began to notice a similarity in their subjects' features. All of the ladies Mr. Jervas had painted resembled the same species of curious bird, something along the lines of a bright-eyed robin. She doubted she would be able to distinguish any of the sitters if she encountered them on the street, the faces in their portraits were so much alike. Seeing this, she suffered a twinge of conscience, for Isabella could afford the best for her likeness. But Hester eased her regret with the reminder that it was St. Mars's fortune that would pay for the work, and that Jeremy's troubles were vastly more important than Isabella's posterity.

Mr. Jervas asked Isabella whether she had given any thought to the pose she would like or to a particular composition. As she was responding, Hester's eye was captured by a singular painting propped against the wall. Leaving the others to discuss the merits of various poses, she walked over to get a closer look.

Though unfinished, the picture of the Virgin Mary had a depth of feeling the other paintings lacked. She had begun to wonder if Mr. Jervas had a secret religious bent when he appeared beside her and said, "That was painted by one of my students. Perhaps you have heard of him? Mr. Alexander Pope? He is a poet, but I have told him that he would make a very fine painter as well."

Hester's heart gave an eager skip. This was exactly the opening she had been hoping for. "Oh, yes, I have heard of Mr. Pope, We were all diverted by his *Rape of the Lock*. I understand he lives here with you?"

"Not at the moment, I'm afraid." Mr. Jervas shook his head. Then, glancing over his shoulder, he caught sight of Isabella, distracting his students, and indicated with a sweep of his hand that they should rejoin her. As they moved towards her, he said in a low voice, "You may not be aware, but dear Pope is a Papist—not the least bit political, I assure you! He was forced to leave London, of course, so he decided to take advantage of his absence to journey to the Bath. I'm afraid his health is never very robust. But I received word from him only yesterday. He's had to cut his trip short and should be on his way to Binfield by now."

The excitement Hester had felt began to deflate. "Do you expect him in London any time soon?" She was afraid she had arranged all this subterfuge for nothing.

Mr. Jervas shrugged, his rather thick neck and sloping shoulders almost concealing the gesture. "Who can say?" He sighed. "I hope it will not be long before he can reside safely in town again."

They had reached Isabella now and the talk at once returned to her sittings, how often they should be and when she should start. Predictably, Isabella wished to be painted as a shepherdess. Since a portrait of Lady Mary, made in the same guise, had been the topic of much discussion at Court earlier that year, Hester hoped this would give her a reason to introduce that lady into the conversation.

But no further opportunity presented itself, and she had to leave

Mr. Jervas's studio frustrated by the wait. Isabella's first sitting would not take place until Friday, by which time her mother surely would have arrived. And there was no way of predicting the many ways Mrs. Mayfield would hamper Hester's activities.

That afternoon brought Hester a different kind of surprise. She was upstairs with Harrowby and Isabella, inspecting St. Mars's old nursery to see what changes should be made for the heir. Hester had suggested the refurnishing as a means of taking Harrowby's mind off his fears of imminent arrest, since his obsessive moping had begun to have a damaging effect on Isabella's moods. It would not be wise to let the expectant mother be oppressed by negative thoughts.

They were discussing new window curtains when she spied the footman Will beckoning to her from the adjoining room. Evidently Will had a secret to impart. Between his beckoning gestures, he darted in and out of sight, clearly trying to avoid his master's eye.

With an anxious pulse starting up in her throat, Hester made a hasty excuse for leaving the others and joined him in the next room.

"What is it, Will?" she whispered. "Has my brother come to visit?" She had begged all the footmen to alert her privately if Jeremy turned up.

"It's not your brother, Mrs. Kean. But there is a person downstairs who's asking to see you. He says he knows you, but I didn't think you'd want me to announce him all the same."

Will's manner was more hesitant than usual, which alerted Hester to his doubts about the visitor. She surmised that there was something about him that Harrowby would not like.

"He says his name is Tubbs. That's all he said, ma'am. Just 'Tubbs.'"

Hester's mind froze in astonishment. Then, before Will could offer to send the man packing, as he appeared eager to do, she said, "Thank you. Yes, I will see him. You did very right in coming to me quietly. Have you left him downstairs in the antechamber? I shall speak to him there."

Fortunately, no one else was in the small, square room where Harrowby's uninvited visitors and supplicants waited to get an audience with the earl. Hester found Mr. Tubbs sitting there, uneasily alone, and bundled up in a moth-eaten cloak with an equally disreputable felt hat in his hands. He jumped nervously to his feet at her entrance, clutching the brim of his hat with desperate fingers and making odd growling noises, which she took to be a form of greeting.

Hester was not at all happy to see him at Hawkhurst House, certain as she was that Harrowby would be tiresome, at least, about his visit—possibly furious, if he ever he found out. But she found she could not purposely be unkind to any fellow creature.

She returned Tubbs's greeting, if such it was, and asked him cordially whether he had brought her a message from her brother, for she could think of no other reason for his coming.

Her question sent him into fits of embarrassment. His face and neck turned red. He shuffled his much scuffed shoes, and his growls became even more unintelligible, to the point that she was moved to pity. Taking a chair herself, she begged him please to sit.

As he did, she said, in as encouraging a voice as she could muster, "Very well, if you have not come with a message from my brother, then I assume that your business is with me." She certainly hoped it was, and not that he had come wishing to meet her cousins again. She had not forgotten Mr. Curry's wish to publish something purportedly by Isabella. "Why don't you tell me what it is, and I will see if I can help?"

Her receptive attitude had a soothing effect on his more grievous habits. He sat down next to her on a gilded chair and cleared his throat, before mumbling, "Came to hear about Blue Satan. Want to write it—y-your abduction, that is."

Taking a few seconds to absorb this, Hester's first reaction was irritation. She thought she had made it perfectly clear that she had no intention of making that episode public. Besides not wishing to have her virtue discussed—which it would be when people speculated on whether a rape had occurred—she did not want to risk saying anything that might give away St. Mars's identity.

She was about to repeat her refusal, when she was halted by the desperate look on Mr. Tubbs's face.

Her irked expression had alerted him to the answer she meant to make, for tears sprang readily to his eyes. His forehead beaded with sweat, and his fists clenched so tightly that his knuckles showed white.

Concern for a fellow human warred with Hester's innate reserve. She felt a deep sense of misgiving, but forced herself to smile. "I should like to be of assistance to you, Mr. Tubbs, but there is simply so little to tell. Please tell me why you are so eager to write about my adventure, and I will see if there is anything I can do."

He swallowed the desperate plea she could see forming on his lips and wiped his streaming brow upon his sleeve.

Hester knew she should invite him to remove his cloak, but she could not allow him to remain long. Thinking of her cousins in need of her assistance upstairs, she was about to put him off when he blurted, "People like to read about them—highwaymen. Thought if I wrote a piece on Blue Satan, might be able to make a bit of money."

She could not help feeling sorry for him. She knew something of what it was to be penniless, which was why she was grateful to Isabella, even if her dignity was often offended by the duties of her dependent position. She wanted to help him, but thought there must be a different way.

"I truly have so little to tell that you would do much better making up a story out of whole cloth. Why don't you do that instead? Using another name than mine, of course?"

Painfully shy, he avoided her gaze and shook his head as if a flea had lodged in his ear. "No—can't. Work better with facts—get the particulars of a crime, so I can write it up."

Now Hester began to understand his problem. If she wanted to help Tubbs, she would have to invent a story herself. But surely she should ask St. Mars's permission before she embellished his false reputation.

"Very well, then," she said, hoping to buy some time in which to consult him. "I shall do what I can." She added hastily, "But since I am occupied with my cousins at the moment, let us agree to discuss this elsewhere. I must return upstairs, or my lord will demand to know what is keeping me. But I know your direction and, as soon as I can get leave to come, I shall send you a message appointing a time."

She had purposely referred to Harrowby in this way in the hope that Mr. Tubbs would understand the difficulties of her position. Not waiting to hear his reaction, she stood to indicate that their interview was over. When he stumbled to his feet, she could see that at least some of his despair had been allayed.

He made her a clumsy bow, which she acknowledged with the barest of nods before asking Will to show him out. As she remounted the stairs, however, a notion came to her that made her give more serious thought to a meeting with Mr. Tubbs.

If she did speak with him, she would have another opportunity to question him about Edmund Curry. She did not truly suspect Mr. Tubbs of murdering his patron. He seemed far too timid for one thing. And it was hard to imagine a motive, when clearly he was desperate for money, and Curry had, at least, supplied him with a roof over his head. In spite of Mr. Tubbs's coming here, which had taken a great deal of courage, he must know how unemployable he was. If a man as attractive and talented as Jeremy had been grateful for Curry's patronage, how much more so must Mr. Tubbs have been, in spite of any suspicion or resentment he had harboured towards his employer?

Hester found his situation somewhat comparable to her own. She had to assume that Mr. Tubbs, like her, had no other option than to work for his bread and butter and, therefore, must accept occasional mistreatment from the only patron he had.

With two motives, then—to help a fellow dependent and to further her investigation—she determined to speak to St. Mars, assuring herself that in spite of the excitement this notion caused her, there was nothing at all frivolous about her decision.

⌀

On Sunday, in his lawyer's garb, Gideon had attended Morning Prayer at St. Dunstan's. Afterwards he had explored the sprawling church, peering into its corners and examining its walls. Marble effigies lined its chapels, and the tombs of centuries of dead filled its floors. He tried to visit the crypt, but the stairs to it were locked. The sexton informed him that the crypt had been sealed up because the ceiling was caving in. This did not surprise him for the whole building emitted a crumbling air.

When there was no more to see inside, he spent an hour strolling about the streets. The first floor of the house the stranger had entered was a barber-surgeon's shop. Gideon was surprised that he had not noticed its red and white pole before now, but, like St. Dunstan's, the building seemed barely to be standing. He had hoped by studying the house to pick up some clues, and he even searched Hen and Chicken Court just past it, but he noticed nothing helpful. Some of the windows in the house had been bricked up, but since it was a common practice to fill in windows to avoid the window tax, he saw nothing sinister in that.

He decided that he should talk to Mrs. Kean again before returning to the bookstall on Monday afternoon. But Monday's rain discouraged him. Mrs. Kean did not make her morning walk, and Gideon decided it would seem suspicious for his fop to brave bad weather.

By the time he did see Mrs. Kean again, Mrs. Mayfield had arrived to complicate their plans.

In Men, we various Ruling Passions find;
In Women, two almost divide the kind;
Those, only fixed, they first or last obey,
The Love of Pleasure, and the Love of Sway.

CHAPTER XIV

Rain came again on Wednesday and with it Isabella's mother, Mrs. Mayfield.

Hester was sewing quietly by her cousin's bed when she heard a commotion so loud that it managed to penetrate the sturdy walls of Hawkhurst House. For a brief moment she thought that the worst of Harrowby's fears had come to pass and that Messengers had stormed the house. Then the harsh notes of her aunt's familiar voice rose above the hubbub and, with a sigh, Hester put down her stitching and prepared to greet her.

It was not hard to imagine the scene that must have transpired downstairs. Mrs. Mayfield would barely have set foot inside the house before calling out for Isabella, and when her daughter did not appear at once, she would have demanded to be shown to Isabella's chamber. The servants' reasonable protests that their mistress was taking a nap would have been indignantly swept aside as impertinent and intentional affronts.

By the time Hester opened the door to Isabella's bedchamber, her aunt had already reached the antechamber. She ignored Hester's greeting in a rush to embrace her daughter, sweeping past her niece in a flutter of ducape skirts, flowing ribbons, and lace cuffs.

The ensuing reunion would have touched Hester's heart, were she not all too aware of her aunt's selfish character. Mrs. Mayfield quite doted on her offspring as long as they complied with her avaricious schemes. Naturally, in marrying an earl, Isabella had fulfilled her mother's fondest wishes; however, Mrs. Mayfield had learned that she could not always rule her daughter's mind. Even so malleable a child as Isabella was capable of asserting her will now and then. There, too, was the problem of Isabella's husband, who held the purse-strings to the immense Hawkhurst fortune. He had tired of Mrs. Mayfield's machinations once, so presumably she had learned to be more careful not to offend him now. But for the near future, her position in the house was safe since she would be needed to attend the birth of the heir.

Hester would have slipped quietly from the room, but she could not afford to offend her aunt, so she stood patiently by until Mrs. Mayfield deigned to greet her.

This she did in her inimitable way, folding her arms at her waist and raking her niece up and down. "Well, Hester," she said, "you are looking mighty fine for a dependent. Not that I can say that green becomes you over much. It was a great deal prettier on my Isabella, as I recall."

Hester thanked her aunt for her frank observation and reminded her that everything naturally looked better on Isabella.

Mrs. Mayfield emitted a smug snort, but her hard smile told Hester that she did well to remember this important fact. Then in a tone more often used for commands than requests, she bid her supervise the maid's unpacking, "for I dare not trust her not to crush my gowns."

Since the maid was perfectly capable of carrying out her accustomed task with no supervision, this was clearly a flimsy pretext to remove Hester from the room and to reassert her authority. Nevertheless, Hester obeyed. Unless she wanted to pit Isabella immediately against her mother, she would have to wait for her cousin to rebel against her mother's highhandedness. Exiting the chamber with a heavy heart, Hester acknowledged that this might never happen if her aunt had benefited from her past mistakes and learned a touch of diplomacy. She only hoped she would not find herself waiting on her aunt as well as her cousin or she might never escape the house again.

For the next few days, the ladies remained close to home. Rain and cold gave them little inclination to venture out, even if the Court had tempted them with entertainment. News that the rebellion had spread into Northumberland had effectively halted all the usual amusements. Their Royal Highnesses with their households had stayed on at Kensington Palace while the King reestablished his Court at St. James's.

In spite of her tendency to criticize Hester's every act, Mrs. Mayfield's visit was at least well timed because she averted some of Isabella's boredom with news of her family. Her brother Dudley had at last become engaged to the daughter of a local squire. It was not the brilliant match Mrs. Mayfield had envisioned for her eldest son, but his landholdings would be increased by it. Hester could only pity the girl, for it was inconceivable that Dudley would make anyone a good husband, but discussion of the settlement the squire had made and the neighborhood jealousies spawned by the match filled a few otherwise empty days.

Parliament met on the sixth of October, only to be adjourned again until later that month. With more than a fortnight's recess granted, Harrowby could no longer avoid a trip to his estate in Kent. To postpone it any longer would expose him to a charge of neglecting his duties, which would not stand him in good stead with the King. Already, he had felt a certain coolness from the Court, since without military experience, he had not raised any men or rushed to fight the rebels. But at least he could be seen to be maintaining his acreage for the Crown. Accordingly, within a few days of Mrs. Mayfield's arrival, he bid his wife a nervous goodbye and set out with more than twice the usual retinue in case he should meet with the Pretender's men on the road.

By this time, Isabella and her mother had caught up with each other's news and were ready to seek more active diversion. The skies cleared, and Isabella made plans to resume her sittings with Mr. Jervas. But before she could even think of appointing a time, an announcement came from the Palace informing them that the Princess of Wales was again with child.

Not wishing to be tardy with their congratulations, and eager for the kind of gossip that only the Court could provide, Isabella and her mother set out on a crisp afternoon for a visit to Kensington. Fortunately, Hester was excluded from the trip, and she learned of their intentions in time to write St. Mars a note, asking him to meet her that day at the New Exchange in the Strand.

The weather had frustrated Gideon's plans, too. Not that he was the least bit daunted by the threat of rain, but the foppish character he had assumed would be unlikely to undertake a shopping expedition under inclement conditions, no matter how charming the shopkeeper. Neither had Gideon expected Mrs. Kean to take her morning walk, so, although he had managed to spend two afternoons at the bookstall, he had suffered from several days of indolence, too. Thus, in addition to the pleasure he received on reading her summons came an intense measure of relief.

He dressed in his fop's clothes, laid paint and patches on thick to disguise his face, and, covering his shoulders with a fur-lined cloak against the increasing chill, took a wherry to Savoy Stairs from where a short walk soon conveyed him into the Strand. At the entrance to the Exchange, he was taunted by a group of loitering soldiers who called after him, "French fop!"

His answering laugh must have surprised them, but looking forward to seeing Mrs. Kean, he did not bother to turn around.

Her choice for an assignation was wise because the New Exchange was no longer the fashionable promenade it had been even ten years ago. Its shops were less likely now to be frequented by the people who knew them. The century-old, Gothic-style building was stained black with soot, which lent its stone galleries an unwholesome look, and the very quantity of its shops, numbering close to a hundred, gave the most particular shoppers reason to doubt their quality.

Gideon made his way upstairs and along one of the two galleries, crowded with females and the occasional fop. Ignoring the pretty shop-girls' calls, he wove through the press of people, until he came to the bookseller's shop Mrs. Kean had appointed. When he caught no sight of her, he bought a news-sheet and, finding a corner in which to wait, perused it for news.

The reports that had reached London had cast an even darker pall over his days of inactivity. The rebels had seized Perth, where the Earl of Mar had proclaimed James King of Scotland. Mar had summoned the Scottish nobility and gentry to appear with men at arms under the standard of James VIII, but without the presence of James himself, Gideon wondered how long Mar would be able to hold onto his troops. Winter was approaching fast, and from all accounts, James still remained at Bar-le-Duc. The news-sheets reported that the French would soon ask the Duke of Lorraine to expel him from his dominions. Whether James's illness, the weather, or the effectiveness of Mr. Walpole's spies was preventing him from joining his men across the Channel, precious time was being lost.

The fact that Mar had proclaimed James King of Scotland only and not the whole of Great Britain seemed significant to Gideon. Perhaps Mar believed that reclaiming Scotland for James would be not only possible, but relatively easy. Discontent across the border over the union with England was certainly widespread, yet none of the West Highlanders had joined the rebellion except the Macdonalds and the MacGregors. The Campbells had already submitted themselves to George.

But now Jacobites in the north of England had risen, too, and King George would be merciless in suppressing the rebellion. He had sent three regiments of dragoons to deal with the newest uprising, and another cache of rebel arms had been seized at Bath. Gideon knew how essential those arms were to the English effort. The English rebels were much fewer in number, too. They would need to converge with Mar's army before government troops caught up with them or their chance of success would be slight.

It seemed that all of Gideon's worst fears had come to pass. The rebellion seemed doomed to failure before its start. Another man might have congratulated himself on escaping his involvement, but Gideon could not watch his father's cause or his father's friends being crushed without a painful sense of guilt.

If he had not been outlawed . . . . If he still had charge of his father's men . . . .

But it was useless to speculate on what he might have done if he had occupied his rightful place. If nothing else, perhaps he should be grateful that he would not have to make such a fateful decision.

"My lord?" The voice of Mrs. Kean roused him, and he started up to find her peering at him from beneath a hooded cloak. Her cheeks were pink with exercise, and her grey eyes were bright with laughter she could not hide.

For a moment Gideon was puzzled by her amusement. Then he remembered how many patches he had affixed to his face, and a chuckle burst from him.

No one else had noticed their greeting. The crush of customers was so noisy and the people so intent on their own business that, Gideon realized, they might say anything they wished and not worry about being overheard.

He bowed with a flourish. "I suppose you find my face ridiculous. But, if you will *persist* in endangering my very life with these public meetings, I can hardly be blamed for the image I am forced to assume."

"Indeed, my lord," she said, accepting his right arm, "it was only because I knew that you would take the most *extreme* measures that I felt secure in naming such a place."

"It was truly that, and not simply a desire to see me make a complete ass of myself?"

She loosed an unguarded giggle, which sent a lightening-bolt through him. "How could you accuse me of such insensitivity, when I have anguished over your safety to the point of making a nuisance of *my*self?"

"Ah, but *that* you could never do, my dear Mrs. Kean! Speaking of which, may I ask to what circumstance I owe the pleasure of meeting you today?"

She was about to answer him, when a shop-girl tried to interest them in her wares. Pretty, as they all were, she bobbed a coy curtsy at him and said, "Does not your lady want hoods? Scarves? Fine silk stockings?"

Mrs. Kean gave a quick shake of her head and tried to hasten past.

Gideon sensed her discomfort. An evil imp prompted him to pull her back. "Yes, my dove. Wouldn't you care to see some green silk stockings?"

The embarrassment that leapt to her face made him want to laugh, but he maintained his pose of the attentive husband while she struggled with a succession of contradictory emotions, ranging from surprise, to amusement and reproach.

She soon regained her poise sufficiently to smile and move past the shop-girl, saying with a dimple, "I do not think you need carry out your masquerade to that extent, my lord. If you did, we should spend all our time here fending off tradesmen and never accomplish our business."

"I was merely trying to blend in. If you did not wish us to be taken for husband and wife, you should have asked me to meet you on the lower floor."

For a moment, he thought he had angered her, for her cheeks looked as if she might explode. Then she burst into an indignant laugh. "You know very well what the reputation of the downstairs gallery is, sir!"

"As an assignation place? Well, if this is not an assignation, Mrs. Kean, I must humbly beg your pardon."

Her eyes twinkled as she strove not to smile. "You persist in teasing me. And with a complete lack of shame! I wonder how you can do it."

"But it gives me such pleasure to see you blush, I fear I cannot help myself."

"Aha!" She gave a triumphant lift of her head. "Now I know you are funning, for I never do blush! I lack the complexion for it."

"I usually find that the complexion is of little consequence. Rosy cheeks are merely an outward manifestation of an inner sensation."

"But how can you tell there is an inner sensation if there *is* no outward sign?"

"I did not say there was none. Only that blushing was but one. Would you like me to describe the others?"

At that her cheeks did fill with pink, contradicting her assertion. Her confusion was so plain that, in spite of his amusement, he almost took pity on her before she said, "Perhaps, instead, we should discuss my brother's business before I have to go."

He *had* pushed her too far, but this time he did not apologize. She did not seem angry—but rather unable to manage her confusion. They would have to talk about her brother's troubles, of course, but Gideon hated for their banter to end.

His disappointment made him grimace. "Is your time still so

constricted then? You have not told me how you managed to get away."

She informed him of her aunt's arrival and the reason for her escape today. The mere thought of Mrs. Mayfield was enough to raise Gideon's hackles. That Mrs. Kean should have to cater to that trollop! His father had tried to tell him that was what Mrs. Mayfield was, but in his stubbornness, he had refused to listen.

The news that Mrs. Mayfield and Isabella had gone to pay their respects to the Princess of Wales, however, meant that Mrs. Kean had much more time than she had allowed. He would permit her to change the subject, but he would not let her put him off entirely.

"Sir, will you buy a fine sword knot?"

Ignoring another shop-girl, Gideon said, "If we don't find a quieter place to talk, I fear we'll be interrupted by every girl in the Exchange."

"That's because you look so very fine." Mrs. Kean was pressing her lips tightly together to keep from grinning. "You must be wearing at least half the goods they sell."

Her mischief made him halt in his tracks. She had never acted this boldly with him before. His pulse quickening, he said, "If we were not in view of most of London, Mrs. Kean, I should be tempted to make you pay dearly for that thrust."

When she chuckled by way of reply, he took her firmly by the elbow and steered her up to a counter. Speaking over her gasped protest, he told the merchant to bring them a selection of fans with India paint.

When the man had stepped away to fetch them, he said, "We shall be less bothered if we stand in one place. It *may* be the extraordinary taste of my clothing, but I assume I am a target for a different reason. There are not many gentlemen present, and those who are, are undoubtedly on errands. In other words, they *intend* to buy something, while nine out of ten of your fair sex are merely idling away their time. I believe the shopkeepers call them 'No Customers.'"

Hester could hardly deny it, when pieces in the *Spectator* and even songs were written about these women, and she had often witnessed their behaviour herself. They would ask to see a merchant's wares until nearly every item in the shop had been displaced, then find something deficient in each and depart without purchasing a thing.

Believing that they were about to do the same, she, nevertheless, responded meekly, "Yes, my lord."

A twitch of his lips told her that he knew she was not as meek as she would have him believe. While the merchant was gathering his wares to show them, Hester used the time to tell St. Mars about her visit to Mr. Jervas's studio.

"Unfortunately, Mr. Pope is out of the city. He's a Papist, so no one can say when he'll return. I would try to ask Mr. Jervas if he knew how Lady Mary's manuscript came into Mr. Curry's hands, but now that my aunt is here, she plans to accompany Isabella to her sittings. At least, I will have a few hours of freedom when they go."

"Why don't you use one of them to call on Lady Mary yourself?"

Hester looked anxiously into his face. "I have never been presented to the lady. Do you think I could approach her?"

"Of course. If you prefer, you can pretend to be on an errand for Isabella, if you're afraid Lady Mary might not receive you. But, provided she is not already engaged, I doubt she would refuse to see you."

She sighed, but she knew he was right. Even if Lady Mary did prove to be haughty or proud, the very least Hester could do as Jeremy's sister was to try.

She told St. Mars about Mr. Tubbs's visit and his surprising request. "I wondered if you would mind terribly if I spun him a false tale about my encounter with Blue Satan. I do not know how else to win his confidence in order to question him, and he must know much more about Mr. Curry than he has been willing to say. Certainly more than Jeremy does."

A frown had darkened St. Mars's face. Thinking she'd offended him, she was about to retract her request, when he said, "I don't like the thought of your meeting him alone. What if he turns out to be the murderer?"

"Oh, we shall not be alone! I'll ask Jeremy to be there as well."

They were interrupted by the shopkeeper, who returned with his wares and laid them carefully on the counter. He proceeded to unfold every fan, tell them where it was made, and point out its unique design. Hester found herself exclaiming over the delicate creations of chicken skin, each painted with an exquisite pastoral scene, but she quickly reminded herself that she was a "No Customer" and mustn't give the poor merchant false hopes. She was relieved when St. Mars told him to leave them alone so they could study the fans at their leisure.

He unfolded one and held it up to her face to see how well it became her. This supposed, of course, that she would use the fan to flirt with instead of to cool herself.

Reverting to the subject they had been discussing, he said, "If your brother will be with you, I have no objections, just as long as you don't saddle my reputation with any additional crimes."

"But that is precisely one of my motives—to prevent Mr. Tubbs from inventing a worse lie himself. I only hope I can compose a story that's sufficiently romantic for his purpose."

His gaze, which had been on the fan, shifted quickly to meet hers. The gleam in his eyes made Hester swallow, as a smile curved his lips.

"What a pity I shan't be there to hear it!" Taking mercy on her briefly, he set the fan down and, unfolding another, held it up the way he had done the first. He gave the impression that there was no greater object in his mind than seeing how well the fan became her.

His scrutiny made her feel uncomfortably warm.

"But you have not asked me what I've discovered," he said with a hint of reproach.

She started. "Have you? Have you already found something out?"

Her eagerness wiped a budding grin from his face. Contrite, he said, "I only wish it were more. I have at least satisfied myself that Sally had no pecuniary motive for killing her husband, and that if she had another, your brother was entirely unaware of it."

Hester bridled, but he forestalled her protests. "I know, you had already assured me, but I had to make certain that your affection for your brother was not blinding you to a fairly common occurrence. If it makes you feel better, I do not believe Sally had any role in her husband's murder."

Hester had to acknowledge the reasonableness of his doubts. She smoothed her ruffled feathers, but had to hide her disappointment. She had hoped he had discovered something of more use.

Then he told her about the man he and Tom had followed to Ozinda's Coffee House, and the nervous customer who had asked to see Mr.

Curry's private store, and her excitement returned.

"You think that Mr. Curry *was* selling Jacobite literature?"

"It is possible, but I can't be sure that the Jacobite we followed has anything to do with the Bell and Bible. It may be just a coincidence that he had business across from the shop. Tom says he will know him again if he sees him, so we will keep a watch."

Hester hated to be skeptical about his discoveries, but had to say, "When Jeremy and Mr. Curry were released from gaol, I remember Jeremy said that Mr. Curry never did publish political tracts. And Sally seemed certain that he did not."

St. Mars smiled and shrugged. "If he were selling something treasonous, it's unlikely he would have told them."

She nodded. "And Sally found a great deal more money in his house than she knew he had."

"Well, there's only one way to uncover where the money came from. We'll have to get into the bookstall and search for Curry's hiding place. That whole area of London is riddled with underground rooms and passages. I looked inside St. Dunstan's to see if I could reach Curry's cellar from the crypt, but the crypt has been closed for years. It's so ancient, its ceilings are crumbling."

"You believe Mr. Curry's private store is under the floor?"

"I can't believe it would be anywhere else." St. Mars unfolded another fan, this one made in France. Its carved ivory sticks were from India, and the scene painted on it was of a lady with her swain in a garden, all in delicate pinks, blues, and greens.

St. Mars gave a satisfied smile. "I think this will be the very one." He held it up to her head and studied its effect.

"It *is* very beautiful," Hester agreed. But, as they were only pretending to buy a fan, she did not allow St. Mars to divert her. "But you think we will find treasonous literature, if we look under the floor?"

"That's the most obvious guess, but it's only one possibility. We'll never know until I can gain entrance to the bookstall. And I should hate to break it open to find out."

Hester pondered this problem, but her mind was too distracted by St. Mars's movements. Not content with studying her until her cheeks grew quite warm, he had now progressed to fanning her. She wondered if he had noticed any of those "outward manifestations" he had spoken so teasingly about.

"I'll see if Jeremy can help me get the key," she said, "but I don't know what to say to keep him from accompanying me."

"Just see if you can. If all else fails, you can tell *him* to look beneath the floor. If there is illegal literature in the shop, it should be burned anyway before the authorities do find it. You might ask Mrs. Sally if the Messengers took up the floorboards when they searched."

Hester's heart gave a skip. "You don't think she knew about her husband's secret store?"

St. Mars shook his head. "I could swear she did not. She was completely flummoxed by the customer's request. I think it frightened her, as if it were one more trap just waiting to close over her head."

Finally, he stopped examining Hester's eyes over the fan. He folded the last one and set it aside. "There is one thing more. Sally is afraid of something that has nothing to do with Curry's secret store. I think the beadle may have threatened your brother again. She seems terrified to be seen with him."

"Jeremy wrote me something to that effect, but not how serious it was."

"I doubt she has told him—probably so he will not do anything to provoke further enmity. Your brother has not seemed aware of any threat the times that I have seen him."

"Oh, you *have* seen him?" Hester did not know why, but she was terribly pleased.

St. Mars smiled and nodded. "Perhaps I should have told you." He did not say what he thought of her brother, but his smile was warm. It was enough.

The owner of the shop came over to ask if they had chosen a fan.

Hester started to express her regrets, but St. Mars spoke first. "Yes, this one. With the ivory from India and the garden scene."

It was the fan he had said would suit her best. If not, Hester would have wondered if he intended it for someone else. Shocked and dismayed, she could not say anything to prevent him from buying it until the merchant left them to wrap it.

"I cannot allow you to purchase that fan, my lord!"

He laughed. "Now, how did I know that you would forbid me? You are much too predictable, my dear. Has no one ever told you that?"

"If they did, I am sure I took it as the greatest of compliments! You must not do this."

"But that would turn me into a 'No Customer,' and I must uphold the honour of my sex."

"Please think, my lord! What would my aunt say, or Isabella say, if I turned up with a fan this fine?"

Her mention of those two seemed to annoy him. He looked torn between a frown and a smile. "I am sure you will think of a credible explanation. Have you not had to cultivate a talent for lies ever since we met?"

She could see how frustrated he was by the constraints that secrecy had imposed upon their friendship. "That is nothing for you to distress yourself with, and it is quite beside the point. I cannot let you buy me such an extravagant gift. It would be improper for anyone in my situation to own such an expensive trinket."

He scowled. "Now that could be a problem. I'm afraid you'll just have to hide it."

She could not keep from laughing. "Hide such a splendid thing? What a waste!"

"You could bring it to our assignations. Then we could meet on the ground floor."

A gurgle rose up inside her, nearly making her burst. It took every shred of her character to manage a stern look, and the grin on his face told her that she had failed miserably. "I must stop you from doing this, my lord. I am grateful, but it will not do. I have already imposed upon you enough by asking for your help. How could I ever ask you again if you persist in this generosity? You would think I was asking to meet you to see what you would give me next. Or if you did not think it, at least I would fear you would."

She had finally said something to make him pause. He obviously did not like it, but he had seen the sense in her words.

He sighed. "Then I shall have to purchase it for myself. If I had known that from the beginning, I would have chosen one that went better with this suit. But it will not be too terrible, do you think?" He looked down at his foppish clothes.

His pitiful look was so ridiculous, she might have laughed, but a certain sadness stopped her. She wished she *could* have accepted St. Mars's gift. She would have treasured it more than any other of her possessions, but she knew that what she had done was correct.

The merchant brought them the fan wrapped up in paper, and St. Mars produced his coins. They left the shop and immediately fell victim to a series of shop-girls before they descended the stairs and made their way out into the Strand.

Hester had walked to the Exchange, so St. Mars accompanied her halfway back to Hawkhurst House. Since she had been obliged to refuse his gift, she could not turn down his escort, but she made him stop before they reached Covent Garden.

"It's not that I fear you will be recognized," she explained, "but that someone who knows me will wonder who my splendid escort is."

"That is two insolent thrusts from you now, Mrs. Kean, that I shall be forced to address. You should be quaking in fear of learning what form my revenge will take."

She *was* trembling, but not from fright, for his voice had conveyed a promise rather than a threat. The thought of what he might do sent a thrill down her spine, but she must not let him see what fancies she had taken into her head.

"I will promise to quake, my lord, but you must promise me something in return."

He paused and faced her, a serious question in his eyes.

"You must promise that you will never use that fan when you are wearing your blue satin cape."

He grabbed her elbows so quickly she gave a little squeak. Then, bringing his face so near that she could see the wicked gleam in his eyes, he whispered, "That makes three, my dearest, and you know what they say about three. I doubt that I can let this one pass."

His voice was so thrilling, it nearly terrified her. There was something in his gaze she had seen before—but not when it was directed at her. It was the look he had once given Isabella. There was fierceness in it, and desire.

He had frightened Isabella with that look, but Hester's heart gave an eager leap. She wanted to see where his look would take them, but then fear of a different sort claimed her. She was afraid she might have misinterpreted his expression. That it might have been made just in fun.

She would not face that disappointment, so she mustered a smile of amusement. The spell broke, and he let her go. Silently, they kept on their way until they parted at the Haymarket, each promising to send the other word when they uncovered something useful.

Before he left her, St. Mars pressed the wrapped parcel into her hands. "Please take this and hide it," he said. "I'll try not to burden you with further gifts. If anyone sees it, you can say your great-aunt Mathilda bequeathed it to you, or that you found it on the floor of a hackney— anything you like. But if Tom catches me with it, he might leave my service and I cannot risk that."

Not giving her any chance to respond, he turned and strode in the direction of the Thames.

Hester watched him until he disappeared around a corner. Then, before she turned to walk home, she raised the parcel and pressed it to her cheek.

As the last image of that troubled heap,
When Sense subsides, and Fancy sports in sleep,
(Though past the recollection of the thought)
Becomes the stuff of which our dream is wrought:
Something as dim to our internal view,
Is thus, perhaps, the cause of most we do.

CHAPTER XV

Even more restless than usual after his meeting with Mrs. Kean, Gideon set out the next day with Tom, hoping to find something new to report. Each time he saw Mrs. Kean, he left her reluctantly, but there was something new in their last meeting that he was eager to pursue.

A change had occurred in her manner. As he pondered what it was, the only conclusion he could reach was that she had seemed more confident, less shy, and much less respectful of his rank. He had always thought her modesty was one of her finest qualities, but he found that he enjoyed this new Mrs. Kean, who had treated him as her equal.

Smiling at the way she had teased him about his disguise, he strolled into the Bell and Bible, leaving Tom to watch the shop from across the street. Sally looked up when he entered, so he hastily composed his features into a haughty leer. Still dressed in black, she was serving three customers with books and pamphlets spread all over the crowded counter. Acknowledging Gideon over their heads with a distant smile and a promise to attend him shortly, she returned to her transactions.

Wedging himself in at the far end of the counter, Gideon coolly studied the other men through his raised glass. Any attempt to hide his scrutiny would have attracted more suspicion than the rudeness he displayed. One customer did seem more interested in the widow than the books he had asked to see, but the other two seemed genuine enough.

When Sally reluctantly stepped over to ask what he wished, he spared her the worst of his leers, merely indicating with a sly wink that he believed they had achieved an understanding of sorts. He asked if she had any more verses by people at Court, and when she answered no, he settled for a book of poetry by an unnamed author.

He had lingered over an hour, alternately perusing the poems and ogling Sally, when a man with a familiar face entered the bookstall.

Gideon hurriedly bent his head over his book. He had not been prepared to find an acquaintance here. But, although at the moment he could not recall where he had met the customer, he knew he had seen him before. The man was dressed like a clerk from the Temple, but Gideon could not recollect meeting any member of that profession.

He had to trust that his disguise would be sufficiently impenetrable to conceal his identity. But the shop was very small, and the stranger was near enough that he might easily see through Gideon's paint. Gideon felt the man's gaze pass over him as he took a glance about. Then he stepped to the counter and greeted Sally with an easy familiarity.

Sally seemed pleased enough to see him, but it was clear from her weary demeanour that his visit came more as a respite than a joy.

"And where is that young gallant of yours this fine morning?" the newcomer asked.

Sally jerked as if a snake had bitten her. "Gallant! I don't know who you're talking about!"

"Don't ya now? Well, the fellow I had in mind has a name that begins with a 'J.' Does that help ya t'place him?"

Sally's hands shook as she picked up a folio her last customer had left and returned it to its rail. "I wish you will not talk such nonsense, Mr. Sullivan. I have my widow's reputation to protect."

He appeared to realize that his teasing had not pleased her, for he gave her a strangely piercing look and said he was sorry if he had offended her.

So, here was the man Mrs. Kean had told him about. While Sullivan's attention was focused on Sally, Gideon surreptitiously studied his features, still convinced that he had seen them before. But their encounter must have taken place somewhere else, or under very different circumstances. He racked his brain, but no recollection came.

Even before Sally had spoken his name, Gideon had heard the lilt in his voice. Mrs. Kean had noticed it even though it was faint, and Gideon could confirm that Sullivan's inflections were Irish.

Sullivan leaned over the counter and idly perused the rails, while posing Sally a series of seemingly innocent questions. He asked her how her business was going, whether she had learned all she needed to run the shop, and if she had found any worthwhile tracts to publish. As she answered his questions, she relaxed and even grew animated when she spoke about her ideas for the bookstall. In one unguarded moment, Jeremy's name nearly slipped from her lips, but Sullivan pretended not to notice.

In a short while he took his leave, making no purchase. Ostensibly he had come in just to see how she was. But something in his air had been more purposeful than that, both in his coming and in his going, which led Gideon to suspect there was another reason for his visit than the frivolous one he'd revealed.

It frustrated him that he could not recall where he'd seen Joseph Sullivan before. He was nearly certain that it had not been in Fleet Street. He decided to ask Tom if he'd noted where Sullivan had gone, so he bid Sally an oily goodbye and left the bookstall.

He did not find Tom where he'd left him, so he strolled up and down outside the other shops in the shadow of St. Dunstan's, glancing into their windows, but taking care to be visible in case Tom returned.

Presently, Tom came striding quickly from the east along Fleet Street. At a nod from Gideon, he disappeared into the relative quiet of Falcon Court where Gideon soon joined him.

"That was him, my lord!" Tom said in an eager, careful voice. "That was the man we followed last Saturday."

Gideon raised his brows. "You're perfectly certain of that, are you?"

"I swear I am, my lord."

"Then things have suddenly become much more interesting. That was the Joseph Sullivan Mrs. Kean asked me about. Did you see where he went?"

"Yes, sir. I followed him for a little ways, but he didn't go into the barber-surgeon's shop. He went up Fleet Street and then headed up the Old Bailey. I should've stayed with him, I guess, but I thought you'd want to know."

Gideon frowned. "You did right. We shall have to watch for him again, that's all—now that we know he has a definite interest in the bookstall. And I swear his interest has nothing to do with Mrs. Curry. The curious thing is that I've seen his face before, and I'm positive it was not the other night."

"You've seen him, my lord? Where?"

"I can't recall, but with any luck it will come to me. At least we're getting somewhere. Let's head back home."

Gideon left the court first, with Tom following soon behind. When they arrived at his house, Gideon threw off his heavy wig and scrubbed the paint from his face before settling down in front of the fire. He asked Katy to bring him a large mug of beer.

Taking an occasional swig, he combed his memories, searching for a hint of Joseph Sullivan's face, but the last image of him inside the Bell and Bible kept intruding. Then, abandoning these unproductive thoughts, he reviewed what he knew.

Sullivan was a Jacobite. Gideon was certain of that because of his late night visit to Ozinda's coffee house and the way he had fled from the authorities. Not that an innocent man would not have run, but with the rebellion underway, only a dedicated Jacobite would have stopped at Ozinda's now. Most Tories who did not want to risk suspicion of treason had gone to ground. They avoided assembling in places that the authorities might be watching.

Sullivan's movements were suspicious, too. He had carried a bundle into the barber's shop under cover of night, and left it without so much as lighting a candle. And he had braved the nighttime streets without hiring a linkboy to light his way. Clearly, he had not wanted to be seen going in or out of the shop, so it was safe to assume he was up to something illegal at the very least.

According to Jeremy Kean, he kept a frequent eye on Curry's bookstall, visiting it often but seldom making any purchase. This made Gideon suspect that something in the bookstall itself held an attraction for him.

Gideon's mind returned to the customer he had seen the previous week, the man who had inquired about Curry's private stock. What if that stock consisted of treasonable material, pamphlets critical of the Crown, or of the government for supporting the usurper George? What if Joseph Sullivan had brought the treasonous literature to the shop so that Curry could spread it for him?

As a theory, it was plausible. Curry's bookstall would have been of valuable help in spreading treasonous ideas, but Gideon would have to search under the floor of the shop to see if it was true.

The fire in his grate had warmed him and made him sleepy. He closed his eyes on the acknowledgement that he might never have thought of searching beneath the floor of the shop if he had not seen the trap in the hall at Westbrook Place. It was cut so perfectly into the floor that no one could see that a door was there. As he started to doze, beneath his eyelids, Gideon again saw Fanny's servant Patrick, using a prise to lift the door, then slowly lowering it over his head.

Then, in that second before sleep came, Gideon recalled where he had seen Joseph Sullivan before—in the hall at Westbrook Place, as he'd moved out of the shadows.

Abruptly Gideon sat up in his chair, his eyes wide open. The scene was clear in his mind. The Irishman who called himself Joseph Sullivan was most certainly conspiring with the Jacobites, and what was even more intriguing was that the man was a Roman Catholic priest.

∅

Hester would have been comforted if she had known that her meeting with St. Mars had resulted in such success. As it was, at the moment she could only feel guilty that while she had been flirting outrageously with St. Mars, poor Jeremy was suffering a deep affliction.

She had taken the very first opportunity—the day of Isabella's next sitting—to appoint a meeting with him and Mr. Tubbs, and she had floated from Piccadilly to Holborn on a sea of daydreams, only to be dashed on the rocks at the first glimpse of her brother's face.

Misery was written into every line of Jeremy's usually sunny countenance. The uncertainty and frustration of his situation with Sally had taken their toll. Perhaps Mr. Simpkins's threats had frightened her brother, too, but Hester did not want to question Jeremy in front of Mr. Tubbs. The best she could do until they were alone was to squeeze his hand and offer him a sympathetic look.

Since she had written Jeremy a note explaining the reason for their meeting, at least he was prepared for that additional disappointment. Hester had recalled that Jeremy had also expressed a wish to write about her adventure, so she felt guilty, too, for giving the story to Mr. Tubbs instead. She detected no hurt feelings in her brother's manner, though. Either his characteristic generosity had overcome his own self-interest, as usual, or he was too distressed about Sally to care much about anything else.

They sat at the simple table in Jeremy's chamber at the Pewter Platter Inn. Although a fire burned in the grate, Hester could not remove her cloak or gloves. The room was distressingly cold, and it was not even November yet. She could only imagine how miserable it would be in another two months.

They started by agreeing to use no names in the story. Harrowby and Isabella would figure in it simply as a "great lord and his lady." Hester would be called the "lady-in-waiting." It would be titled, *A Full, True and Particular Relation of the Abduction of a Young Lady by the Highwayman Blue Satan, Being an Account of a Merry Prank by that Great Robber of England.*

"Do you think Mrs. Curry will publish it?" Hester asked the two men.

Mr. Tubbs did not answer, but turned to Jeremy for his opinion.

Jeremy responded with a sigh, "I cannot speak for Mrs. Curry, Tubbs. I am not in her confidence. I should think she would wish to sell it, for that kind of story always sells well. But if she will not, I do not doubt you could sell it to Mr. Dicey in Aldermary Churchyard. His chapbooks are generally successful."

Hester lowered her gaze. She knew Mr. Dicey's chapbooks well. For the story she was about to relate, she had heavily borrowed from the one she had read about the highwayman Captain James Hind.

As Mr. Tubbs took notes, she faithfully related how Harrowby's carriage had been stopped by two masked men, since there had been too many witnesses to dispute those details. As she had done once before, however, she was careful to alter the appearance of St. Mars's beloved horse. Anyone who had seen Penny, a horse of exceptional breeding and a coppery coat, might recognize her description and guess the true identity of Blue Satan.

From this point, her story would diverge widely from the truth.

"Where were we?" she asked Mr. Tubbs. She'd had to pause often in her relation to give him time to catch up.

Tubbs had overcome his shyness from the instant he had started to write, so there was hardly a stammer in his voice when he replied, "The man in the blue satin cape pointed his pistol through the carriage window and said, 'Your money or your life.'"

"Yes, I remember now. This is why I think the whole thing was a prank, you see, for instead of waiting for us to hand over our jewelry, he made us all descend from the coach."

Jeremy's ears pricked up. "Just a prank? Do you think he was acquainted with someone in the carriage?"

"Oh, no!" Hester feared she might have protested too much. She said more evenly, "I cannot believe that he did. He treated us all too much like strangers."

"What was he like? Could you see any of his features?"

"Well, he was very polite. Quite a 'gentleman of the road,' but I got the impression that it was all a pose. His accent seemed a little foreign."

"You mean, French?" Tubbs looked so horrified that Hester thought she'd better improve upon this aspect. She supposed a French highwayman would never appeal to English readers.

"No, not as foreign as that. Simply northern . . . or, perhaps, from the West Country? I'm afraid I cannot recall, but I remember being struck with it at the time. But he was very courteous."

"Then what? Did he ask for your jewels?" Tubbs demanded impatiently.

"Well, he was about to, I believe, when my lord protested this ill-treatment. He spoke very forcibly to Blue Satan—you must know that it was my lord who gave the robber that name." Harrowby would not in the least mind having his courage exaggerated, so Hester went on, "I believe it was my lord who said that he and his lady had just been wed, and perhaps it was this fact that persuaded Blue Satan not to rob us."

"What did her ladyship do?"

Isabella had been too hysterical to do much of anything or even to remember details about the incident. "She was entirely silent," Hester lied, "although, as I recall, she tried to comfort her mother, who was really and truly beside herself with fright." She could not resist this one embellishment.

"So then, Blue Satan got back on his horse?"

"Goodness, no! It was nothing so prosaic! He gave a great leap, and with the most graceful swoop you ever saw, he flew onto his horse's back and started to gallop past me."

"Wait there!" Bent over his paper, Tubbs scribbled furiously, cursing his pen every time it emptied.

Even Jeremy seemed cheerful as he leaned over his colleague's shoulder. "Here. You mustn't say it like that. I'm sure we can put it better than Hester did."

Tubbs jerked away from him and moved his paper where Jeremy could not see it. His face took on a purplish hue. "Just taking it down," he growled. "Can fix it later. Don't need your help."

Looking over his friend's head at Hester, Jeremy rolled his eyes and smiled, but he only said, "I know you can do it, Tubbs. I'm only trying to give you a few hints." Then his face screwed up with puzzlement. "But I still don't understand why he rode away with you," he said to Hester.

She shook her head, trying to appear as mystified as he. "I have thought and thought about it, and I can only suppose that he took me for a kind of shield. The coachman had not been injured, and Harrowby must have had a pistol primed in the coach. Either one of them could have fired a shot at Blue Satan as he rode away."

Jeremy frowned. "Doesn't make for a very entertaining reason."

Tubbs looked up at him, and his square-featured face betrayed alarm. "Then, we must give him another! But what could it be?"

Forgetting that he had just refused Jeremy's aid, he listened desperately as Jeremy began to weave a tale. "What if he was in love with Isabella—the countess, I mean? And since her lord had just given him news of their marriage, he swept off in despair and took Hester— I mean the lady-in-waiting—out of fury."

This was so near the truth that Hester jumped. "Oh, no! You mustn't write that! My lord would not like it at all!"

"But we're not using his name," Tubbs protested.

"It doesn't matter," she said. "He is certain to recognize the story, and if he gets angry enough, he might cast me out."

There was enough genuine desperation in her voice to make Jeremy retract his idea, though reluctantly. "Then what if we say he took a fancy to you?"

Her desperation turned to panic. "No, I cannot allow you to say that! What would—what would people think of me? No, I think it much better to say that on learning about the wedding that had taken place, Blue Satan grew merry and decided to play a prank on the newly wedded pair by riding off with their servant."

Tubbs and Jeremy pondered this and eventually agreed that, even though it was not as romantic as Jeremy's ideas, they supposed it would do. From that point, the three went on to discuss what might have taken place next, with Hester chiefly steering them away from any resemblance to the truth, Tubbs acting solely as transcriber, and Jeremy providing most of the imagination and the narrative. Tubbs appeared to have no objections to using Jeremy's work as long as no one pointed out that he was doing it.

When they had finished, Hester tried to turn the conversation round to the bookstall. "What sort of pieces did you write for Mr. Curry?" she asked Tubbs.

His cheeks filled with a ruddy colour, and he stood to gather up the pages of his manuscript, mumbling protests all the while.

One would think I had asked him the most intimate of questions, Hester thought

Jeremy gave a laugh. "Oh, it's no use your asking Tubbs about his work," he said. "He guards his privacy, but he is simply being modest. He's quite the hand at translations. You should see him work with French. I was embarrassed to confess that I didn't speak a single word of it."

Instead of responding positively to this praise, Tubbs glowered at Jeremy and told him to "mind his own business."

Jeremy laughed heartily as he clapped him on the shoulder, "See how Tubbs hates to be praised? But I tell him there's no flattery in it. Mr. Curry told me himself how talented Tubbs is."

Tubbs stood with his shoulders bent, looking angry and mortified, but Hester thought there was more to his reluctance to talk about his work than simple modesty could explain.

Perhaps he had been employed in translating treasonous material from France. The language used at the Pretender's court presumably was French, and certainly there were French priests and nobles involved in his cause. If Mr. Curry had kept a secret stock of political pamphlets, Mr. Tubbs might have been involved in producing them, and with Jeremy's not knowing a word of French, Tubbs could have translated them right under his nose.

She tried again to get him to speak about Mr. Curry, but he had closed his mouth as tightly as an oyster and would not open it for her. He muttered something about having business in the City and bustled away.

As they heard his treads receding down the passageway, Hester turned to her brother and sighed. "Not very chatty, is he?"

"Who? Tubbs?" Jeremy gave her a defensive look. "You mustn't blame Tubbs for being a bit on edge right now, Hester, not when he's lost his patron. If he can't find something to write, he'll be beggared. I've had to pay his share of our lodgings these past few weeks, as it is."

Hester knew that it would be useless to point out the lack of wisdom in doing that, so instead she asked him what had him so dispirited.

As she had supposed, the problem was with Sally. Jeremy had started to doubt that she had any tender feelings for him at all.

"Lately she's been treating me like a leper," he complained. "If I go by the bookstall, she cannot get rid of me soon enough. And she never smiles any more when I'm about. She'll scarcely even look at me."

"Could it be because of what I said? Do you think she's afraid she'll be accused of throwing her cap at you?"

He shrugged miserably. "How can I know if she won't tell me?"

Hester felt nearly as sorry about the situation as her brother looked. What if she *had* been the cause of Sally's coolness?

Jeremy must have seen the guilt in her face for he said, "I really don't know what's wrong, so you mustn't assume it's anything you did.

If she would only tell me . . . ."

"What about Mr. Simpkins? Is he still making threats?"

Jeremy's face hardened. "Whenever I see him on his rounds, he shouts all kinds of offensive things at me." He gave her a wistful smile. "It's not very pleasant, I can tell you, to have a beadle pointing his staff as if he were Moses, and yelling, 'There he is, the murderer!'"

"Oh, Jeremy!"

"It's true! Sometimes I think he must have convinced Sally that I did kill her husband."

"She would never think that! Not if she knows you at all."

"I thought she did," he said, with such despair in his voice that her heart nearly broke.

"Try not to worry, Jeremy. We'll find out who did it, and then everything will turn out well."

The smile he gave her showed that, though he was grateful for her attempt to comfort him, he could not quite believe her. How could he, when she had done nothing to help him yet?

Hester felt so full of remorse that she vowed she would not see St. Mars again until she had discovered a clue. With winter approaching and the days shortening, Mr. Jervas had asked Isabella to sit for him more frequently while he could take advantage of the light. Hester used the next of these occasions to call on Lady Mary Wortley Montagu.

She wrote and asked permission to visit her ladyship on a matter of some importance, regarding the publication of her "Court Ecologues." She signed the letter, indicating her relationship to the Countess of Hawkhurst, and asked one of the footmen to deliver it to Lady Mary's House in Westminster not far from St. James's Square. A few days later, having received permission to call, Hester hastened over at the appointed hour, only to have to wait downstairs for above a quarter of an hour while Lady Mary finished with her dresser.

Finally, she was taken up to the withdrawing room where Lady Mary received her guests. Accustomed as Hester was to her cousins' extravagance, she found the chamber rather plain for the daughter of the Duke of Kingston, but Lady Mary, who was seated on a love-seat beneath a portrait of her sister Lady Mar, was as beautiful as ever, with her large, almond-shaped eyes, clear skin, and full lips. Her figure was still slim and girlish, despite the birth of her first son, and she had a particularly graceful neck, which her dresser had set off with a low décolletage surmounted by ruffles.

She received Hester coolly, merely nodding at her curtsy and giving her a rather reluctant invitation to sit.

Hester perched on the edge of a damask chair and clasped her hands in her lap to keep from fidgeting. She had debated with herself about the best way to broach the topic of Lady Mary's poems, but she needn't have bothered for the lady sprang to the subject herself.

"I was surprised to learn that your mistress had any dealings with that scoundrel Curry," she said, bristling at the name. "I shouldn't have thought her taste ran to books, but if it does, perhaps I should have expected it to be in accord with his."

Hester was momentarily struck dumb by this attack on Isabella, but she hastened to correct Lady Mary's misinterpretation of her note. "I beg your pardon, but I have not come here on my cousin's business. She knows nothing of Mr. Curry's books, and indeed, she found him as repellent in life as I am certain you did—as we all did."

"Then what is your reason for disturbing me?"

As an invitation to unburden herself, Hester found it distinctly lacking in sympathy. Still, she took advantage of the opening, merely clenching her hands more tightly in her lap.

"I wonder if you will tell me how Mr. Curry came into possession of your verses, for I suspect it was not with your approval."

She had obviously said something right, for Lady Mary unbent. Easing back on the loveseat, she waved a dismissive hand. "No, it most certainly was *not* with my approval. I wish I knew how he did come by them. I had only shown them to a very few friends, and I had no intention of their ever being printed." She gave Hester a rueful look. "The portraits I drew of . . . certain . . . rather important people were not very flattering, as I'm sure you know."

Hester did not like to confess that she had not read them, so made no particular response. "Is it possible that one of your friends showed them to Mr. Curry?"

Lady Mary scoffed. "If they had, they would no longer be numbered among my acquaintance. But I cannot believe any of them would, for they despised the man as much as I did. I cannot tell you what satisfaction it gave me to hear that he had been murdered. If I were a man, I would have strangled him myself."

Narrowing her eyes, she fixed them on Hester. "What is your interest in this, Mrs. Kean? Why are you posing me these questions?"

Hester had already determined how to answer this particular query if she was asked. "Like your ladyship, my brother Jeremy is a writer, and Mr. Curry published some of his work. Unfortunately, someone is spreading a vicious rumour that it was Jeremy who killed Mr. Curry."

"Then your brother should be a very popular man."

Hester did her best to hide her anger at this comment. "Alas, no," she said with a brittle smile. "No matter how reviled Mr. Curry was, his killer is certain to be even more so. Fear alone would make people shun him. And, if the worst should happen, he could be charged with a crime he did not commit."

"Do you mean to say that someone is bothering to discover who did it? I cannot imagine why anyone would."

Hester restrained a sigh. "His widow has offered a reward for information, but the person I am speaking about has a grudge against my brother and is using Mr. Curry's death to persecute him."

A spark of interest lit Lady Mary's eyes. "I see. And you wish to know how my verses came into Curry's hands because it might throw some light on his murder?" She frowned. "I would tell you if I knew, but I fail to see how it could. I have one friend who vowed to avenge the affront, but I'm certain he had nothing but a prank in mind. And, besides, he was not in London when the killing occurred."

"I know it sounds very flimsy, my lady, but I feel I must try to uncover everything I can about Mr. Curry's unsavoury dealings. And I have little else to go on. Someone must have stolen your verses, and Mr. Curry obviously had no scruples about using them."

"Very well." Lady Mary languidly drew herself up in her seat. "I will tell you all I know, but I doubt that you will find it useful. I gave the verses to a friend, Mr. Alexander Pope. He promised to read them and give me his opinion of their worth. He says he did read them, but he was obliged to leave London, so he posted them back to me. I never received them, so I assumed the Post Office had seized them. If I had known Mr. Pope had posted them soon after he'd read them, I should have been in a quake, I assure you. But by the time I discovered it, time enough had elapsed that I was reasonably certain I would not be taken up for treason."

When saying this, she spoke with a wry, amused tone, but Hester imagined that Mr. Wortley, if not his wife, would have been genuinely terrified by the possibility. Favourite or not, Lady Mary would not have been the first of King George's courtiers to be arrested under suspicion of being a Jacobite. If Harrowby were to be believed, even the most powerful Whigs in the government were afraid that something they had thoughtlessly committed to paper could be misinterpreted as treason. But if government agents had read Lady Mary's verses, they must not have understood her satire.

Hester asked a few more questions, but when she took her leave, she was not one step closer to finding out how Mr. Curry had obtained Lady Mary's work. She tried to accept that she might never find the answer, but the puzzle plagued her mercilessly. She could not escape the feeling that the information was important.

"Yet, Chloe sure was formed without a spot"—
Nature in her then erred not, but forgot.
"With every pleasing, every prudent part,
Say, what can Chloe want?"—She wants a Heart.

CHAPTER XVI

His discovery that Joseph Sullivan was a Popish priest gave Gideon
fresh theories to consider. He would have liked to discuss them
with Mrs. Kean, but he knew she could not meet him every time a new
line of inquiry opened up. Besides, he felt a need to achieve some result. He could not stand to be idle when all about him other men were
acting.

He was almost certain that Sullivan had not penetrated his disguise.
If Gideon himself had been thrown by the difference between the circumstances of their two meetings, the priest must have been even less
able to recall him, when before he had seen him in groom's clothing
with neither patches nor paint. Fortunately, Tom was a complete stranger
to him, so Gideon instructed him to follow Sullivan continually and
see where he went.

When Tom set about this chore without a grumble, but looking as
if a lifetime of waiting stretched before him, Gideon relented enough
to speak to Katy the next morning. Within Tom's hearing, he told her
to ask the neighbours to recommend a doctor who could physick his
servants. For this consideration, he was rewarded when he heard Tom
whistling a cheerful country song on his way to the river stairs.

After seeing him depart, Gideon put on his tricorn hat, a woolen cloak, and muffler, and walked to the stables to greet his mare. Penny playfully tossed her head, as if indignant over his neglect, but she eventually accepted a lump of sugar from his hand and allowed herself to be coaxed into a bridle. This did not prevent her from stamping her hooves and flicking her tail ominously while he saddled her, but her high spirits only made him laugh.

"Ready for a gallop, I see." He stroked her neck, being careful to keep a watch in case her impish mood led her to bite. "Well, let's see if we can't relieve some of your fidgets while I sift this matter out."

She sidled after he mounted her, but she was far too eager to run to waste her time with silly tricks. Gideon made her weave through country paths on his way to Kennington Lane. It would never do to let her get heated too fast. The morning was cold, and he did not want her to get a stitch.

Once they were clear of the nearest farms, he loosened his tight grip on the reins and let her gallop until she showed signs of wanting to slow. Then he turned her back towards home, alternating her pace between a canter and a walk.

The fresh air helped to clear the cobwebs from his brain, which continued to dwell on the Popish priest. The most likely reason Joseph Sullivan would have an interest in the bookstall was if he had brought Curry treasonous pamphlets to sell. But if he had, and Curry was useful to him, then why would he murder him? And would a Roman Catholic priest kill?

Gideon knew there were a few in that sect who might be able to convince themselves that the killing of a fellow human would be justified by all the souls that would be saved if England were returned to Mother Church. But even if Sullivan—if that was truly his name— were one of those, that fact would not address the issue of Curry's usefulness.

Why would anyone, priest or not, murder an accomplice? What if Curry had threatened the priest or his cause in some way? If, after his near brush with the law, he had decided not to sell the pamphlets any longer, would he not simply have told the priest? What if, instead of simply backing out of their arrangement, he had threatened to report Sullivan to the authorities? Not because he had developed a civic conscience, but because he feared arrest himself. Gideon doubted that any-one would be so foolish to give advance warning of such a move, unless for a good reason.

Someone appeared to have known about the secret cache of publi-cations, for that person had reported them to the authorities. Presum-ably, whoever it was had not known where they were hidden, or he would have included that detail in his note. One thing Gideon could be certain of was that the priest would not have been the one to alert the law. Even if he had wished to punish Curry for some reason, he would never have worked against the cause.

Leaving aside for now the question of who had written the anony-mous note, Gideon returned his thoughts to the priest, whose very presence in London was illegal. If Curry had threatened him with ex-posure—possibly agreeing to keep the secret in exchange for money— would that have been enough to make Sullivan kill him when he might more easily have left the City? Again, the question all came back to the priest's willingness to kill.

Penny shied at a swirl of blowing leaves, and almost unseated him. Gideon had to abandon his musings in order to soothe her before moving on. He had let the puzzle distract him, when Penny was not a horse on which a rider could afford to be inattentive, even after she had been thoroughly exercised. He kept his focus on her the rest of the way home, and he talked to her, praising her for her good behaviour with generous pats.

Later, though, as he rubbed her down inside her stall, he recalled one detail about the murder that had escaped his mind. Whoever had killed Curry had troubled to lock the stall behind him, which could mean that he had not wanted Curry's stock to be stolen, or for an inquisitive thief to discover the secret cache. For now, the only lead they had to follow was Joseph Sullivan and whatever his interest in the bookstall was, which meant that Gideon and Tom had many days of waiting and watching to look forward to.

§

"The Earl of Scarsdale sent to the Tower . . . Sir William Wyndham in the Tower . . . the Lord Duplin in the Tower . . . ."

"And the Duchess of Montague delivered of a son."

Isabella's contribution to Harrowby's list did not seem as inapt to him as it did to Hester. He sighed and said to his wife, "Very true, my dear. We can only hope our own little George does not disappoint us."

He had returned to town in time for Parliament to meet on the twentieth of October. In spite of having survived his journey into Kent, he had not remained in a cheerful mood for long. That night, the Court had celebrated the anniversary of his Majesty's coronation with the usual ringing of bells, bonfires, and illuminations, but beneath the official demonstrations of joy, anxious feelings had roiled.

Members of the Prince of Wales's household had whispered that the rebels in Northumberland had overwhelmed the local forces. According to Lady Cowper, one of the Princess's ladies, her friends in Newcastle had been pleading with King George for help which had never arrived. And, now, Jacobites in Lancashire and Yorkshire had risen, too.

Lord Townsend and Mr. Walpole seemed so intent on beating down reports of the rebellion as almost to confirm the worst.

But relations between the Prince and his father's ministers were so strained that it was impossible to know whom to believe. Even with war being waged in the North, their Royal Highnesses had been using every bit of influence they possessed to get people loyal to them into government posts. The King's ministers were so incensed by their interference that Baron Bernstorff, his Majesty's German aide, had warned the Princess not to meddle any further in the government's business.

As the days grew colder and darker, everyone's spirits seemed to fail. For most of the next fortnight, even Mrs. Mayfield and Isabella kept to the house, for few ladies felt safe going about now. Huts had been built in the park to house the soldiers, along with stables for their horses, and the vicinity of the Palace had taken on the appearance of a military camp. With nothing to celebrate but the solemnization of the Prince of Wales's birthday at the end of October the ladies grew exceedingly bored, and Hester was kept busy day and night trying to amuse them.

She was soon frustrated, too, for Isabella's sittings with Mr. Jervas came to an abrupt end. The artist informed her that he had made enough progress to be able to finish the portrait from memory. Even though Hester had obtained the information she had wanted from Lady Mary herself, the sittings had been useful for the hours of freedom they had provided her. Now, without those regular meetings, Hester did not know when she would be able to escape the house again. She was tempted to break her vow and ask St. Mars to meet her in a church, since that was the only place she could get leave to go, but tied to the house as she had been the past few weeks, she had discovered nothing new to help Jeremy's case.

She realized how desperate she had become when Harrowby's gossip came as a welcome relief.

As they sat in the withdrawing room after dinner one evening, he talked about the latest scandal at Court. His Grace the Duke of Somerset was reported to have resigned his place as Master of the Horse, but, according to the Duke's version, he had been unwillingly relieved of his post.

"He said that Lord Townsend came to him, pulling a sad face, and said that the King had no more need for his services."

"How impudent!" Mrs. Mayfield scoffed. "To pretend to be sorry, when those two have always been at daggers drawn. Did his Grace say why he'd been dismissed?"

"He said Townsend had turned the King against him with his lies, and that he accused Townsend of it directly to his face. But I have my doubts about that."

"Why?" Isabella asked.

"Because Townsend's a very touchy sort. He drew his sword on Walpole once, and Walpole's his *brother-in-law.* No." Harrowby shook his head. "I'd say that if Somerset had spoken to Townsend like that, blood would surely have been spilled."

"But what does Lord Townsend say?"

"He says that his Grace was seen in Sir Edward Northey's chambers, consulting with him about the proof against Sir William Wyndham before he surrendered himself. Said that amounted to treason. But I heard they only suspect that the Duke was there because his coach was seen waiting in the street, and he could have been in Lechmere's chambers instead."

"Isn't Sir William the Duke's son-in-law?" Hester asked.

"Yes. And he says he was promised that Wyndham would not be

imprisoned if he gave himself up. He was indignant about that, I can assure you."

"So the Duke did resign his post, after all?" Isabella was not the only one confused.

Harrowby's tension began to show. "How the deuce should I know? I've just told you what I heard, but they all could have invented a pack of taradiddles for all I know!" He screwed his lips into a pout. "I'll tell you what, though. If the Whigs aren't careful, they'll bicker and quarrel until they're no better off than the Tories. After all we've witnessed, you'd think they'd have more sense than that."

For once, Hester agreed with her cousin, but she understood why so many families connived and bribed for places at Court. Without the income from those posts, some would have little income at all. At the very least, they would not be able to afford the luxuries that raised them above their servants. She could be grateful that the Hawkhurst estates produced enough wealth to shelter her family from the petty rivalries that ruled the Court, even if her conscience always smote her for accepting a living that was not really Isabella's to give.

"Oh, by the way," Harrowby said, looking warningly at his mother-in-law and his wife. "I heard that Lady Mary Wortley has been stricken with the smallpox. I hope you have not been in her company of late."

As Hester's stomach took a sudden plunge, Isabella released a laugh. "Of course, I have not, silly. You know that she and I have never taken a liking to each other."

Mrs. Mayfield said, "And it's no wonder, my pet, for I have never met a lady as grasping as her. If she did not speak French, I don't believe the King would have taken such a fancy to her, for she's not half as pretty as you . . . I guess she won't be after this." She gave a mean laugh, before a calculating gleam came into her eye. "Maybe it's time you learned a little bit of French. Hester could teach you."

As they all turned their eyes on Hester, she felt a heavy lump in the pit of her stomach. Ignoring Mrs. Mayfield's remarks, she said, "But I have seen her. I spoke to Lady Mary just a short while ago. I sat in a room with her and talked for a half hour or more."

There was a stunned silence in the room, before all hell broke loose. While Harrowby scrambled over a chair to distance himself from her and Isabella began to wail, Mrs. Mayfield leapt to her feet with the look of an avenging fury, spilling her needlework onto the floor.

"Out! Get out!" she screamed, pointing to the door. "You will leave this house at once. If you have dared to harm the heir—"

She did not finish, but she had said enough to make both Harrowby and Isabella turn pale. Their cries of worry were added to her vicious voice, and, frightened already, Hester ran for her room.

Once there, in her haste she slammed the door behind her and stood against it until her panicky breathing could subside. In the shock of hearing about Lady Mary, a dozen separate thoughts had flitted through her brain. How long ago had she seen Lady Mary? Was it two or even three weeks ago? Harrowby had not said when Lady Mary had been stricken, and Hester doubted that he knew.

In her father's parish Hester had been exposed to the smallpox before and had never caught it. No one could say why some people did and others did not, or why some cases were light when so many were fatal. She had been fortunate up until now, and even if her good luck were to end, there was nothing she could do to avert the change. But, given all she had learned from the cases in her father's parish, she did not truly believe that she had been exposed.

Surely Lady Mary would have noticed if she had had any blisters that morning. Her dresser must have noticed them, even if she had not. And if the pox had not erupted yet, Hester doubted she would be at risk.

Mrs. Mayfield's mention of Isabella's child had worried Hester much more than fear for herself. Hester would never forgive herself if Isabella's baby should be lost due to any deed of hers, even if her intentions had been good. Even more applicable, perhaps, she would never be forgiven by her family.

But beyond these fears was her grief for Lady Mary. Although she had not struck Hester as particularly kind, she was nonetheless an intelligent and beautiful young lady with a husband and an infant son. Her death—should it occur— would be tragic, and if she survived, her beauty could be ruined. The smallpox was no respecter of wealth or status. The great were taken along with the poor. But at least Lady Mary could command the very best medical attention, and Hester was in no position to offer her even so little a thing as her sympathy.

She had to figure out where she could go. She had the small bit of money James Henry had given her. She could use that to pay for lodgings until the risk of contracting the disease was past, at which point she hoped to be welcomed at Hawkhurst House again.

A knock on her chamber door moved her to open it. Will stood there, looking ill at ease.

"Sorry to disturb you, Mrs. Kean," he said, "but Mrs. Mayfield was asking—that is, she sent me to discover—"

Hester took pity on him and finished his sentence. "She wants to know if I've left the house yet?"

Will looked miserably down at the floor. "Yes, that's it."

"If you could find me a hackney, I'll be ready to leave in a minute. I need to gather some belongings first."

He bowed and apologized again before letting her get on with her task. Hester quickly folded a clean Holland smock and a bodice into a bag. She had no hoops to burden her, but she took another pair of stockings and garters in case hers became soiled, and a cap. Then, after throwing in a hairbrush and a few other personal items she donned the warmest cloak and mittens she had and, carrying her bag, tip-toed down the stairs, hoping to escape the house unseen. As she descended, she thought comfortingly of the fan St. Mars had given her, hidden safely in the pocket tied beneath her skirt.

Will was waiting for her at the door, ready to hand her into the coach. His unselfish gesture, when he must have known the reason for her banishment, caused a few tears to fill her eyes, and she thanked him as he took her elbow to guide her in.

"Where shall I tell him you wish to go?" he asked.

Hester had not the slightest idea. She yearned to appeal to St. Mars who, she was sure, would be willing to help, but she could not inflict herself upon him. The only other friend she had in London was her brother Jeremy, and though she did not wish to burden him either, she thought she could ask his advice about an inn. So she gave Will the name of the Pewter Platter Inn, and settled back on the hackney seat, while he shut the carriage door and instructed the driver. Then, as the coach pulled away from Hawkhurst House, she waved goodbye.

On the way to Holborn, she thought how much she had recently yearned for the freedom to come and go at Hawkhurst House. But she had never envisioned leaving it under these circumstances, and she wondered how she would be able to help Jeremy now.

Arrived in Holborn, she paid the driver to fetch her brother, while she waited outside in the coach. She could not be certain that Jeremy would wish her to enter his room if there was any chance she'd been infected.

He appeared, and the sight of his welcoming face almost prompted her to tears, but she kept him standing in the street while telling him her tale through the carriage window. She should have known that, after listening to her, he would barely pause before urging her to come in, but in spite of her thankfulness for this proof of his affection, she refused.

"I cannot in good conscience," she explained. "I only came to you in the hope that you could advise me where I should stay until the uncertainty is past."

When his renewed urgings failed, he stood and thought a moment before a happy thought struck him. Then, ignoring her earnest warnings, he opened the hackney door and joined her inside.

"Jeremy, no! Don't! What are you doing?"

"I'm taking you to see Mrs. Sally. She's had the smallpox, so you needn't fear giving it to her. And she will know better than I where a delicately nurtured female can stay safely in London."

Hester wondered then whether his sudden cheer had come from the thought of solving her problem or the prospect of speaking to Sally, but his suggestion had given her hope. Mixed with her trepidation now was a growing feeling that she might be able to turn her new circumstances to good account. But she could not easily shake off the possibility that she might fall deathly ill.

The coach pulled up in Fleet Street, and after telling Hester to wait, Jeremy jumped down. He was not gone two minutes before he reappeared with Sally on his arm. She immediately invited Hester to stay with her in her house in Bell Yard and even closed the bookstall to help her settle in. The street that had seemed so dirty and forbidding earlier appeared like a haven to Hester today.

Sally's house was as tidy and as well-furnished as before. She gave Hester her husband's old chamber to use as her own.

Fortunately, Sally's one maidservant had been hard at work and had scrubbed his quarters from top to bottom, so that no lingering scent of him remained. Hester was ashamed of the relief she felt when this became evident, but she hoped that by finding out who had killed Mr. Curry, she would earn forgiveness for her uncharitable thoughts.

After showing her where to put her things, Sally left her to return to the shop, saying she would return that night after nine o'clock. Before she went, Hester asked for pen and paper so she could write to Mrs. Dixon, the Hawkhurst housekeeper. She wanted to ask her to pack more of her clothing and have it sent to Sally's house. There was a second letter she meant to write, too, but she kept that information to herself.

As soon as she had put away the few things in her bag, she sat at Mr. Curry's desk and composed a note to St. Mars informing him of her new address. Since she did not wish to alarm him, she did not mention her exposure to the smallpox. He would not be surprised to learn that Mrs. Mayfield had cast her out, but she even had to make light of this if she did not wish to incite his temper. The thought of what he might be tempted to do to her aunt if his anger was aroused made her smile, but she would never purposely provoke him. He had acted rashly before, and he must do nothing more to reveal himself. Consequently, her letter was a mixture of obfuscations and omissions, with its principal message being that now she was conveniently placed to search for Mr. Curry's murderer.

Indeed, she reflected, as she sealed the letter with a wafer, she finally found herself in a position to do her brother some good.

※

Gideon opened her note and scanned it eagerly. Then he frowned and read it a second time.

There was something Mrs. Kean was concealing. So much was clear. But the news that she had escaped her aunt's surveillance gave him a thrill all the same. When he saw her next, which would be soon, he would insist on knowing why she had left the comforts of his house, but for now, he and Tom had business to discuss.

Taking turns, they had watched the Bell and Bible for the past fort-night and the barber-surgeon's shop at night. Once Gideon had seen the priest enter the barber's shop again—again with a parcel, which he had left somewhere inside the shop in the dark. After he had exited, Gideon had followed him to a house just outside Temple Bar, presumably his lodgings, as he had not emerged again that night. From that day on, Tom had waited every morning outside the house and had seen Sullivan leave on his way to chambers in Pump Court in the Inner Temple. He had done nothing outside his usual habits until today, when Tom had followed him from the Bell and Bible all the way to Windmill Hill.

Gideon had just begun to question Tom about this news when the boy had brought Mrs. Kean's note. Now he returned his attention to Sullivan's actions, and asked, "Did he speak to anyone?"

"No, my lord." Although he always refused to sit in his master's chamber, Tom had unbent enough to warm his hands at the wood fire, for keeping watch outside in these wintry temperatures could freeze a man. "He didn't talk to no one that I could see, and all he did was to walk about Moor Fields."

"As if he were simply taking exercise?"

Appearing to be at a loss, Tom shrugged. "It could be, my lord. He went to the top of the hill and started straight back down. He might've spotted me on his way back 'cause he surprised me when he turned 'round. I was staying a good bit behind, for if he'd noticed me on the way up, he might have thought it was queer, since there's nothing much along Finsbury there but those open fields. So I let him get past me, and kept on till I was pretty sure he'd be a fair bit on the way to Moorgate before I turned back. Then I nearly caught up with him at the first corner."

Gideon's interest was piqued. "You mean, he walked more slowly on the way down?"

"He must have, my lord."

"Either that or he stopped somewhere. Would you have noticed if he had?"

Tom shook his head. "Not before I started back down, and when I caught up with 'im, he was still walking . . . almost strolling like."

"Is there anything there? Of any particular interest, I mean?"

Rubbing his hands to get the blood moving again, Tom tried to remember, then gave a rueful grimace. "I wasn't looking for nothin' like that, my lord. I was just tryin' to keep 'im in sight and not be spotted myself."

Gideon was frustrated that he had not been there with Tom. "It's understandable that you would not, but can't you recall anything at all?"

A red piece of coal fell out of the fire and onto the hearth. Gazing down absently at it, Tom kicked it back in with the toe of his boot. "There was an inn . . . the Castle, I think. And there was some kind of smithy about. I heard some hammerin' and smelled the smoke."

Gideon gave a nod. "Well . . . we'll just have to make a trip up there ourselves. That's very good work, Tom. You may go ask Katy for your dinner now."

"Thank you, my lord. But there's sommat else I ought to tell you."

At Gideon's inquisitive stare, he went on, "When this Sullivan—the priest—when he was on his way back, he didn't pass through Moorgate."

Gideon drew his brows together. "What do you mean? How else would he enter? The old city wall is still intact around there."

"I know it is," Tom said, appearing eager, "but Moorgate's not the only way through it. There's a pair of postern gates a little way to the west."

"He used one of those? Why?"

"I really couldn't say, my lord." Tom scratched his head. "I thought he'd go back the way he'd come, but just as he got past the Artillery Ground, he turned right. I hurried after 'im and nearly lost 'im 'cause he turned again—left that time. Then I really had to keep close, for he turned again and again till he got to London Wall. That's when I saw 'im go in by the postern gate."

Gideon frowned, prepared to be annoyed. "Perhaps he'd spotted you and was trying to shake you off his trail."

"No, my lord." Tom sounded definite. "He was going along too slow for that. If he'd wanted to lose me, seems he would've moved faster."

"Could you retrace his steps? There might be something along that route to interest us."

"I'm sure I could, my lord, but I don't think there'll be anything."

Gideon studied him. "Why?"

Uncertainty drifted across Tom's face. "I don't know . . . he just didn't seem to be that fixed on anything he was passing. It was more as if he was just trying *not* to go by Moorgate, but I know that don't make any sense."

Gideon chewed his lips and thought. Then, he said, "I don't know. I suppose there could be a good reason."

Tom grunted. "Maybe he's afraid somebody'll run out of Bedlam and nab him. That's the only thing that's up there."

Gideon smiled. "I don't think so. If he were really afraid of Bedlam, why would he have passed so close to it on his way up?" He shook his head to loosen the cobwebs. "It is a mystery, but one that we shall have to clear up. Tomorrow you'll have to show me everywhere he went, and with luck we'll notice something."

He dismissed Tom to his meal, crossed his booted ankles in front of the fire, and spent another few minutes trying to imagine what Sullivan could have been doing on Windmill Hill. Gideon did not believe that the priest had simply been taking exercise, for a number of reasons—mainly, because of the impression he'd got from seeing him in the book-stall. While Sullivan might have seemed to be doing nothing important, there was always something firm in his manner, as if he was a man with a very serious purpose.

If he had taken the time to walk up Windmill Hill and to use an alternate route back, then whatever he was planning had something to do with that walk.

Search then the RULING PASSION: There alone,
The Wild are constant, and the Cunning known . . .

CHAPTER XVII

The next morning, Sally was up and dressed before six to do the daily marketing. Then she had a quick breakfast and departed for the bookstall. She faced a hard day of work that would not bring her home until long after dark. With no cook and only one maid to help with the cleaning and laundering, the last thing she needed she was an idle guest.

Hoping to be of some use to her hostess, Hester was putting away the breakfast dishes when she heard a knock at the door. She hesitated before answering it, but reflecting that the visitor might be bringing something Sally wanted, she opened the door.

Outside on the pavement she found a man dressed in Quakers' clothes—a plain black suit, plain woolen cloak, and high-crowned, broad-rimmed hat. His short bob wig had a heavy dusting of grey, and his brows looked thick and black, but the thin, hawkish features and the laughter in his blue eyes revealed him as St. Mars.

With a joyful gasp, she quickly motioned him inside, then took a careful look up and down the street before closing the door.

She turned to find him waiting in the small entryway. Flustered by the surprise of seeing him, she gave a nervous smile. "I see you received my note, my lord, but I hope you did not consider it a summons of any kind. You must know I would never be that impertinent."

"What nonsense you do talk, my dear Mrs. Kean! I welcomed it for the chance to speak to you without our usual difficulties. But, perhaps, in this particular disguise I should address thee as Hester?"

She laughed at that. "You do have the look of a Quaker, sir. I swear I would not have known you, had I not seen you in that garb before."

"I think it a rather good costume myself." He pulled off his dark cloak and hat, hooked the cloak over his arm, and cocked his head at the stairs. "Now that we have thoroughly discussed my disguise, do you intend to invite me up?"

Hester felt a rush of warmth that flowed to the roots of her hair. She had been pondering the awkwardness of their situation. It had been weeks since she had been truly alone with St. Mars, and since then something between them seemed to have changed.

She was, also, acutely aware that this was not her house.

Then, she recalled the risk of smallpox and gasped, "Please forgive me, my lord, but I should never have admitted you!"

"No?" He gave her a teasing look. "If you are worried that Sally will come home and discover me, I assure you she won't. I made certain she had opened the bookstall before I dared to come. And as much as I have watched the Bell and Bible over the past few weeks, I can promise you she never quits it before noon."

"It's not just Sally, my lord." Hester wrung her hands. "Oh, I should never have opened the door!"

His smile vanished rapidly. "I knew there was more to your being here than you said in your note. What is it? Why did you leave Hawkhurst House?"

"It was . . . for the best. And it shall not be for long. But, my lord, I must not keep you standing here."

"Then, by all means, let us go up. But I will not leave until you tell me why you're here." Before she could stop him, he turned and took the stairs.

Hester had no choice but to follow him, but she dreaded his reaction when she told him the truth.

He waited for her on the landing and let her precede him into the parlour that Mr. Curry had used. She apologized for not being able to offer him any refreshment.

"Pray do not be ridiculous," he said, glancing about the simple room before seating himself on a straight, leather-seated chair near the fire and pointing to its match across from him. "Come now . . . out with it."

Hester remained standing. "I will tell you, my lord, if you will promise to go."

His stare reflected concern rather than offence, but her obstinacy *had* begun to annoy him. "I make no such promises, Mrs. Kean, but I will have your answer."

With a sigh, she told him about her visit to Lady Mary, and about Harrowby's subsequent announcement of the lady's illness.

Alarm flashed in St. Mars's eyes. He came rapidly to his feet, but he made no move to leave. Instead, he grasped her hands and held them firmly. "But what about you? Are you ill? Have you called for a physician?"

His worry was so immensely gratifying that Hester hated to spoil it. She gave an embarrassed laugh. "No, I feel perfectly well, I assure you. And I sincerely doubt that the infection will spread to me. In my experience, in order to communicate it to me, Lady Mary should already have had an eruption, which I am persuaded she did not. She had just been dressed by her maid, who should have seen the blisters if she had."

Although St. Mars loosened his grip on her hands, he was clearly not satisfied for he posed her a series of questions. How long ago had she spoken to Lady Mary? Had the lady seemed ill? Did her servants betray any sign of distress?

Hester shook her head at the last. "I do not believe anyone in the house had taken ill yet. I have visited houses where the smallpox was present and no one at Mr. Wortley's house had that fearful look."

She could feel him relaxing. Still holding her hands, he gave them a shake and said, with an encouraging smile, "Then I see no cause for you to banish me from this house. If you had erupted in the smallpox yourself, you would not be standing here."

"Of course I would not. But when Jeremy told me that Sally had already had the smallpox, I thought it would be safer for everyone at

Hawkhurst House if I came here for a while. I do not truly believe that I'm in danger, or I would not have forgotten it so easily when you surprised me at the door."

"There," he said abruptly. "That's much more sensible talk. But perhaps you thought I would be so afraid that I would trample you in my haste to get away?"

She chuckled. "I thought no such thing! But I did not expect you to react foolishly either. It would be no more than prudent to stay away from me until the risk of infection is past."

"Well, since we have already been imprudent, it is too late to alter that now. I shall promise not to— *No*, on second thought, I refuse to swear to anything. You, on the other hand, must promise to notify me the instant you do begin to feel ill or if you see a blister of any kind."

"I will certainly warn you to stay away."

He looked sternly down at her. "That is not my meaning, and you know it. I want to be told so I can fetch a doctor to you right away."

Hester's dimples would not be contained, though she felt very shy. *Compare his chivalrous behaviour to my relations'*, she thought. She thanked him prettily and promised to do as he asked.

"There, that's settled." St. Mars led her to the chair he had wanted her to take before and resumed his seat. Before releasing her entirely, however, he raised her hand to his lips and planted a firm kiss upon it. The gesture took Hester completely by surprise, but when she looked at his face to see what he meant by it, he did not meet her gaze.

Changing the subject, he told her about having seen Joseph Sullivan at Lady Oglethorpe's country house where he was known to be a Roman Catholic priest, then about his strange nighttime activities and Tom's most recent discovery.

"A Roman priest!" Dismay filled her breast. "Then we are no closer to a solution, for he certainly could not have murdered Mr. Curry. No man of the cloth would."

St. Mars's smile was cynical. "No? Have you never heard of the Inquisition? And what about the burning of witches, which some of our clergy still do? Although in general I would agree with you, the world is full of religious men who believe that no sin attaches to killing an unbeliever."

"Mr. Sullivan doesn't appear to be so ardent."

"Nor, I presume, does he appear to be a priest." Leaning forward in his chair, St. Mars turned serious. "I have met a number of the Pretender's men, and I can tell you that there is no more zealous man than a priest who believes he can regain the whole of England and Scotland for Rome. No, my dear, make no mistake. This priest who calls himself Joseph Sullivan is likely as dangerous a man as you will ever meet. If his mission for the Pretender was thwarted, I do not doubt that he could find it in his conscience to kill Edmund Curry."

A shudder ran through Hester. She had to believe what St. Mars had said—that a priest might see the murder as a case of trading one despicable life for thousands of souls.

"Now," he went on, leaning back again, "what I need is for you to obtain the key to Sally's bookstall for me."

Hester's stomach gave a lurch, but she could not afford to let her courage fail her. "When will you require it?"

"The sooner, the better. Could you pass it to me tonight?"

She shook her head. "Not so soon. Not until I've learned more about Sally's habits. I would have to pass it to you in the middle of the night, and I do not even know where she keeps it. I recall Jeremy spoke of a hook where Mr. Curry left the key for his wife, but with Mr. Curry gone, she may have moved it."

St. Mars nodded, but his eagerness to search the bookstall was almost palpable. "Then you must tell me when to expect it. I shall come every morning to ask."

An unwelcome thought struck Hester, and she was forced to say, "I—I do not think you should come to the door again, my lord. One of the neighbours might notice your visits and tell Sally about the man I entertained."

The corners of his mouth curved up. "And who knows what Sally would think, eh?" But before she could argue further, he sighed and said, "No, I see that you are right. I promise I shall not come in again. I'll either stand outside or send someone else to the door."

Changing the subject again, he asked her how Jeremy was doing.

Hester told him about her visit to her brother and Mr. Tubbs, and how little she had learned from either. "Except how miserable my brother is. He's afraid Sally has no tender feelings for him, but I am certain that she does. I only wish I knew what has caused her to be so frightened. This morning she looked as pinched as Jeremy, and I cannot believe she is happy not confiding in him. She seems very lonely. I believe even my visit was welcome to her."

"I do not doubt that it was." His smile was gently teasing. "Perhaps you can use your visit here to discover what is troubling her."

She promised to try. Then they discussed other suspects, but it was clear that Joseph Sullivan's actions were the most suspicious.

"There is one thing I cannot understand," Hester mused aloud. "If there is something of value to him hidden in the bookstall, then why would he have called the authorities' attention to it by laying information against Jeremy and Mr. Curry?"

St. Mars, whose manner had grown distracted, frowned, until she reminded him of Jeremy's arrest. "I agree," he said, staring off into space. "That makes no sense."

"Then someone else must have done it."

She waited for a response, but he was not attending. Something was clearly disturbing him, for he seemed unable to keep his mind on their discussion. After a short silence, he rose to leave, with his mien sober. And he refused to allow Hester to accompany him to the door, insisting that he could throw the latch behind him. He ordered her to rest.

"For I make no doubt," he said, his face set in grim lines, "that Mrs. Mayfield has had you at her beck and call since I saw you last."

Hester could not deny it, but she made no complaint. She was free of her aunt for now.

St. Mars stared her in her eye. "By the bye, you did not tell me why you really left Hawkhurst House."

When Hester could not think promptly of an answer, he clenched his jaw tightly and said, "Never mind. I believe I know what must have happened."

He took her right hand in both of his and carried it to his lips again. Then cradling it, he fixed her with an anxious gaze. "You will not forget that you promised?" It was both a command and a plea. "And if you should find yourself too sick to write, you will tell Sally to fetch me?"

"I promise I will, my lord, but I am sure there is nothing to fear."

"There had better not be. I will not take it lightly if you become ill, my dear Mrs. Kean." He squeezed her fingers and turned to descend the stairs. Soon she heard the front door close behind him.

In spite of the words he had uttered, his manner had been strangely distant. She was almost afraid he had regretted visiting her. But if he had, why had he risked infection more by touching her? A suggestion of desperation had been in his parting gaze—as if his dearest friend had threatened to leave him.

※

The moment Gideon entered his house he called loudly for Katy and found her upstairs in his bedchamber, putting away the scarlet coat she had just pressed.

He cut through her cheerful greeting and said, "Did you locate that doctor I asked you to get?"

Taken aback, she stammered, "Yes, my lord, I did."

"Then fetch him—now. Tell him I have some urgent questions to put to him. If he's reluctant to come, tell him I'll pay him handsomely for his trouble."

Katy bobbed him a hurried curtsy. Then, looking mystified and not a little worried, she hastened from the chamber. He heard her rapid descent of the stairs and, less than a minute later, the sound of the door shutting behind her. She must have sensed his worry, for she had barely taken long enough to grab her cloak.

As he waited for the doctor, Gideon paced up and down in his chamber. Mrs. Kean had lulled him into thinking she would be all right with her talk of no eruptions, but the longer he had sat there, the faster his fears had mounted. It was as if his reaction to the shock had been delayed, but as he had silently contemplated the possibility of her illness, with the direst of probable outcomes, anxiety had seized at his heart and he had been unable to remain sitting still any longer. He had needed to do something that instant. But, what?

There was nothing he *could* do to protect her from an enemy he could not see, or an exposure that might already have occurred. He had barely been able to look her in the eye for fear of communicating his worry. And, until he had some reassurance that she would be safe, he would find it impossible to think of anything else.

The wait for the physician seemed interminable, but at last a Dr. Colley appeared, a sober-looking, bespectacled man in brown coat and breeches with curly, reddish hair standing thinly on his head. It took all of Gideon's restraint not to pounce on him at once, but he politely greeted the doctor and invited him to sit.

When he explained Mrs. Kean's situation and his concern that "his friend" might have contracted the disease, Dr. Colley placed the tips of his fingers together and gave the problem his serious consideration. He asked Gideon to describe this friend of his.

"Is he—or she, if it's a lady—a choleric individual?"

Taken aback, Gideon assured him that she was not.

"Would you say melancholic, perhaps?"

Impatient with these questions, Gideon glowered. "No."

Evidently pleased with this answer, Dr. Colley gave a satisfied nod. "Then, in my opinion, he—or she, as the case may be—is unlikely to have contracted the smallpox. You see, Mr. Mavors, one of the most basic tenets of medicine is that persons with an excess of certain humours are far more vulnerable to disease than others, and since you are so certain that your friend falls into neither of the susceptible groups, I can assert with a reasonable degree of accuracy that even if the disease were communicated to this individual, he or she is unlikely to experience any illness."

Gideon breathed deeply for the first time since Mrs. Kean had delivered her news. Feeling as if a cartload of stones had been lifted off his chest, he thanked the doctor and invited him to drink a glass of Madeira. While they conversed amiably over their cups, he recalled the plan he had made with respect to Katy and related it to Dr. Colley, who agreed to come later that week to physick both of Gideon's servants and to examine Katy for signs of the pox.

By the time he left and Gideon was able to redirect his thoughts, it was late in the day. He had been so disturbed by Mrs. Kean's news that he had neglected to eat, and now he felt ravenous. Katy brought him the dinner she had been keeping warm, and he tore into a stew of pigeons and cabbage, before demolishing a hare with a savory pudding and a hot, buttered apple pie.

When he had finished eating, it was much too dark for Tom to show him the route Joseph Sullivan had taken the day before. Deciding they would have to wait until another day, Gideon got his pistols out to clean. He had a matched pair of wheel-locks made in Edinburgh with ornate silver-mounted hafts. Single-barreled, they were fairly accurate at twenty paces, and relatively easy to handle, taking a heavy bullet but requiring only a light charge of powder.

He had meant what he'd said when he had told Mrs. Kean that Joseph Sullivan was a very dangerous man. Something told him now that it was time to prepare for action.

As he sat at the table, packing the barrel of one gun with rod and rag, the simple nature of his task began to calm him. He had been wound like a watch spring all day, first with the anticipation of seeing Mrs. Kean alone, then with worry and impatience until the doctor's pronouncement had set him at ease. He had not experienced such strong feelings since learning of his father's death in March, and he was amazed at how the thought of losing Mrs. Kean had wrenched him inside out.

At times, his chest had felt so constricted that he had scarcely been able to hold a breath, while his heart had beaten against his ribs like a caged, wounded animal. The worst had been knowing that if the disease did take her in its grip, there would be nothing he could do to stop it. And the knowledge that neither Mrs. Mayfield nor Isabella had been willing to care for her had nearly made him burst with anger. Only thoughts of retribution had brought him solace.

His emotions had been far too painful. He would not reflect on the possibility of losing his dear friend again.

☙

When Sally came home later that day, Hester had dinner cooked and the table laid. She had not cooked much since leaving her father's house, but she had been sufficiently trained in the kitchen to present Sally with a roasted pullet, a dish of stewed mushrooms, and fried smelts. Sally was so grateful for the attentiveness that she almost burst into tears.

Sitting at the board across from Hester, she wiped her eyes with her apron and begged Hester to forgive her foolishness.

"Nonsense," Hester said. "It is I who should beg your forgiveness for not offering you any assistance after Mr. Curry's death."

Sally gaped at her. "But why should you, when we had only just met?"

Making a sudden decision, Hester said, "I should have done it for my brother's sake."

A question leapt into Sally's gaze.

"He is very fond of you, you know."

Sally buried her face in her hands and gave a sob. When she did not reply, Hester said, "I'm sorry if I've distressed you. I thought I had detected—but if you do not—"

Sally raised her head quickly and said, "It's not your fault! But I can't—I mustn't—"

She looked so miserable that Hester stood and went round the table to take her in her arms. Cradling Sally's head, she said, "I wish you would tell me what has you so frightened."

Sally gasped. A shiver ran through her before she gently pulled away. "It's nothing, I beg you not to notice if I appear distracted, but so much has happened, and there's been so much work to do and so much to learn." She blew her nose, her cheeks covered with splotches.

Seeing that she was no longer needed, Hester released her and went back to her chair. She gave Sally a few moments to collect herself, then said, "Has Mr. Simpkins accused Jeremy of your husband's murder again?"

Sally's face went rigid. Then, through tightened lips, she said, "Yes."

"But he has no proof," Hester protested.

The other woman shook her head. "Of course he does not. How could he when Mr. Kean has done nothing wrong? But Mr. Simpkins has dropped hints about something else—something he says can do us harm. He says if I—that is, if Mr. Kean were to—" she faltered.

"That's quite all right. I think I know what you mean."

Sally coloured, but seemed grateful not to have to explain. "He says he knows something he could tell the authorities, which will make them suspect the worst. And he says that no one will believe me if I defend Mr. Kean, for they will think that we are lovers."

Hester could not hide her indignation. "Despicable man! Well, we shall have to find out what he knows."

Sally's splotched cheeks turned pale. "But how can we?"

Brought back to earth, Hester merely said, "I do not know yet, but until we think of something, you must not let him worry you overmuch."

Sally made a valiant effort. "I shall try not to, but—" she flushed— "that is why I have not appeared as . . . grateful . . . to Mr. Kean as I truly feel."

"I do understand the reason for your forbearance. And I thank you for it. I would not wish to see Jeremy in Newgate again, which is why I have begged him not to plague you until we know who murdered your husband and Mr. Simpkins's accusations cannot do any harm."

Sally appeared more cheerful on hearing this, which made Hester glad that she had confided this much to her at least. Their dinner had grown very cold by now, so together they collected the dishes and took them back downstairs to heat. Then Sally had to finish hers quickly in order to open the shop again, which left them no time for more talk.

What lay unspoken between them was the fear that Mr. Curry's killer might never be caught.

✆

Two days later, at nine o'clock at night, Gideon and Tom stood again in the shadows of Falcon Alley. Hiding their tools under their cloaks, they waited for Sally to pass them on her way to Bell Yard. Then they headed for the Bell and Bible where Mrs. Kean had promised to meet them.

The shop was dark and its shutters were closed, but as they knocked she quickly opened the door. She motioned them through it and carefully latched it again behind them. "We shall have to work fast," she said, reaching for the single candle she had left burning in a sconce. "I told Sally I would lock up the stall and be directly behind her."

"How did you convince her to leave you the keys?" Gideon removed his cloak and threw it onto the counter. It was already growing cold inside, for the fire had been extinguished, but he would need freedom to maneuver if they found a trapdoor. That was why he had worn the simple homespun he had got from Fanny's groom.

"She didn't need any urging. Poor Sally is very tired. Since Mr. Curry died, she's been shouldering the work at her house and the bookstall alone. When I asked if she'd allow me to help her in the bookstall, she agreed to it right away. Then I suggested that if she opened the shop in the morning, I could close it for her at night, once she showed me how."

While they'd been speaking, Mrs. Kean had used her candle to light a lantern, which she now handed to Tom.

Gideon moved behind the counter with the prise he had brought, and Tom held the lantern high so he could examine the floor. The wood was rough-hewn and riddled with flaws, which effectively hid any intentional notch. At first glance, Gideon could detect no difference between the boards that would suggest any opening, so he ran his fingers over them, giving an occasional tap with the dull end of his bar to listen for a hollow sound.

When he was certain he had found the right area to explore, Mrs. Kean addressed him nervously from across the counter. "I hope it won't be necessary to damage any wood, my lord. I should have a hard time explaining it if you did."

A bubble of laughter welled up inside Gideon's chest, but he restrained himself to a smile. "No need to worry, Mrs. Kean. I'm sure it won't be anything that a carpenter can't fix."

With the light from the lantern directed at the floor, he could not see her reaction, but Tom said, "Now don't go payin' him any mind, Mrs. Kean. That's just his lordship's way of teasin'."

"*Thank* you, Tom," she said, with a virtuous emphasis. "I am glad that one of you, at least, can appreciate the seriousness of this situation."

Gideon chuckled, and would have retorted, but just then his fingers came upon a suspicious nick. Stepping off the hollow area, he placed the sharp end of his prise between the two boards at that spot and gave it a gentle push. A piece of the floor budged, so he pushed down harder until he could slide his hand under the now visible trapdoor.

"You've found it, my lord!" There was pleasure in Tom's voice as he set the lantern down and bent to take the door from Gideon's hands.

"You truly have?" Mrs. Kean, who had been staying out of their way, peered over the counter at Gideon's work.

"Come see for yourself." He reached for her hand and pulled her around so they could both look down inside. Then taking the lantern up, he held it over the opening.

The top of a ladder was visible, with the rest disappearing into the darkness below. Gideon slowly moved the beam of light across the void, but it could not penetrate the areas beyond the perimeter of the opening itself.

He handed Tom the lantern again and said, "Hold this, while I climb down." Tom abhorred narrow spaces to the point of irrational fear, and Gideon would not embarrass him in front of Mrs. Kean by sending him down. Besides, Gideon wanted to see the space for himself.

He quickly climbed half-way down and reached up for the lantern before continuing down to the floor. Beneath his feet, surprisingly, he felt stones, which made him believe that he had landed in a section of the ancient crypt. As he turned in a circle, holding the lantern up, he saw what looked like a rabbit warren of passages, some blocked by fallen stones, which should give anyone pause who wished to explore. Layers of grit and dust covered the stones, which ground further beneath his boots. From the lack of footprints in the dust beyond a small area, he doubted that Curry had ever bothered to go farther.

At the base of the ladder stood a few wooden boxes with their lids down. If Curry had possessed a "private stock," this assuredly would be it. Gideon raised one of the lids and found it full of pamphlets and unbound books. He extracted one and, expecting a Jacobite tract, began to read. It took him only a few seconds to see that the pamphlet in his hand had nothing to do with politics or the Crown. Tossing it back, he chose another from a different box, and found the same kind of material. Then, chuckling to himself, he checked the other boxes to make certain he hadn't missed anything, but the boxes all contained the same type of literature.

Up inside the Bell and Bible, Hester waited impatiently. Although St. Mars had lost no time in locating the trapdoor, she was aware that the ticking seconds raised the risk that Sally would return to see what was keeping her.

When Hester saw St. Mars's head and then his shoulders appear through the trap, she eagerly inched forward, but he said nothing as he climbed the ladder back into the shop. Then, handing the lantern back to Tom, he stood and faced her with a curious expression on his face.

"Well, my lord . . ." she said, breaking the silence, "did you find it? Are there treasonous pamphlets down there?"

St. Mars took a deep breath, and she could see that he was trying not to smile. "Treasonous . . . ? No . . . I found nothing of that nature."

Surprised and let down, she said, "Then, there is nothing?"

"Oh, there is something. A great deal of something, in fact. But there are no Jacobite pamphlets in Curry's cellar."

"Is it something else illegal?"

Leaning against the counter with arms folded, he considered this. "Probably . . . inasmuch as the pamphlets seem to have escaped the stamp tax, and unless I am much mistaken, the original versions may have escaped the customs officials."

"Original versions?" Confused and frustrated, Hester's anxiety got the better of her. She tried not to snap at him. "My lord, you are teasing me. Pray enlighten me as to what you discovered below, or I shall look for myself."

He started up, as if to block her way. Then, seeing she had made no move, he laughed. "I shouldn't go down there, if I were you, Mrs. Kean. But I would tell Sally that you stumbled upon a cache of objectionable material, and I would urge her to burn it before the authorities are called again."

Hester wrinkled her brow. She was about to ask what he meant by "objectionable" when an offended huff from Tom and a grin from St. Mars suddenly made her understand. "Do you mean indecent material?" she asked.

St. Mars nodded. "I believe the Society for the Reformation of Manners would consider it so. It is not illegal to print it, but it might as well be, for a bookseller could be hounded for selling it." As she stared incredulously at him, he added sympathetically, "I believe it is a case wherein 'a man may be allowed to keep his poisons in his closet, but not publicly to vend them as cordials.'"

Hester shook her head, which was foggy with confusion. "Then, nothing makes any sense, for I don't see why a priest in danger of arrest for treason would bother himself about a cache of obscene books."

"True, but it could explain Sally's customer from the other day."

"But this—this literature surely has no bearing upon the murder."

"Perhaps not, but possibly."

Before she could ask him how, the lantern spluttered, and they turned to find that it was about to go out. Hester remembered Sally and said, "Oh dear! I have been too long, and Sally is sure to ask questions."

As they snatched up their cloaks and prepared to leave the shop, St. Mars said, "Before she does, you can tell her about the cache you found, which will explain why you left the bookstall so late."

This advice soothed Hester as she locked the door behind them. "Now I must only think of a plausible scenario for finding the trapdoor when it took you a minute examination of the floor and a crow bar to do it."

"Tell her you struck your toe against the notch I found, and when you bent down to see what it was, you noticed the seam in the floor. I suspect she will be too worried by what's beneath it to waste her breath questioning how you found it."

"I hope so," Hester said. She looked about them, but the adjoining shops were all closed. The pedestrians in Fleet Street were too far away to hear and they appeared no clearer than shadowy shapes in the dark. With St. Mars's face similarly protected by the night and the prevalent haze of coal smoke, she accepted his escort as far as the entrance to Bell Yard. Wrapping their cloaks about them, they set quietly on the way, with Tom walking a few paces behind.

"What did you mean when you said that the original versions might have escaped the customs officials?" she asked.

"Only that I suspect they came from France. Salacious stories are banned in France, but their authors find a way to sell them here."

Hester gave a shudder, but she refrained from expressing her distaste aloud. "I still do not understand why Mr. Sullivan would care about Mr. Curry's store if that is what it contains."

"Nor do I, for certain, but I have a theory I'd like to explore."

Before Hester could ask him about it, they arrived at Bell Yard. She did not dare tarry, so he promised to get in touch with her at the bookstall as soon as he had any more information to impart.

As soon as Hester saw Sally, she told her about the printed material she had found beneath the floor. As St. Mars had predicted, Sally was too upset over the existence of anything for which she might be pilloried or taxed to wonder how Hester had seen a seam in the floor that she herself had missed. She agreed at once that the material must be destroyed, and sent a note to Jeremy asking him to come the next morning to burn it for her.

"I knew that Mr. Curry had been sent to the stocks," she said later, as they supped on bread and cheese, "but I never knew why. He never told me."

"You never suspected that he might be selling anything else?"

"No . . . but he always insisted that I should leave him to close the shop. I guess that is when his lecherous customers would come—in the dark after I had gone home."

It seemed so revolting to Hester, especially when she thought how repulsive Mr. Curry was. But more than one person must have known about the stock. The customers who bought it and anyone else they might have told. There was also the question of who had printed the indecent material, for Mr. Curry had no printing press.

Another thought occurred to her. "Do you think that Mr. Simpkins could have known about it? Could that be the secret he's been threatening you with?"

Sally raised her head with a jerk. "It could be! And if he does know about it, he could inform the authorities any day."

"Then the sooner it is burned the better. And that will be one less thing to worry you," Hester said. "I also can't help wondering whether your husband's murderer might have known about the stock beneath the shop. If the customers who bought it always came later when you were here at home, they would have known that your husband would be alone in the bookstall that night."

Sally loudly sucked in her breath. "Do you think it was a customer who killed him?"

Hester shook her head, impatient with herself. "I shouldn't speculate about something so important. There is no way to know. I am simply trying to make sense of the things that confuse me."

The main circumstance that troubled her was the fact that the killer had locked the bookstall behind him. Why? Had he worried that a stranger might see Mr. Curry's body and stumble across the trapdoor. He might have worried that the material would be stolen before he could return for it. But return to do what with it? And why would a customer have murdered Mr. Curry?

Or what if the killer had been looking for the hiding place himself and Mr. Curry had caught him in an attempted theft? If so, he might have panicked and throttled the bookseller to avoid arrest. But in that case, again, why lock the shop?

Perhaps, it was simply a result of the killer's panic, and she was fumbling for reason in a situation that did not follow any logic. There were still too many questions to be answered, but there was one thing Hester could be grateful for. Now that she was living with Sally, she stood a far better chance of answering them.

Not therefore humble he who seeks retreat,
Pride guides his steps, and bids him shun the great:
Who combats bravely is not therefore brave,
He dreads a deathbed like the meanest slave:
Who reasons wisely is not therefore wise,
His pride in Reasoning, not in Acting lies.

CHAPTER XVIII

G ideon *had* developed a theory about Joseph Sullivan's interest in the bookstall, but to prove it he would have to do something that would alarm Mrs. Kean.

The maze of stone passageways under the Bell and Bible had given him a notion he meant to explore. If the Bell and Bible had a portion of the old crypt of St. Dunstan's beneath it, it was possible that the house across from it did as well.

More than once now, he and Tom had observed the priest disappearing inside that house with a bundle which he had deposited inside—possibly beneath the ground floor? There was only one way to find out, and that would be to search the cellar of the barber's shop to see what he might be hiding. But gaining entry to the house would be more difficult than asking Mrs. Kean to borrow a key. On the other hand, St. Mars had fewer qualms about breaking into the barber's shop. If he was unable to find anything incriminating in the process, he could always find some way to pay for the damage he had done.

He knew better, however, than to concern Mrs. Kean with his plan. Telling Tom would be ticklish enough. He flirted with the idea of not including Tom in the venture, but Tom had helped him out of too many dangerous situations to be left in the dark. He might not approve of his master's actions, but his tendency to scold had grown weaker as he had accustomed himself to their lives as outlaws.

To soften him up, the next evening before they set out, Gideon informed him that he had engaged the doctor to examine Katy. Unfortunately, no matter how happily Tom received this news, it did nothing to stem his reaction to a notion he considered more foolhardy than rash.

As soon as Gideon told him what he planned to do that evening, Tom gaped at him and said, "Have you lost every penn'orth of sense you was born with?"

This was an unpromising response, so Gideon asserted his authority. "Now, Tom, you know I have remonstrated with you before about addressing me in such a disrespectful way."

Tom was too mad, and feeling too ill-used, to consider this as much of a threat. He gave an indignant huff. "So, I suppose you mean to turn me off for speaking my mind? When it's me what has kept you from breaking your neck too many times to count?"

"No . . . ." Gideon did his best to sound reasonable. He should have known that Tom would see through his wiles. "But you might reflect that I could have gone on this escapade without you. I did think of doing it, but it is precisely because I do rely upon you to guard my back that I did not."

This statement did have a palliative effect. At least, the anger faded from Tom's face, leaving only a bit more than his usual disgruntlement, which Gideon took for a step towards resignation.

He pursued his advantage. "I have to have a look under that barber's shop. If I'm right, the priest is hiding something illegal there. I doubt he had any interest in Curry's dirty business. If he had, he would simply have found a way to alert the authorities to its existence without calling their attention to himself. But his behaviour suggests that he is more anxious to see that Curry's secret cache goes undiscovered. And unless he has a passion for dirty literature himself, which I sincerely doubt, he must fear that if Curry's secret is discovered, his own may be, too."

"But I don't see why you have to concern yourself with that, when it means he didn't kill Mr. Curry."

"We still don't know that. You should have seen the warren that runs under that shop. Now that I have, I've thought of another possible motive for Sullivan. I wonder if Curry could have heard him or someone moving about in the cellar of the shop across from his. No more than twenty-five paces separate the two. It is dark down there and stones and timbers have fallen to block the passageways, but that doesn't mean that noises couldn't carry. If Curry heard something and got curious enough to investigate, he might have stumbled across whatever Joseph Sullivan has planned. And if his plans are important enough to risk exposure as a Roman priest, when priests have been banned from London, they might be important enough to Sullivan at least to kill for."

It was clear that Tom had the picture now, but he was still not happy with his master's dangerous plan.

"Believe me, Tom, when I say that it will be much less risky to search the cellar from the barber's shop than to try to reach it from the Bell and Bible. That crypt was closed off for good reason."

He could almost see Tom's inward shudder at the thought of exploring that crypt.

Gideon went on to press his case for a few more minutes, and Tom eventually grumbled, "Well, it's plain you've got your head set on it, so how do we go about it?"

"I'll tell you on the way."

The air on the Thames after midnight was bitterly cold. Few watermen were still plying their trade. Without the seasonal traffic from Spring Gardens at Vauxhall, none could be induced to dock this far from the City in hopes of a fare. Gideon had prepared for this by engaging an oarsman for the night. With Tom carrying the equipment they needed, they found the boat waiting for them at Vauxhall Stairs.

Gideon waited until the boat had disgorged them on the opposite bank before telling Tom the details of his plan. Fortunately the need for silence hushed the protests he could feel emanating from his groom in the dark.

Slinking through alleyways to avoid the watch, they quietly felt their way to Fleet Street in a night made blacker by a fog and no moon. At this hour between the taverns' closing and the markets' opening, the streets should have been still, but in the City there was always life. An occasional hackney coach rattled through the mist with its late-night fare. The sounds of a brawl could be heard not too far away, probably the result of a constable's attempts to convey drunkards to the Poultry. Anyone caught walking the streets this late could be suspected of drunkenness, submitted to a catechism, and carted off to the roundhouse for the night.

As Gideon and Tom drew near the Bell and Bible, a group of urchins who'd been huddling on a doorstep for warmth saw them pass and began to beg loudly. Gideon hastily fished some coins out of his pocket to silence them, and Tom shooed them away. Then they pressed on, the brims of their hats pulled low and their cloaks pulled high about their jaws to conceal the pallor of their faces.

In Fleet Street, they halted in the shadow of a building to peer about.

The Bell and Bible and the barber-surgeon's shop were both shrouded in mist. Here the smelly fog was thinner than it had been on the water, but every bit would help to obscure their activities. Nothing moved in the street at the moment but a bedraggled dog that was digging at a wall to worry a rat.

Gideon took a deep breath, and said, "Give me the sack."

As Tom lowered it to the ground, Gideon removed his woolen cloak and wound it tightly into a bundle. He bent to feel inside the sack and found his blue satin cape. He pulled it out and threw it around his shoulders, before reaching for the black half-mask Tom was holding out.

Tom said in a low voice, "I still don't see why you have to dress like a criminal."

Gideon knotted the mask behind his head and the cape strings across his chest, "If anyone sees me breaking in, I want them to think I was looking for something to steal. I don't want to alert the priest to our suspicions, and we will if he questions my motive for breaking into a barber's shop at night."

"But the barber-surgeon lives upstairs! It'll be burglary, my lord, as soon as you put your hand inside his window. They'll hang you for sure!"

"Not if no one catches me, and that's where you come in, Tom. The moment the watch is alerted, I want you to make yourself as visible as possible. Cross to the barber shop as if you've been attracted by the noise, and try to keep anyone from coming in. Stand in the doorway if you have to and shout that you saw me fleeing through the side window. Shout until you're blue in the face if you have to. Then when you're certain that no one will search the shop, lead them around the side. Be sure to tell them you saw a mask and a blue cape, so when I emerge without them, they won't suspect me."

"You're never going to leave them inside!" A hopeful note rang in Tom's voice.

"No, hate to disappoint you, but I'm not ready to retire Blue Satan yet." Gideon tucked his rolled-up cloak beneath his left arm, then gathered up the chisels they had brought.

"I wish you wouldn't do this, my lord."

Tom's anguish gave him pause, but the blood in Gideon's veins was thrumming with the need for action. Ignoring Tom's words, he bade him not to forget his instructions and crossed the street, covering his pale face with his cape until he reached the corner shop, where he put his tools down on the pavement to feel at the door with both hands.

He had noted the age of the building before, for the Great Fire had spared it. The windows that had not been bricked up were casements, built before the double sliding-sash had been brought to London by the Dutch. The panes were small and the shutters inside looked stout, so Gideon hoped he could find a way to enter by the door.

As he ran his hands around the jamb, splinters poked into his fingers. If he had to, he could probably split the wood with his crow, but with the barber asleep upstairs, Gideon hoped to make as little noise as possible. He found the hinges—two—and felt for their pins.

As he had hoped, both had worked their way out a fraction of an inch, as pins tended to do over time, giving him the space he needed to insert his chisel. Kneeling, he picked up the shorter of his instruments, wedged it beneath the head of the bottom pin, and tapped on its handle, feeling occasionally to see what progress he had made.

He had wrapped his palms in layers of cloth, both for warmth and to cushion them from repeated blows. This lower hinge was the harder since kneeling and bending robbed him of some of his strength. By the time he felt the pin give sufficiently that he could pull it from the top, he could feel the bruise on his palm where the handle had struck his frozen flesh. Leaving the pin partially in, he stood and started on the top one, which gave suddenly as if it had recently been oiled.

Fumbling with frozen fingers in the dark, he managed to catch it before it reached the ground. Gaining control of it finally, he set it quietly down on the pavement, then removed the lower pin and placed it with the first.

Now that the easiest part was over, he took a few breaths and peered about. To his right he thought he saw the dim glow of a lantern breaking through the mist in a swinging arc. Then he heard the watch call out the hour, surely no more than ten houses away. The man was still invisible, his figure cloaked by the murky fog that had muffled his approaching steps, but soon Gideon could make out the sound of his shuffling and the grumbling under his breath.

As the watch came closer, Gideon heard him banging on doors and shouting, "'Tis one of the clock, and all's well." Evidently resenting the fact that he had to be out on such a cold night, the watchman was determined that no one else should enjoy his sleep.

Gideon took advantage of one of these bangings to pick up his tools and slip around the side of the shop, where he flattened his back against the wall. The cold of the stone seeped through the thin satin of his cloak and turned his shoulder blades to ice. It was almost more than he could do to keep from shivering. If he had been given more warning, he might have sought a better hiding place, but without a light he could not see where to go, and the possibility that he might drop a chisel and make noise seemed the greater risk. If he remained perfectly still, the watchman might pass by without seeing him. But if he held his lantern up and peered around the corner, Gideon would be caught.

He had never dreamed of assaulting the watch, but as the man drew nearer, Gideon prepared for the necessity. He could drop the tools he had brought, and he had no doubt that he could overcome the man, who sounded half drunk. Then he realized what the greatest danger would be. If the watchman knocked upon this door, without any hinge pins the door would give. The resulting crash would bring not only the barber-surgeon, but every able-bodied man within hearing.

He prepared to run, but before he could worry any more, the watch, in the shape of an elderly drunkard, shuffled past. Muttering curses against the cold, and someone who might have been his wife, he peered neither right nor left, but wove an unsteady path across to St. Dunstan's and beyond where he was swallowed up again by the fog. Relieved that he would not have to add assaulting the watch to the list of crimes he was wanted for, Gideon waited until he was certain the man would not return before slipping round the front of the shop again.

After setting one of his tools down, he used the other to pry the door from its jamb. This proved to be much harder than he had expected, for it was securely locked from the inside. He took one side of it off its hinges and tried to ease it out of the latch, but it wouldn't give, so in the end he had to use force to prise it open.

When he did, before he could stop, the door let loose with a loud crack as if the screws that held the lock had split the wood. Sudden noises erupted in the projecting room above his head—footfalls, the thunk of a bolt, the creak of window hinges—and a man's voice cried down, "Who's there?"

Gideon froze, sheltered from the occupant's view by the overhanging story of the ancient house. Thinking fast, he considered and rejected the idea that keeping silent would throw the barber off. The noise Gideon had made had been loud enough to wake him, and he would not be satisfied until it was explained.

Then a bolder notion occurred. He held the door steady with one hand and knocked loudly on it with the other. "'Tis one of the clock and all's well!" he slurred in a grumbling voice.

Even from where he stood, he could hear the other man's sigh of exasperation. "You cursed fool! How many times have I told you not to disturb decent people in their sleep? I'll talk to the beadle about this— just see if I don't!"

The window creaked shut again, with a sound on closing that resembled the wrenching of a vise, as if the barber-surgeon had given the crank a last angry push. Gideon waited breathlessly, but no further noises came from upstairs. He was so relieved by the success of his ploy that he wanted to laugh, but he knew he had used up any indulgence Providence was likely to grant.

Carefully now, he lowered the hinged side of the broken door to the pavement a fraction of an inch at a time to smother all other unusual sounds. Then, when he had balanced it somehow on one bottom corner, he groped in his pocket for his tinder box and a candle stub and struck a light.

The interior of the barber's shop looked unremarkable by the faint beam of his candle, with a large chair in the centre of the room, and cabinets wherein presumably he kept his gruesome instruments. A combination of rushes and hair covered the floor, but the tangy odor of blood still seemed to hover over all. Beyond casting a look about to get his bearings, Gideon wasted no time in the front room of the shop. If his theory was correct, he would find the evidence to support it underneath. Moving as quietly as he could, he searched for an opening that would lead him to the cellar, and located it in a small room just off the first. Then he quickly extinguished his candle and felt the floor until his fingers encountered two hinges. Relieved that he would not have to prise this trap out of its place, he found a metal ring at the other end and pulled it up.

The trap lifted with no sound. It had obviously been recently oiled, a mistake on the barber-surgeon's part, but one which worked to Gideon's advantage. Smelling the dank air that rose up from the ground, Gideon felt about the opening for the top of a ladder, and as soon as he had found it, started down, pausing only to lower the trapdoor behind him. When both his feet had landed soundly on stone, he lit his candle again and took a look about.

The space he found himself in was very like the one beneath the Bell and Bible, but larger and put to greater use. Since no attempt had been made to conceal it, Gideon was not surprised to discover that it held what appeared to be several pieces of old, broken furniture. He was dismayed, however, by the thought of the time it would take to search it, for the watchman should return in an hour. And even drunk as he was, he was likely to notice a door that had been taken off its hinges. Gideon also worried that with the door now open, cold air would be pouring into the warmer house and might wake the barber again.

He was ready to start looking in chests, when his candle picked up a trace of footprints in the dust. Gideon held his beam higher and saw that they led behind some bales of wool, incongruously lined up in a row, and disappeared into an arched passageway inside the old crypt. This area did not appear to be blocked, so with his heart quickening he followed the tracks, stooping so as not to bump into the stone arch over his head.

He had not gone many paces before he began to see stacks of small barrels lined against the wall. They were easily of a size that a man could carry alone, and might be Sullivan's bundles. Before Gideon stopped to see what they contained, he crept farther along the passageway—really an aisle of the crypt he saw now, with ancient tombs lodged in its walls—to see if he could reach the cellar beneath the Bell and Bible. Moving only as fast as the feeble glow from his candle would advance, he had the feeling that the bookstall lay in this general direction, but the farther he went, the more debris he found. In a few more steps, he came to the end of any possible exploration for he encountered a tall pile of large stones, too formidable to attack. Other pieces had been stacked before the blockage, making him think they had been cleared from the section through which he had passed. Dirt and stone dust falling on his head made him retreat, but he thought he had seen enough.

The blockage was not so complete that sounds could not have travelled through it. Perhaps Edmund Curry had been down in his cellar and had heard the priest talking to the barber-surgeon in here. He might have heard details about whatever plot they'd been hatching.

Gideon retraced the few steps to where he'd found the barrels stacked. He squatted near one and held his candle up to look for a label that might betray its contents. Then he saw a metal strip attached to one end, and he sprang backwards, his heart leaping into his throat.

The barrels were gunpowder kegs, which he should have seen immediately if his light had been stronger—or, if he had not been so intent in exploring the crypt, he admitted wryly. He could have ignited one with his flame and brought the whole building crashing down.

Thoughts of what the kegs could be for filled him with dread. The powder could be for guns, but if it was, where was the shot that should go with it? There were no weapons down here. If Sullivan was arming a group of local Jacobites, surely he would have stored everything they needed as well. So it followed that blowing-up something was more likely his aim. Whatever the priest had in mind, something was destined for destruction. And at the cost of how many lives?

Whatever his target could be was something Gideon did not have to figure out here. Just being in the presence of so much gunpowder made him nervous. Determined to leave, he made a quick count of the kegs and returned to the main cellar. There he extinguished his candle before reaching for the ladder.

No sooner had he stepped upon the first rung than the sound of muffled shouts reached him from above. He paused, and his pulse began to race. He knew he must move in the right direction, for an error could expose him at just the wrong moment. The thick floor had kept him from hearing the initial outcries, in which case others beside the watch would have gathered, and the barber would have been roused. Gideon quickly thought of what he would do if it were he who had an illegal store of gunpowder under his shop. The first thing he would do, on learning that his shop door had been breached, would be to see if the intruder had discovered his cache.

Gideon stepped back down just at the moment a closer noise sounded above him. The shouting seemed to have stopped, which should mean that Tom had carried out his instructions. But the barber was still in the shop. Gideon moved quickly, feeling in the dark for one of the large pillars that supported the vault, just as the trapdoor above him was raised and the glow of a lantern shone down. The sudden burst of light allowed him to slip behind the pillar without stumbling over a broken chair, while he assumed the barber's eyes would have to adjust to the relative darkness. He knew how poorly a lantern shed light down into a hole.

Then the lantern was extinguished, and Gideon heard a footstep on the ladder. The barber was coming down to see if the burglar had discovered his cellar.

He quieted his breathing, though the pace of his pulse made him want to take a huge gulp of air. The air in the cellar was thin as it was, but if he could avoid being caught he could wait until the tumult had died. The brilliance of his hiding place was that the barber would never dare ask the watch or a constable to search the cellar for the intruder.

But the barber himself might be armed. If worse came to worst, Gideon would try to overpower him, but that would alert the priest that his plot had been uncovered—a complication Gideon wished to avoid.

He heard the barber's boot reach the cellar floor. There he paused as if to listen. If he lit his lantern, Gideon wondered if his body would cast a shadow and alert the other man to his position. The lingering scent from the candle he had lit could also give him away. He was getting ready to spring from his hiding place if need be, when a voice up in the shop called out something that sounded like, "'Oy!"

Immediately, the barber started to hurry back up the ladder. When he reached the top, he climbed out and lowered the trapdoor behind him with a thud.

Gideon took the few deep gulps of air he had craved before deciding that he had spent long enough in this hole. He lit a candle only long enough to pick his way back to the base of the ladder. Then, extinguishing it again, he quickly climbed until his head touched the door. With barely a pause—for he had had enough of this space—he silently raised the trapdoor an inch with inward thanks to the barber for oiling its hinges.

The first voice that greeted his ears was Tom's. Tom appeared to be posing as a concerned Londoner who, on his way past, had discovered the barber's door off its hinges and had alerted the watch. He was explaining that the watchmen and a constable who had been at the watch house had taken off after the burglar they had seen fleeing the shop.

The powers of invention required to revise their story into this version impressed Gideon very much. He wondered, though, how Tom would ever get the barber to leave his shop.

"Did you see him, too?" the barber asked.

Tom said, "Yes," and described Gideon's mask and blue satin cape.

"Then it was a burglar!" the barber said, relief in his voice.

"Who else would it be?"

At this question, the barber denied any particular meaning. He thanked Tom for the service he had done him, clearly with the intention of sending him about his business. But Tom said he had promised the constable to stand guard at the shop. He wondered aloud that the owner of the house wouldn't want to follow the watch to see if he could help in the capture of the burglar.

While Tom was distracting the barber, Gideon eased the trapdoor all the way open, climbed quietly out, and lowered the door into its place. Through the doorway into the main room he could see the barber with his back towards him, and Tom facing him, standing just outside the door to the shop. They appeared to be at an impasse, with the barber trying to rid himself of Tom and Tom failing to budge the barber. It would be only a matter of time before the barber began to suspect Tom of being an accomplice. And when the watchmen did not pick up Blue Satan's trail, they would soon be back.

Making a quick decision, Gideon emerged from his hiding place and crept up on the man still facing Tom. With the room in darkness, the only light coming from a link in Tom's hand, Gideon was almost within reach of his goal when Tom spied him. In his surprise, a gasp escaped him. The barber whirled to see what had prompted it, and Gideon greeted him with a punch to the jaw.

His blow knocked the barber flat. Gideon leapt over his prostrate body and, without pausing to see if the man raised himself, ran with Tom. Reaching the alley across Fleet Street, they picked up the sack with Gideon's clothing inside. Then, as they felt their way towards the Thames, Gideon stripped off his mask and exchanged his cape for the woolen cloak.

There was no hue and cry behind them. Gideon didn't know if he had knocked the barber unconscious or if the man had decided he'd better not call out for the watch, who would want to see where Blue Satan had been hiding. By now the barber would know that his cache of gunpowder had likely been discovered, and he would wonder what interest a highwayman had in it. But certain as Gideon was that the barber would never call the law down upon him, the barber was, too, that no criminal would alert them to his store.

The waterman Gideon had hired for the night rowed them back towards Vauxhall Stairs. Then, before they reached the landing, he lifted his oars out of the water and allowed the boat to glide. Facing them in the cold and the dark, he cleared his throat. "I don't ask ye wot the two of ye're doin' sneakin' about in the middle of the night," he said.

Gideon, whose strength had been fired by the danger, but whose blood had already started to cool, had to bite his tongue to keep from swearing. He ought to have foreseen that the waterman would become suspicious. At least the fellow had not alerted the law, but he certainly knew enough to bring the authorities to them.

"Why are we slowing?" Gideon tried to buy time to think.

"I thought mebbe we could have a little chat."

When Gideon did not respond, the waterman continued, "Ye don't look much like footpads t'me. 'Course, I could be wrong."

"If that is what you think, you would be." A harsh wind was whistling past their ears and the cold night air with its sulfury smell was nearly intolerable. But, short of tossing the waterman into the Thames, Gideon could think of no alternative to listening to him.

He asked the man what he wanted.

"Spoken like the gen'leman I took ye for," he answered cheerfully. "And if ye weren't up to no mischief, the better it'd be for me—not that I'm askin' to know yer business. All I was goin' to say was that a waterman's business an't as good as it used ter be, see. What with them carridges the tufts are ridin' in now, and all the rich men's ladies clammerin' for one . . . well, a man 'as got ter find 'is business where he can find it, see?"

"You want to work for me?" Relieved to meet with a fairly gentle form of blackmail, Gideon decided to cut through his monologue. "If that is all you want, couldn't we discuss it in a warmer place? If you do not get us off this river soon, we might have to murder you to keep from freezing to death."

The man gave a jerk before he understood Gideon's jest. Then he pulled on his oars with a powerful stroke, and chuckled. "Don't mind if I do. Name's Nathaniel, but people call me Nate." In a few more seconds, he had brought them to the landing below Gideon's house.

As he climbed out of the boat, Gideon told Tom to wait while Nate tied up, and then lead him up to the house. There he would ply the waterman with beer from Southwark's finest brewer and offer him a fixed wage to be available whenever called, and as long as the proposed wages were more than Nate could expect to make in a year on his own,

Gideon had no doubt his offer would be accepted. But it was nearly dawn, and he would have to deal with this matter before he gave any more thought to Joseph Sullivan's plans

As he mounted the bank to his house, he reflected with a touch of wry humour that his little household would insist on growing, despite his need to hide.

Who suffer thus, mere Charity should own,
Must act on motives powerful, though unknown.
Some War, some Plague, or Famine they foresee,
Some Revelation hid from you and me.

CHAPTER XIX

Hester had little time to wonder what plan St. Mars was considering, for the next morning all of Fleet Street was alive with the news that the highwayman Blue Satan had broken into the barber-surgeon's shop across from St. Dunstan's. The first customer who came in to buy a book told her everything he had heard from the gingerbread peddler on the corner. Hester did not have to feign surprise for the thought of how rashly St. Mars had acted left her aghast. Just the day before she had assisted Jeremy in burning the books in Mr. Curry's hidden store . . . and now, this.

"Did they capture him?" Her heart stopped in the middle of a beat while she waited for his answer.

"No, he escaped. And he did not manage to steal anything." As he left, the customer tipped his tricorn to Sally saying, "Consider yourself fortunate that he did not break in here."

Hester released her pent up breath.

Across the counter Mr. Tubbs, who was in the bookstall trying to persuade Sally to publish his chapbook on Blue Satan, wriggled with excitement. His voice was even intelligible as he insisted that this news would create more interest in his story. The version he had written of Hester's "abduction" was ready to print, and he was convinced it would make his fortune. Hester had never seen him so cheerful, but no matter how pleased she was for the odd little man, whose rags alone demanded her compassion, she could not be sanguine about St. Mars's exploit. She would have some very strong words to say to him the next time they met.

Sally had only risked her inheritance on one publication—another collection of Jeremy's *Tales from the Dead,* for which a healthy audience had already been proven. But she was clearly intrigued by Tubbs's idea. She had developed a good sense of business and knew what kind of tale the public liked. "I suppose I could publish it," she said, "although I don't really know how to go about it."

"The printer can advise you, and I will go with you to see him," Tubbs pressed. "Only have to decide how many copies you want . . . and pay of course." He nervously pulled on his hair with ink-stained fingers.

While Sally was mulling over her answer, the door opened and Joseph Sullivan walked in. Unprepared, Hester did her best to greet him as if she knew nothing of his secrets. As he tucked his hat under his arm and loosened the cloak about his shoulders, his smile seemed strained. For the first time, she thought she saw a hardness in his eyes. Addressing the room at large, he asked if they had heard the news of the robbery.

"Robbery?" Hester said. "But I thought that nothing was taken." Blue Satan had enough mistruths spread about him. He did not need any more.

Sullivan lifted a brow. "Is that right, now? Well, perhaps ya've heard more than me. I just learned of the break-in myself and came to see if ya'd noticed anything strange."

While Sally denied having known about the incident until a few minutes ago, Hester took the opportunity to watch the priest. He had to be lying, but he did it so smoothly, she would never have suspected a lie if she had not already known the truth. Now she began to see why St. Mars believed the man was dangerous.

Then Tubbs blurted, "M-Mrs. Curry is going to p-publish the book I have written about Blue Satan—when he abducted Mrs. Kean."

A gasp of outrage escaped her. With a jerk Sullivan swung his head around, all trace of his affability gone.. "Begorrah!" he exclaimed. "Is that right?"

Hester threw Tubbs a resentful look, but he avoided her gaze. "It was hardly an abduction, as I clearly informed Mr. Tubbs. In fact, the story he's written bears little resemblance to the truth. But he did want to write it, and Jeremy and I agreed to help him, as long as he did not use my name."

Tubbs muttered an apology, but the worried looks he darted were aimed principally at Sally. He was more concerned that she would refuse to publish his writing than repentant for betraying Hester.

But Sullivan had no interest in Tubbs's offence. Taking a step closer to Hester, he said, "But what intrigue is this? I promise I'll not tell a soul, if ya tell me what occurred."

Hester hoped he would interpret her reluctance to speak as the natural embarrassment a maiden should feel when an abduction was linked with her name. "Blue Satan stopped my lady's carriage on our way to Rotherham Abbey last spring. Since Lord Hawkhurst's men were still armed, the highwayman took me up as a kind of shield and left me to make my way back to my lady on foot. But there was no real abduction. He left me as soon as he was safely out of reach and rode away."

"Not very chivalrous, was it?" Sullivan insinuated. "Sure, and it's a remarkable coincidence, though. That ya'd be the victim of a highwayman, and not a year later, the same villain would appear in London across from this shop?" He looked as if he would have tried to force Hester into confessing to a conspiracy, if there had been no witnesses to see him. He would be looming over her if the counter had not been between them.

"It is strange," she admitted, hoping her agreement would satisfy him. "Stranger still that he should risk being caught in London."

"Right ya're. Come to think of it, I wonder why a highwayman would try to rob a barber-surgeon's shop." He fixed Hester with a piercing look, before doing the same to Tubbs. "He could not have expected to find much to steal."

The little man was taken aback by this curious aspect, which he had obviously not considered. Frowning, he mumbled, "Could've mistaken the house."

"Ya think?" Hester noticed that Sullivan's Irish accent was more evident today, perhaps because he was upset. "How peculiar! But maybe the boy's right," Sullivan said, shaking his head. "The fog was thick last night, and if he did not know his way about, perhaps he mistook it for a different shop—this one, ya think?"

Sally gave a shudder and asked how the burglar had got in. When Sullivan related how the door had been taken off its hinges, she gasped. "How did he ever do it without being heard?"

He pretended not to know. "But I shouldn't have frightened ya," he said soothingly. "After all, it was not so very long ago that this shop was broken into." A thought seemed to strike him and he added, "I wonder if it was that blue devil who murdered yar husband?"

Hester gave a start. "But why should he?" she asked.

Sullivan disclaimed any understanding of a criminal's mind. "But, as I recollect," he added, "there was nothing taken on that occasion either."

Sally's hand moved to her throat. "But how could we ever prove it?" She turned to Hester and her expression said that Sullivan had convinced her. She seemed to be reminding Hester about the store of indecent material she had found under the floor. She didn't know what a highwayman would have had to do with it, but the coincidence of two break-ins being made by two different criminals was clearly too much to accept.

If St. Mars had been there in that minute, Hester would have had a hard time not lecturing him on the consequences of acting rashly. Now, even Sally thought he might have throttled her husband. There was nothing she could say to deny it, for it would appear strange for her to defend a highwayman. It almost seemed as if the priest were trying to provoke such a reaction from her.

Tubbs scowled and chewed his cuticles through the holes in his gloves. Hester could almost hear the struggle going on inside his brain as he hesitated to speak. If Sally believed that Blue Satan had killed her husband, she might be less interested in publishing his book, though it could make the story more attractive to another bookseller.

"Hoare's Bank is just across Fleet Street," Hester said. "Perhaps Blue Satan got turned about in the fog."

Support for this latest fabrication came from an unexpected source.

"Sure and it's a plausible notion you have there, Mrs. Kean." Sullivan had resumed his amiable pose. "Whatever the villain wanted, it was not inside the barber-surgeon's shop, I'll warrant. And I doubt he'll return to plague us. If he does, we'll all have to be ready for him next time." He smiled and rubbed his gloved hands together as if eager for a fight, but his eyes held a threat, which she believed he thought she would pass on to the intruder.

She felt relieved on the one hand. If nothing *was* missing from the shop, he could afford to forget the incident. But the threat in his gaze made her nervous. She did not doubt he would be on his guard in case Blue Satan interfered with his plans.

Again St. Mars's warning about the priest echoed in her head.

He replaced his hat, fastened his cloak, and took his leave. In the doorway he passed a gentleman entering, in a bright red coat that showed beneath his cloak. He wore thick white paint on his face, and a profusion of patches from forehead to chin. This new gentleman took no notice of the departing Mr. Sullivan, but arrogantly strolled through the door without so much as a thank you for the man who held it ajar.

Behind Hester, Sally issued a low groan. Hester thought she might break into hysterics herself, for the newcomer was none other than St. Mars, whom she had seen disguised this way before. After her encounter with the priest, she did not think she could handle any more challenges. But here he was, and she would have to pretend not to know him, when she had been terrified by his latest exploit.

He minced the few steps to the counter, emitting enough scent to fill a perfumer's shop, and raised a glass to his eye, through which he studied each of the remaining three in turn. Poor Tubbs received a sneering look. He glowered, grunted, and turned red. St. Mars then turned his focus on Sally and attempted to engage her in a flirtation, but she excused herself, gesturing for Tubbs to join her at the far end of the counter. "If you will forgive me, sir, this good man and I must conduct a little business."

"Well . . . if you must." St. Mars stifled a yawn with his gloved hand. Then his gaze fell on Hester, and he said, "But what delightful creature have we here? Another nymph? Well, I shan't be left to amuse myself then, shall I?" This last was tossed at Sally as if he hoped to make her jealous.

Passing behind Hester on her way to the other side of the stall, Sally whispered in a persecuted voice, "Could you please attend to him, Mrs. Kean? I don't think I could bear to do it again."

It took all of Hester's fortitude not to smile. She moved to stand across from St. Mars and said, "May I assist you in finding a book, sir?"

"Of course you may, my dove, but there's no need for haste. Here, let me take a good look at you first." He ogled her unmercifully through his glass, while she had to improvise the proper reaction. In the end she raised her chin and spoke haughtily, "Sir?"

The corner of his mouth twitched, before he reluctantly put down the glass. "So that's the way it's to be, is it? Well, then, if you're not of a mind t'be friendly, y'can find something that's likely to amuse me."

Hester searched behind her for something that might appeal to a rake and came across one of Jeremy's *Tales of the Dead*. When she turned back around, she discovered that St. Mars had raised his glass again to study her posterior. She choked on a smothered laugh and felt herself flushing to the roots of her hair, but he leered and gave no sign of being contrite.

"Aha!" he said, laughing loudly. "There's more than one way to catch a nymph, my dear!"

Hester wanted to laugh . . . and to cry because she must not betray the fact that she knew him. Words blistered her tongue, but she didn't dare utter them. She had never felt so frustrated. She tried to draw more anger from her frustration, but only succeeded in suppressing another giggle.

"Here you are, *sir!*" She slapped the book upon the counter. She would have left it—and him—but he grabbed her hand and pulled her close.

Lowering his lips to her right ear to hide his whisper from the other two, he said, "I need to see you. Can you close the shop again tonight?"

Hester needed to see him, too—to deliver the scathing lecture that had formed on her lips. "I should like to oblige you, sir," she said with spirit, "but I can do nothing until you release me."

"Shall I take that as a yes?" He whispered, his eyes dancing with mischief.

"Sir," Hester said firmly, "if you do not release me this instant, I shall fall down in a fit of *hysterics.* Perhaps *you* are not aware of the *fright* we have had this morning. Perhaps *you* did not hear that the notorious highwayman, Blue Satan, *was seen breaking into that shop* just across from us? Why the news is *all over town!"*

"Well, if that is all that is bothering you, my dear, I say posh!" With his free hand he snapped his fingers. "I should like to meet up with that paltry villain. Then I should teach him a thing or two."

Hester wanted to scream. It seemed he would not be satisfied until he had given them both away. So, she resorted to begging. "Will you never release me, sir?" she said on the verge of tears.

"There, there now!" Alarm sprang into his eyes. "I did not mean to plague you, confound it! I was only indulging in a bit of fun." As soon as he saw the appeasement on her countenance, he said, "Come, let us have a kiss upon it." And before Hester could stop him, he reached over the counter, grabbed her by the waist, and planted a kiss upon her cheek.

Her nerves, which had been on edge, were too excited to accept this calmly. Bursting into hysterical laughter, which she smothered with both hands over her face, she pulled away, just as Sally said, "Fie upon you, sir! Do you not see that you have upset her? And Mrs. Kean is a lady. She is not accustomed to your kind of impertinence. You had best be off," she scolded, "and you can take your business elsewhere. I can do very well without it."

St. Mars protested this treatment in an indignant voice, chiding Sally for her jealousy, "For it's as plain as a pikestaff, you don't relish the competition, my dear." When, with fire in her eyes, Sally threatened to send for the constable, he finally agreed to take himself off.

By this time Hester had recovered sufficiently to peer at him through her fingers, though she did not trust herself enough to lower her hands. Sally came and put an arm about her, making comforting sounds. She advised Hester not to let such a debauched gentleman fluster her, for his good opinion was not worth it.

When Hester thought of St. Mars and the charge of debauchery she wanted to laugh even more, so she tried to think of something to depress her spirits instead. Sullivan's threat came quickly to her mind, as well as the notion that he might spread the rumour that Blue Satan had murdered Mr. Curry. This tactic of his, which could help Jeremy in the short run, would never definitively solve his problems, and would only make things worse for Blue Satan if he was ever caught.

The tears that laughter had drawn into her eyes were taken as proof of her distress. Hester begged Sally not to concern herself, and she changed the subject by asking Sally whether she had decided to publish Tubbs's book. It seemed the anger that St. Mars had provoked had taken the effect of boosting Sally's courage as well, and she had agreed to venture the money. As soon as Hester had recovered from St. Mars's visit, she encouraged the two of them to visit the printer, for she did not doubt Tubbs was correct when he supposed that a book about Blue Satan would sell very well. Eventually she was left in relative peace to compose herself to face St. Mars again that night.

Gideon left the Bell and Bible, bundled up against the cold and feeling very pleased with himself. He had managed to embrace Mrs. Kean, and he had done it with a credible excuse. He fully expected that she would challenge his behaviour that evening, but he would tell her how necessary the kiss had been to maintain his pose as an obnoxious rake. And while she might not believe him, the thrill he had got from squeezing her waist was certainly worth her reproach.

In truth, while he had gone to the bookstall to make an assignation with her that evening, he had been ready to encounter Joseph Sullivan as well. He had expected the priest to try to discover all he could about the supposed burglary, and since he would not wish to be seen entering the barber-surgeon's shop, the Bell and Bible was his best alternative.

Unfortunately, Gideon had missed the priest's visit by only a few minutes. But in the hope of finding him there, he had brought Tom to track him again. Meanwhile, Gideon had enjoyed the chance to tease Mrs. Kean. One look at her face had been enough to tell him that she had heard of his risky adventure, and the temptation to cajole her out of her ill humour had simply been too great to resist. He was not surprised by her reaction, but his presence in the shop should have assuaged any worry she had felt on his account. If she intended to be angry with him, however, he'd decided to make it worthwhile. The taste of her cheek was still on his lips, and her sweet scent lingered in his nostrils in spite of the cold. He almost felt the need to strut.

While he waited for Tom to return, Gideon perused the other bookstalls in the shadow of St Dunstan's, as always keeping an eye out for anyone who might know him, even painted and bundled up as he was. At one shop, he was obliged to turn away when he saw two gentlemen he knew jesting with a neighbouring bookseller. In another, he thought he caught a customer studying his face. The trouble with having a price on his head was that anyone who had seen him once might try to find him, even if the two of them had never exchanged speech.

Gideon was back out in the street, huddling to keep warm, when he heard the giants in St. Dunstan's tower strike the hour of eleven. Thoroughly chilled, he was growing impatient for Tom and was considering entering a coffee house, when a clamour off to his right arrested him. A boy, wearing the livery from the Palace and bearing a message, was struggling to make his way along Fleet Street from Temple Bar, but he was hampered by a crowd who was pestering him for news.

Not wishing to risk being spotted by the boy, who might have seen him once at Court, Gideon kept a safe distance, but as the boy pushed past, he could hear the questions his followers were shouting into the crisp autumn air.

"Is it over then?"

"Have they caught him? The Pretender?"

"How many have they captured?"

"Is Derwentwater caught?

"Any news of Forster?"

His exhilaration of the morning fading, Gideon did not need to hear the boy's replies to guess what had taken place. The names he had heard belonged to James's followers in Northumberland, the leaders of the English who had answered his call when the Earl of Mars had raised his standard in Scotland. If they had truly been taken, then the rebellion in England had failed before James had even set foot on British soil. Sick at heart, Gideon felt sure the next time he would see the valiant men who had rallied to their king across the water, would be when their heads were posted on London Bridge.

The day, which had seemed sunny in spite of the cold, turned gloomy and bitter. The sky clouded over, and he shivered beneath his cloak.

He sensed a warm presence at his side and turned to see Tom. When he noted the agitation in Tom's expression, he said, "What news have you heard?"

Tom was breathing hard as if he had been running. "There's all kind of tumult in the street, my lord. There's men as say General Wills has captured the rebels at a place called Preston in Lancashire. They say as how they've took their leaders, too."

"What about the priest? Did you follow him?"

Tom nodded. "And he didn't look too happy to hear the news. I followed 'im just like I did the other day—same way, same stop. Then I stayed with 'im all the way back to his lodgings, but when we got near the Old Bailey, we saw the messengers carryin' the news. You should've seen 'im, my lord! Looked like he could've strangled 'em with his bare hands. Then I had to race to keep up with 'im before I came back here to you."

If the rebellion had failed, then surely Sullivan would alter his plans.

"Well, show me this route of his, and let's see if we can make any sense of it."

Following Tom's lead, Gideon covered the ground at a brisk pace. With the news that was out, no one would think it odd to see a gentleman making haste. There was not a calm visage in the streets. People were either rejoicing, cursing, or weeping. Church bells had begun to ring. Enough Londoners would understand the significance of the captures to spread the word that the greatest danger was over.

As Gideon made his way north past the Old Bailey, the first news-sheets to report the defeat at Preston appeared on the street. He fumbled in his jacket for a coin, and tossed it to a boy who was selling them, before moving on with his purchase. With cold, gloved hands, he folded the paper and stuffed it in his capacious pocket to read later.

By the time they had reached London Wall and passed through Moorgate, with Bethlehem Hospital on their right, there was little traffic in the street. Moor Fields stretched along beside them with the Artillery Ground left and beyond. When he had first heard of Sullivan's strange promenade in this direction, the proximity of the Artillery Ground had made Gideon wonder if it could be his target, but there was no logical reason to attack what in essence was nothing more than a frost-covered field.

They did not stop to study it, therefore, but continued on up Windmill Hill. Here, where no one was likely to notice two apparent strangers speaking to each other, Tom waited until Gideon caught up with him and said, "Here it is, my lord, the place where the Papist turns around."

Pausing with his hands on his hips, Gideon took a good look in every direction. Over the puffs of his own breath, visible in the frigid air, he tried to see what had attracted Sullivan to the site. Although the windmills for which the hill was named were long gone, the area was still rural with orchards, market gardens, and pastures all about. Burial grounds lay to both east and west, and nearby fields were used for men to practice their archery or exercise their mounts. To his right, in the distance were tenter fields, where yards and yards of new cloth were stretched over frames on hooks—hardly a tempting target for a spy. South was Bedlam, of course, with its lunatics, but a priest should have no reason to harm them.

"Let's retrace our steps," he said. "If Sullivan does intend to blow-up something, it's likely he wouldn't stop right in front of it at the risk of drawing unwelcome attention. Whatever it is, we must have missed it."

They started back down. When they were almost at the corner of Hog Lane, Gideon spotted a wooden sign for the Castle Inn. He stopped and beckoned to Tom. "You are certain that he never stops here?" he said, indicating the wooden sign.

"Never. I've never seen 'im even glance that way, my lord."

Gideon sighed and took another look round.

Somewhere across the street he heard the hammer of a blacksmith, which meant that a forge was nearby. Crossing to find it, he followed the sounds which led him around the corner. With the north end of Moor Fields on his right, he noted that on his left across the street and facing it, was not simply a smithy, but a large foundry, bearing a sign with the name "J. Bagley" written above the gate. He could not see over its walls, but its nearness to the Artillery Ground posed a question that begged investigating. With mounting eagerness, he motioned for Tom to follow him back to the Castle Inn.

"Wait outside a minute or two. Then go in and order a drink. I have to speak to the innkeeper, and there's no sense in your freezing out here."

"Thank you, my lord."

When Gideon walked into the inn, his entrance caused something of a stir. Most of the men who were eating and drinking there appeared to be labourers, and they stared as if they had never seen his ilk before.

For a moment, Gideon inwardly cursed the costume he had worn, but he recovered quickly and, lifting the glass to his eye, surveyed both the room and its company with a sneer. "Egads!" he swore. "Now I'm in for it, for a filthier set of yokels I never have seen." To the man in the apron who ran forward, cringing, he said, "You there! Is this your hostelry?"

The keeper of the Castle bowed and scraped and swore that it was.

"Well, I am lost," Gideon whined. "I was told by a gentleman not too far from here that if I followed this miserable lane, leading out from Bedlam, I should emerge at St. Giles Cripplegate."

A few guffaws greeted his idiocy, but the innkeeper shushed them and apologized as if Gideon's mistake had been his fault. He explained in a superfluity of detail how both Finsbury and Fore Street led away from the hospital, but in different directions.

"Yes, yes!" Gideon said, finally cutting through the man's complicated speech. "I can quite see my error now, but ye gods, I'm famished! I must have been walking for miles, and I'm frozen to the core. What sort of refreshment can you give me?"

Delighted, but also frightened by the prospect of entertaining such a fancy gentleman, the innkeeper blinked while he wondered what he possibly could serve such a vision. Then with a burst of pride, he declared that his wife had just dressed a pullet, which he thought the gentleman might like, seeing as its neck had only been wrung that morning. He also promised him a mug of warm sack.

Gideon sat down to an early dinner of pullet and sack, while at another table Tom drank a mug of cock ale. When the innkeeper came to see if everything was to the gentleman's liking, Gideon sent his compliments to the man's wife and asked him to tell him about the neighbourhood he had found himself in.

"Just before I sought directions from you, I heard the most infernal racket coming from over there." He waved a hand in the direction of the foundry. "What is the fellow making? Church bells?"

"Mr. Bagley, ye mean? Oh, aye, he do cast a bell or two now and then, and great, big things they are! He's working on one now, he says, for St. Alban's—that is, him and his son. But that's not the most of what he does. No, sir—" and here the innkeeper lowered his voice, not so much in secrecy as in awe— "our Mr. Bagley, he makes just about every gun the government uses—army and navy, both."

So, here it was, Joseph Sullivan's plot. The audacity of it nearly robbed Gideon of breath. To blow-up the only source of English guns. If he succeeded, once it was known abroad, the French would have less reason to resist James's pleas for aid. Since their terrible losses in the war fought over the Spanish Succession, they had not dared to challenge England's superiority. But how different the Regent might feel if he could be assured that the supply of English guns had been cut off.

Sobered by his discovery, Gideon paid his bill of fare with a generous tip for his host. Tom joined him outside within a few minutes, and they started back into London through Finsbury with Gideon thinking the whole while. Everything made sense now, even the alternate route Sullivan had used to return, since once the explosion had occurred, he would want to avoid the city gates.

Afraid of being overheard, he said nothing to Tom about his discovery until after Nate the waterman had deposited them on the opposite shore. Gideon ordered Nate to return for him that evening at nine o'clock. Then, as he and Tom hurried up the bank towards the house, he told him about Mr. Bagley's foundry.

Tom's jaw fell open, but he quickly closed it again to keep his tongue from freezing. "You never think—"

Gideon cut in grimly, "Yes, I'm afraid I do."

"But he must be mad to think he could get away with it!"

"Not necessarily, though I grant the difficulties would appear to be great. No doubt he has a plan for moving the powder—some way to disguise it in a cart perhaps." He recalled the bales of wool he had seen in the barber-surgeon's cellar and the tenter fields above Moor Fields, and one possibility occurred. "All it would take would be one cartload and a tinder box. And think of the havoc he would cause, not to mention the trouble for his Majesty's army."

"Who knows?" he added, as they entered the house. "If he succeeded, and then arms arrived from France, then perhaps more Englishmen would decide to revolt."

Or would have revolted, he thought as he shed his cloak inside the door, handed it to Tom, and headed up the stairs. Now, with their most devoted leaders captured, even this great a venture would be futile. Gideon entered his parlour and stood to warm his hands before the fire, wondering what Sullivan would do now that the rebellion in the North had been defeated. The rising in the West had already been thwarted. Ormonde had not managed to land, and James had not found a way through France to the coast. Even if he did soon, it was November now and the crossing would be too hazardous. As Gideon had feared, even if King George had not outsmarted the rebels, the rebellion had been launched too late in the year to succeed.

Would Sullivan wait for instructions, abandon his plot, or go through with his plan of destruction? What if someone at the foundry were killed? Possibly Mr. Bagley or his son? Their wives or their children? Did they live on the site?

Thoughts like these made him realize that he would have to stop the priest. It did not matter that he had once worked for James himself. To cause a fire or an explosion this near to London, close to where people lived and worked, to rob the Bagleys and their employees of their livelihoods—perhaps even of their lives—was something Gideon could never condone. He thanked God he had been banished from James's service. If he had not, he would have had to consider his allegiance, and he did not want to think how different his decision might have been.

No, his duty was clear. Even though he owed nothing to King George or to his Whigs, who had robbed him of his birthright, he still had to think of his fellow Englishmen. The rebellion had failed. It was time for the killing and the destruction to stop.

That night, as he waited in the dark and the cold across Fleet Street, with the collar of his greatcoat pulled over his face, Gideon was dismayed to see Mrs. Kean leaving the shop with Sally and heading towards Bell Yard. The urge to speak with her was eating a hole inside his stomach, and he had counted on their meeting tonight. He began to wonder if he had truly offended her. He'd thought she had only been pretending, for he had spied laughter in her eyes, but the recollection of the liberty he had taken made him think he might have gone too far to be forgiven.

The night was so cold that his breath was freezing. Icicles were forming on the woolen muffler over his lips. If the winter worsened at this rate the Thames would soon be frozen. For once in his life, he wished he had worn a wig, but he had changed into his workman's clothing and had nothing but his own hair and a felt hat to keep his head warm.

It would look strange on a night like this for anyone to loiter, but he was not ready to give up on Mrs. Kean yet. Fortunately, in their hurry to get indoors no one was paying much attention to anybody else. He crossed the street and, as soon as the area was relatively clear, ducked into the doorway of the bookstall next door, the shutters of which had ready been locked. The niche he had found was not very big, and he was still visible to anyone who bothered to look, but at least his back was protected from the wind.

He had not waited long when the cloaked figure of Mrs. Kean came hurrying around the corner of St. Dunstan's towards him. He waited until she had unlocked the door to the Bell and Bible, and taken a quick look about, before moving from his doorway to join her. She barely caught a glimpse of him before he threw an arm about her shoulders and bustled her inside.

It was pitch dark inside the shop and silent, except for the sound of her quick breathing. As she hastened to the counter to light a candle, Gideon could almost sense her shivering, but her presence gave him a sense of real warmth. He heard her try to strike a spark three times before he moved to take the tinder box from her hands. As soon as the wick flickered with light, Mrs. Kean picked the candle up inside its dish and held it between them, facing him with a skittish air.

His appearance seemed to disconcert her. Then he recalled that for once he had not bothered to disguise his face. The shy smile that transformed her into a mysterious woman dawned briefly on her countenance before she seemed to note a speck of dust on the counter. "I mustn't be long." As she brushed the spot with her mitten, her voice sounded breathless. "I told Sally I had forgotten to see that the fire was out. She wouldn't go home without me tonight, and I couldn't think of any reason to insist. I am always afraid that she may become worried and come looking for me."

She seemed determined not to mention the kiss. Afraid of frightening her, Gideon did not raise the subject. "I am sorry to detain you on such a bitter evening, but I had to tell you what I discovered."

Her head flew up. "When you broke into the barber-surgeon's shop?"

He pretended not to notice the edge in her tone. "Yes, then . . . and today when Tom and I retraced Sullivan's walk." He described what he had found in the barber's cellar, and his theory that Mr. Bagley's foundry was the priest's intended target.

She looked horrified. "But he must be stopped! Someone could be injured!"

"I agree, but we must think carefully how to go about it."

"Why shouldn't I simply inform the authorities? The only difficulty will be in explaining how I came about the information."

"No, we cannot afford to do that," Gideon said. "Not when that won't clear your brother."

She tilted her head in confusion. "But won't that prove Mr. Sullivan's guilt?"

"No. In fact, the more I think about it, the less I see him as our culprit."

Her face fell. "Why?"

"Because I do not see how Curry could have discovered what Sullivan was up to. When I was down below the barber's shop, I tried to make my way through the crypt to the cellar of the Bell and Bible, but the passage was completely blocked. It is possible that a voice could have carried through the rubble, but no one could have seen what Sullivan was hiding, and I cannot believe he would have been so foolish as to speak of it aloud. It's possible he might have heard Curry, but he's much too clever to have given his plot away that easily.

"Think about it." He leaned back against the counter and folded his arms across his chest. "Think how hard it was for us to uncover his plans. And if the most important thing to Sullivan was to keep his plot a secret, why would he do anything to attract the authorities' attention to St. Dunstan's?"

She sighed. "I suppose you are correct, which would mean he had no reason to report Jeremy and Mr. Curry to the authorities either." Then she gave a start. "I really must not tarry. Sally is bound to get suspicious if I stay any longer."

"Then, let's go. But we shall have to meet again tomorrow, for we have much to discuss." He put his hands to his mouth and tried to warm them with his breath.

Mrs. Kean saw this and threw him a shocked look. "Where are your gloves? Do not tell me that you came here without them."

He laughed. "And how would I explain having a good pair of gloves when I'm supposed to be a servant?"

She gave her head a disapproving shake. "You know that is a feeble excuse. After all the taradiddles you have had to invent, I suspect you could have thought of something. Your fingers will get frostbitten if you're not careful!"

While she was scolding him, she arranged her cloak more tightly about her, picked up the candle, and started for the door.

He followed her, chuckling. "You could always warm them up for me, if you like."

He heard her sudden intake of breath, but she did not turn around. "A better idea would be to tuck them inside your sleeves."

As he stepped through the doorway behind her, he glanced across at the barber-surgeon's shop, but he saw no sign of life. He said, "You haven't told me if we can meet again. Tomorrow night? Here?"

"It does not have to be as complicated as that, you know. I am not really accountable to Sally."

Her amusement made him realize what a fool he had been. As she closed and locked the door behind her, he excused himself for forgetting that she was free to come and go, for he had been so used to the trouble she had escaping Hawkhurst House, he had forgotten how different her status at Sally's was.

"We can meet in St. Bride's," Mrs. Kean, said, turning to face him. "What time?" she asked, as he offered her his arm.

The wind nipped at them as it whipped around the church. They huddled closer for warmth as they started for Bell Yard. Gideon wished he could simply put both arms about her and hug her to him, but the knowledge of what he would want to do next prevented him.

They agreed on a time. Then, both shaking from the cold, they did not speak again until their arrival at the entrance to Bell Yard. Recollecting how recently he had feared for Mrs. Kean's health, he sent her on her way, just watching her long enough to see that she entered the house safely before hastening back to the Thames where Nate awaited him in his boat.

In vain sedate reflections we would make,
When half our knowledge we must snatch, not take.
Oft, in the Passions' wild rotation tost,
Our spring of action to ourselves is lost:
Tired, not determined, to the last we yield,
And what comes then is master of the field.

CHAPTER XX

In the morning, Hester was about to leave the Bell and Bible for her meeting with St. Mars, when the door to the bookstall opened and James Henry walked in. At any other time, she would have been delighted to see him, but thinking of St. Mars, who should even now be waiting for her in the nave of St. Bride's, she hardly managed to greet him with a smile.

Fortunately, James Henry did not seem to notice, for his mind was intent on something else. With a heavy frown on his aquiline features, he approached her, saying, "My dear Mrs. Kean, I came as soon as I heard the news. I was never so shocked in my life as I was when Mrs. Mayfield told me she had driven you from the house."

His distress was real, and she was touched. Of all the members of Harrowby's household, he was the only one who had bothered to come see her.

She thanked him, but begged him not to worry about her. "For Mrs. Sally has taken me in, as you see, and taken very good care of me."

Sally, who had watched their interchange with a speculative eye, laughed and said, "I'm not certain that it is *I* who have been taking care of *her*, for I do not know what I would have done without her this past week."

James Henry forced a smile, but his temper was obviously not appeased. "I'm certain that no one who knows Mrs. Kean will be surprised to hear it. She has been greatly missed at Hawkhurst House. In fact, I am come to take you back with me," he said. "Mrs. Mayfield" —a note of distaste entered his voice— "requested me specifically to beg you to return at once."

A feeling of panic rumbled up in Hester's stomach. "At once?"

He gave her a wry look. "I was instructed to inquire about your health, and if it appeared that the danger of contagion was past, which I assured her it was, then to fetch you back. I believe Mrs. Mayfield finds herself in need of your services. God willing, it won't be long before Lady Hawkhurst is brought to bed, and apparently her confinement weighs heavily upon her spirits."

"She wants me to entertain Isabella?"

James Henry could not entirely hide his grimace. "I believe that is what she wants, yes. And then, there are the tradesmen to deal with over the furnishing of the nursery, which is not yet completed."

Hester heaved a sigh, which she did not bother to conceal. "I will have to return, I suppose."

He frowned and darted a glance Sally's way before asking, "Would you rather remain here?"

Although he could not say it in front of Sally, Hester knew he was asking if she truly preferred residing with a bookseller's widow and working with her in a bookstall to living in Hawkhurst House with all its luxuries.

For a moment, Hester did not reply. It was not that she still feared coming down with the smallpox, for surely it had been more than two weeks since she'd spoken with Lady Mary, and that should be long enough. Since she had never intended to leave Hawkhurst House permanently, however, it had never occurred to her to examine her feelings on the subject. In truth, in some ways she *was* happier here. In Sally's house, she was an equal, despite her dependency, better educated certainly and, therefore, treated with respect. In Hawkhurst House, she lived at the beck and call of two very self-centred women. Mrs. Mayfield's feelings for her did not bear thinking about, and Isabella, though fonder, must regard her more and more as a servant instead of the near cousin she was. None of her relatives would ever show more than a mild affection for her, and seldom even that, while Sally and she were on the road to becoming real friends.

Even the work in the bookstall had been more enlivening than her tasks in Hawkhurst House. The thought of returning to her aunt's service oppressed her so greatly that for a moment she wondered if she might not remain where she was.

But despite what Sally had said, Hester realized, she could not expect to live with her forever. If Mr. Curry's murder could be solved, Jeremy and she would marry, and Hester would become the maiden aunt of the household, kindly treated perhaps, but also perhaps eventually despised. She did not really know that Sally would want her to stay once Jeremy could work in the bookstall. It did not appear to be a business that could support three.

She also had to admit that there were luxuries to living at Hawkhurst House that she missed, especially the cook and the maids. If she were to stay at Sally's she would have to earn her keep with jobs of a much more basic and taxing nature, such as laundering—certainly the most arduous in a city where it rained more often than not and the air was too dirty to breathe.

And, besides, Hester thought, if she did not return to her place, who would St. Mars rely upon to keep him informed of the goings-on in his own house?

As these thoughts passed through her mind, her face must have betrayed a portion of them, for James Henry's frown had deepened. He looked as if he wanted to speak, but was afraid of saying something that might offend Sally.

Hester owed him some explanation, as the only member of the household to care about her welfare. It was possible that he had even urged her aunt to send for her. And she would have to send her Aunt Mayfield an answer back.

Turning to look at a clock on the wall, she said, "My goodness! Look at the time. I wanted to attend church this morning, and if I do not hurry, I shall be too late. Will you walk out with me?" she asked James Henry, as she pulled her cloak on and picked up her gloves.

He readily agreed. Then, after waiting for her to come from behind the counter, he ushered her out into the street.

The weather was still wretchedly cold, but no snow had fallen. It seemed almost too cold to snow, if that were possible.

"Mrs. Kean, I know—" James Henry started as they walked up Fleet Street, as if he would apologize for the cruelty of her family.

She interrupted him. "I will return to Hawkhurst House, certainly, but I must not abandon Sally yet. She took me in when I had nowhere else to go, and I owe her much."

He gave an angry grumble, so she hurried on. "And besides Sally, there is my brother who needs me."

When James Henry looked surprised, she said, "Not like before, when you so kindly rescued him." She smiled her thanks again. "But it is something serious nonetheless."

"Yes, I heard about Mr. Curry's murder. You should have told me before I left for Northumberland." His voice was full of self-reproach.

Hester laughed. "And asked you not to act in your lord's interest? I would never be so selfish!"

She had expected him to laugh, but his tone was earnest when he said, "No, you are not at all like—" He broke off when he saw her startled look. She had never heard him speak so unguardedly.

They walked in silence for a moment, dodging other pedestrians who, heads down against the wind, were scurrying about their business. The traffic in the street was light due to the absence of casual strollers and the desire of most people to remain indoors. Those who had to go outside did not stop on their way to shop or chat, but hastened to their destinations. Even the peddlers for whom London was so well known barely uttered a cry.

"So you will not go back with me?" he said at her elbow.

"I cannot immediately. Not now." Hester had to trust him. He had proved himself her ally once and she knew he would do so again. "No one has been able to discover who murdered Mr. Curry, and because my brother has a . . . a fondness for Sally, harmful rumours have been flying about. He is living under a heavy cloud of suspicion, and I cannot in good conscience leave him now."

"Even though he left you to fend for yourself after your father's death?"

Hester would have been offended by his implication, if beneath it, she had not sensed his concern on her account. But the question was unworthy of someone who wished to be her friend, as he seemed to want. If he truly knew her, he would understand her inability to turn her back on her brother's misfortunes.

Choosing to ignore it in the hope he would never raise the subject again, she said, "I would be grateful if you would tell Isabella that I shall return as soon as I know the danger is past." She gave him a conspiratorial look. "You needn't say which danger I'm referring to."

She did not want James Henry to escort her all the way to St. Bride's for fear of his meeting St. Mars. No matter how well St. Mars had disguised himself, she knew James Henry would be able to recognize his half-brother. She could only imagine the number of times he must have studied the younger man's features, knowing the history of their relationship so many years before St. Mars discovered it. So, as soon as she spotted St. Bride's spire, with Sir Christopher Wren's unusual design of octagonal tiers, she stopped and held out her hand.

"Do you think you could make her my excuses without my aunt there to insist?"

Reluctantly, as if he had intended to remain with her longer, he took the hand she offered and held it in his large one. "I can manage it precisely as you like. Never fear. All I would say— if I cannot persuade you—again is that you are missed. The level of . . . harmony . . . in the household is not quite the same when you are not there."

Gideon, who had begun to fret at her tardiness and had started out to find her, spied her standing in the street, looking up at James Henry, her eyes alight with warmth and her hand engulfed in his. Seeing her in such intimacy with his brother caused his temper instantly to flare, and he almost forgot that he should not let James Henry see him. He took a few angry steps towards them before, recalling his situation, he turned to peer in a shop window. In the reflection of the glass, he kept an eye on the couple. Mrs. Kean was bidding James Henry goodbye, but even from this distance, Gideon could sense his brother's reluctance to let her go. He would clearly have liked to prolong their *tête-à-tête,* if keeping her in the street would not lead to their both catching cold. He bent and kissed her hand, a courtly gesture Gideon had never known him to use. It provoked another spurt of his temper, but he consoled himself with the knowledge that Mrs. Kean's hand was gloved and she would not have felt the kiss. Then James Henry tipped his hat to her and headed towards the other side of St. Dunstan's where the coach undoubtedly awaited him.

"*My* coach, I suppose," Gideon grumbled to himself, although he never gave it a thought. He had always preferred a saddle to being bounced and jolted over uneven roads. But suddenly, it seemed grotesquely unfair that James Henry should be able to use anything that was his.

He felt almost like leaving, but aware of how ridiculously childish such behaviour would be, he turned to greet Mrs. Kean, he hoped with no outward semblance of his feelings.

She apologized for making him wait. "You'll never guess who kept me," she said, as they turned to make their way into the church.

"Oh?" He despised himself for pretending ignorance, but he wanted to see what she would say about his brother.

"It was James Henry," she whispered as they entered the main door.

Unwilling to feign a response, Gideon paused to look up at the interior of the church. An elliptical barrel vault rose over the nave, which was long and rectangular and extended right to the altar with neither chancel nor screen intervening. The morning service was coming to an end, so they waited near the door while the congregation knelt for the blessing. Then, as the worshippers left, they took seats in one of the pews reserved for visitors, its high wooden walls providing them with a semblance of seclusion.

"What did James Henry want?" Gideon finally asked.

"He came to offer to take me home. Apparently my aunt has decided to send for me."

Gideon bit back a rude remark, as she continued, "He promised to make her my excuses, but I shan't be able to remain with Sally much longer, or else my aunt may prevail upon Isabella to have me replaced."

"Did James Henry say that?" It sounded like blackmail.

Hester chuckled. "Of course not. That is my conclusion, but I know my Aunt Mayfield."

"I don't see why James Henry had to come. Why couldn't she simply have written you a letter, or come herself?"

She looked amused. He hoped it wasn't because he sounded jealous. He wasn't jealous. He just did not like the way James Henry had held her hand.

"I'm afraid my aunt's writing is not always what it should be," she replied, and he breathed again. "No doubt she's missed my assistance. But we did not come here to talk about her, so will you please tell me what you intend to do about Mr. Sullivan?"

Gideon would have liked to ask her more about James Henry's conversation, but not knowing how he could without sounding queer, he moved on.

"I shall have to confront him," he said. "If we interfere with the priest's plot, he may escape the country, and we cannot afford to let him go until we discover what he knows about the murder."

"But I thought you believed him to be innocent."

Gideon shrugged. "Even if he is, he could know something. With his own secret to hide, he might have kept any information to himself."

She pondered this, and said in a dubious tone, "Would a priest abet a murder that had nothing to do with reclaiming souls?"

"Now, *that* I do not know, but I shall do my best to discover the truth."

The look she gave him was brimful with misgivings. It conveyed her concern, but, like Tom, she was beginning to accept that he would do things his own way, no matter how much his methods frightened her.

Instead of pleading with him to take care, therefore—though he could see the words forming on her lips—she said, "I cannot help the feeling that we would know who killed Mr. Curry if we thoroughly understood the details of the crime."

"You mean, we should be able to identify the murderer by examining the deed itself?"

"Not his identity, perhaps, as much as his motive. Then once we understood the motive, perhaps the correct name would come to us."

Thinking about this idea, Gideon ran his mind over the details of the crime. It had been a while since he had given them any thought.

"Curry was not robbed," he said, "which suggests that the killer knew him, of course."

"And he did not pause to take money, even to conceal whatever his motive was."

"On the contrary, everything about the killing suggests haste, which means it was not premeditated—another reason I find it hard to see Sullivan in the role. If he wanted Curry dead, I believe he would have planned the murder more cleverly. Instead it was both dangerous and untidy. More like a crime of passion."

Beside him, Mrs. Kean gave a jump. "If it is passion we are looking for, then Mr. Simpkins could be the culprit. He has certainly pursued Sally, both before and since her husband's death, and he was so angry when she refused him that he tried to get Jeremy arrested, when he knew that could lead to Jeremy's death."

"He is certainly without scruples, but there are other kinds of passions, don't forget. Simple anger, a strong desire for revenge . . . ."

"According to Lady Mary, Mr. Curry had any number of enemies. But how can we ever uncover them all before I have to go back to Isabella?"

Her tone was so hopeless, that he took up her hand and gave it a little shake. "You mustn't despair. If we have to find them, we will, and in that case, you might be better positioned at Court to hear of them—think of all you learned from Lady Mary."

She gave him a grateful look, but he could see that the thought of returning to her servitude made her unhappy. He could only imagine what living at the mercy of Mrs. Mayfield's tongue must cost her.

"What about this Tubbs fellow, the one who wanted to write the history of your abduction?" he asked, in part to make her smile. "You told me once that he had no love for Curry."

"No, and he's made it plain enough. I believe there was hatred there, and passion, but without Mr. Curry's employ he might have starved. I know that Jeremy has had to pay their rent, and I shouldn't be surprised if he fed Mr. Tubbs, too. If Tubbs did kill his employer, he was taking an enormous risk. As it was, he was desperate to write that piece about you."

Her smile, which she tried to restrain and failed, teased him. He gave her a threatening look.

"It is finished, you know." Apparently, his glare was not threatening enough. "He was talking to Sally about publishing it when Mr. Sullivan came in, and that was what they were discussing when you assaulted me over the counter."

"Assault!" He was very tempted now to show her just what a true assault would be. But they were sitting in a church, and the verger, who was sweeping the nave, had already sent them disapproving looks. Using his Majesty's churches for trysts was generally frowned upon, but common nevertheless. It gave a greater air of respectability than meeting in a commercial place. It was certainly much safer for the female involved. Perhaps that was why Mrs. Kean had chosen St. Bride's today. He had teased her too much about some of her earlier choices.

"Shall I save you a copy of Mr. Tubbs's story when it's ready?" she asked, in a tone too innocent to be believed.

"Please do." He hoped to intimidate her when he added, "I should like to see how I've been portrayed—from your description of me, of course."

Her flustered behaviour told him he'd succeeded. "You must not look for a word of truth in it, for I had to deceive him, as you know. I tried not to give him any idea of you—or of me, for that matter."

"So, if the story says I was handsome and gallant, I should take it that you find me both offensive and coarse?"

She stifled a laugh. "It would mean nothing of the sort!"

"Then you said I was coarse, because you really find me handsome?"

She smiled, but her voice was trembling. "For shame, my lord! You are trying to confuse me, but I have told you before that I do not blush."

"No, in general you don't, but I think I detect a slight change in your colour. Just here, on your right cheek." He brushed it lightly with the back of one finger.

She had pressed her lips together tightly, but she could not hide the dimple in her cheek. She tried to compose herself. "You stray too far from the subject of our intercourse, my lord."

He was tempted to make a pointed reply, but recollecting where they were, he reined in his high spirits. "I beg you to forgive me, of course, but if you will persist in arranging these trysts, Mrs. Kean, I really shall not know what to think."

Her mouth fell open, and she regarded him with indignation. "'T'was you who said we should meet, and you know it!"

He furrowed his brow. "Was it?" He pretended to scratch his head. "Well, then of course I beg your pardon."

She gave him a scolding, sideways glance, before her face took on a guilty expression. "I must do something soon to help Jeremy, but what can it be? I mustn't leave all the tasks to you."

They had played long enough. He mustn't forget that her brother's happiness would depend on the success of their efforts.

"The best thing you could do would be to discover more about Mr. Simpkins. You mustn't ever be alone with him. According to Tom, Sally is not the only woman he pesters with unwanted attentions."

She nodded. "I should have pressed Sally to tell me more, and now I shall, but I thought we had found our murderer in Mr. Sullivan." She gave him a concerned glance. "And we have not entirely ruled him out yet. If Mr. Curry suddenly threatened to expose him, in his zeal the priest might have throttled him, so please be wary when you do confront him. How will you do it?" she asked.

Gideon frowned and thought. "I have not decided that yet. He must have seen me at Lady Oglethorpe's, in which case he knows who I am. I'm not sure if he knows that I am no longer working for James."

Mrs. Kean gave a violent start. "Were you?" she said. "Oh, dear!"

He'd forgotten that he'd never told her about his involvement in the cause. He would have berated himself for his indiscretion, if he had not found her reaction so amusing. With a grin, he said, "Yes, I was . . . but in no significant way. And he was not very pleased with my efforts for he turned me off."

"Thank God!"

Her fervent exclamation made him laugh. "Yes, again, I suppose. Given the outcome of the rebellion, I suppose I should be grateful he did."

Her face filled with sympathy. "Are you terribly disappointed?"

Unprepared for this question, he said, "I—I hardly know." His feelings with respect to James and his cause were too complex to unravel. He shook his head to clear it. "But that doesn't matter. The greater tragedy is the men who are fighting for his cause—the faithful, honourable men who have risked everything for him and will lose it all."

That was a pain he could comprehend, but at least he had no family to suffer for his mistakes as those men had. As the wives and children of traitors, they would forfeit their wellbeing, too.

She gave his hand a squeeze. He returned it, though he had not meant to draw her attention to his problems again.

He straightened and smiled. "So you will endeavour to learn more about the beadle, Mr. Simpkins, while I confront the priest?"

She nodded and prepared to leave. They agreed to meet each other every morning at St. Bride's at ten-thirty o'clock.

She would not have this freedom much longer. As he watched her leave, Gideon sighed to think of her returning to Hawkhurst House, as that meant he would seldom see her.

On her way back to the Bell and Bible, Hester tried to restrain the exhilaration she felt every time she saw St. Mars. It was wrong of her to enjoy his company when Jeremy was so miserable. He seldom saw Sally now. Except for the day he had burned Mr. Curry's store of indecent material for her, her brother had hardly dared set foot in the bookstall. It was a prudent decision, she knew. If Mr. Simpkins had killed Mr. Curry in a jealous rage, what would stop him from throttling Jeremy, too? That was not Jeremy's reason for staying away, of course. He did so because his visits distressed Sally. At least, his absence spared her the worry that he might be murdered, too.

She was horrified, then, when she approached the shop, to hear angry voices coming from within—if she was not mistaken, one of them Jeremy's. She threw the door open to find him and Mr. Simpkins, lunging and shouting at each other, with Sally in between, trying to keep them from coming to blows. Mr. Simpkins's clothing was greatly disordered, his wig askew on his head. Jeremy's face was contorted with rage and his hair had escaped its ribband.

They did not notice Hester's entrance until, finding her voice, she clapped her hands together loudly and yelled, "Stop it! Stop it this instant! What is the meaning of this disgraceful conduct?"

Recalled to his senses, Jeremy stopped shoving and turned to face her, his face flushed. "It's this blackguard's fault! I just came in and found him forcing his attentions on Mrs. Sally."

"That's not true, is it, my dear? Me and the widow were just gettin' to know each other a little bit better, that's all, when this ruffian crashed in and assaulted me."

"You miserable liar!" Jeremy shouted. Hester had never seen him so furious. "Don't you dare insult this virtuous lady!" He put his arm about Sally's shoulders, and she buried her face on his chest.

Seeing her choice, Mr. Simpkins curled his lip. "Lady, eh? Hmmph! She weren't so lady-like when she lured me in 'ere."

Sally shot him a look of pure venom and stamped her foot in frustration. "I *never* lured you. I tried everything I could to shake you off."

"Is that so?" A spiteful gleam lit his eyes. "That's not 'ow I remember it, missy. Nor what your 'usband said to me. 'E was always a-hintin' at 'ow much you admired me. Now tell me why would 'e do a thing like that?"

Shuddering, she answered miserably, "I don't know. But he wasn't being truthful—*if* he said it, which I doubt."

"You *know* 'e did, you slut! And you encouraged me, too—with all your smiles and your wiggles."

"No!"

Sally's cry was part a refutation of his statement, part an attempt to stop Jeremy from lunging forward again, as he growled, "Shut your mouth *now,* or I'll do it for you!"

"Enough!" Taking up the poker from the hearth, Hester wielded it between them. This startled them both enough to silence them for a moment. Taking advantage of the quiet, she told Jeremy to hold his tongue, giving him a look that she hoped would convey a strong warning, before turning back to Mr. Simpkins.

She could not order him about so easily. He *was* a beadle of the ward, even if he did abuse his office. It galled her to have to treat him with a respect he did not deserve, but seeing no alternative, she tried to soothe his ruffled feathers to get him to leave the shop.

"There have been some serious misunderstandings here, but they cannot be resolved while your tempers are roused. Perhaps if you were to return when you both have had time to cool, we could try to sort this out."

Mr. Simpkins would have none of this. "Don't think you can play your tricks on me. You're just abetting your rascal of a brother. But I've got 'im where I want 'im now. I'll go fetch a constable and clap 'im in gaol again. Just see if I don't!"

"Upon what charge? I don't suppose a magistrate will think he did anything wrong to defend a widow from assault. And he will have both Sally's testimony and mine." Even for her brother, Hester would not perjure herself, and she had not seen Mr. Simpkins attack Sally, but Mr. Simpkins did not know this.

He glared at Sally with his mean, little eyes. "If she does speak against me, I'll tell 'im what a slut she is. I warned you I would now, didn't I?"

"You can say whatever you want. I don't care any more." With tears in her eyes Sally forced her chin into the air. "I will tell him the truth whether he believes me or not. You can't scare me any more."

"And what about your fine young gen'leman, eh? Will 'e want you, when everyone in Lunnon knows you for a trollop?"

Jeremy's face turned red and the knuckles on his fists were white. Hester put out a hand to restrain him, saying, "Don't let him bait you, Jeremy. He's hoping you'll do something to get yourself arrested."

Speaking to Mr. Simpkins again, she said, "You have said all you can to insult our defenceless friend. You force me to remind you that our cousin is a very powerful man, very high in his Majesty's opinion. If you do not stop your persecution of Mrs. Curry, it will take no more than a word on my part, and Lord Hawkhurst will see that you lose your place."

She hated to make use of Harrowby's name, especially when she doubted he would trouble himself to help them, but she had prevaricated in a worthy cause and it appeared she could get rid of Mr. Simpkins no other way. He seemed ready to tell any range of lies to avenge himself on Sally, and to hurt Jeremy, too.

Her threat did make him pause. He studied her with a mixture of fury and fear. She tried to soothe the former out of him by offering him the same graceful exit she had at first. Eventually, he straightened his wig and his clothes, took up his staff, and stormed out of the bookstall, promising to return with a warrant from the magistrate.

As soon as he left, Sally collapsed onto a stool and covered her face. Jeremy hurried to comfort her, and cradled her head to his chest.

Hester allowed them a moment of peace. Then, afraid that Mr. Simpkins would return before they had prepared their defence, she latched the door so no one could interrupt them and went to sit on another stool facing Sally.

Taking hold of both of Sally's hands, she prompted her to look up. "We must talk now. You must tell us why you've been so afraid of Mr. Simpkins."

Sally sighed and nodded. She appeared so exhausted, it was easy to see how much he had oppressed her. There was almost an apathy in her expression when she said, "He's been threatening me with all those lies you heard him say. He said that no one in the city would trade with me if he told them what a harlot I was. And if he did, I didn't know what I would do! Without this bookstall, I would starve!"

"What reason did he give for threatening you?"

Sally shook her head and wiped her nose with her handkerchief. "He didn't need a reason. He was only angry because I refused him." She gazed pleadingly at Jeremy. "I swear I never lured him the way he said."

"Do you think I believed that for one moment?" He took her hand and raised it to his cheek. "I could have killed him for the way he talked about you!"

Hester closed her eyes and prayed for patience, then opened them again to say, "I know how angry you must be, Jeremy, but please do not employ that expression again. Sally and I both know you don't mean it, but someone else might believe you."

These words reminded them that Mr. Simpkins had threatened to return with a warrant. They glanced fearfully at Hester, then back at each other.

"We will be better prepared to refute his charges," she said to Sally, "if you tell me everything he's done since this whole business began."

A flicker in Sally's gaze prompted Hester to ask, "Is there any truth at all to what he said?"

"Hester!" Jeremy gasped in outrage.

"No, it's all right, Mr. Kean." Sally composed herself. "The only thing he said that might be true is that my husband could have said that I admired him."

"But—why?" Jeremy's frown was disapproving.

Sally heaved a shaky breath and addressed them both. "I've already told you that Mr. Curry liked me to be amiable to his customers. He insisted on it, even when they offended me. He wanted me to be friendly to Mr. Simpkins, too. *Particularly* friendly, he said."

"Did he ever tell you why?"

"No . . . but after you found those books he had beneath the floor, I wondered if maybe that wasn't the reason."

"You think he knew Mr. Simpkins had learned about the indecent literature he sold, and would be willing to overlook it as long as he was enamoured of you?"

Sally nodded and took another wobbly breath. "He had been pilloried once, and you saw what the crowd did to him. He didn't want to be placed in the stocks again."

"But to imply that you fancied Mr. Simpkins!" Jeremy was shocked. "I've never heard of anything so despicable!"

"Mr. Curry wasn't a very admirable man. The only good thing about him was that he did love books."

Jeremy shook his head in distress. He could not reconcile Mr. Curry's offences with a lover of books. Hester had a similar problem, but the facts were what they were. There was no understanding human beings.

"I tried to be a good wife, and do what he wanted of me," Sally continued, her eyes filling with tears, "but after the night Mr. Simpkins came to the house—" Glancing up at them suddenly, she broke off, then stared down at her hands—"I just didn't want to be friendly to him any more."

Her voice trailed off feebly. Over her head, Jeremy exchanged a troubled glance with Hester, who leaned forward and said, "Mr. Simpkins came to your house? When?"

Sally was obviously reluctant to tell the story, but when she did, she spoke to Jeremy. "That night—the night you were both carried off to Newgate."

"What did he want?"

She winced at his angry tone and knotted the handkerchief in her lap. "What he always wanted, I suppose. He said he would tell our customers I had invited him to come, and that I'd made certain that my husband wouldn't be at home."

"That . . . that cur!" Jeremy curled his hands into fists as if he wanted to throw a punch.

"He said that?" Hester asked. "Had you told him about their arrest?"

"No, but he had heard about it. I suppose that's why he thought it would be safe to come."

A possibility occurred to Hester that made vastly more sense. What if Mr. Simpkins had written the anonymous letter to the authorities? If he had wanted to seduce Sally, he would have had to get rid of her husband. And if he already suspected that Jeremy was a rival for her affections, he would have needed to get rid of him, too.

"Did he hurt you?" Jeremy waited tensely for her answer.

"No . . . not very much. I know something about defending myself. I hurt *him* though, enough that he's minded his distance until today. But he was so furious, I thought he would try to kill me. Instead, he threatened to tell everybody those lies."

"Which no one who knows you would believe! Why couldn't you have confided in me?"

She looked up at Jeremy and her lips trembled as she smiled. "I didn't want you to think ill of me."

"As if I ever could!"

The tenderness in his voice made Hester feel distinctly *de trop*, but she was afraid that Mr. Simpkins might return with the constable soon. She let them gaze happily into each other's eyes for a moment longer, before saying, "We must prepare ourselves in case he tries to charge Jeremy with assault."

Recalled to Jeremy's peril, Sally swore that she would testify on his behalf and tell the magistrate how Mr. Simpkins had tried repeatedly to molest her. "For I am not afraid of what he'll say now." She beamed up at Jeremy's face. Now that her fear that Jeremy might believe Mr.

Simpkins's lies had been laid to rest, she could brave his slander.

As they waited to learn the consequences of Jeremy's temper, Hester took comfort in the knowledge that Sally's assertions would carry all the weight of truth.

And yet the fate of all extremes is such,
Men may be read as well as Books, too much.
To observations which ourselves we make,
We grow more partial for the Observer's sake;
To written Wisdom, as another's less;
Maxims are drawn from Notion, these from Guess.

CHAPTER XXI

G ideon left St. Bride's in a quandary. When he had told Mrs. Kean
he did not know how best to confront Joseph Sullivan, he had
spoken the truth. Turning the matter over in his head, he rode in Nate's
boat back to his house on the Thames, and arrived to find Dr. Colley
taking his leave.

The doctor appeared quite startled to see him. Puzzled at first by his
reaction, Gideon then recalled that the only time they had spoken, he
had been garbed much more simply, like a Quaker. But remembering
his promise to Tom, he invited the doctor back inside for a glass of
wine and offered no explanation for his altered appearance, deciding to
let him wonder all he liked about the eccentric Mr. Mavors.

Once Katy had left them alone with their cups, Dr. Colley informed
Gideon that he had examined her and discovered no sign of the pox.
"In my opinion, she is as healthy a woman as I have ever seen." He
sipped his Madeira appreciatively before adding, "Just the perfect balance
of humours. I have physicked her as you requested—and I could always
bleed her—but I doubt she would benefit much from it. Generally, I
find employers prefer that I not bleed their servants. The procedure
can produce a lassitude, which can last for several days and cause
unwelcome interference with a servant's duties."

"Don't bleed her on my account!" Gideon had always found the practice repugnant. He had no opinion concerning its medical worth, but he did not care to think of blood. He did not fear shedding it in honest competition, but there seemed something repulsive about taking it in such a cold-blooded fashion.

"While I am here, shall I physick you, too?" Dr. Colley asked.

"Who, me?" Gideon sat up straight. "No, thank you. I am perfectly well."

The doctor directed him a speaking look over his glass. "I should have said that your servants were quite well, too—remarkably well fed and not particularly over-exercised—but an occasional physick can do you no harm. And we can never know how many ailments it prevents."

Gideon discovered that he was ready for the doctor's visit to end. Declining the offer of his services politely, he downed his drink in one gulp, meaning to inspire the physician to do the same.

This was obviously not the first time Dr. Colley's services had been refused. He quickly finished off his Madeira and took his leave, expressing his wish to be of service should anyone in Mr. Mavors's household ever need a physician.

After he left, Gideon heaved a great sigh of relief, which was only partly due to his escape from being physicked. It would be a pleasure to tell Tom that as far as Katy's health was concerned, he could marry her whenever he wished. Tom was not in the house now, for Gideon had set him to watch Joseph Sullivan's lodgings in case he made an unexpected move. Logic told him that the priest would alter his plans now that the rebellion in England had been quashed, but whether it would spur him to greater haste as long as the Scottish revolt was still viable, or lead him to abandon his plot altogether, was impossible to guess.

Sitting in his bedchamber in front of a mirror, Gideon removed the dozen patches from his face. He called for Katy to bring him water, and scrubbed off his rouge and white paint, before donning a simpler shirt and breeches.

In the parlour again, as he poured himself another glass of wine, Gideon weighed his options. His escapade at the barber-surgeon's shop had made a similar outing to confront Sullivan impossible. The watch would be alert for any glimpse of Blue Satan, and both Sullivan and his accomplice, the barber-surgeon, would be on their guard. It would be equally difficult to break into Sullivan's house, since its location in the Temple meant that the neighbours would never be asleep. The students at the Inns of Court were notorious for the strange hours they kept, staying up all night and lying abed in the mornings, until they rolled into the coffee houses mid-day still wrapped in their sleeping attire. It seemed the only chance Gideon would have to confront the priest would be to waylay him somewhere other than his normal haunts.

Besides the problem of where to confront him, Gideon had to consider how he should present himself. If he did not go masked, he risked being recognized and betrayed to the authorities. Surely by now, the Oglethorpes and their Popish friend had heard that he'd been dismissed from James's service. It would be useless to appeal to the priest as a fellow Jacobite, and if Gideon was no longer one of James's men, Sullivan might happily sacrifice him to the law. Another consideration was that Sullivan might wonder how Gideon had come to hear of the powder cache. If he put two and two together, he could easily divine Blue Satan's identity, which would place Gideon at even greater risk.

Gideon considered the possibility of wearing one of his disguises, but it was possible, even probable, that Sullivan would see through it, once he focused his attention on his assailant's face, which he certainly would if Gideon interfered with his plans. That the priest was a clever man, Gideon had no doubt. That his cleverness was combined with ruthlessness was likely. No matter how carefully he must avoid being exposed as a Roman Catholic—not to mention a Jacobite spy—he was clever enough to think of a way to betray Gideon without betraying himself.

Even without all these difficulties, Gideon still wondered how he could manage to get the priest to confess to Edward Curry's murder.

Half the afternoon passed, and he had still not arrived at a satisfactory plan, when near three o'clock he heard Tom's voice below, followed by a hurried tread upon the stairs. Tom burst into the room and said breathlessly, "He's gone, my lord. Hired a horse at a livery and headed west."

Gideon bounded to his feet. "Do you know where?"

"No, my lord. I followed him to the stables, but I couldn't go inside without him seeing me. As soon as he left, though, and I'd seen which way he'd rode, I went in and tried to ferret it out of the liveryman, but I misdoubt he knew. I asked 'im how soon before that horse would be available to hire—like I'd taken a fancy to it, see. He said it should be back in tomorrow, but since he didn't know how far it would get rode, he couldn't say as how fresh it would be."

"You did well," Gideon said, racking his brain to think what he should do. It appeared that Sullivan had decided on a course of action. "He didn't take a waggon or a cart with the horse?"

"No."

"Then he mustn't intend to move the powder." That news came as a relief. "But he's due back tomorrow, so he can't have gone too far. I wonder . . ." An idea had just occurred to him. The last time the rebels had suffered a setback, Sullivan had gone to consult Lady Oglethorpe. Whether she knew about his plot or not, clearly they were in league. He might be relying on her for communication, or even for orders. So far, neither Tom nor Gideon had seen any messengers arrive at his lodgings. They could have missed them, of course, but Gideon had a strong hunch that the priest would seek all the information he could obtain from the conspirators around London.

"He may have gone to Lady Oglethorpe in Godalming. This could give us the chance I need. Saddle Penny for me, and take Beau. Be sure to rub some blacking into Penny's coat, and see if you can disguise Beau's fetlocks. We'll ride west, and see if my hunch is correct."

Tom left the room immediately, and Gideon called down to Katy who came at once. He told her to go to the river stairs and tell Nate he was free for the day. He also told her to take Nate's boat to St. Bride's in the morning and carry a message to Mrs. Kean that he would meet her there again on the following day.

As he issued these orders, he extracted his pistols from their case. Watching him, Katy's eyes grew round and her lips curved down. She obeyed without a word, but as she left, the hand she held to her stomach reminded him that she had just been physicked, and that it would be mere kindness to leave her alone for the rest of the day. Fortunately,

Tom had not been home when the doctor had come, or Gideon would have had to leave him behind.

He checked his supplies of powder and shot. He pulled on boots, cloak, hat, and gloves, and wrapped a thick woolen scarf around his neck. Then he hesitated over his mask and blue satin cape, before grabbing them and hurrying out to the stables.

By the time he arrived, Tom had saddled both horses, and was in the process of rubbing blacking into the coppery coat of Gideon's mare. On seeing her master, Penny's nostrils flared and she irritably tossed her beautiful head.

"Sorry, my girl." Gideon smiled as he stroked her nose. "But you're much too pretty ever to be forgotten." Beau's white fetlocks had already undergone a similar treatment and were now the colour of mud.

As soon as Tom had finished, Gideon untied his horse's reins. "If Sullivan rode west, he probably took the horse ferry across. We'll have to avoid the Portsmouth Road since the troops will be using it. It's possible that we can intercept him before Guilford." He handed one of his pistols to Tom. "I hope you won't have to use this, but I don't have to tell you how dangerous he is."

Tom acknowledged the warning with a sober nod. He took Gideon's pistol and buried it in the deep right pocket of his greatcoat. His head and neck were wound with a long woolen cloth that covered his hat and most of his face.

They led their horses out into the yard, mounted, and urged them out into the lane that paralleled the Thames.

It was just after mid-afternoon, but soon it would be dusk. The roads in Surrey were so few and so poorly dug, they would need to hurry before darkness made the route even more treacherous. Gideon never needed to urge Penny to run. Got by Mr. Darley's famous Arabian, she leapt instantly to a gallop the moment he touched his heels to her flanks, but he would not sacrifice her legs for the sake of a few minutes or even a few hours gained. When darkness fell, he would have to rein her in, but cold would be their enemy, too. If they did not reach Guilford in time to catch Sullivan there, they would have to find shelter for the night and keep watch for his return.

Winter was already here, and with a particular viciousness. Gideon could not recall ever experiencing such cold. People were predicting that the Thames would freeze. Already ice was forming along its banks, which was one of the reasons Nate had pressed him for a retainer. With the river frozen, all the watermen would be out of work.

Gideon avoided the Vauxhall Turnpike where troops had built lines to fortify the town in case of invasion. Riding overland, they cut across to Towting where they started along the road to Arundel. Now, the faster Gideon urged his horse, the more pitilessly the cold bit at his flesh. Before they had covered any distance, his eyes were stinging and his lips were turning raw. If not for his gauntlets and his thick leather boots, his hands and feet would already be frozen.

Through the remainder of the daylight, they flew over the wheel-rutted roads, keeping a sharp eye out for the deeper pits that could lame their horses. Gideon thanked the fates that they were heading into the sun and neither north nor east, where dark had already fallen.

But no horse could outrun the sun. Night came soon, and they were forced to slow their pace. Now they had to maintain an uneasy balance between the hazards of the road and the risk of cooling their horses too quickly.

Up until this point, they had barely spoken. But now Gideon paused his mount for Tom to come abreast.

"I hoped you dressed warmly enough," he said, as they walked their horses. They would need time for their eyes to grow accustomed to the dark, and their ability to see would decrease over the next half hour.

"I wasn't born yesterday, my lord."

"That's right, you weren't." Gideon chuckled. "I was forgetting what an old man you are, but that must be the effect of your bachelor status. Once you and Katy are married, I shall have to think of you as ancient."

"What's that, my lord?"

Tom's eagerness caused Gideon another twinge. Was it jealousy of his lifelong groom's devotion? Or envy, that Tom would have the intimate companionship he lacked?

Gideon didn't know, but he would not begrudge Tom his happiness. He said immediately, "Dr. Colley came today, and he assures me that Katy is as sound as a woman can be. Now the rest is up to you."

"Yes, my lord." He heard a tremor in Tom's voice. Then he sighed as if a millstone had been lifted from about his heart.

"Sorry I had to drag you away on such a propitious night, but perhaps you could use the time to work on your proposal."

"That I could, my lord."

"Just don't let your mind wander too much. We've got to stay alert."

"Don't you worry about me, my lord. I won't let nothin' interfere with my duties."

He sounded so relieved that Gideon was reassured. He had not realized how much Tom's mind had been occupied with worry about Katy, but now that his fears were over, it was true that he might be more, not less, attentive to his work.

The night and the miles wore on. This portion of their route took them past groves, lodges, and retreats built for the wealthiest merchants of London. The houses were all shut up now, their windows and doors shuttered, and the furniture taken down. In summer, they would be full of mirth, but for now, with the leaves off the trees and the roads deep and stiff when dry, and slippery when wet, the families had removed themselves to town. Gideon did not have to worry about calling attention to their passage, since along this road the villages were sparse. They used a lantern when needed and extinguished it whenever enough moonlight was present to guide their way. But riding grew even more fatiguing since they had to pick their way through the sloughs.

Hills rose to the south, but their path remained below where the roads were clogged with clay. Sometime before seven o'clock, he guessed, they reached Leatherhead, a little thoroughfare town with a bridge over the River Mole. Over the next ten miles to Guilford, they passed a continuous line of gentlemen's houses, one after another, their leafless parks and gardens stretching off into the dark.

By this time Gideon was nearly frozen and tired from fighting the cold. It was late, and so far, there was no sign of Sullivan. They pressed on, keeping an ear out for the sound of hoof beats to the rear. He had no way of knowing if Sullivan had already passed them, but given an earlier start, he might have—if he had, in fact, gone to Lady Oglethorpe's.

They avoided the market town of Guilford, circling it through fields and pushing their way through hedges to pick up the road to

Godalming. Here they had joined the Portsmouth Road.

When the sleepy town was behind them, Gideon brought Penny to a halt and waited for Tom to catch up. "We'll have to find a place to rest the horses." He took a look about.

"You don't want to stop at the inn?"

"No. I've stayed in Godalming before. The landlord at the King's Arms would know me." He told Tom about the underground passage that linked the inn with Westbrook Place, the Oglethorpes' house. He could sympathize with the disappointment in Tom's voice when he acknowledged, "Then I reckon that's no place to stop."

"Not unless we want Lady Oglethorpe to discover Blue Satan's identity. And I'm afraid I can't trust her with that knowledge. If I'm correct and Sullivan *has* come here, he is sure to use the secret passageway. He may even stop at the inn overnight."

Now that he knew he would have to wait until tomorrow to confront Sullivan, Gideon realized the delay was for the best. If they had stopped the priest on the road, he would have ended by going on to Westbrook Place and informing the Oglethorpes of Blue Satan's interest in the powder cache. Though Gideon was leery of the Oglethorpe ladies, he would never underestimate their intelligence. Arousing their curiosity about Blue Satan would surely be a mistake.

There would be a way now, he realized, to discover if their journey had been in vain. "The men at the inn might remember me, but they don't know you, and they don't know Beau. If Sullivan has reached Godalming, he will already have left for Westbrook Place and his horse will be stabled in the barn. Would you know the horse if you saw it?"

Tom grunted in amusement. "You know I would, my lord."

"Then ride into the village. Tell them you think your horse is about to throw a shoe, but you can't see it in the dark. Ask if you can examine it inside out of the cold. As soon as you've taken a good look round the stables, meet me back here."

When Tom had gone, Gideon walked Penny back and forth along the road to keep her warm, and searched for a place they could shelter for the night.

By the time Tom returned, having cooled Beau with a walk, Gideon had found a derelict sheep pen just a few paces from the road. A shearing shed was attached with room enough to stable the two horses. After leading Tom to it, Gideon removed Penny's tack in the dark and let her nibble on the stale hay scattered on the floor while Tom reported what he had seen.

"It's the horse from Lunnon. I could swear to it, my lord."

"Good. Then we have not come all this way for nothing." Gideon picked up his saddle and carried it into the corner nearest the highway. "We can take turns sleeping and keeping a look out for Sullivan." He wrapped himself in his heavy woolen cloak and lay on the hard-packed floor, using his saddle for a pillow. He told Tom to awaken him in an hour.

Numbed by the cold, he slept, in spite of the frantic squeaks and rustlings occasioned by their invasion of the abandoned shed. He awoke a few hours later to find Tom still sitting nearby with his back against the wall. Without a light Gideon could not see his watch to discover the time, but judging by the intensity of the dark it was still far from morning. Ordering Tom to rest, he propped himself against the same wall to stay awake. Refreshed by his nap, he worked his fingers inside his gloves to thaw them while listening to the wind stir the thatch above his head.

Tom dozed, but unable to settle into a deep sleep, he eventually sat up and brushed the straw out of his hair.

Taking this as a signal that the night was over, Gideon stood and stretched, before saddling and bridling Penny again. Tom took similar care of his mount, and together they led both horses out into the night.

"I'll ride ahead," Gideon said, throwing his leg over Penny's back. "I want to find the best place for an ambush. Stay here and follow Sullivan after he rides by, but take care he doesn't hear you. When you catch up with us, keep out of sight in case I need your help. Think you will be able to distinguish him in this light?"

"Aye, my lord."

Gideon gave Tom a nod and turned Penny out onto the road. Disturbed by their unusual night time adventure, she tossed her head and danced sideways before yielding to his hold on the reins. As he guided her, Gideon noticed how poorly he could feel the leather strips through his gloves. He had tried to warm his hands, but his fingers were still half-frozen.

He let Penny alternate between a trot and a canter to settle her down until he came to a turn in the road, shaded by an ancient oak tree. Pausing there, he guided Penny behind it, dismounted, and removed his cloak. In its place he put on the blue satin cape that Pierre had ordered for him and tied on the black half-mask. He wished he could keep his woolen cloak on, too, but knowing how little warning he would receive of Sullivan's approach, he folded it and stuffed it inside his saddle-bag.

He remounted and waited with his pistol drawn, fighting the need to shiver.

He was nearly solid ice when the first sound of hoof beats broke the still of the morning. The sky was still dark, but a glimpse of dawn to come had lightened the night. By this time, Gideon's eyes were so accustomed to the gloom that he could easily make out shapes. He did not fear mistaking another man for his quarry, but if his ambush was to succeed, there must be no error.

The instant Joseph Sullivan came around the turn, riding at a daring pace for a man travelling in the dark, Gideon spurred Penny out from behind the tree and blocked the road.

"Stand!" He called, reining her to a sudden halt and brandishing his pistol. "Stand where you are!"

"You!" Sullivan's hired horse was no match for Penny, but he did not seem to care. He tried to ram his way past her, ignoring the gun in Gideon's hand.

"Hold! Or I shall fire!"

His threat seemed to work. He could almost hear Sullivan's teeth grate as he pulled on his reins. "Who are ya? And why have ya followed me?"

Frightened by the rough treatment, the hack shied, trying to escape from the devil in the flapping blue cape, and nearly threw Sullivan off.

Gideon did not reply until both horses had calmed, but he kept his pistol trained on the priest. When he finally had Sullivan's attention, he said, "I am a friend of Edmund Curry."

Sullivan's head jerked. "Curry's dead," he said.

"Indeed. And I should like to know why."

"What does his death have to do with me? And why did ya break into an innocent man's house?"

Gideon scoffed, partly to hide the chattering of his teeth. "Hardly the innocent barber he seems. I was much intrigued by the gunpowder he keeps under his shop."

"That has nothing to do with Curry's murder!"

"No? That is not the reason you throttled him?"

Sullivan gasped. Then he growled, "I am not a common murderer. I did not kill Edmund Curry."

"What about your friend the barber-surgeon?"

"Of course he did not! I would never be a party to such a sin!"

"Because you're a priest? Yet, you would destroy Mr. Bagley's foundry—perhaps with him and his workers inside."

Shocked surprise radiated from the man in front of him. Sullivan seethed with impotent rage. The horses felt it, too, for they both began to fret. "What do ya want?" Sullivan demanded, as soon as he had brought his hack back under control.

"I want to know why you've been keeping such a close watch on Curry's bookstall."

The other man barked a laugh. "That should be obvious, me boy. I had to make certain he had not discovered our store."

"And did he? Did he confront you? Is that why he died?"

"No! His murder, right there in the bookstall, could not possibly serve our cause. If I had wanted to kill him, do ya think I would have been such a fool as to kill him there? When his body was discovered, I feared we should be discovered, too."

"Are you certain he did not hear you talking in the cellar and threaten to report you to the authorities?"

"No, I tell ya! I know nothing about his murder! He never did find us out. But I heard *him* though—once, when he was speaking to someone in the section of the old crypt beneath his shop. That's when I discovered that he was hiding something there, too. It did not take me long to learn what. But I suppose ya know, for you must be the one who brought him that filth he sold from hallowed ground."

Gideon ignored the insult. If Sullivan thought the indecent books were the reason for his interest in Curry's bookstall, so much the better. But the priest's revelation that he had heard Curry's voice in the cellar was a possibility that Gideon should never have overlooked. It made perfect sense. He should have considered that noise could be carried both ways. Sullivan's responses nearly had him convinced of his innocence in the murder, for his logic was clear. After hearing Curry's voice through the rubble, Sullivan and the barber would have been even more careful not to be overheard when they were in the cellar.

Gideon asked, "How did you learn what Curry was hiding?"

"Do not forget that I'm a priest. I know a great deal about men's sins—more even than men like you. And I'm familiar with all the causes of guilt. There was no mistaking the way some of his customers would slink into his shop, then hurriedly make their escape, as if the Devil himself were on their tails. An attraction to obscene images can be an addiction to a disturbed mind."

"Then, you have no notion who murdered him?"

"No . . . . For all I know, it could have been you."

Stung, in spite of his better judgement, Gideon could not avoid an angry retort. "If you are so knowledgeable about men's sins, then you must know how mistaken that would be."

A tense silence filled the air, before the priest said, "Then, me boy, ya should have no objection if I continue on my way."

"None at all. But I should advise you and your friend the barber-surgeon to make for the coast with all haste. I am sympathetic to James, but I cannot allow you to blow-up Mr. Bagley's foundry."

An exclamation burst from Sullivan's lips. His horse gave a leap.

Gideon tightened his grip on Penny's reins, unconsciously ready for her reaction, but as she shied, the sudden movement knocked the pistol from his paralyzed fingers. He fumbled with it in the dark, and it tumbled towards the ground. As he bent to catch it, a shot cracked the air.

A sudden pain seared its way across his ribs. Then, he realized that Sullivan had been the one to fire. In the dark Gideon had not seen the pistol in the priest's hand.

As Penny bolted forward, Tom burst out from behind the oak with his pistol raised. He fired above Sullivan's head, and the priest turned and spurred his horse towards London.

With the burning pain in his side it was all Gideon could do to settle Penny. A warm trickle ran down his ribcage, but it was quickly stemmed as the blood congealed and froze.

"Are you hurt, Master Gideon?" Tom frantically asked.

"Not seriously, but it's a good thing you were here."

A rare string of oaths spewed from his servant's mouth. "I should have killed the lousy bugger!"

"I was rather tempted to myself, but we mustn't be caught here. You'd better help me off with this cape. Someone's likely to have heard those shots."

Tom leapt off his horse. Gideon dismounted more slowly. He felt gingerly along his ribs, but the bleeding had already stopped—a relief when he thought of the long ride ahead.

"We'd best get you some place where that can be dressed, my lord."

"No need. I swear there isn't. Just take this blue thing off and hand me my cloak."

When the warmer garment was around him, and the satin cape safely stowed inside Tom's bag, Gideon asked for a leg up. He was well enough now to ride. For a second, he had felt a touch of lightheadedness.

"Better take off that mask, too, my lord." Tom sounded worried. "Are you sure you're all right?"

Caught with his booted foot in Tom's hands, Gideon grinned. "'O thou of little faith!' Very well, then, if you insist." He untied the mask with one hand and stuffed it inside the pocket of his coat before pushing off from the ground.

He must have been more shaken by the bullet than he'd realized. The absurdity of his error made him laugh. As soon as Tom was in the saddle, Gideon touched his heels to Penny's flanks, and they made haste up the dark road. They had ridden long and hard to accomplish very little, but except for the fact that he'd been grazed, Gideon could not regret that they had come. At least, some of his most important questions had been answered. And his own feelings about Sullivan's motive—or lack of one—had been confirmed. All this had been accomplished with little risk of Gideon's exposing himself.

The danger was not entirely behind them. The late dawn was still their ally, but just in case Sullivan had laid information against Blue Satan up the road, they would take a long, winding route back to London, the vision of a warm bed and a hot meal urging them forward.

Yet, in this search, the wisest may mistake,
If second qualities for the first they take.
When Catiline by rapine swelled his store;
When Caesar made a noble dame a whore;
In this the Lust, in that the Avarice
Were means, not ends; Ambition was the vice. . .

CHAPTER XXII

A lthough Hester and Jeremy had remained at the Bell and Bible till the end of the day, Mr. Simpkins had never returned with a constable. His failure to make good on his threats could have been taken as proof of his guilt, if Hester had not threatened him with her cousin's influence, for anyone might fear losing his position, even if innocent of any crime. He was guilty of something, at least, if only of forcing his attentions on a woman who had made it patently clear that she wanted nothing to do with him.

To Hester, his actions branded him as a coward, for he had tried to take advantage of Sally when no man was there to protect her, and had used the power of his office as a threat. Thinking about Mr. Curry's murder, she wondered what might have provoked Mr. Simpkins, a man who was both a coward and a bully, to kill. If Mr. Curry had discovered that the beadle was the person who had set the authorities upon him, might there not have been a confrontation? And, if Mr. Curry had attacked him or threatened to report how he had abused his post as beadle, would Mr. Simpkins have been afraid enough to throttle him?

Surely Mr. Curry must have wondered who had sent the anonymous letter? Could he have discovered the truth? Sally swore that she did not tell her husband about Mr. Simpkins's visit the night of his arrest, but might he not have guessed?

When Hester went to St. Bride's the following morning, hoping to discuss these questions with St. Mars, she found Katy waiting for her just inside the door to the nave. She hid her disappointment and, after hearing St. Mars's message, thanked Katy before sitting in a pew to wait for the next service. She had tried not to worry about his confrontation with the priest, for worry wouldn't help, but fears for his safety were never far from her mind.

Katy had assured her that, wherever he was, Tom was with him, as if nothing could possibly harm him with Tom along. Hester prayed that this was so, but St. Mars's recent revelation that he had been in the Pretender's employ, had given her another reason to fret. Now, she recalled that he had mentioned seeing Joseph Sullivan at Lady Oglethorpe's house. Hester's experience with that lady had left her with a bitter taste, and she could not welcome the news that St. Mars was still in touch with her.

But no matter how friendly she and St. Mars had become of late, she had no right to all his secrets. Heaven only knew what else they were.

She went back to the Bell and Bible and worked until dinner time. Then together, she and Sally secured the bookstall before heading home for their afternoon meal. As they entered Bell Yard, huddling arm in arm against the cold, Hester noticed a small, curious figure descending from a carriage across the way.

He was the tiniest gentleman she had ever seen, richly clothed and beautifully coifed with a fine, shoulder-length peruke, but standing surely no higher than her chin. The head above his fur-lined cloak seemed too large for his fragile body, which was pitifully twisted in the shoulders and the back. As he stepped down from his coach and approached the house across from Sally's, he moved as if every step cost him pain.

Beside her, Sally gasped and pulled back. Hester glanced at her, startled, but Sally held onto her and whispered, "Pray, wait a moment, Hester, until he has gone inside."

"But why?" Hester whispered in return. "Who is that gentleman?"

"It's Mr. Pope." When Hester's stare questioned her, she added, "He's that poet you've no doubt heard of. And he hated Mr. Curry. I'd rather not have to face him."

Hester turned to look at the small figure again. She supposed she ought to have recognized Mr. Pope, for she had heard of his deformities. Her pulse quickened. She had wanted to ask him about Lady Mary's poems, and here he was, right here in Bell Yard. She wondered what he could be doing in such a dingy passage.

She thought of calling out and stopping him, but the door to the house he was visiting had opened and a servant was assisting him inside.

"What is he doing here?" she asked, as Sally resumed her steps. Perhaps it would be better to speak to him on the way out, after she discovered why Sally was afraid to see him.

"His friend Mr. Fortescue lives there. The barrister." They reached the house and Hester followed Sally into the kitchen. "Mr. Pope visits him occasionally, but this is the first time I've seen him in months."

"He had to leave when the papists were ordered out of the City. I had heard he might be returning soon." As Sally busied herself, lighting a fire for their meal, Hester removed her cloak and cap and asked Sally why Mr. Pope had such animosity towards her husband.

Sally reached into the larder for a loaf of bread, reluctant to answer. Finally, she gave a shrug and said, "He accused Mr. Curry of stealing some verses from him. I didn't pay any attention at the time, but now I think maybe it was true."

"Did he say which poems they were?"

"Yes. The ones Mr. Curry published 'By a Lady of the Court'. First Mr. Curry attributed them to Mr. Pope, but after Mr. Pope accused him, he changed the name of the author to 'A Lady'."

"Do you know who the real author is?"

"No, and I don't care to know. Mr. Curry said for me to tell the customers that Lady Mary Wortley Montagu had written them, and perhaps she did. But whoever wrote them, it's too late to do anything about it. Mr. Curry had them printed, and I have to sell them."

Hester had no trouble believing that these poems were the ones by Lady Mary that Mr. Pope had lost. What she wanted to know was how he had lost them. If she did not get her question answered today, she might never know, and something told her the information could be important.

Gathering up the cap and cloak she had just set down, she startled Sally by saying she would not be able to sit with her because she had to keep a look out through the parlour window.

"But what about your dinner? And a look out for what?"

"Something I hope may benefit Jeremy." Hester headed for the stairs so she could sit at the parlour window and watch for Mr. Pope to emerge. "You can save some dinner for me, if you please, and I will heat it up when I'm through."

She would have waited for Mr. Pope outside, but the weather was so harsh she didn't dare. Besides, if she hurried downstairs the moment she saw him open the door, she was certain to reach him before he got settled in his carriage.

It was two hours later, and Sally had returned to the bookstall alone, when the door to Mr. Fortescue's house finally opened and Mr. Pope emerged. Hester's stomach had been rumbling for half that time, and she had regretted missing her dinner. She was almost dizzy with hunger, but she had had no way of knowing how long Mr. Pope's visit to his friend was likely to last.

She hastily put her cap back on and laced it beneath her chin. Then grabbing up her cloak, she hurried down the stairs.

When she reached the other side of the poet's carriage, he was just leaning to climb inside. His coachman stood to hold the door open for him, wrapped in wool from crown to toe with only a slit left for his eyes.

"Pardon me, Mr. Pope. Please!"

Surprised by a voice he didn't recognize, the poet looked up, and Hester was struck at once by his expressive eyes.

Coming in behind him as they had entered Bell Yard, she had not been granted a good view of his face. Now, only a few feet from him, she noted not only the hugeness of his eyes but the carved sensuality of his lips. She had never beheld such sensitive features.

In spite of the cold wind that rimmed his eyes and a nose tipped with red, he did not appear to be annoyed that she'd accosted him. On the contrary, he looked intrigued. He studied her features as if trying to recall where they had met. Then his gaze dropped briefly to her left hand before he responded with a graceful bow, in spite of his twisted back. "I do not believe I have had the pleasure . . ." he said on a questioning note.

"No, sir," she admitted ruefully. "We have never met. I have only recently heard news of you from a friend of yours, Lady Mary Wortley Montagu, and it is about her that—"

"You have news of my lady?" With a start he stepped forward and grasped at her hand. "Can you tell me how she is?"

Guilt sliced through Hester with a sharp pang. In her need for information, she had forgotten all about Lady Mary's illness. Her thoughtless speech must have raised his hopes. The sorrow in his eyes begged for relief, and his thirst for news revealed his deeper—perhaps illicit—feelings.

She had not expected his reaction. If she had, she might never have mustered the courage to address him, but now that she had, she had to make the best of it. With her free hand, she gripped her cloak more tightly round her throat.

"No, sir. I wish I could give you news, but my conversation with Lady Mary took place before she became ill, and I have heard nothing since then that the whole world does not know."

The flame in his gaze died before he curtained it with long-lashed lids. He released his hold on her hand, and an uncomfortable silence fell.

Hester shivered as a blast of cold air swept through Bell Yard. She should not keep him standing there for long. His health had always been delicate, she had heard people say, and she could see for herself how fragile he was.

"I know it was presumptuous of me to call out to you, Mr. Pope, but my brother's welfare is at stake. I must ask you if you know how Mr. Edmund Curry came to have Lady Mary's verses."

When he recoiled, suspicion flickering in his gaze, she said, "I have Lady Mary's permission to approach you. She tried to help me, but she did not know how her poems had come into his possession, and quite soon after we spoke she fell ill."

Another gust of wind raised dust into the air. It swirled about their heads. Hester threw up a hand to shield her eyes. Pope's lips were turning blue.

She started to apologize for detaining him in the street, but he forestalled her by saying, "Why don't we finish this conversation inside my carriage?" He indicated the door, which his servant was still holding ajar.

Grateful and freezing, Hester did not hesitate, but preceded him into the coach and made space for him on the seat beside her. It was still bitterly cold inside the carriage, but at least they were out of the wind. The coachman spread blankets over their laps, while she fumbled for a handkerchief and dabbed at her running nose.

Before his servant shut the door, Mr. Pope advised him to get the horses moving. "Take us on a brief turn, then bring us back here."

"Now," he said, facing Hester, "you have the advantage of me. I do not yet know your name." His manner was courtly. He appeared to have recovered from the disappointment she had dealt him and seemed not at all averse to having a strange young lady in his coach.

She introduced herself, telling him her relationship to Lady Hawkhurst, and explaining how she had come to approach Lady Mary. Then, timorously, she admitted her connection to Jeremy and his to Mr. Curry.

The kindness in his expression vanished. He stared at her coolly, but waited for her to go on.

She told him about the books Jeremy had written for Mr. Curry, and how desperate her brother had been for the bookseller's patronage. Then she explained that Mr. Simpkins had tried to accuse her brother of the murder, and told him how she had learned about Mr. Curry's shady endeavours.

"It is my belief, sir, that his unsavoury business may have given someone a reason to kill him."

Pope's features had softened with an amused kind of wonder as she'd regaled him with the story of her detection. His sensitive lips curled in a smile. "You are a most remarkable young lady, Mrs. Kean."

"Not at all, sir. It is only that my brother's safety is at stake. I have tried to imagine every possible reason why someone would want to kill Mr. Curry, but there are still mysteries about his business that I have been unable to uncover . . . such as how he managed to obtain Lady Mary's verses."

His beautiful mouth gave an angry twist. "He stole them. I do not know how he managed it, but Curry was a devious rogue, in addition to being a savage. I cannot pretend to be sorry that he is dead."

"You truly have no notion how he managed it?"

He looked rueful, and shook his head. "That was not the first time he'd stolen papers from me. I tried to discover his methods, but had no success. I confronted him immediately, but he would only say that they had fallen into his hands. Then certain circumstances made it necessary for me to leave London. Otherwise, believe me, I would have made him pay for embarrassing such a great lady in the eyes of the Court."

His vague answers were frustrating Hester. She tried to coax the details from him. "Perhaps he obtained them from someone else?"

"No, for I only showed them to my friend Gay, and he swears they were never out of his hands. You see, the three of us, Lady Mary, Gay, and I, have come into the habit of sharing our work in its infant stages. We might suggest a different word or adjust a troublesome phrase. It has even amused us to collaborate on a few harmless verses."

"So you sent Lady Mary's poems to Mr. Gay? And, then what?"

"He posted them back to her. Or at least, he said he did. And although dear Gay can be haphazard with his own affairs at times, I have no reason to doubt his word."

"So, in order for Mr. Curry to get them, he would have had to interfere with the post?"

Pope raised a delicate shoulder. "So it would seem, but the penalty for stealing from his Majesty's post would be stiff, and I cannot imagine Curry having the courage to risk it."

"Unless," Hester said, half to herself, "he got someone else to take the risk?"

Just then, the carriage pulled to a stop. Looking through the window, Hester saw that they had returned to Bell Yard.

"That sounds like the sort of cowardly thing Curry would do," Mr.

Pope said, just as his coachman called down to ask if he should walk the horses again.

"No," his master called up. "We are nearly done." He looked at Hester, who nodded and smiled her agreement. But one more question occurred.

"Where did Mr. Gay post the poems?"

Mr. Pope looked taken aback. He pondered for a moment. "I cannot say with any certainty, but I believe he usually posts his letters from the Rainbow Tavern."

A burst of excitement nearly escaped her, but not knowing what to make of her discovery, she concealed her response. She did not want to provoke any questions from him before she had reasoned the information out. When the coachman opened the door, she thanked the poet sincerely for his aid. He expressed the hope that they might meet again and bowed his head as his coachman handed her down from the carriage.

Outside, the wind nearly swept the hood from her head, but Hester's thoughts were racing so furiously, she barely noticed the cold. Something Mr. Pope had said had stirred her memory, and suddenly pieces of the puzzle she had been pondering for weeks all seemed to fit. As she ran across Bell Yard and bustled back into Sally's house, she prayed that St. Mars would meet her at St. Bride's on the morrow.

∅

Tom woke up late the next morning, surprised to find a hint of dawn in the sky. As soon as he recalled what day it was, his heart began to turn somersaults in his stomach. He leapt out of bed, ignoring the cold that turned his breaths to frost, and started pulling on his clothes.

St. Mars and he had reached home after dark, nearly frozen to the bone. They had been forced to walk their horses most of the thirty miles back from Godalming to spare them after their hard ride the day before. Unable to find them any forage either, they had not wanted to press them, but after so many hours in the cold, their strength had been sapped. Tom had thought he might never thaw again, and St. Mars had limped from the stable to the house as if his feet were blocks of ice. With Katy's help Tom had dressed the wound on his master's ribs, which thankfully was shallow, but blood had frozen his shirt to it, and they'd been obliged to open it again to get his clothing off.

On his way home, although Tom had worried for his master, a part of his mind had never stopped working on the proposal of marriage he wanted to make to Katy. Their late arrival and St. Mars's injury had made him postpone its delivery until today when Gideon would go to his meeting with Mrs. Kean. But now the day was here, and Tom was on the fret to get the business done.

He dressed with unusual care, making sure his hands and face were clean and using a soft twig to clean his teeth. He finished by putting on a clean shirt and taking a comb to his hair. Then, when he judged himself as presentable as he was ever likely to be, he threw a woolen cloak about him and bracing himself against the cold, stepped out into the wind. Rehearsing under his breath all the way, he crossed the yard to the kitchen door and determinedly went inside.

There, to his annoyance, he found Nate the waterman, settled in a chair before the hearth, smoking a clay pipe and cradling a mug of beer in his lap. Katy stood near him, bending over a pot on the fire and chatting as if Nate and she had been friends for years.

They barely paused at Tom's entrance, though Katy looked over her shoulder and tossed him a smile. Nate greeted him with a solemn nod, as if he owned the place. He ignored Tom's scowl.

"What are *you* doin' in here?" Tom growled.

Katy turned an astonished gaze on him. "For shame, Mr. Barnes! Why shouldn't poor Mr. Peevey warm himself at our fire? He's come to speak to the master, and it's too cold to make him wait outside."

Stung by her reproach, Tom could only grumble, "Well, I don't see what business he's got to do that when the master's already told 'im to be here at ten o' the clock to row him into town. There's time enough to talk on their way into Lunnon."

Nate gave him a stare he couldn't read. Then speaking around the pipe-stem between his teeth, he said, "That's the wery thing I be here about. Your master'll thank me for comin', just you wait an' see. So best you let me speak to 'im soon as 'e wakes."

Tom could think of no satisfactory response—at least none that wouldn't offend Katy more—so swallowing the deep snarl that welled in his throat, he turned and headed for the stairs. Now he would have to wait until later to pose his question, and he had already started on the wrong foot. He'd overcome his misgivings about bedding Katy, but he could not be sure that she would agree to have him. With the wages St. Mars was paying her and a sound roof over her head, what need did she have to marry, especially a bad-tempered oaf like him? She had been born into a finer trade than Tom's—the drapers' trade—and now that she'd escaped the consequences of her past mistakes, might she not aspire to a better match? Why would she settle for a servant to an outlaw? The more he thought about these things, the darker the cloud that settled on his head.

When Gideon awoke, he saw Tom crouching on his heels before the fire, and stoking it viciously with a poker. As Gideon sat up and stretched, Tom told him that Nate the waterman was waiting below.

"Is it ten o'clock already? Why didn't you wake me?" Gideon tossed the covers aside.

"It's not but eight, my lord. But he's been sittin' down there since cock crow, as far as I can tell."

Tom's brow was as black as Gideon had ever seen it. Clearly something had upset him, but Gideon's brain was too fogged to indulge Tom's ill humour yet, at least not until he had broken his fast. Not only that, but he wanted to focus on his meeting with Mrs. Kean. So far, his suspicions about Curry's murder had not led to a solution, yet he could not help the feeling that they were near to solving it, if only they could put their heads together. Tom's ill humour would have to wait.

Gideon wrapped himself in a fur-lined morning gown and told him to send Nate up with his chocolate. As Tom stood to leave, the idea struck Gideon that his mood could have something to do with Katy. He hoped she had not refused him. For a moment Gideon felt an inkling of the pain her rejection would cause Tom, and he shrank from knowing more. It was bad enough that Tom had been cut off from his home and everyone he knew without suffering a broken heart, too. Gideon thought of calling him back, but he did not know what to say.

When Katy came up with his tray, he searched her face for signs that something was amiss, but she seemed her usual cheerful self. Then

Nate came trudging up the stairs, and Gideon put his concern aside. The waterman shuffled into the room with an almost defiant air, but he clutched his woolen cap nervously between his fingers and his pipe seemed almost crushed between his teeth. Something had upset him as well. Gideon had the feeling he would not be glad to hear what Nate had to say.

He greeted him and took a few sips of his chocolate, while Nate delivered his news.

The Thames was frozen.

Gideon let loose with an oath. This cursed weather was playing havoc with his plans. Not only had his frozen fingers nearly led to his death the day before, but now the river was conspiring to prevent him from seeing Mrs. Kean.

It was not the first time in his lifetime that the river had frozen. When he was four, the winter had been so severe that snow had fallen on London for weeks. The river had frozen solid then, too, but the temperatures had been so brutal, no one in his family had travelled up to London to see it. Then, seven years ago, it had frozen again, and Gideon had seen it, but the ice had not lasted long. Long enough to rob the watermen of their income, it was true, and it was said that some had starved to death, which was no doubt why Nate had come to see him this morning.

While Gideon drank more of his chocolate, he listened to Nate's concerns, the chief of which, it soon became obvious, was that Gideon would renege on their agreement since Nate could no longer provide the service he wanted.

Nate did not admit this, of course. Instead, he offered to be of use in a different way.

"Now, I don't s'pose that just 'cuz the river's gone an' froze that ye won't be wantin' to cross her," he said.

"No, indeed." Gideon could see how worried Nate was, no matter how hard the man tried to hide it. Every man had his pride, and apparently Nate had too much to beg to keep his place. "In fact, I have an appointment in Fleet Street this very morning, which means that I shall have to take my horse across the bridge."

"Now, that's where ye're wrong, see. If ye try to ride yer nag across that bridge, ye'll get all tangled up wif them troops an' all them other folks 'oo've got to use it, too."

Gideon heaved a sigh. "There is that," he agreed, "but at the same time, I want to keep that appointment. I can't just wait for the ice to break up now, can I?"

"Just as I thought." Nate gave a satisfied nod. "An' that's why I took the trouble to come see ye so early this mornin'. I thought ye might be needin' me."

"Do you have a better notion?"

"Don't I just! What ye'll need, see, is fer somebody to guide ye over that river. Ye can't be takin' a walk on that ice wifout ye goes wif somebody like me who knows her."

"You mean, we could walk across? Is it strong enough to hold us?"

Nate gave him a cautious nod. "In places she is, but it'll take an eye as sharp as mine to find 'em. Ye can't be sure that it's good and froze all the way acrost. Ye might fall in, and then where would ye be?"

"Well, presumably I'd be in the Thames. But if you will undertake to see that I do not meet my fate as a block of ice, I shall be very happy to accept your guidance." As he reached for the watch resting on his table, Gideon could almost feel Nate's relief. Then he saw how quickly the morning had disappeared and he leapt to his feet. "It's time for me to dress. Wait below, and we'll see how strong this ice of yours is."

The ice, which had been forming along both banks for weeks, had spread rapidly since Gideon had last laid eyes upon it. Now it glistened before him in a vast silent sheet. The river, which was usually jammed with boats of all kinds, lay eerily empty and still, like a looking glass turned up to reflect the sky.

Gideon would have taken more time to marvel over the phenomenon if he had not had to watch his footing so closely. He and Nate had both tied rags over their wooden heels, the better not to slip, but still he had to take care in the placement of each step.

They moved along the southern bank for a while until the City came into view, then zigzagged over the glistening surface, with Nate testing the river with his pole and using his eye to watch out for thinner ice. In places their way was more treacherous. Wind had sculpted curved ridges into the frozen sheet. Near the center of the river, the water was visible under the ice. Another day or two of frost, and the surface could be as solid as a rock, but for the moment a misstep would cost them dearly. Once, Gideon held his breath when the ice under Nate's foot started to crack. The waterman retreated and circled gingerly for another place to cross.

A few other souls had ventured timidly out onto the Thames. Near the banks children with their fingers and noses turning blue slid and fell as if skates were attached to their feet. Watermen lurked about, staring gloomily down at the mistress who had betrayed their devotion. A few youths tried to pull their sweethearts out onto the ice and raised shrieks of terror from the girls.

Gideon was relieved when at last they made it past the middle and the ice felt more solid beneath his feet. Soon thereafter, they arrived at White Friars Stairs. He dug in his pocket for a coin and told Nate to wait for him at a tavern in Water Lane. Then, he hurried to St. Bride's, arriving only seconds before the bells rang eleven o'clock. He took a seat in the visitors' pew at the back, where they had sat before, just as Morning Prayer ended. From there, he kept an eye out for Mrs. Kean.

In a few minutes she came and spotted him instantly. Her face lit with relief. Gideon stood and opened the door to the pew, then sat down beside her on the bench.

"Thank goodness!" she said breathlessly, as she pulled back the hood of her cloak. There was an air of nervous excitement about her. "I worried that you might not come with the river frozen over. I hope you did not risk your neck to do it."

He chuckled. "No more than is my habit, I suppose."

A flicker in her eyes gave way to a hint of dimples. "I do not refer to your usual risk, my lord," she whispered, "but to the danger posed by the ice."

"Ah, that! Why, yes, I admit that did catch me off guard, but I was assisted by an expert, who persuaded me not to ride across the bridge. But you should know I would come when we have so much to discuss."

Hester was more relieved to see him than she would admit. She was bursting with news, but urged him to deliver his first.

He told her about his trip to Godalming and his conversation with the priest. She wondered how he had managed to extract any information from Sullivan. There must have been more to the tale than he was telling, but she did not pester him for it.

"So, you see," he said, "it was not as I suspected. If Sullivan was telling the truth, Curry never did stumble across their plan. Instead, it was Sullivan who heard Curry in his cellar, which was why he kept such a careful watch on the bookstall. I had to believe him when he said that Curry's murder could only pose a risk to his project, so I find it hard to imagine him as the culprit."

"After speaking to him, did you find him even capable of murder? I cannot forget that he is a priest."

With what seemed an unconscious gesture, St. Mars laid his left hand across his ribs before giving her a rueful smile. "I would not say I found him incapable of it, no. He claimed he would never take part in such an evil deed, but he was certainly prepared to defend his cause."

"What's to be done about it now?"

His tone was serious. "I've given the matter some thought, and cannot reconcile my conscience to letting him proceed, if for no other reason than that surely the foundry's owner does not deserve such wretched treatment. I think a letter, much like the one their lordships received about Curry and your brother, should bring the King's Messengers down upon the barber-surgeon's house. I've already warned Sullivan that I intend to report him, so if he has any sense, he is already halfway to France.

"But what about you?" he said, turning fully towards her. "I can tell you have something important to say."

"*Several somethings,* I believe, but since you mentioned the anonymous letter, I will start with that." She told him of her suspicions that Mr. Simpkins had sent it. "He was trying to get Mr. Curry and Jeremy out of the way so he could seduce Sally without their interference. Then, when she rejected him—and finally with enough force to convince him that he stood no chance with her—he threatened to tell everyone that she had tried to seduce him. Poor Sally was afraid he would be believed, which was the reason she did not tell us any sooner. The moment she saw that Jeremy believed her story, out it spilled."

"So his letter had nothing to do with Curry's murder?"

"I think not. But I believe I may have guessed who our murderer is." With a tremor of excitement, she quickly told him about her encounter with Mr. Pope and the verses of Lady Mary's that were stolen out of the mail at the Rainbow Tavern.

He frowned, unconvinced, until she said, "When I heard that the verses had been stolen, I wondered who could have done it. I could not see Mr. Curry in the role. For one thing, his physical presence was so remarkable that it's likely he would have been recognized. And I knew how badly he wished to avoid any punishment if caught. Then I recalled a comment he made the day I met him. He was speaking of Mr. Tubbs, and he said something about how light a touch he had. I thought he was speaking of Mr. Tubbs's writing, but Mr. Tubbs did not act as if he was complimented by the remark."

"You think he was speaking of Tubbs's ability to steal?"

"Yes. And Mr. Tubbs was entirely dependent upon Mr. Curry, his only patron, the man who paid for his lodgings. His talent for writing is simply not good enough to warrant that support, as Jeremy and I discovered when we had to help him write the chapbook about you, At the time, I should have asked myself why Mr. Curry employed him. The only talent I know he possesses is to speak French."

St. Mars's ears perked up. "Some of the material I found in the cellar was in French. Perhaps he employed Tubbs to translate it into English."

Hester had forgotten this, but now that she recalled, it made sense. "I never thought to look in the bookstall for any publications by Mr. Tubbs, but this morning I did and there were none except his chapbook about you."

"Not about me, my dear," he teased her. "You told me you made up a fantasy."

She laughed shyly. "No, it was not about you. But it finally struck me as odd that Mr. Curry would support Mr. Tubbs when there was no evidence of his work. He was not at all generous. I believe you are right. He must have translated the indecent material you found."

St. Mars pondered this, and as he did, he began to jiggle his right leg. "It all fits!" he exclaimed in a whisper. "If Tubbs had translated that literature, he would not want anyone to discover it."

Hester tumbled quickly to his meaning. "That was why after he murdered Mr. Curry, he bothered to lock the bookstall. Perhaps he meant to sell the material himself."

"Possibly, but I suspect he was more concerned that it not be found for fear that someone would guess he had written it, as we have just done. He panicked, for he had not planned to kill Curry, had he?"

St. Mars's thoughts were running parallel to her own. "I believe not," she agreed. "I think something enraged him so thoroughly that he attacked his patron without thinking. Why else would he kill the only person who would pay him for his work?"

"And he was so panicked by what he had done that he did not even think to rob the shop. That's why Curry still had money on him. Yes, the more I look at it, the better it fits. We have been searching too hard for a motive when it was nothing but frustrated anger. Anger is the motive that fits the details of this crime."

"But what provocation could have made Mr. Tubbs so far forget his welfare that he would murder his only patron? I've been assuming all along that he could not have killed the man whose support he needed. Do you think Mr. Curry threatened to tell someone about the illegal tasks Mr. Tubbs had performed for him?" She paused. "But no, that would make no sense, for in doing so, he would implicate himself."

"I don't think we need to look too far into what made Tubbs go beyond reason if Curry liked to taunt him as you said. Constant belittlement can work any man into a suppressed passion. If his anger had been suppressed long enough, it might not have taken much to tip him over the edge. "

"I daresay you are right. I believe Mr. Curry did enjoy humiliating him." Hester could almost understand Mr. Tubbs's passion, too, for she knew what it was like to be at the beck and call of someone who despised her. How many times had her aunt embarrassed her with ungrateful and insulting speeches? Not that she would ever murder her aunt, but neither was she as miserable and peculiar a creature as Mr. Tubbs.

She had seen his fury when Jeremy told him about Curry's wealth. How much bitterness must that knowledge have caused him? If he had not already been provoked to throttle Mr. Curry, that new information might have angered him enough. Still, she knew it was more likely that Mr. Curry had insulted him just one too many times on the evening he was killed.

"I can understand how intolerable his position must have been, but I cannot forgive him for letting Jeremy live under suspicion, when Jeremy has always been so kind to him. What should we do now? How can we prove these conjectures when even the French literature has been destroyed?"

St. Mars looked at her. "We shall have to make him confess."

"But how?"

He smiled. "I believe I have an idea."

"All this is madness," cries a sober sage:
But who, my friend, has reason in his rage?
"The ruling Passion be what it will,
The ruling Passion conquers Reason still."

CHAPTER XXIII

They hastily laid their plans. Then, in the morning Hester sent a messenger with a note for Mr. Tubbs, saying that she had learned something more about Blue Satan which he might like to include in a second chapbook about the notorious highwayman. She said she would be working late at the Bell and Bible and could give him the information, if he would come to the shop at closing time.

Later that evening, she found it easy to persuade Sally that she should walk out with Jeremy to see the moonlight on the frozen Thames. All day, customers had come in talking excitedly of the possibility that a frost fair might be held if the weather remained this cold. Some thought a fair would be a fitting celebration for his Majesty's triumph over the Pretender's men. One older man recalled a similar one in his youth when bull baiting, puppet plays, and even horse and coach races had been staged on the river's ice, and although to him nothing could ever match the thrill of those days, he agreed that this year was the first to approach that earlier one for cold.

With all the cheerful speculation, no one but Hester noticed the absence of Joseph Sullivan, although one man remarked that the barber-surgeon's shop across the way seemed to be closed.

In order to forestall Sally's protests that it would be wrong to leave

Hester alone to close the shop, Hester had taken time that morning to go see the river for herself. The day was bitterly cold, but nothing could stop fun-seekers from playing on the ice. Children pulled their friends up and down on makeshift sleds and people slid about on Dutch skates. They remained near the banks where the ice was hard, for towards the middle one could still see the water flowing under thinner patches.

Hester had been too nervous about her evening plans to stand and observe it long, but she could honestly urge Sally to go see it, even in the dark. "For there are certain to be plenty of others there, as rare a sight as it is. And, if there are truly to be booths built upon the ice, you might want to open a bookstall there."

"As if it were not already cold enough in this one." Sally shivered, gazing up happily into Jeremy's face. "But I should like to see it soon, in case the weather changes and it thaws."

"Then, please, do go," Hester said, "and take advantage of my being here. I've heard from Isabella again, and if I don't want to lose my place, I can't stay many days longer."

Jeremy, who had lingered about most of the day, was only too eager to escape with Sally now that there was a flourishing understanding between them. Since the moment she had confessed her reason for keeping him at arm's length, they'd spent little time apart. Mr. Simpkins's failure to carry out his threats had eliminated most of their doubts. If only Sally had been open with Jeremy before, there would have been no need for Hester and St. Mars to search for Mr. Curry's killer. But now that Hester was almost certain of his identity, she could not turn her back on solving the crime—if for no other reason than she could never be easy knowing that Jeremy counted a murderer among his friends.

By the time she saw the couple off, it was many hours after dark. The solstice was approaching and the sun had set before four o'clock. Now it was nearing closing time, and outside all was black as midnight. As the giants in St. Dunstan's tower struck nine. Hester pulled the shutters nearly closed, leaving only one chink through which St. Mars could peek into the shop. Then she stirred up the coals to get more heat, for in spite of the fire that had burned all day, the harsher chill of night had dampened its effect. She didn't know how much of her shivering was due to the cold and how much to nerves, for she had only a vague idea of what she would say to Tubbs, even if she had led St. Mars to believe that her script was all set.

He had not been thrilled with the changes she had made to his plan, but in the end he had agreed to them when she'd convinced him it was the only way to get Tubbs to confess. He had only made her promise not to let Tubbs come within two paces of her and had cautioned her not to rile him.

The door of the shop opened, making her turn with a start. As Tubbs blew in on a gust of frosty air, she composed her trembling features into a smile.

"Good evening, sir. I see that you received my note."

He gave her one of his shy grunts, which she took for all the greeting she was likely to get. Then he moved to the center of the shop, and she noticed how cold he was, hunching his shoulders beneath a cloak that was too thin to fight such miserable weather. The lamplight shone on the tips of his fingers, which poked through his gloves, and he blew on his hands as he hurried over to the fire.

Hester fought the pity that welled up inside her at the sight of his want. But recalling her promise to St. Mars, she retreated until the counter stood between them.

As soon as Tubbs had warmed his hands, he turned his back to the fire. Only then did he seem to notice that they were alone. His gaze bounced repeatedly from the door to the walls, then to the rails hung with folios behind Hester's head. Sally's absence seemed to make him even more jittery than usual.

He stammered, "Wh-what do you know about B-Blue Satan? What have you found?"

Hester hoped she had not guessed wrong, for she had nothing to give him but lies. "It is not that I have found anything," she said, acting purposefully mysterious. "But I have developed a theory or two."

Eyeing her suspiciously, he glowered, but his curiosity was still piqued. "What book can I write with that?"

"I'm not perfectly certain, but I may know something that would be of interest—to the authorities, I mean." Turning her gaze upon him, she stared into his eyes, hoping to use his guilty conscience against him. That last bit had come in a moment of inspiration. If she could throw him off balance before St. Mars appeared, maybe he would be more likely to confess.

Her mention of the law made him jump, but she could almost hear him reminding himself that they were speaking of the highwayman. "What?" He was disappointingly brief.

"Blue Satan's interest in the barber-surgeon's shop . . . And in this one, too."

This caused his brow to shoot up. "Here? He's been in here?"

She did not answer him directly, but said, "I heard he searched the cellar beneath the shop." Her intent was to make him think of the translated books Mr. Curry had hidden. She wondered if Jeremy, in his *naïveté,* had told his friend Tubbs what they'd found.

"Wh-Who told you?"

Again she ignored him. "It was very curious what he found."

"What—what did he find?" Fear had entered his tone.

In planning this confrontation, this was the point at which Hester's ingenuity had given out. She did not know how to lead him on further without giving away all she knew and the fact that she had no proof.

She remained silent, letting her gaze speak for her.

His jaw fell slack. He worked his lips. His eyes reminded her of a frightened animal's. A more confident person would have waited to see what she would say next, but Tubbs did not possess that coolness. He took a few steps towards her, his hands clenching and unclenching. "You promised me another story I could write," he said.

The door of the shop burst open and a masked figure swept inside. A tricorn hat shaded his gaze. French lace curled at his cuffs and at his throat. And a blue satin cape swirled from his impressive shoulders to the doe-skin at his knees. Even expecting his arrival, Hester gave a gasp, for the ferocity in Blue Satan's movements always shook her.

Tubbs had whirled around at the sound of the door, and now he backed as Blue Satan advanced towards him into the shop. "You!" Excitement mixed with fear in his voice.

"I hope you were not thinking of harming Mrs. Kean—the way you throttled Mr. Curry," St. Mars said in a menacing tone. It thrilled Hester even as she shrank from its threat.

"H-How did you—I-it's not true!" Tubbs stumbled backwards as Blue Satan kept coming, a jewel-hilted sword in his grasp.

His smile looked cruel beneath the black of the mask. "Too late for that, I'm afraid. You were going to ask how I discovered your crime. But I know all about the books you translated for your employer, and the verses you stole for him. What did he do to enrage you? Did he refuse to pay you, or did he debase you one too many times?"

"He refused to let me write the chapbook about you!" Tubbs cried, abandoning his attempt to dissemble. "It was *my* idea to write the account of Mrs. Kean's abduction, not Kean's! But he said that Kean would do it better—that I had no talent for writing what the public wants to read."

For a moment, St. Mars was speechless. And Hester felt a stab in her breast. She winced to think that if she had never stepped into this miserable creature's life, he would not be a murderer now. Then she reminded herself that in time something else would have caused Tubbs to explode. It was Curry's preference for Jeremy's talents that had made him snap. And Curry—no matter how unnecessarily cruel he had been—had been right. Tubbs did not have the talent to invent stories.

His ability to translate was his only strength. But he could not see that, and he had compromised himself by stealing to gain favour with his patron in the hope of being given other opportunities—which Curry might have given him, if he had not learned that Jeremy was related not only to Hester but to the Earl and Countess of Hawkhurst. From what she knew of him, Hester supposed he would have urged Jeremy to pen the story about Blue Satan even if Tubbs had been the one with the talent for fiction. His proclivity for using people to enrich himself was entirely without sympathy or honour.

"So you throttled him, here, in front of the counter." St. Mars had recovered his voice. "Then, when you saw what you had done, you remembered the indecent literature that Curry hid under the shop, and you panicked. You couldn't stay about. If someone had heard Curry's struggle and come to investigate the noise, you'd be discovered. But you did not want to leave the shop unlocked in case someone came, and in searching found Curry's cache. You knew that Mrs. Curry had no knowledge of it, so you wanted her to be the one to discover the body. Then there would be less risk of the material being uncovered."

"I thought I might retrieve it later and sell it myself. God knows, it's mine! Curry always underpaid me. He loved to say that beggars can't be choosers, but it's *my* work on those pages. You can say that he paid to house me, but like an animal in a cage! *You* with your lace and your sword—you would *never* live like that." Tubbs's voice took on an unfamiliar, assertive tone. "So I sometimes stole for Curry, but you don't dare tell anyone I killed him, or you'll end up on the scaffold, too."

Blue Satan's smile did not change. "But what about Mrs. Kean behind you? I'm afraid she's heard your confession."

Tubbs's head spun round. He stared at Hester with wide, frightened eyes. He had forgotten she was there.

His manner changed again. Gone was the confident note, as he stammered, "I l-lost my temper. I d-didn't mean to kill him."

"I know you didn't," Hester said, scarcely able to persist. Her heart had wept at his story. "But you would have let Jeremy take the blame, and I cannot allow him to live under that cloud." It was only because of her interference that Mr. Simpkins had not taken him before a magistrate. She shuddered to think what might have happened next.

"I-I can go away! If you let me, I can sign a confession, and you can use it as long as you give me time to escape."

Hester could barely stand to see him begging like this. His notion tempted her.

Then, before she could decide anything, the door flew open with a bang. Jeremy rushed in and threw himself at Blue Satan, pinning his arms behind his back.

Hester cried, "Jeremy, no!"

Tubbs hesitated only an instant before ducking around the two grappling men and disappearing into the night.

As St. Mars fought to free himself from the taller man's grip, he let loose with a stream of oaths. Trying to fling Jeremy off his back, he sent them crashing about the tiny shop. A coat stand went clattering onto the floor. The andirons clanged. Then, Sally came running into the bookstall, and added her frightened shrieks to the madness.

Rushing from behind the counter, Hester yelled at her brother to stop. She tried to explain that it was Tubbs who had murdered Mr. Curry, but the noise the men were making was so loud he could not hear. He threw her a puzzled glance, and she could almost read the thoughts that must be running through his head. The man he had jumped was armed—Jeremy was not. If he mistook his sister's words and released the bandit, they might all pay for the error with their lives.

Finally, with a mighty shove St. Mars knocked Jeremy's head against the wall. With a painful grunt Jeremy loosened his grip long enough for Blue Satan to wriggle from his grasp. Then in silence, his cape flapping like wings behind him, Blue Satan dashed out into the night in the wake of the killer.

Sally ran to bend over Jeremy, who had slumped to the floor. "Mr. Kean, are you hurt?" She frantically checked him over for injuries, and seeing none, called over her shoulder to Hester to fetch the watch.

Exhausted by the display she had witnessed, Hester did not instantly respond. She would have preferred to run after St. Mars, but knew she must stay to keep the other two from calling down the law upon Blue Satan. She stumbled over to a stool and sat down to rest.

Jeremy, who must have had the breath knocked out of him, gradually recovered it He threw his sister a confused look.

She said, "I'm sorry you were hurt, Jeremy, but that man you saw was only trying to help."

"Help?" He stared incredulously and Sally turned to her with a frown. "But we saw him through the opening in the shutter. Wasn't that the robber, Blue Satan?"

Hester did not know what answer she should give. St. Mars's secrets were not hers to divulge. Besides Jeremy was such a poor judge of character, she didn't know if he could be trusted with information that could cost another man his life.

"That man you saw was not a highwayman or even a thief," she said. "The real villain, I'm afraid, is your friend, Mr. Tubbs. It was he who throttled Mr. Curry."

"Tubbs? But you cannot be right! Why poor old Tubbs wouldn't harm a flea."

Hester gave him a pitying smile. "I'm sorry, Jeremy. But you must believe me, even though his treachery will come as a shock. He confessed to the murder just before you burst in."

When Gideon ran out of the shop, he was met by Nate, carrying a torch, who pointed him towards the Temple, crying, "He ran into King's Bench Walk. Yer groom is on 'is tail."

Gideon hurried after the two men. He didn't dare take a moment to remove his cape and mask or he would never stand a chance of catching up with them. He knew his behaviour was reckless, but his temper was so riled by Jeremy Kean's ill-timed interference that he would have run straight into Newgate if doing so would relieve his frustration.

Tubbs and Tom had only had a few seconds gain, but they could easily lose him in the maze of courts and walks that made up the Temple. The courts, not principal streets, were only lit at the whim of the tenants who inhabited them—a good situation for hiding Gideon from the law, but much to Tubbs's advantage as well. Gideon hoped that Tom could manage to stay with him through the dark.

The night—so cold his breath froze on his lips—was clear and dry. The stars shone with a crystalline crispness. With neither fog nor clouds to cloak it, the three-quarter moon provided a steady glow to light his way through an alley that was usually black with menace. As Gideon tore through Mitre Court, he could almost make out the features of the men who stumbled out of the Mitre Tavern. One caught sight of his caped figure and paused to stare. Gideon prayed the man could not see the blue of his cape, but he knew that anyone running at night would be suspected of evil. Then, as he burst out onto King's Bench Walk, he heard a shout behind him and knew that someone had called out for the watch. It would not be long before they came to see what all the shouts were about.

He had not expected to find so many pedestrians out in the cold, but with the Thames iced over, the curious had gathered to see it even at this late hour. Every stairwell from every group of chambers spewed forth a few occupants. A coach and four traversed the walk in front of him, another pulled up in front of a door. Steam blew out of the horses' nostrils, giving them a dragon-like appearance. The walkers he passed carried links, which brightened the ambient light. Gideon slowed and tried to turn his face away from them, but when a group passed close, he heard an exclamation, then another, and knew that his luck had run out.

He had planned to weave a quick path through the darkened courts and exit by Middle Temple Lane in the hope of spotting Tom, but he heard running feet, then the rattle of the watch behind him in Mitre Court, and he knew he must flee for his life.

As he reached the middle of the vast walk, three shadowy figures started merging towards him from the right, their weapons out. Gideon quickly drew his sword and parried a thrust from the closest man. Then, with a feint he ducked around Sir Robert Sawyer's Buildings with the others fast on his heels.

"Ye gods! It's Blue Satan! After him!"

"There's a fat price on his head!'

Their voices followed him as he flew onto the terrace of the Inner Temple. There, through the dark he could make out groups of students, laughing and talking with their friends. As the commotion reached them, they turned their necks, and froze like the shadows of actors in the wings. Gideon's mind quickly counted—there were far too many of them to slip past. Pivoting too rapidly, then, he slid on a patch of ice. His fingers hit the ground before, without a pause, he recovered his balance, and praying he wouldn't fall again, headed left for the entrance to the gardens and the Thames.

The gate to the garden was closed. Running to a spot near the stone piers with their griffin engravings, he grabbed hold of two of the wooden posts to vault into the garden below. He landed hard. Luckily still erect, he ignored the fresh pain in his ankles and the bite of the cold air in his lungs, and ran full out for the Thames. The sound of pursuit behind him had grown fainter, undoubtedly while his chasers fumbled with the gate. He did not turn around to see if any had copied his rash vault. If they had, they could be on him before he could look forwards again.

He had just passed the last building on his right when a movement in Middle Temple Lane beyond caught his eye. Two men were hastening towards the river, one short and one square, the larger man in pursuit. As their paths converged with his, Gideon saw that Tom was the second man and that he had almost caught up with Tubbs.

Whether Tubbs had panicked and forgotten that the river was frozen, or whether he simply had nowhere else to run, there was nothing to carry him down the Thames but his own two feet. He did not seem to have noticed Gideon's approach on his left, as he disappeared through the arch to Temple Stairs just moments before Gideon reached the garden wall. Preparing to climb, Gideon turned his head briefly to see a mob of men, a regular *mobile vulgus,* chasing after him, but none was close enough to worry him. Crowding so many men through the gate must have slowed them down. He turned to reach across the thick wall, then gripping the top with his forearms, he jumped and hooked one knee over before pulling himself the rest of the way up.

Tonight, the drop down the other side was an equal distance. Normally, anyone leaping the wall would find himself deep in the River Thames, but thanks to the cold, Gideon landed on solid ice. Tubbs must have paused when he had seen it for he was only now at the bottom of the stairs, ready to step out. A few people stood on the frozen bank, but at this late hour, no one cared to test its strength farther out.

Gideon glanced one more time over his shoulder and was relieved to see that a few of his pursuers had slipped on the grass. He caught a fleeting glimpse of a jumble of bodies before he turned back to his own quarry, thanking God he had tied the soles of his boots with rags. The other men in their high wooden heels could not keep their balance.

Now, on the river there were no city lights to guide them. No carriage lamps and no links. Just the moon shining down on the glistening surface with one desperate man fleeing, and two others—only slightly less desperate—in pursuit. Instantly, Gideon assessed his advantage. If he veered only slightly from his present course, he should be able to cut Tubbs off. Then, with Tom behind him, they should be able to trap the fleeing killer who would not dare venture too far out on the ice.

Tubbs obviously knew that Tom was after him, even if he did not know who his pursuer was, else he might have stopped running minutes ago. Terror had given him speed, while Tom, more accustomed to riding than walking, was losing ground with every stride.

In another second, Tom spied his master converging on his path, and crying out with relief, clasped his ribs with one hand and began to slow his pace. A painful stitch must have taken hold of his side. He moved as if every breath stabbed him like a dagger.

Gideon, too, was suffering from the cold. Miniature icicles had formed and reformed on his lips with every exhalation of his lungs. Only the heat made by his running body had melted them. But the cold on the ice was so intense, his chest burned with every gulp of air. He knew that Tubbs would not be in better shape, and as his pace brought him closer to Curry's killer with every running step, he looked for signs that his quarry would soon collapse.

These thoughts flew through his mind in seconds, as he tried to catch up with the slipping, sliding pair. Now, as he sped past Tom at an angle, he realized that Tubbs had not turned yet, but was still heading towards the middle of the river where the darkness was more profound. The Thames was at its widest here, well over a thousand feet across. If Tom could not keep up, Gideon would have to catch Tubbs by himself, no matter which way the killer ran.

Tubbs turned his head once, and saw Blue Satan at his heels. Then, with a burst of panicked speed, he abandoned any logic that might have restrained him. He ran as if salvation waited for him on the southern bank, slithering and scrambling sometimes with his hands as well as his feet.

Just an hour ago, Gideon had crossed the Thames at the narrowest point, with Nate testing the ice with every step. They had safely made it across, but in this wide section there were sure to be thinner spots. Tubbs must have known this. Except for the defeat of the Pretender's men, few other subjects had been on Londoners' lips all day, for everyone was eager to see if the river would get solid enough for the frost fair they wanted. Yet, on Tubbs ran, hurtling towards the other bank with no sign of caution. Gideon had gained on him, but he did not like the direction they were taking.

He called out, "Wait! The ice may give!"

He might have been shrieking at a deaf man for all the sign Tubbs gave. With no more than a slight break in his stride, he headed for the middle where the ice was surely thinnest.

Then beneath his own feet Gideon heard a crack. Fear jolted his thoughts, but he reacted immediately, diving and flattening his body on the ice. He slid for several feet. Cruel cold bit into his elbows and knees, but with his weight spread over a wider area, the ice beneath him held.

Behind him, Tom gave a cry of fear, but when Gideon peered back over his shoulder, he saw that Tom's worries were only for him. He called back, "I'm safe. Don't come any farther!"

In front of him Tubbs was pushing on. Dark had almost cloaked him, but Gideon knew there was nothing more he could do. He knew when he was beaten. Carefully, he pushed himself backwards gradually until the ice beneath him felt firm. He slowly rose to his hands and knees, and then to his feet.

Tom, who had come to a halt not far from him now, breathlessly said, "I'm sorry I couldn't catch him, my lord."

Gideon looked about but through the dark he saw no one else. The men who had chased him must have given up when he and Tubbs had ventured out onto the ice. "No matter," he said. "Mrs. Kean heard him confess to killing Curry. It's a pity he escaped, but the fact that he ran will confirm her story when she informs the law."

A figure came towards them through the darkness. It was Nate, with his pole and Gideon's fur-lined cloak And not a moment too soon, for Gideon's teeth had begun to chatter.

He was about to hail the waterman when he heard a strangled cry coming from somewhere on the ice behind him. A voice shrieked frantically. Then it stopped. Turning, he peered out into the gloom, but the night defeated his gaze. The moon had painted a glistening path through the point where he stood, but everything beyond it was black.

⅌

Later that week, St. Mars went into London to see the captured Jacobite rebels marched in.

Tom stayed behind and worked up his courage again. As soon as his master left, he cleaned himself up and went into the house to find Katy.

This time, when he saw Nate sitting at her kitchen hearth, it took every bit of his restraint not to throw the worthless beggar out. But he knew that Katy, who was sitting across from him plying her needle, would be angry if he was mean to the old man, so he asked him instead why he had not gone with the master to make sure he got safely across the ice.

Arms crossed, Nate puffed twice on his pipe before answering slowly. "Said he wouldn' be needin' me today. Said he thought the ice was thick enough." He puffed a few times more. "Told 'im he didn' ought to go takin' risks like that. Said I was sure ye wouldn' like it if I let 'im go alone, but 'e said 'e had a bit o' business in town." *Puff. Puff.*

"You could've followed 'im . . . made sure he made it across."

When Nate still sucked on his pipe, Tom thought he just might strangle him. What would it take to get the old blackguard to leave him and Katy alone? He practically haunted the house now that he couldn't row his boat, and Katy seemed cheered to have him around.

"S'pose I coulda done it," Nate finally spoke. "But then who woulda kep this pretty girl comp'ny?" As he pointed at Katy with the stem of his pipe, a flirtatious gleam lit his eye.

Katy blushed, as if some young, handsome buck had chucked her under the chin. She gave a girlish laugh.

Tom felt like exploding. He smothered an oath. If he strangled the bugger, Katy would never forgive him. He knew he must look like a grumbling fool, but he didn't know how to make Nate disappear.

The waterman studied him for a while through the smoke he steadily released from his mouth. When Tom was all set to give up and to work out his frustration grooming the horses, Nate finally spoke up again.

"Looks t' me like ye could use a little help out in that barn o' yers."

Tom's head jerked up and he scowled. If Nate thought he was going to stick his confounded head inside St. Mars's stables . . . .

Tom gritted his teeth. "I thank you kindly for the offer, but I don't need no help."

"Not me, ye idiot." Nate pointed his pipe stem at Katy again. "It's 'er I mean. Thought ye might need 'er fer somethin' out there in that barn."

Katy shot Tom a nervous glance and turned a pretty shade of pink. Then she bent over her needle and gave a little wriggle in her seat. "Mr. Barnes doesn't need anyone's help," she said, her neck all stiff.

But Tom did. He was such a bloody fool that he'd needed this old man to tell him how to court a female.

He stalked her and watched as she raised her head in surprise. When he stopped no more than a few inches away, he swore he could see her gulp.

"Mr. Barnes?" Her voice trembled, making his knees shake in response.

"Mrs. Katy" —Tom held out a hand to her— "would you step outside for a bit with me, please?"

Her big brown eyes were wide as saucers. Then she looked about, as if searching for help. She glanced at Nate, who said nothing, though out the corner of his eye, Tom thought he saw the old man nod. Then Katy fumbled with the stitching in her lap. "I s-suppose I could step out with you, Mr. Barnes—if you be needing me. I shall have to get my cloak first, or I just might catch my death."

She was talking a different way, like a lady who was flustered. It made Tom happy to think he could fluster her.

"And I'll need my pattens for the mud—"

"No, you won't." Tom wrapped her in his coat, scooped her up into his arms, and carried her to the door. A little flustering was all right, but he couldn't let her go on and on.

"Mr. Barnes!" Her gasp of delight set up a burning in his loin. "You shouldn't lift me! Why, a man of your age—"

He halted mid-stride in the middle of the yard. "My age?" he said, growling down at the woman in his arms. "What the devil's my age got to do with it?"

A dimple popped into each of her cheeks, and she bit her lower lip. "Why, nothing, I do believe!"

He resumed his stride. "You'd better know it." He said nothing else until they reached the stables. Then while he negotiated the door, he added, "If we're goin' to be married—and the master says it's all right— I don't aim to disappoint you."

He set Katy down with her feet in the hay, keeping her within the warmth of his coat. His heart was pounding now, but not from exercise as much as desire—which to show her how much he had come to respect her, he would keep in check until their marriage was blessed.

Sooner than later, he hoped.

Katy wrapped both arms about his waist and rubbed her cheek against his chest. Then lifting her face, she said, "I could never be disappointed with you. Not after—"

He shushed her, bending his forehead down to hers. "I don't want to hear it. Not now—not ever. I'm not proud of the way I treated you, but I was just that scared—scared of wantin' you."

Tears filled her eyes, and for a moment he was afraid he had hurt her again. Then she smiled through her tears. "But you're not afraid of me any more." She gazed up at him with confidence and joy.

He shook his head and whispered with his lips brushing hers, "No, not any more."

∅

The principal rebels taken at Preston in Lancashire had been brought to London with their servants, and today they were paraded through the streets. Among them were the earls of Derwentwater, Nithsdale, Winton, and Carnwath, Viscount Kenmure, the Lord and the Master of Nairn. Their hands were bound behind them, and each of their horses with its bridle removed was led by a soldier. Upwards of a hundred men, most Scots or Papists, made the fatal march with them. All the way down from Highgate to the gaols that would house them—the Tower, Newgate, the Marshalsea, and the Fleet—they were met by a vast throng of people who jeered and teased them. A man carried a warming pan before the procession—to mock James Stuart, who was rumoured to have been smuggled into his mother's birthing chamber by that means. Though the rebels responded with spirit to the insults that were flung at them, Gideon soon had to turn away from the humiliation of these honourable men who had taken up the banner of their rightful king. Being witness to their defeat was simply too painful.

Dressed as a stonemason, he made his way to St. Thomas's Church in Kingly Street, where he had arranged to meet Mrs. Kean. With most Londoners and members of Court distracted by the spectacle in the streets, they hoped to find a quite moment in which to talk. As cold as it was, they had to meet indoors, and since Mrs. Kean had returned to her duties at Hawkhurst House, Gideon had suggested St. Anne's as the nearest church outside St. James's parish. St. Thomas's had been built to serve the needs of the less fashionable members of the parish, whose nobler members might be praying at St. Anne's, so Mrs. Kean had recommended the poorer church to avoid their being seen by a courtier.

Gideon found her in the back, seated in the pews reserved for visitors and the poor. As he had hoped, the church was empty, though it gave him no pleasure to think of the crowds who had chosen instead to go jeer at the prisoners.

As he approached the pew, her smile expressed a sympathy that warmed his heart. He returned it with no attempt to hide his sadness, then opened the door of the pew and joined her on the bench.

"Did you see them?" she asked. Her voice came in a low tone rather than a whisper.

He nodded, then lacing his fingers, he leaned to rest his elbows on his knees. "Would to God I had not."

Her silence was the greatest solace he could imagine, and for a long while they simply sat, Gideon appreciating the peace she brought him, as much as the excitement he usually felt in her presence. Finally, he said, "Tell me what occurred after I left you at the Bell and Bible. I hope your brother wasn't much hurt."

She leaned back, and a twinkle lit her eyes. "After you soundly smashed him into the wall? No, my lord, he was only dazed, but I had a hard time convincing him and Sally that Mr. Tubbs was the villain and not you."

He chuckled. "I imagine you did. How did you stop him from issuing a call for the watch?"

"That was the easy part, for the watch came by when he heard the noise and did not need to be called. Fortunately, by then I had convinced Jeremy that you were not the highwayman you appeared to be, but a friend who had helped me uncover Tubbs's guilt. He was so stunned to learn of his friend's villainy, he allowed me to say what I wanted to the watch. By then, of course, others were crying out that Blue Satan had been seen fleeing through the Temple, and the watchman took off after you, undoubtedly dreaming of the reward for your capture, and ignoring me when I tried to tell him about Tubbs."

"Yes, I heard him or one of his confederates behind me, but I lost them when I ran into the gardens. So, who did you tell your brother I was?" He trusted her so implicitly that he would not have minded if she had confided his identity.

But she regarded him seriously and said, "I told him nothing else, beyond the fact that he would have to trust that you would do none of us any harm. I love Jeremy, of course, and I would trust him with my life. But I cannot be confident in his choice of friends. He is far too gullible."

"It's strange, isn't it, how different you are?"

Her smile was surprisingly rueful. "Yes, but I am not always the one who knows best. But fortunately, we agree on the things that truly matter."

"Did Mr. Kean go with you to report Tubbs's confession?"

"Yes, and Sally went, too. And just to make certain we were believed, I asked Mr. Henry to accompany us to give me a good character. I hope you do not mind, for I know how uncharitable you are towards him, but I thought the testimony of a gentleman from Lord Hawkhurst's household would carry more weight than either my word or Jeremy's.

"And I'm glad I did," she continued, as he concealed his irritation at the thought. "The Lord Mayor, who took our testimony at the Guildhall, clearly did not look with favour upon two females without husbands and a scribbler of chapbooks."

"Well, with such a sterling character as James Henry with you, I hope he believed you."

"I believe he did. At least, he acknowledged that Tubbs was most likely the culprit since he had fled. Now, you," she said. "It's your turn to tell me what you can about his disappearance."

Gideon had debated whether to share his suspicions about Tubbs's end with Mrs. Kean. He did not know how much the truth would disturb her, but if Tubbs had not fallen through the ice, he would be awaiting the hangman's noose instead.

He decided to tell her as much as he knew, starting with the moment he had spied Tom chasing Tubbs through the gate at Temple Stairs.

"I was sure he would turn eventually and run parallel to the bank. He must have known how dangerous it was to risk the ice in such a wide part of the river. But he never paused. I called out to him to stop, but he kept going. Then, when I heard the first sound of cracking under my feet, I knew I had to stop. I thought he might have made it across, but I couldn't see that far in the dark."

When he mentioned the cracks in the ice, she gasped and her hand flew out to grasp his arm. "I never want you to risk that sort of danger again, my lord. I had much rather see the villain escape than for you to lose your life."

He grinned at her concern, which was impractical at this point, but he still had to tell her about the cry he had heard.

When he did, she gave a shiver and released his arm. "Poor, poor Tubbs," she said, her face covered with pity. "If there ever was a miserable creature, it was he. Mr. Curry used him abominably, and I suppose I shall always wonder how differently they would have ended if Jeremy had never entered their lives. But he is not to blame for the consequences of Mr. Curry's greed on the one hand, or Tubbs's violent resentment on the other. And I cannot forget that Tubbs would likely have let Jeremy hang for his crime if Jeremy had been charged with it. In spite of the feelings of pity someone like him must always arouse, I do not think his character was very good."

"No, just because we pitied him doesn't mean he deserved it. He did, after all, lie and steal and kill. And, as you said, he was prepared to let your brother suffer for his sins, when your brother had helped pay his rent. I do not know what his background was or why he was so desperate. I can only wonder how much of his situation was due to his own faults."

"More than I realized, as it turns out. I learned more about him when we laid information before the Lord Mayor. Apparently, he had broken with his father, who had tried to apprentice him to a clockmaker in Bristol. But that was the reason Jeremy felt so much sympathy for him, for their situations appeared to be the same. I doubt he ever felt much else. Certainly, he could never have enjoyed Tubbs's companionship. But Jeremy's heart is very big. Much bigger than mine I'm afraid."

He scolded her with a teasing look. "It is never wrong to take care with the associations one makes. Just look at the trouble your friendship with me has caused you. The last thing you need is another escaped felon for a friend."

"How right you are! *One* must certainly be enough. But I cannot help thinking how useful your friendship can be at times."

He loved the sly way she slanted her eyes when she said this. "I could say the same about you. But I believe I should reserve judgement until I see what other benefits our friendship brings."

He heard a catch in her breath as her eyes grew wide, but considering where they were sitting, he did not elaborate.

The End

AUTHOR'S NOTE

That 1715 was one of the most apprehensive years in British history is confirmed by the very dearth of letters, personal papers, and diaries chronicling its events. The few entries in various collections spanning that year make it explicitly clear that people were afraid to commit their thoughts to paper. Aware that the English government was opening the mail in search of Jacobite activities, letter writers were either grossly circumspect or completely silent on the subject of Jacobite activities or King George. Writing at a later, safer date, the niece of Lady Cowper, wife of George's Lord Chancellor, explained that the hysteria was so severe that even the Whigs that were very high in George's favor burned their papers for fear that their enemies might find something in them to justify an accusation of treason. Working with the few personal accounts I found, including Lady Cowper's, plus the basic facts reported in the news-sheets, I have tried to convey the fear and uncertainty that must have roiled English society that autumn.

The character and physical description of Edmund Curry were derived from an eighteenth-century bookseller by the name of Edmund Curll, owner of the Dial and Bible, a bookstall up against St. Dunstan's Church. A thoroughly distasteful creature, Curll was known to put up his translators "three a bed at the Pewter Platter Inn in Holborn." This quoted phrase appears repeatedly in collections of anecdotes of the time, but try as I did, I could not locate a Pewter Platter Inn in Holborn. There was one further north near St. John's Gate, but the Holborn location seemed more convenient, so I used it. Curll published "disgraceful books and forged letters," and was put in the pillory at least once. He did steal verses from Alexander Pope and printed them without the poet's permission. I do not know how he executed his thefts, but he so riled Pope that he took an uncharacteristically physical act of revenge.

Pope offered to meet Curll at the Swan Tavern to patch up their differences. There he lulled Curll into believing all was forgiven while he poured an emetic into his canary, rendering him miserably sick. I suppose Curll might have died as a result, but as practical jokes were much in vogue in the eighteenth century, the prank was reckoned a very good joke by Pope and his friends.

The idea for Joseph Sullivan came from a contemporary newspaper report that one Loree, alias Doulee, an Irish priest, was arrested for a plot to blow-up his Majesty's magazine of gun-powder at Greenwich. Logistically, that site would not work for my novel, but Mr. Bagley's foundry did. His foundry did make all guns for the government. Both father and son died the following year as the result of an accident in the casting of a cannon, though not at the hands of a Jacobite agent. The danger of permitting such a business to operate within the precincts of London became apparent and eventually the fabrication of the king's arms was moved out of the city.

According to some accounts, the barber-surgeon shop across from my fictional Bell and Bible, now 186 Fleet Street, was later the shop of Sweeney Todd, the barber-surgeon who slit the throats of his clients. The tunnel under his shop which led to the crypt of St. Dunstan's, gave me the idea for Curry's hidden stock. Amazingly, all the area about St. Dunstan's is riddled with tunnels, which were used for all kinds of nefarious purposes in the eighteenth century. The tunnel St. Mars used to go from Westbrook Place to the King's Arms in Godalming was also real.

My portrayal of Lady Mary Wortley Montagu is based on the opinion I formed by reading her letters. Although intelligent and beautiful, she struck me as conceited and smug. The annotated set of her letters points out numerous items of damaging and mistaken gossip, which she would report as fact. Nevertheless, thousands, if not millions, of Britishers owe Lady Mary their lives, for it was she who persuaded the English to innoculate themselves for smallpox. In 1716, her husband, Edward Wortley Montagu, was named Ambassador to the Ottoman Empire. There she witnessed the effectiveness of innoculation as practiced by the Turks, and given her own near death in 1715, on returning to England, she risked every bit of her social prestige to bring about its acceptance. For convenience to my plot, I had to move her infection up by a couple of weeks. I doubt any reader will mind, but it's always wise to admit taking liberties with history.

Lady Oglethorpe and her daughters Anne, Eleanor, and Fanny are real historical figures, of course, as are the Duke of Ormond, Viscount Bolingbroke, and James's courtiers. I could not conceive of setting a novel in 1715 without at least mentioning these figures who were so central to the history of that year. Because they were the eventual losers in this conflict, their existence has all but been forgotten, but for the cleverness of Robert Walpole and his spies, they might have gone down as the heroes who restored the Stuarts to their throne. To be fair, wherever possible, I have tried to put their own words into their mouths, especially in the case of Fanny and Bolingbroke who left sufficient correspondence that their opinions and personalities were easier to capture. For the rest, I was forced to rely upon others' interpretations to approximate their characters.

James himself is often dismissed as weak and ineffective. When he eventually reached Great Britain, the men who had sacrificed everything for his cause were shocked to find that the prince they had championed was such a weak, pallid creature. It was only on reading a thorough biography on James that I learned the cause of his weakness. Whether his illness was never mentioned for fear of discouraging his adherents or whether it was too common to be worth mentioning, I believe it explains a great deal about James's failure and that he deserves recognition for his courage in forging ahead in spite of his difficulties.

A note about usage. As I have mentioned in earlier notes, in the early eighteenth century, unmarried women were still addressed as "mistress." Since this is abbreviated as Mrs in Restoration plays, I have used that style for convenience. For the most part, I have tried to use English spellings, although I may have missed some, and since my audience is primarily American, I have used American punctuation. In other words, I've made a hodge-podge, but hope it conveys a suitable flavor.

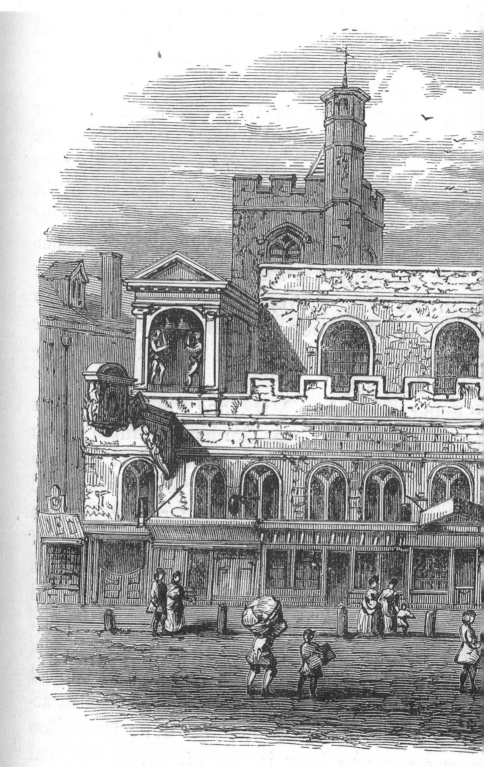

OLD ST. DUNSTAN